dark
visions

dark visions

THE STRANGE POWER

THE POSSESSED

THE PASSION

L.J. SMITH

SIMON AND SCHUSTER, LONDON

SIMON AND SCHUSTER
First published in Great Britain in 2009 by Simon & Schuster UK Ltd,
1st Floor, 222 Gray's Inn Road, London WC1X 8HB
A CBS COMPANY

Published in the USA in 2009 by Simon Pulse,
an imprint of Simon & Schuster Children's Division, New York.

The Strange Power copyright © Lisa J. Smith, 1994
The Possessed copyright © Lisa J. Smith, 1995
The Passion copyright © Lisa J. Smith, 1995
These titles were originally published individually by Simon Pulse.

A CIP catalogue record for this book
is available from the British Library

ISBN 978-1-84738-682-3

10 9 8 7 6 5 4 3 2

Printed by CPI Cox & Wyman, Reading, Berkshire RG1 8EX

CONTENTS

THE STRANGE POWER

For Max,
who brought sunshine

CHAPTER 1

You don't invite the local witch to parties. No matter how beautiful she is. That was the basic problem.

I don't care, Kaitlyn thought. *I don't need anyone.*

She was sitting in history class, listening to Marcy Huang and Pam Sasseen plan a party for that weekend. She couldn't help but hear them: Mr. Flynn's gentle, apologetic voice was no competition for their excited whispers. Kait was listening, pretending not to listen, and fiercely wishing she could get away. She couldn't, so she doodled on the blue-lined page of her history notebook.

She was full of contradictory feelings. She hated Pam and Marcy, and wanted them to die, or at least to have some gory accident that left them utterly broken and defeated and miserable. At the same time there was a terrible longing inside her. If they would only let her *in*—it wasn't as if she insisted on being the most popular, the most admired, girl at school. She'd settle for a place in the group that was securely her own. They could shake their heads and say, "Oh, that Kaitlyn—she's odd, but what would we do without her?" And that would be fine, as long as she was a *part*.

But it wouldn't happen, ever. Marcy would never think of inviting Kaitlyn to her party because she wouldn't think of doing something that had never been done before. No one ever invited the witch; no one thought that Kaitlyn, the lovely, spooky girl with the strange eyes, would *want* to go.

And I don't care, Kaitlyn thought, her reflections coming around full circle. This is my last year. One semester to go. After that, I'm out of high school and I hope I never see anyone from this place again.

But that was the other problem, of course. In a little town like Thoroughfare she was bound to see them, and their parents, every day for the next year. And the year after that, and the year after that. . . .

There was no escape. If she could have gone away to college, it might have been different. But she'd screwed up her art scholarship . . . and anyway, there was her father. He needed her—and there wasn't any money. Dad needed her. It was junior college or nothing.

The years stretched out in front of Kaitlyn, bleak as the Ohio winter outside the window, filled with endless cold classrooms. Endless sitting and listening to girls planning parties that she wasn't invited to. Endless exclusion. Endless aching and wishing that she *were* a witch so she could put the most hideous, painful, debilitating curse on all of them.

All the while she was thinking, she was doodling. Or rather her hand was doodling—her brain didn't seem to be involved at all. Now she looked down and for the first time saw what she'd drawn.

A spiderweb.

But what was strange was what was *underneath* the web, so close it was almost touching. A pair of eyes.

Wide, round, heavy-lashed eyes. Bambi eyes. The eyes of a child.

As Kaitlyn stared at it, she suddenly felt dizzy, as if she were falling. As if the picture were opening to let her in. It was a horrible sensation—and a familiar one. It happened every time she drew one of *those* pictures, the kind they called her a witch for.

The kind that came true.

She pulled herself back with a jerk. There was a sick, sinking feeling inside her.

Oh, *please,* no, she thought. Not today—and not here, not at school. It's just a doodle; it doesn't mean anything.

Please let it be just a doodle.

But she could feel her body bracing, ignoring her mind, going ice-cold in order to meet what was coming.

A child. She'd drawn a child's eyes, so some child was in danger.

But *what* child? Staring at the space under the eyes, Kait felt a tugging, almost a twitch, in her hand. Her fingers telling her the shape that *needed* to go there. Little half circle, with smaller curves at the edges. A snub nose. Large circle, filled in solid. A mouth, open in fear or surprise or pain. Big curve to indicate a round chin.

A series of long wriggles for hair—and then the itch, the urge, the *need* in Kait's hand ebbed away.

She let out her breath.

That was all. The child in the picture must be a girl, with all that hair. Wavy hair. A pretty little girl with wavy hair and a spiderweb on top of her face.

Something was going to happen, involving a child and a spider. But where—and to what child? And *when?*

Today? Next week? Next year?

It wasn't enough.

It never was. That was the most terrible part of Kaitlyn's terrible gift. Her drawings were always accurate—they always, always came true. She always ended up seeing in real life what she'd drawn on paper.

But not in time.

Right now, what could she do? Run through town with a megaphone telling all kids to beware of spiders? Go down to the elementary school looking for girls with wavy hair?

Even if she tried to tell them, they'd run away from her. As if Kaitlyn brought on the things she drew. As if she *made* them happen instead of just predicting them.

The lines of the picture were getting crooked. Kaitlyn blinked to straighten them. The one thing she wouldn't do was cry—because Kaitlyn never cried.

Never. Not once, not since her mother had died when Kait was eight. Since then, Kait had learned how to make the tears go inside.

There was a disturbance at the front of the room. Mr. Flynn's voice, usually so soft and melodious that students could comfortably go to sleep to it, had stopped.

Chris Barnable, a boy who worked sixth period as a student aide, had brought a piece of pink paper. A call slip.

Kaitlyn watched Mr. Flynn take it, read it, then look mildly at the class, wrinkling his nose to push his glasses back up.

"Kaitlyn, the office wants you."

Kaitlyn was already reaching for her books. She kept her back very straight, her head very high, as she walked up the aisle to take the slip. KAITLYN FAIRCHILD TO THE PRINCIPAL'S OFFICE— AT ONCE! it read. Somehow when the "at once" box was checked, the whole slip assumed an air of urgency and malice.

"In trouble again?" a voice from the first row asked snidely. Kaitlyn couldn't tell who it was, and she wouldn't turn around to look. She went out the door with Chris.

In trouble again, yes, she thought as she walked down the stairs to the main office. What did they have on her this time? Those excuses "signed by her father" last fall?

Kaitlyn missed a lot of school, because there were times when she just couldn't stand it. Whenever it got too bad, she went down Piqua Road to where the farms were, and drew. Nobody bothered her there.

"I'm sorry you're in trouble," Chris Barnable said as they reached the office. "I mean . . . I'm sorry *if* you're in trouble."

Kaitlyn glanced at him sharply. He was an okay-looking guy: shiny hair, soft eyes—a lot like Hello Sailor, the cocker spaniel she'd had years ago. Still, she wasn't fooled for a minute.

Boys—boys were no good. Kait knew exactly why they were nice to her. She'd inherited her mother's creamy Irish skin and autumn-fire hair. She'd inherited her mother's supple, willow-slim figure.

But her eyes were her own, and just now she used them without mercy. She turned an icy gaze on Chris, looking at him in a way she was usually careful to avoid. She looked him straight in the face.

He went white.

It was typical of the way people around here reacted when they had to meet Kaitlyn's eyes. No one else had eyes like Kaitlyn. They were smoky blue, and at the outside of each iris, as well as in the middle, were darker rings.

Her father said they were beautiful and that Kaitlyn had been marked by the fairies. But other people said other things. Ever since she could remember, Kaitlyn had heard the whispers—that she had strange eyes, evil eyes. Eyes that saw what wasn't meant to be seen.

Sometimes, like now, Kaitlyn used them as a weapon. She stared at Chris Barnable until the poor jerk actually stepped backward. Then she lowered her lashes demurely and walked into the office.

It gave her only a sick, momentary feeling of triumph. Scaring cocker spaniels was hardly an achievement. But Kaitlyn was too frightened and miserable herself to care. A secretary waved her toward the principal's office, and Kaitlyn steeled herself. She opened the door.

Ms. McCasslan, the principal, was there—but she wasn't alone. Sitting beside the desk was a tanned, trim young woman with short blond hair.

"Congratulations," the blond woman said, coming out of the chair with one quick, graceful movement.

Kaitlyn stood motionless, head high. She didn't know what to think. But all at once she had a rush of feeling, like a premonition.

This is it. What you've been waiting for.

She hadn't known she was waiting for anything.

Of course you have. And this is it.

The next few minutes are going to change your life.

"I'm Joyce," the blond woman said. "Joyce Piper. Don't you remember me?"

CHAPTER 2

The woman did seem familiar. Her sleek blond hair clung to her head like a wet seal's fur, and her eyes were a startling aquamarine. She was wearing a smart rose-colored suit, but she moved like an aerobics teacher.

Memory burst on Kaitlyn. "The vision screening!"

Joyce nodded. "Exactly!" she said energetically. "Now, how much do you remember about that?"

Bewildered, Kaitlyn looked at Ms. McCasslan. The principal, a small woman, quite plump and very pretty, was sitting with her hands folded on the desk. She seemed serene, but her eyes were sparkling.

All right, so I'm not in trouble, Kait thought. But what's going *on?* She stood uncertainly in the center of the room.

"Don't be frightened, Kaitlyn," the principal said. She waved a small hand with a number of rings on it. "Sit down."

Kait sat.

"I don't bite," Joyce added, sitting down herself, although she kept her aquamarine eyes on Kait's face the entire time. "Now, what do you remember?"

"It was just a test, like you get at the optometrist's," Kaitlyn said slowly. "I thought it was some new program."

Everyone brought their new programs to Ohio. Ohio was so representative of the nation that its people were perfect guinea pigs.

Joyce was smiling a little. "It *was* a new program. But we weren't screening for vision, exactly. Do you remember the test where you had to write down the letters you saw?"

"Oh—yes." It wasn't easy to remember, because everything that had happened during the testing was vague. It had been last fall, early October, Kait thought. Joyce had come into study hall and talked to the class. That was clear enough—Kait remembered her asking them to cooperate. Then Joyce had guided them through some "relaxation exercises"—after which Kaitlyn had been so relaxed that everything was foggy.

"You gave everybody a pencil and a piece of paper," she said hesitantly to Joyce. "And then you projected letters on the movie screen. And they kept getting smaller and smaller. I could hardly write," she added. "I was *limp*."

"Just a little hypnosis to get past your inhibitions," Joyce said, leaning forward. "What else?"

"I kept writing letters."

"Yes, you did," Joyce said. A slight grin flashed in her tanned face. "You did indeed."

After a moment, Kaitlyn said, "So I've got good eyesight?"

"I wouldn't know." Still grinning, Joyce straightened up. "You want to know how that test really worked, Kaitlyn? We kept projecting the letters smaller and smaller—until finally they weren't there at all."

"Weren't there?"

"Not for the last twenty frames. There were just dots, absolutely featureless. You could have vision like a hawk and still not make anything out of them."

A cold finger seemed to run up Kaitlyn's backbone. "I saw letters," she insisted.

"I know you did. But not with your eyes."

There was perfect silence in the room.

Kaitlyn's heart was beating hard.

"We had someone in the room next door," Joyce said. "A graduate student with very good concentration, and *he* was looking at charts with letters on them. That was why you saw letters, Kait. You saw through his eyes. You expected to see letters on the chart, so your mind was open—and you received what he saw."

Kaitlyn said faintly, "It doesn't work that way." Oh, *please,* God . . . all she needed was another power, another curse.

"It does; it's all the same," Joyce said. "It's called remote viewing. The awareness of an event beyond the range of your ordinary senses. Your drawings are remote viewings of events—sometimes events that haven't happened yet."

"What do you know about my drawings?" A rush of emotion brought Kait to her feet. It wasn't fair: this *stranger* coming in and playing with her, testing her, tricking her—and now talking about her private drawings. Her very private drawings that people in Thoroughfare had the decency to only refer to obliquely.

"I'll tell you what I know," Joyce said. Her voice was soft, rhythmic, and she was gazing at Kaitlyn intently with those aquamarine eyes. "I know that you first discovered your gift when you were nine years old. A little boy from your neighborhood had disappeared—"

"Danny Lindenmayer," the principal put in briskly.

"Danny Lindenmayer had disappeared," Joyce said, without looking away from Kait. "And the police were going door to door, looking for him. You were drawing with crayons while they talked to your father. You heard everything about the missing boy. And when you were done drawing, it was a picture you didn't understand, a picture of trees and a bridge . . . and something square."

Kaitlyn nodded, feeling oddly defeated. The memory sucked at her, making her dizzy. That first picture, so dark and strange, and her own fear . . . She'd *known* it was a very bad thing that her fingers had drawn. But she hadn't known why.

"And the next day, on TV, you saw the place where they'd

found the little boy's body," Joyce said. "Underneath a bridge by some trees . . . in a packing crate."

"Something square," Kaitlyn said.

"It matched the picture you'd drawn exactly, even though there was no way you could have known about that place. The bridge was thirty miles away, in a town you'd never been to. When your father saw the news on TV, he recognized your picture, too—and he got excited. Started showing the drawing around, telling the story. But people reacted badly. They already thought you were a little different because of your eyes. But this—this was a whole lot different. They didn't like it. And when it happened again, and again, when your drawings kept coming true, they got very frightened."

"And Kaitlyn developed something of an attitude problem," the principal interjected delicately. "She's naturally rebellious and a bit high-strung—like a colt. But she got prickly, too, and cool. Self-defense." She made *tsk*ing noises.

Kaitlyn glared, but it was a feeble glare. Joyce's quiet, sympathetic voice had disarmed her. She sat down again.

"So you know all about me," she said to Joyce. "So I've got an attitude problem. So wh—"

"You do *not* have an attitude problem," Joyce interrupted. She looked almost shocked. She leaned forward, speaking very earnestly. "You have a gift, a very great gift. Kaitlyn, don't you understand? Don't you realize how unusual you are, how wonderful?"

In Kaitlyn's experience, unusual did not equate to wonderful.

"In the entire world, there are only a handful of people who can do what you can do," Joyce said. "In the entire United States, we only found five."

"Five what?"

"Five high school seniors. Five kids like you. All with different talents, of course; none of you can do the same thing. But that's great; that's just what we were looking for. We'll be able to do a variety of experiments."

"You want to *experiment* on me?" Kaitlyn looked at the principal in alarm.

"I'm getting ahead of myself. Let me explain. I'm from San Carlos, California—"

Well, that explained the tan.

"—and I work for the Zetes Institute. It's a very small laboratory, not at all like SRI or Duke University. It was established last year by a research grant from the Zetes Foundation. Mr. Zetes is—oh, how can I explain *him?* He's an incredible man— he's the chairman of a big corporation in Silicon Valley. But his real interest is in psychic phenomena. Psychic research."

Joyce paused and pushed sleek blond hair off her forehead. Kaitlyn could feel her working up to something big. "He's put up the funds for a very special project, a very *intense* project. It was his idea to do screening at high schools all over the country, looking for seniors with high psychic potential. To find the five or six that were absolutely the top, the cream of the crop, and to bring them to California for a year of testing."

"A *year?*"

"That's the beauty of it, don't you see? Instead of doing a few sporadic tests, we'd do testing daily, on a regular schedule. We'd be able to chart changes in your powers with your biorhythms, with your diet—" Joyce broke off abruptly. Looking at Kait directly, she reached out and took Kait's hands.

"Kaitlyn, let down the walls and just *listen* to me for a minute. Can you do that?"

Kait could feel her hands trembling in the cool grasp of the blond woman's fingers. She swallowed, unable to look away from those aquamarine eyes.

"Kaitlyn, I am not here to hurt you. I admire you tremendously. You have a wonderful gift. I want to study it—I've spent my life preparing to study it. I went to college at Duke—you know, where Rhine did his telepathy experiments. I got my master's degree in parapsychology—I've worked at the Dream Laboratory at Maimonides, and the Mind Science Foundation in San Antonio, and the Engineering Anomalies Research Laboratory at Princeton. And all I've ever wanted is a subject like *you.* Together we can prove that what you do is real. We can get hard, replicable, scientific proof. We can show the world that ESP exists."

She stopped, and Kaitlyn heard the whir of a copier in the outer office.

"There are some benefits for Kaitlyn, too," Ms. McCasslan said. "I think you should explain the terms."

"Oh, yes." Joyce let go of Kaitlyn's hands and picked up a manila folder from the desk. "You'll go to a very good school in San Carlos to finish up your senior year. Meanwhile you'll be living at the Institute with the four other students we've chosen. We'll do testing every afternoon, but it won't take long—just an hour or two a day. And at the end of a year, you'll receive a scholarship to the college of your choice." Joyce opened the folder and handed it to Kaitlyn. "A very generous scholarship."

"A *very* generous scholarship," Ms. McCasslan said.

Kaitlyn found herself looking at a number on a piece of paper. "That's . . . for all of us, to split?"

"That is for you," Joyce said. "Alone."

Kaitlyn felt dizzy.

"You'll be helping the cause of science," Joyce said. "And you could make a new life for yourself. A new start. No one at your new school needs to know why you're there; you can just be an ordinary high school kid. Next fall you can go to Stanford or San Francisco State University—San Carlos is just half an hour south of San Francisco. And after that, you're free. You can go anywhere."

Kaitlyn felt *really* dizzy.

"You'll love the Bay Area. Sunshine, nice beaches—do you realize it was seventy degrees there yesterday when I left? Seventy degrees in winter. Redwoods—palm trees—"

"I can't," Kaitlyn said weakly.

Joyce and the principal both looked at her, startled.

"I can't," Kait said again, more loudly, pulling her walls close around her. She needed the walls, or she might succumb to the shimmering picture Joyce was painting in her mind.

"Don't you want to get away?" Joyce said gently.

Didn't she? Only so much that she sometimes felt like a bird beating its wings against glass. Except that she'd never been quite sure what she'd *do* once she got away. She'd just thought, There must be some place I belong. A place where I'd just fit in, without trying.

She'd never thought of *California* as being the place, California was almost too rich, too heady and exciting. It was like a dream. And the money . . .

But her father.

"You don't understand. It's my dad. I've never been away from him, not since my mom died, and he needs me. He's not . . . He really needs me."

Ms. McCasslan was looking sympathetic. Ms. McCasslan knew her dad, of course. He'd been brilliant, a philosophy professor; he'd written books. But after Kaitlyn's mother had died, he'd gotten . . . vague. Now he sang a lot to himself and did odd jobs around town. He didn't make much doing them. When bills came in, he shuffled his feet and ruffled his hair, looking anxious and ashamed. He was almost like a kid—but he adored Kait and she adored him. She would never let anything hurt him.

And to leave him so soon, before she was even old enough to go to college—and to go all the way to California—and for a *year*—

"It's impossible," she said.

Ms. McCasslan was looking down at her plump hands. "But, Kaitlyn, don't you think he'd want you to go? To do what's best for you?"

Kaitlyn shook her head. She didn't want to listen to arguments. Her mind was made up.

"Wouldn't you like to learn to control your talents?" Joyce said.

Kaitlyn looked at her.

The possibility of control had never occurred to her. The pictures came when she wasn't expecting them; took over her hand without her realizing it. She never knew what had happened until it was over.

"I think you can learn," Joyce said. "I think you and I could learn, together."

Kaitlyn opened her mouth, but before she could answer, there was a terrible sound from outside the office.

It was a crashing and a grinding and a shattering all together. And it was a *huge* noise, so huge that Kaitlyn knew at once it could come from nothing ordinary. It sounded very close.

Joyce and Ms. McCasslan had both jumped up, and it was the plump little principal who made it to the door first. She rushed out through the office to the street, with Kait and Joyce following her.

People were running up on either side of Harding Street, crunching through the snow. Cold air bit Kaitlyn's cheeks. The slanting afternoon sunlight threw up sharp contrasts between light and shadow, making the scene in front of Kaitlyn look frighteningly focused and distinct.

A yellow Neon was facing the wrong way on Harding Street, its back wheels on the sidewalk, its left side a wreck. It looked as if it had been broadsided and spun. Kaitlyn recognized it; it belonged to Jerry Crutchfield, one of the few students who had a car.

In the middle of the street, a dark blue station wagon was facing Kaitlyn directly. Its entire front end was accordioned. The metal was twisted and deformed, the headlights shattered.

Polly Vertanen, a junior, was tugging at Ms. McCasslan's sleeve. "I saw everything, Ms. McCasslan. Jerry just pulled out of the parking lot—but the station wagon was going too fast. They just hit him. . . . I saw everything. They were going too fast."

"That's Marian Günter's station wagon," Ms. McCasslan said sharply. "That's her little girl in there. Don't move her yet! Don't move her!" The principal's voice went on, but Kait didn't hear any more.

She was staring at the windshield of the station wagon. She hadn't seen before—but she could see now.

People around her were yelling, running. Kaitlyn hardly noticed them. Her entire world was filled with the car windshield.

The little girl had been thrown up against it—or maybe it had crunched back up against her. She was actually lying with her forehead touching the glass, as if she were looking out with open eyes.

With wide eyes. Wide, round, heavy-lashed eyes. Bambi eyes.

She had a small snub nose and a round chin. Wavy blond hair stuck to the glass.

The glass itself was shattered like a spiderweb, a spiderweb superimposed on the child's face.

"Oh, no—please, no . . ." Kaitlyn whispered.

She found herself clutching, without knowing what she was clutching at. Somebody steadied her.

Sirens were wailing closer. A crowd was gathering around the station wagon, blocking Kaitlyn's view of the child.

She knew Curt Günter. The little girl must be Lindy, his baby sister. Why hadn't Kait realized? Why hadn't her picture shown her? Why couldn't it have shown her cars crashing, with a *date* and a *place,* instead of that pathetic kid's face? How could it all be so *useless,* so completely freaking *useless* . . . ?

"Do you need to sit down?" the person holding her asked, and it was Joyce Piper, and she was shivering.

Kait was shivering, too. Her breath was coming very fast. She clutched harder at Joyce.

"Did you mean that, about me learning to control . . . what I do?" Kait couldn't call it a talent.

Joyce looked from her to the accident scene with something like dawning realization. "I think so. I hope so."

"You have to *promise.*"

Joyce met her gaze full on, the way people in Thoroughfare never did. "I promise to try, Kait."

"Then I'll go. My dad will understand."

Joyce's aquamarine eyes were brilliant. "I'm so glad." She shivered violently. "Seventy degrees there, Kait," she added softly, almost absently. "Pack light."

That night, Kaitlyn had a strangely realistic dream. She was on a rocky peninsula, a spit of land surrounded by cold gray ocean. The clouds overhead were almost black and the wind blew spray into her face. She could actually feel the wet of it, the chill.

From just behind her, someone called her name. But when she turned, the dream ended.

CHAPTER 3

Kait got off the plane feeling giddy and triumphant. She'd never been on a plane before, but it had been easy as anything. She'd chewed gum on takeoff and landing, done twists in the tiny bathroom every hour to keep limber, and brushed her hair and straightened her red dress as the plane cruised up to the gate. Perfection.

She was very happy. Somehow, once the decision to go was made, Kait's spirits had lifted and lifted. It no longer seemed a grim necessity to come to the Institute; it was the dream Joyce had described, the beginning of a new life. Her dad had been unbelievably sweet and understanding—he'd seen her off just as if she were going to college. Joyce was supposed to meet her here at San Francisco Airport.

But the airport was crowded and there was no sign of Joyce. People streamed by. Kaitlyn stuck close to the gate, head high, trying to look nonchalant. The last thing she wanted was anyone to ask if she needed help.

"Excuse me."

Kaitlyn flicked a sideways glance at the unfamiliar voice. It wasn't help; it was something even more disturbing. One of those cult people who hang around airports and ask for money. He was wearing reddish robes—Tuscan red, Kait thought. If she were going to draw them.

"I'd like a moment of your time, please." The voice was civil, but persistent—authoritative. It sounded foreign.

Kait edged away—or started to. A hand caught her. She looked down at it in amazement, seeing lean fingers the color of caramel locked around her wrist.

Okay, jerk, you asked for it. Outraged, Kait turned the full power of her smoky blue, strangely ringed eyes on him.

He just looked back—and when Kait looked deeply into *his* eyes, she reeled.

His skin was that caramel color—but his eyes were slanting and very dark, with an epicanthic fold. The phrase "lynx-eyed" came to Kaitlyn's mind. His softly curling hair was a sort of pale shimmery brown, like silver birch. None of it went together.

But that wasn't what made her reel. It was a feeling of *age* from him. When she looked into his eyes, she had the sense of centuries passing. Millennia. His face was unlined, but there were ice ages in his eyes.

Kait couldn't remember ever really screaming in her life, but she decided to scream now.

She didn't get a chance. The grip on her wrist tightened and before she could draw a breath, she was jerked off balance, moving. The man in the robes was pulling her backward into the jetway—the long corridor that led to a plane.

Except that there was no plane now and the corridor was empty. The double doors closed, cutting Kaitlyn off from the rest of the airport. She was still too shocked to scream.

"Don't move and you won't get hurt," the man in the robes said grimly. His lynx eyes were hard.

Kaitlyn didn't believe him. He was from some cult and he was obviously insane and he'd dragged her into this deserted place. She should have fought him before; she should have screamed when she had the chance. Now she was trapped.

Without letting go of her arm, the man fumbled inside his robes.

For a gun or a knife, Kaitlyn thought. Her heart was pounding violently. If he would just relax his grip on her arm for an instant—if she could get to the other side of those doors where there were people . . .

"Here," the man said. "All I want is for you to look at this."

He was holding not a weapon but a piece of paper. Glossy paper that had been folded. To Kaitlyn's dazed eyes it looked like a brochure.

I don't believe it, she thought. He *is* insane.

"Just *look*," the man said.

Kaitlyn couldn't help looking; he was holding the paper in her face. It seemed to be a full-color picture of a rose garden. A walled rose garden, with a fountain in the center, and something thrusting out of the fountain. Maybe an ice sculpture, Kaitlyn thought dizzily. It was tall, white, and semitransparent—like a faceted column. In one of its many facets was the tiny, perfect reflection of a rose.

Kaitlyn's heart was still pounding violently. This was all *too* weird. As frightening as if he were trying to hurt her.

"This crystal—" the man began, and then Kaitlyn saw her chance.

The iron grip on her arm loosened just the slightest bit as he spoke, and his eyes were on the picture. Kaitlyn kicked backward, glad that she was wearing pumps with her red dress, slamming a two-inch heel into his shin. The man yelped and let go.

Kaitlyn hit the double doors with both hands, bursting out into the airport, and then she just ran. She ran without looking behind her to see if the man was following. She dodged around chairs and phone booths, heading blindly into the crowd.

She didn't stop until someone called her name.

"Kaitlyn!"

It was Joyce, heading the other way, toward the gate. Kait had never been so relieved to see anyone.

"I'm so sorry—the traffic was terrible—and parking in this place is always—" She broke off. "Kaitlyn, what's wrong?"

Kaitlyn collapsed in Joyce's arms. Now that she was safe, she somehow wanted to laugh. Hysteria, probably, she told herself. Her legs were shaking.

"It was too strange," she gasped. "There was this guy from some cult or something—and he grabbed me. He probably just wanted money, but I thought—"

"He *grabbed* you? Where is he now?"

Kaitlyn waved a hand vaguely. "Back there. I kicked him and ran."

Joyce's aquamarine eyes flashed with grim approval, but all she said was, "Come on. We'd better tell airport security about this."

"Oh—I'm okay now. He was just some nut. . . ."

"Nuts like that, we put away. Even in California," Joyce said flatly.

Airport security sent people looking for the man, but he was gone.

"Besides," the guard told Joyce and Kaitlyn, "he *couldn't* have opened the doors to the jet bridge. They're kept locked."

Kaitlyn didn't want to argue. She wanted to forget all about it and go to the Institute. This was *not* how she'd planned her grand entrance to California.

"Let's go," she said to Joyce, and Joyce sighed and nodded.

They picked up Kaitlyn's luggage and carried it to a sharp

little green convertible—Joyce's car. Kait felt like bouncing on the seat as Joyce drove. Back home it was freezing, with twenty inches of snow on the ground. Here they drove with the top down, and Joyce's blond hair ruffled like down in the wind.

"How's the little girl from the crash?" Joyce asked.

Kaitlyn's spirits pitched.

"She's still in the hospital. They don't know if she'll be okay." Kaitlyn clamped her lips together to show that she didn't intend to answer any more questions about Lindy.

But Joyce didn't ask any more questions. Instead, she said, "Two of your housemates are already at the Institute; Lewis and Anna. I think you'll like them."

Lewis—a boy. "How many of the five of us are boys?" Kaitlyn asked suspiciously.

"Three, I'm afraid," Joyce said gravely, and then gave Kait a sideways look of amusement.

Kaitlyn declined to be amused. Three boys and only one other girl. Three sloppy, meaty-handed, too-big-to-control, hormone-crazed Power Rangers.

Kaitlyn had tried boys once, two years ago when she was a sophomore. She'd let one of them take her out, driving up to Lake Erie every Friday and Saturday night, and she'd put up with what he wanted—*some* of what he wanted—while he talked about Metallica and the Browns and the Bengals and his candy-apple-red Trans Am. All of which Kait knew nothing about. After the first date, she decided that guys must be an alien species, and just tried to deal with him without listening to him. She was still hoping that he'd take her to the next party with his crowd.

She had it all planned out. He'd escort her into one of those big houses on the hill that she'd never been invited to. She'd wear something a little dowdy so as to not show up the hostess. With her boyfriend's arm around her shoulder, she'd be modest and self-effacing, complimenting everything in sight. The whole crowd would see she wasn't a monster. They'd let her in—maybe not all at once, but over time, as they got used to her being around.

Wrong.

When she brought up the party, her lake-loving boyfriend blustered around, but eventually the truth came clear. He wasn't going to take her anywhere in public. She was good enough alone in the dark with him, but not good enough to be seen with him in the daylight.

It was one of the times when it was hardest not to cry. Stiff-lipped, she'd ordered him to take her home. He got angrier and angrier as they drove. When she jerked the car door open, he said, "I was going to dump you anyway. You're not like a normal girl. You're *cold*."

Kait stared after the car when it had gone. So she wasn't normal. Fine, she knew that already. So she was *cold*—and the way he'd said it made it obvious that he didn't just mean her personality. He meant more.

Well, that was fine, too. She'd rather be cold all her life than feel anything with a guy like that. The memory of his humid palms on her arms made her want to wipe her own hands on the skirt of her red dress.

So I'm cold, Kait thought now, shifting in the front seat of Joyce's convertible. So what? There are other things in life to be interested in.

And really, she didn't care how many boys were at the Institute. She'd ignore them—she'd stick with Anna. She just hoped Anna wasn't boy-crazy.

And that she likes you, a small, nerve-racking voice in her head added. Kaitlyn squashed the thought, tossing her head to feel the wind snapping her hair back, enjoying the motion and the sunshine.

"Is it much farther?" she asked. "I can't wait."

Joyce laughed. "No, it's not far."

They were driving through residential streets now. Kaitlyn looked around eagerly, but with a tingling in her stomach. What if the Institute was too big, too sterile, too intimidating? She'd pictured a large, squat redbrick building, something like her old high school back in Thoroughfare.

Joyce turned the convertible in to a driveway, and Kait stared.

"Is *this* it?"

"Yup."

"But it's *purple.*"

It was extremely purple. The shingled sides were a cool but vivid purple, the wood trim around the windows was darker purple; the door and wraparound balcony were glaring high-gloss purple. The only things that weren't purple were the slate gray roof and the bricks in the chimney.

Kait felt as if someone had dropped her into a swimming pool full of grape juice. She didn't know if she loved the color scheme or hated it.

"We haven't had time to paint it yet," Joyce explained, parking. "We've been busy converting most of the first floor to labs—but you can have the full tour tomorrow. Why don't you go up and meet your housemates?"

Thrills of nervousness wound through Kait's stomach. The Institute was so much smaller, so much more intimate, than she'd imagined. She'd really be *living* with these people.

"Sure, that's fine," she said, and held her head very high as she got out of the car.

"Don't worry about the luggage yet—just go on in. Go straight past the living room and you'll see a staircase on your right. Take that upstairs—the whole second floor is for you kids. I told Lewis and Anna that you can work out the bedroom situation for yourselves."

Kaitlyn went, trying not to either dawdle or hurry. She wouldn't let anyone see how nervous she was. The very purple front door was unlocked. The inside of the house wasn't purple—it looked quite ordinary, with a large living room on the right and a large enough dining room on the left.

Don't look at it now. Go on up.

Kaitlyn's feet carried her down the tiled foyer that separated them, until she reached the staircase.

Take it slow. Just keep breathing.

But her heart was going quickly, and her feet wanted to leap up the steps. The stairs made a U-turn at a landing and then she was at the top.

The hallway was crowded with odds and ends of furniture, piled haphazardly. In front of Kait and to the left was an open door. She could hear voices inside.

Okay, who *cares* if they're nice? They're probably creeps—and I don't care. I don't need anyone. Maybe I can learn to put curses on people.

The last-minute panic made her reckless, and she plunged through the door almost belligerently.

And stopped. A girl was kneeling on a bed without sheets or blankets. A lovely girl—graceful and dark, with high cheekbones and an expression of serenity. Kaitlyn's belligerence seeped away and all the walls she normally kept around her seemed to dissolve. Peacefulness seemed to come from the other girl like a cool wind.

The girl smiled. "You're Kaitlyn."

"And you're . . . Anna?"

"Anna Eva Whiteraven."

"What a wonderful name," Kaitlyn said.

It wasn't the sort of thing people said back at Warren G. Harding High School—but Kaitlyn wasn't at Warren G. Harding High School anymore, and Anna's serene expression broke into another smile.

"*You've* got wonderful eyes," she said.

"Does she?" another voice said eagerly. "Hey, turn around."

Kait was already turning. On the far side of the room was an alcove with a bay window—and a boy coming out of it. He didn't look threatening. He had a cap of black hair and dark, almond-shaped eyes. From the camera in his hands Kaitlyn guessed he'd been taking pictures out the open window.

"Smile!" A flashbulb blinded Kaitlyn.

"*Ouch!*"

"Sorry; I just wanted to preserve the moment." The boy let go of the camera, which bounced as the strap around his neck caught it, and stuck out a hand. "You do have kind of neat eyes. Kind of weird. I'm Lewis Chao."

He had a sweet face, Kaitlyn decided. He wasn't big and gross, but rather small and neat. His hand wasn't sweaty when she took it, and his eyes weren't hungry.

"Lewis has been taking pictures since we got here this morning," Anna said. "We've got the entire block on record."

Kaitlyn blinked away blue afterimages and looked at Lewis curiously. "Really? Where do you come from?" It must be even farther away than Ohio, she thought.

He smiled beatifically. "San Francisco."

Kaitlyn laughed, and suddenly they were all laughing together. Not malicious laughter, not laughing *at* anyone, but wonderful torrents of giggles *together.* And then Kait knew.

I'm going to be happy here, she realized. It was almost too big a concept to take in at once. She was going to be happy, and for a year. A panorama opened before her. Sitting by the fireplace she'd seen downstairs, studying, the others all doing their own projects, everyone joined by a warm sort of togetherness even while they did their own things. Each of them different, but not minding the differences.

No need for walls between them.

They began to talk, eagerly, friendship flying back and forth. It seemed quite natural to join Anna sitting on the bed.

"I'm from Ohio—" Kait started.

"Aha, a Buckeye," Lewis put in.

"I'm from Washington State," Anna said. "Near Puget Sound."

"You're Native American, aren't you?"

"Yes; Suquamish."

"She talks to animals," Lewis said.

Anna said gently, "I don't really talk to them. I can influence them to do things—sometimes. It's a kind of thought projection, Joyce says."

Thought projection with animals? A few weeks ago Kait would have said it sounded insane—but then, wasn't her own "talent" insane? If one was possible, so was the other.

"I've got PK," Lewis said. "That's psychokinesis. Mind over matter."

"Like . . . spoon bending?" Kait asked uncertainly.

"Nah, spoon bending's a trick. Real PK is only for little things, like making a compass needle deflect. What do you do?"

Despite herself, Kaitlyn's heart bumped. She'd never in her life said aloud the thing she was going to say.

"I . . . kind of see the future. At least, I don't, but my drawings do, and when I look back at them, I see that they did. But usually only after the thing has already happened," she finished incoherently.

Lewis and Anna looked thoughtful. "That's cool," Lewis said at last, and Anna said, "So you're an artist?"

The relief that flooded Kaitlyn was painful, and its aftermath left her jubilant. "I guess. I like to draw."

I'd like to draw right now, she thought, dying to get hold of some pastels. She'd draw Anna with burnt umber and matte black and sienna. She'd do Lewis with blue-black—his hair was that shiny—and some sort of flesh-ocher mixture for his skin.

Later, she told herself. Aloud she said, "So what about the bedrooms up here? Who goes where?"

"That's just what we've been trying to figure out," Anna said. "The problem is that there are supposed to be five of us students, and they've only got four bedrooms. There's this one and another one even bigger next door, and then two smaller ones on the back side of the house."

"And only the big ones have cable hookup. I've explained and explained," said Lewis, looking tragic, "that I *need* my MTV, but she doesn't understand. And I need enough outlets for my computer and stereo and stuff. Only the big rooms have those."

"It's not fair for us to take the good rooms before the others even get here," Anna said, gently but firmly.

"But I *need* my MTV. I'll *die*."

"Well, I don't care about cable," Kaitlyn said. "But I'd like a room with northern light—I like to draw in the mornings."

"You haven't heard the worst part—all the rooms have different things," Lewis said. "The one next door is *huge,* and it's got a king-size bed and a balcony and a Jacuzzi bath. This one has the alcove over there and a private bathroom—but almost no closet. And the two rooms in back have okay closets, but they share a bathroom."

"Well, obviously the biggest room should go to whoever's rooming together—because two of us are going to *have* to room together," Kaitlyn said.

"Great. I'll room with either of you," Lewis said promptly.

"No, no, no—look, let me go check out the light in the smaller rooms," Kaitlyn said, jumping up.

"Check out the Jacuzzi instead," Lewis called after her.

In the hallway, Kait turned to laugh at him over her shoulder—and ran directly into someone cresting the top of the stairs.

It wasn't a hard knock, but Kaitlyn automatically recoiled, and ran her leg into something hard. Pain flared just behind her knee, rendering her momentarily speechless. She clenched her teeth and glared down at the thing that had hurt her. A nightstand with one sharp-edged drawer pulled out. What was all this furniture *doing* in the hall, anyway?

"I'm really sorry," a soft southern voice drawled. "Are you all right?"

Kaitlyn looked at the tanned, blond boy who'd run into her. It *would* be a boy, of course. And a big one, not small and safe like Lewis. The kind of boy who disturbed the space around him, filling the whole hallway with his presence. A very *masculine* presence—if Anna was a cool wind, this boy was a golden solar flare.

Since ignoring was out of the question, Kaitlyn turned her best glare on him. He returned the look mildly and she realized with a start that his eyes were amber-colored—golden. Just a few shades darker than his hair.

"You *are* hurt," he said, apparently mistaking the glare for suffering. "Where?" Then he did something that dumb-founded Kaitlyn. He dropped to his knees.

He's going to apologize, she thought wildly. Oh, God, everyone in California *is* nuts.

But the boy didn't apologize—he didn't even look up at her. He was reaching for her leg.

"This one here, right?" he said in that southern-gentleman voice.

Kaitlyn's mouth opened, but all she could do was stare at him. She was backed against the wall—there was nowhere to escape.

"Back here—this spot?" And then, deftly and uncere-moniously, he turned up the skirt of her red dress. Kaitlyn's mind went into shock. She simply had no experience that had prepared her to deal with this situation—a perfect stranger reaching under her dress in a public place. And it was the *way* he did it; not like a grabby boy at all, but like . . . like . . . a doctor examining a patient.

"It's not a cut. Just a knot," the boy said. He wasn't looking at her or the leg, but down the hallway. His fingers were run-ning lightly over the painful area, as if assessing it. They felt dry but warm—unnaturally warm.

"You'll have a bad bruise if you leave it, though. Why don't you hold still and let me see if I can help?"

This, at last, catapulted Kait out of silence.

"Hold still? Hold still for what . . . ?"

He waved a hand. "Be quiet, now—please."

Kaitlyn was stupefied.

"Yes," the boy said, as if to himself. "I think I can help this some. I'll try."

Kaitlyn held still because she was paralyzed. She could feel his fingers on the back of her knee—a terribly intimate place, extremely tender and vulnerable. Kait couldn't remember *anyone* touching her there, not even her doctor.

Then the touch changed. It became a burning, tingling feeling. Like slow fire. It was almost like pain, but—

Kait gasped. "What are you *doing* to me? Stop that—what are you *doing?*"

He spoke in a soft, measured voice, without glancing up. "Channeling energy. Trying."

"I said *stop*—oh."

"Work with me, now, please. Don't fight me."

Kaitlyn just stared down at the top of his head. His gold-blond hair was unruly, springing in curls and waves.

A strange sensation swept through Kait, flowing up from her knee and through her body, branching out to every blood vessel and capillary. A feeling of refreshment—*of renewal.* It was like getting a drink of clean, cold water when you were desperately thirsty, or being drenched with delicious icy mist when you were hot. Kaitlyn suddenly felt that until this moment, she had only been half-awake.

The boy was making odd motions now, as if he were brushing lint off the back of her knee. Touch, shake off. Touch, shake off. As if gathering something and then shaking drops of water off his fingers.

Kaitlyn suddenly realized that her pain was completely gone.

"That's it," the boy said cheerfully. "Now if I can just close this off . . ." He cupped a warm hand around the back of her knee. "There. It shouldn't bruise now."

The boy stood up briskly and brushed off his hands. He was breathing as if he'd just run a race.

Kaitlyn stared at him. She herself felt *ready* to run a race. She had never felt so refreshed—so alive. At the same time, as she got another glimpse of his face, she thought maybe she ought to sit down.

When he looked back at her, she expected . . . well, she didn't know what. But what she *didn't* expect was a quick, almost absentminded smile from a boy who was already turning around to leave.

"Sorry about that. Guess I'd better go down and help Joyce with the luggage—before I knock anyone else over." He started down the stairs.

"*Wait* a minute—who are you? And—"

"Rob." He smiled over his shoulder. "Rob Kessler." He reached the landing, turned, and was gone.

"—and how did you *do* that?" Kait demanded of empty air.

Rob. Rob Kessler, she thought.

"Hey, Kaitlyn!" It was Lewis's voice from the bedroom. "Are you out there? Hey, Kaitlyn, come quick!"

CHAPTER 4

Kaitlyn hesitated, still looking down the stairs. Then she gathered her self-possession and slowly walked back into the room. Lewis and Anna were in the alcove, looking out the window.

"He's here," Lewis said excitedly, and brought his camera up. "That's got to be him!"

"*Who's* here?" Kaitlyn asked, hoping no one would look at her too closely. She felt flushed.

"Mr. Zetes," said Lewis. "Joyce said he had a limo."

A black limousine was parked outside the house, one of its rear doors open. A white-haired man stood beside the door, dressed in a greatcoat which Kaitlyn thought must be terribly hot on this Californian afternoon. He had a gold-topped cane—a real gold-topped cane, Kaitlyn thought in fascination.

"Looks like he's brought some friends," Anna said, smiling. Two large black dogs were jumping out of the limo. They started for the bushes but came back at a word from the man and stood on either side of him.

"Cute," Kaitlyn said. "But what's *that?*" A white van was turning in the driveway. Lettering on its side read DEPARTMENT OF YOUTH AUTHORITY.

Lewis brought his camera down, looking awed. "Jeez. That's the California Youth Authority."

"Which is . . . ?"

"It's the last stop. It's where they put the *baaaaad* boys. The hard-core kids who can't make it at any of the regular juvie places."

Anna's quiet voice said, "You mean it's jail?"

"My dad says it's the place for kids who're on their way to state prison. You know, the murderers and stuff."

"Murderers?" Kait exclaimed. "Well, what's it doing here, then? You don't think . . ." She looked at Anna, who looked back, serenity a bit clouded. Clearly, Anna did think.

They both looked at Lewis, whose almond-shaped eyes were wide.

"I think we'd better get down there," Kaitlyn said.

They hurried downstairs, bursting out onto the wooden porch and trying to look inconspicuous. No one was looking at them, anyway. Mr. Zetes was talking to a khaki-uniformed officer standing by the van.

Kaitlyn could only catch a few words of what was said—"Judge Baldwin's authority" and "CYA ward" and "rehabilitation."

". . . your responsibility," the officer finished, and stepped away from the van's door.

A boy came out. Kaitlyn could feel her eyebrows go up.

He was startlingly handsome—but there was a cold wariness in his face and movements. His hair and eyes were dark, but his skin was rather pale. One of the few people in California without a tan, Kaitlyn thought.

"Chiaroscuro," she murmured.

"What?" Lewis whispered.

"It's an art word. It means 'light and shade'—like in a drawing where you only use black and white." As Kaitlyn finished, she suddenly felt herself shiver. There was something strange about this boy, as if—as if—

As if he weren't quite canny, her mind supplied. At least, that's the phrase people back home used to use about *you,* isn't it?

The van was driving off. Mr. Zetes and the dark-haired boy were walking up to the door.

"Looks like we've got a new housemate," Lewis said under his breath. "Oh, boy."

Mr. Zetes gave a courtly nod to the group on the porch. "I see you're here. I believe everyone has arrived now—if you'll come inside, we can commence with the introductions." He went in, and the two dogs followed him. They were rottweilers, Kaitlyn noted, and rather fierce-looking.

Anna and Lewis stepped back silently as the new boy

approached, but Kaitlyn held her ground. She knew what it was like to have people step back when you walked near them. The boy passed very close to her, and turned to give her a direct look as he did. Kaitlyn saw that his eyes weren't black, but a very dark gray. She had the distinct feeling that he wanted to unsettle her, to make her look down.

I wonder what he did to get in prison, she thought, feeling chilled again. She followed the others into the house.

"Mr. Zetes!" Joyce said happily from the living room. She caught the old man's arm, smiling and gesturing with enthusiasm as she spoke to him.

Kait's attention was caught by a blond head near the stairs. Rob Kessler had a duffel bag—*her* duffel bag—slung over his shoulder. He saw the group that had just come in, and started toward them . . . and then he stopped.

His entire body had stiffened. Kaitlyn followed his gaze down the foyer—to the new boy.

Who was equally stiff. His dark gray eyes were fixed on Rob with complete attention and icy hatred. His body was held as if ready for an attack as Rob came closer.

One of the two rottweilers by Mr. Zetes began to growl.

"Good dog, Carl," Lewis said nervously.

"*You,*" the new boy said to Rob.

"*You,*" Rob said to the new boy.

"You two know each other?" Kaitlyn said to both of them.

Rob spoke without looking away from the other boy's pale,

wary face. "From a ways back," he said. He let the duffel bag down with a thump.

"Not a long enough ways," the other boy said. In contrast to Rob's soft southern tones, his voice was harsh and clipped.

Both dogs were growling now.

Well, there goes any chance of harmony between housemates, Kaitlyn thought. She noticed that Mr. Zetes and Joyce had broken off talking and were looking at the students.

"We all seem to be together," Mr. Zetes said rather dryly, and Joyce said, "Come over here, everybody! This is the moment I've been waiting for."

Rob and the new boy slowly turned away from each other. Joyce gave the group a brilliant smile as they gathered around. Her aquamarine eyes were sparkling.

"Kids, it's an honor and a privilege to introduce you to the man who brought you all here—the man who's responsible for this project. This is Mr. Zetes."

Kaitlyn felt for a moment as if she ought to applaud. Instead, she murmured "Hello" with the others. Mr. Zetes bent his head in recognition, and Joyce went on.

"Mr. Zetes, these are the troops. Anna Whiteraven, from Washington." The old man shook hands with her, and with each of them as Joyce introduced them. "Lewis Chao from California. Kaitlyn Fairchild from Ohio. Rob Kessler from North Carolina. And Gabriel Wolfe from . . . here and there."

"Yeah, depending on where the charges are pending,"

Rob drawled, not quite aloud. Mr. Zetes gave him a piercing look.

"Gabriel has been released into my custody," he said. "His parole allows him to go to school; for the rest of the time, he's confined to this house. He knows what will happen if he tries to violate those conditions—don't you, Gabriel?"

Gabriel's dark gray eyes moved from Rob to Mr. Zetes. He said one word, expressionlessly. "Yes."

"Good." Mr. Zetes looked at the rest of the group. "While you're here, I expect you all to try to get along. I don't think any of you can realize, at your age, just how great a gift has been given to you. Your one job here is to see that you *use* that gift wisely, and make the most of it."

Now for the pep talk, Kait thought, studying Mr. Zetes. He had an impressive shock of white hair on his handsome old head and a broad and benevolent brow. Kaitlyn thought suddenly, *I* know what he looks like. He looks like Little Lord Fauntleroy's grandfather, the earl.

But the earl wasn't giving any ordinary pep talk. "One thing you need to realize from the start is that you're different from the rest of humanity. You've been . . . chosen. Branded. You'll never be like other people, so there's no reason even to try. You follow different laws."

Kaitlyn felt her eyebrows pull together. Joyce had said similar things, but somehow Mr. Zetes's words had another tone. She wasn't sure she liked it.

"You have something inside you that won't be repressed. A hidden power that burns like a flame," he went on. "You're *superior* to the rest of humanity—don't ever forget that."

Is he trying to flatter us? Kait wondered. Because if he is, it isn't working. It all sounds . . . hollow, somehow.

"You are the pioneers in an exploration that has infinite possibilities. The work you do here may change the way the entire world looks at psychic powers—it may change the way the human race looks at itself. You young people are actually in a position to benefit all humankind."

Suddenly Kait felt the need to draw.

Not the ordinary need, like the desire she'd had to draw Lewis and Anna. This was the need that came with an itch in her hand—and the internal shiver that meant a premonition.

But she couldn't just walk away while Mr. Zetes was talking. She glanced around the room in distraction—and met Gabriel's eyes.

Right now those eyes looked dark and wicked, as if something in Mr. Zetes's speech amused him. Amused him in a cynical way.

With a shock, Kaitlyn realized that he looked as if he also found Mr. Zetes's words hollow. And the way he was gazing at her seemed to show that he knew she did, too.

Kaitlyn felt herself flushing. She looked quickly back at Mr. Zetes, freezing her face into an interested, deferential expression. After all, he was the one paying her scholarship.

He might be a little eccentric, but he obviously had a good heart.

By the time the speech was over, her need to draw was gone.

After Mr. Zetes was finished, Joyce said a few words about how she wanted them to do their best in the next year. "I'll be living at the Institute with you," she added. "My room is back there"—she pointed to a set of French doors beyond the living room that looked as if they led outside—"and you can feel free to come to me at any time, day or night. Oh, and here's someone else you'll be working with."

Kaitlyn turned and saw a girl coming through the dining room. She looked college age, and had tumbled mahogany hair and full lips which looked a bit sullen.

"This is Marisol Diaz, an undergrad from Stanford," Joyce said. "She won't live here, but she'll come daily and help with your testing. She'll also help me cook. You'll find a schedule for meals on the dining room wall, and we'll go over the other house rules tomorrow. Any questions?"

Heads were shaken.

"Good. Now, why don't you go upstairs and fix up your rooms? It's been a long day, and I know some of you must be tired from jet lag. Marisol and I will throw together something for dinner."

Kaitlyn *was* tired. Although her watch said 5:45, it was three hours later by Ohio time. Mr. Zetes said good-bye to each of them, and shook their hands. Then Kait and the others headed upstairs.

"What did you think of him?" she whispered to Lewis and Anna as they reached the second floor.

"Impressive—but a little scary. I kept expecting him to introduce 'Masterpiece Theater,'" Lewis whispered back.

"Those dogs were interesting," Anna said. "Usually I can sort of read animals, tell if they're happy or sad or whatever. But those two were very guarded. I wouldn't want to try to influence them."

Something made Kait glance behind her—and she found that Gabriel was looking at her. She felt disconcerted, so she immediately went on the attack.

"And what did *you* think?" she asked him.

"I think he wants to use us for his own reasons."

"Use us how?" Kaitlyn said sharply.

Gabriel shrugged, looking bored. "How should I know? Maybe to improve his corporation's image—'Silicon Valley Company Benefits Humankind.' Like Chevron financing wildlife programs. Of course, he was right about one thing— we *are* superior to the rest of the human race."

"And some of us are more superior than others, right?" Rob asked, from the stairs. "Some of us don't have to follow the rules—or the laws."

"Exactly," Gabriel said, with a rather chilling smile. He was walking around the hallway, glancing into each bedroom.

"Well, Joyce told us to pick our rooms. I think I'll take . . . this one."

"Hey!" Lewis squawked. "That's the biggest room—the one with the cable hookup and the Jacuzzi and . . . and *everything*."

Gabriel said blandly, "Thanks for telling me."

"It's much bigger than any of the others," Anna said with quiet heat. "We decided it should go to whoever rooms together."

"You can't just grab it for yourself," Lewis finished. "We ought to *vote*."

Gabriel's gray eyes narrowed and his lip lifted in something like a snarl. With one step he was close to Lewis. "You know what a lockup cell looks like?" he said, his voice cold and brutal. "It has a two-foot-wide bed and a metal toilet. One metal stool attached to the wall and one built-in desk. That's all. I've been in a cell like that on and off for two years. So now I figure I'm entitled. Are *you* going to do something about it?"

Lewis scratched his nose, looking as if he were considering it. Anna pulled him back a step.

"MTV isn't worth it," she told him.

Gabriel looked at Rob. "You, country boy?"

"I won't fight you, if that's what you mean," Rob drawled. He looked half-disgusted, half-pitying. "Go ahead, take the room—you sad bastard."

Lewis made a faint sound of protest. Gabriel stepped inside

his newly acquired room and began to shut the door.

"By the way," he said, turning, "everyone else had better keep out of here. After you spend so much time in lockup, you get to like your space. You get kind of territorial. I wouldn't want anybody to get hurt."

As the door closed, Kait said, "Gabriel—like the angel?" She could hear the heavy sarcasm in her own voice.

The door opened again, and Gabriel gave her a long, measuring look. Then he flashed a brilliant, unsettling smile. "*You* can come in any time you like," he said.

This time after the door slammed, it stayed shut.

"*Well,*" Kaitlyn said.

"*Jeez,*" Lewis said.

Anna was shaking her head. "Gabriel Wolfe—he's not like a wolf, really, because they're very social. Except for a lone wolf, an exile. One that's been driven out of the pack. If wolves get driven out far enough they go a little crazy—start attacking anything that comes near them."

"I wonder what his talent is," Kaitlyn mused. She looked at Rob.

He shook his head. "I don't really know. I met him back in North Carolina—at a place in Durham, another psychic research center."

"Another one?" Lewis said, looking surprised.

"Yeah. My parents took me to see if they could make any

sense of the weird stuff I was doing. I guess his parents did the same thing. He wasn't interested in working with the staff, though. He just wanted his own way, and the hell with other people. A girl ended up . . . getting hurt."

Kait looked at him. She wanted to ask, "Hurt *how?*" but from the closed-off expression on his face, she didn't think she'd get an answer.

"Anyway, that was over three years ago," Rob said. "He ran away from the center right after it happened, and I heard he just went from state to state, getting in a heap of trouble everywhere. *Making* a heap of trouble everywhere."

"Oh, terrific," Lewis said. "And we've got to live with this guy for a *year?*"

Anna was looking at Rob closely. "What about you? Did that center help you?"

"Sure did. They helped me figure out just what it was I was doing."

"And just what *is* it you do?" Kaitlyn put in, staring significantly from him to her leg.

"Healing, I guess," the blond boy said simply. "Some places call it therapeutic touch, some places call it channeling energy. I try to use it to help."

Looking into his steady golden eyes, Kaitlyn felt oddly ashamed. "I'm sure you do," she said, which was as close as she could come to saying "thank you." Somehow she didn't want the others to know what had happened between her and Rob earlier. She felt strangely confused by him—and by her reaction to him.

"I'm sure we all do," Rob said, again simply. His smile was slow but infectious—irresistible, in fact.

"Well, we *try*," Anna said. Kait glanced at Lewis, who just widened his eyes without saying anything. She had the feeling that, like her, he hadn't worked too hard at helping people with his powers.

"Look," Lewis said, clearing his throat. "I don't want to change the subject, but . . . can I pick my room next? Because I'd like . . . ummmm, that one."

Rob glanced into the room Lewis had indicated, then stepped down the hall and looked into two other doors. He turned and gave Lewis an oh-come-on look.

Lewis wilted. "But this is the only one left with cable. And I *need* my MTV. And my computer and my stereo and—"

"There's only one fair thing to do," Rob said. "We should make that room a communal place. That way, everybody can watch TV—there isn't one downstairs."

"But then what do *we* do?" Lewis demanded.

"We double up in the small rooms," Rob said briefly.

Kaitlyn and Anna glanced at each other and smiled. Kaitlyn didn't mind rooming with Anna—she was actually glad. It would be almost like having a sister.

Lewis groaned. "But what about my stereo and stuff? They

won't even fit in one of those small rooms, especially if there's two beds in there."

"Good," Rob said relentlessly. "Put 'em in the common room. We can all listen to them. Come on, we'd better start moving furniture."

The first thing Gabriel did was scan the room, prowling around it with silent, wary steps.

He looked in every corner, including the bathroom and closet. It was big, and luxurious, and the balcony offered a quick escape route—if it turned out that escape was necessary.

He liked it.

He flopped on the king-size bed and considered whether he liked anything else about this place.

There was the girl, of course. The one with the witch eyes and the hair like flame. She might be an interesting diversion.

But something inside him twisted uncomfortably. He found himself on his feet and pacing again.

He'd have to make sure it was *just* a diversion. That kind of girl might be too interesting, might tempt you to get involved. . . .

And that could never happen again.

Never. Because . . .

Gabriel wrenched his thoughts away. Aside from the girl, there wasn't much to like here—and several things to hate. Kessler. The restrictions on his freedom—being under house arrest. Kessler. The stupidity of the whole study these people had planned. Kessler.

He could do something about Kessler if he wanted. Take care of him permanently. But then he'd have to run, and if he got caught, he'd end up in lockup until he was twenty-five. It wasn't worth it—not yet.

He'd see how annoying Kessler turned out to be. This place was tolerable, and if he could last out the year, he'd be rich. With that much money, he could *buy* freedom—could buy anything he wanted. He'd wait and see.

And as for them testing his powers—he'd see about that, too. Whatever happened, it was their problem. Their fault.

He settled down on the bed. It was early, but he was tired. In a few minutes he was asleep.

Kait and the others didn't get much moved before Joyce called them down for dinner. Kait rather liked the feeling of eating at the big dining room table with five other people—five, because Gabriel hadn't come out of his room, ignoring all knocks at his door. It was like being part of a large family, and everyone seemed to have a good time—except maybe Marisol, who didn't talk much.

After dinner they went back to furniture arranging. There was plenty of furniture to pick from; the jumble in the hall and rooms seemed to include every style ever invented. Kait and Anna's room ended up with two mismatched single beds, a cheap pressed-wood bookcase, a beautiful French Provincial chair, a Victorian rolltop desk, and the nightstand that had attacked Kait in the hall. Kaitlyn liked all of it.

The bathroom in between the two small rooms was designated the girls' bathroom—by Rob's decree. "Girls need to be nearer to their stuff," he said obscurely to Lewis, who by then only shrugged. The boys would use the bathroom off the common room.

Going to bed, Kaitlyn was happy. Indirect moonlight came in the window behind her bed—*north* light, she noted with pleasure. It shone on the beautiful cedar-and-cherry-bark basket Anna had placed in their bookcase, and on the Raven mask Anna had hung on the wall. Anna herself was breathing peacefully in the other bed.

Kaitlyn's old life in Ohio seemed worlds away—and she was glad.

Tomorrow's Sunday, she thought. Joyce promised to show us the lab, and after that, maybe I'll do some drawing. And then maybe we can look around town. And on Monday we'll go to school and I'll have a built-in set of friends.

What a *wonderful* idea. She knew that Anna and Lewis, at least, would want to eat lunch together. She hoped Rob would, too. As for Gabriel—well, the farther off *he* was, the better. She didn't feel sorry for him at all. . . .

Her thoughts drifted off. The vague discomfort she'd felt

about Mr. Zetes had entirely disappeared. She slipped easily into sleep.

And then, suddenly, she was wide-awake. A figure was standing over her bed.

Kaitlyn couldn't breathe. Her heart seemed to fill her mouth and throat, pounding. The moonlight was gone and she couldn't make out any details of the figure—it was just a black silhouette.

For a wild instant—without knowing why—she thought, *Rob? Gabriel?*

Then a dim light came through the window again. She saw the halo of mahogany hair and the full lips of Marisol.

"What's wrong?" she whispered, sitting up. "What are you *doing* here?"

Marisol's eyes were like black pits. "Watch out—or get out," she hissed.

"*What?*"

"Watch out . . . or get out. You kids think you're so smart— so *psychic*—don't you? So superior to everyone else."

Kaitlyn couldn't speak.

"But you don't know anything. This place is different than you think. I've seen things . . ." She shook her head and laughed roughly. "Never mind. You'd just better watch out—" She broke off suddenly and looked behind her. Kaitlyn could see only the black rectangle of the doorway—but she thought she heard a faint rattling sound down the hall.

"Marisol, what—"

"Shut up. I've got to go."

"But—"

Marisol was already leaving. An instant later, the door to Kaitlyn's room silently closed.

CHAPTER 5

The next morning, Kait had forgotten about the strange visit.

She woke up to a distant clanging, feeling as if it were very late. A glance at her bedside clock showed that it was seven-thirty, which, of course, meant it was ten-thirty in Ohio.

The clanging was still going on. Anna sat up in bed.

"Good morning," she said, smiling.

"Good morning," Kaitlyn said, feeling how wonderful it was to have a roommate to wake up with. "What's that noise?"

Anna cocked her head. "I have no idea."

"I'm going to find out." Kaitlyn got up and opened the bathroom door. She could hear the clanging more clearly now, and along with it, a weird shouting voice—and a sound like *mooing*.

Impulsively she knocked on the door that led from the bathroom into Rob and Lewis's room. When she heard Rob's voice calling, "Yeah, come in," she opened the door and peered around it.

Rob was sitting up in bed, his rebellious blond hair tousled into a lion's mane. His chest was bare, Kaitlyn noticed with an unreasonable feeling of shock. In the other bed there was a lump of blankets which presumably contained Lewis.

Kaitlyn suddenly realized she was wearing a T-shirt nightgown that only came down to her knees. It had seemed quite natural to walk around in it—until she was confronted by the indisputable reality of *boys*.

She looked desperately around for the source of the clanging and mooing as a distraction. Then she saw it.

It was a cow. A cow made of white porcelain, with a clock in its stomach. The measured, hoarse voice coming from it was shouting in a marked Japanese accent, "Wake . . . *up!* Don't sleep your life away! Wake . . . *up!*"

Kaitlyn looked at the talking alarm clock, and then she looked at Rob. Rob smiled his slow, infectious smile—and suddenly everything was all right.

"It *has* to be Lewis's," Kait gasped, and began to giggle.

"It's great, isn't it?" said a muffled voice from under the blankets. "I got it at Sharper Image."

"So *this* is what I can expect from my housemates," Kait said. "Mooing in the morning." She and Rob were both laughing together now, and she decided it was time to shut the door.

After she closed it, she looked at herself in the bathroom

mirror. She didn't usually spend much time at mirrors, but just now . . .

Her hair was rather disheveled, falling in fine tangles to her waist. Wispy red curls had formed on her forehead. Her strangely ringed eyes looked back at her sarcastically.

So you don't care about boys, huh? they seemed to ask. So how come you're thinking that next time you ought to brush your hair before barging in on them?

Kaitlyn turned abruptly toward the shower—and that was when she remembered Marisol's visit.

"Watch out or get out. . . . This place is different than you think. . . ."

God, had that really *happened*? It seemed more like a dream than anything else. Kaitlyn stood frozen in the middle of the bathroom, her happiness in the morning draining away. Was Marisol crazy? She must be—she must have some kind of mental trouble, creeping around in the middle of the night and standing over people in bed.

I've got to talk to someone about it, Kait realized. But she didn't know who. If she told Joyce, Marisol might get in trouble. It would be like snitching—and then again, what if it *had* all been a dream?

In the sunlit, bustling morning, with sounds of laughing and washing all around, it was impossible to even consider the idea that Marisol's warning had been genuine. That there really was something wrong at the Institute.

Marisol herself was in the kitchen when Kait went down for breakfast, but she returned Kaitlyn's questioning look with one of sullen blankness. And when Kait said politely, "Marisol, could I talk to you?" she just frowned without looking up from the orange juice she was pouring.

"I'm busy."

"But it's—it's about last night."

She was more than half expecting Marisol to say, "What are you talking about?"—which would mean that it *had* all been a dream. But instead Marisol shook back her mahogany hair and said, "Oh, *that*. Didn't you get it? That was a joke."

"A joke?"

"Of course, stupid," Marisol said roughly. "Didn't you know that? You superpsychics are all so stuck-up—couldn't you tell?"

Kaitlyn's temper hit flashover.

"Well, at least we don't sneak around at night acting like lunatics!" she snapped. "The next time you do that, *you'd* better watch out."

Marisol smirked. "Or what?"

"Or . . . you'll see!" Just then the others began arriving for breakfast, so Kaitlyn was spared having to think up a more specific threat. She muttered, "Nut," and snagged a muffin.

Breakfast was lively, just as dinner had been the night before—and just like the night before, Gabriel didn't show up. Kaitlyn forgot all about Marisol as Joyce told them the house rules and described some of the experiments the kids would be doing.

"We'll do one session of testing this morning, just to get some baselines," Joyce said. "But first, anybody who wants to call their parents can do it now. Kaitlyn, I don't think you called your dad yesterday."

"No, but this would be a great time. Thanks," Kait said. She was actually rather glad to get away from the table—looking at Rob's hair in the morning sunlight made her feel strange. She called her father from a phone at the foot of the stairs.

"Are you having a good time, hon?"

"Oh, yes," Kaitlyn said. "It's *warm* here, Dad; I can go out without a sweater. And everybody's nice—almost everybody. Most people. Anyway, I think it's going to be great here."

"And you've got enough money?"

"Oh, *yes*." Kaitlyn knew her father had scraped together everything he could for her before she left. "I'm going to be fine, Dad. Honest."

"That's terrific, honey. I miss you."

Kaitlyn blinked. "I miss you, too. I'd better go now—I love you." She could hear voices in the room just in front of her. She went around behind the staircase and saw an open door in the little hallway below the landing. Joyce and the others were in a room beyond.

"Come on in," Joyce said. "This is the front lab, the one that used to be a family room. I'm just giving the grand tour."

The lab wasn't at all what Kait had expected. She'd envisioned white walls, gleaming machines, tile floor, a hushed atmosphere. There *were* machines, but there was also an attractive folding screen, lots of comfortable chairs and couches, two bookcases, and a stereo playing New Age music.

"They proved a long time ago at Princeton that a homey atmosphere is best," Joyce said. "It's like the observer effect, you know—psi abilities tend to fade any time the subject is uncomfortable."

The back lab, which had been a garage, was much the same, except that it also had a steel room rather like a bank vault.

"That's for complete isolation in testing," Joyce said. "It's soundproof, and the only communication with the inside is by intercom. It's also like a Faraday cage—it blocks out any radio waves or other electronic transmissions. If you put someone in there, you can be *sure* they're not using any of their normal senses to get information."

"I bet," Kaitlyn murmured. She could feel a creeping sensation along her spine—somehow she didn't *like* that steel room. "I . . . You're not going to put me in there, are you?"

Joyce glanced at her and laughed, her eyes sparkling like green-blue jewels in her tanned face. "No, we won't put you in there until you're ready," she said. "In fact, Marisol," she added to the college girl behind Kaitlyn, "why don't you go bring Gabriel down here—I think we'll test him in the isolation room for starters."

Marisol left.

"Right, everybody, show time," Joyce said. "This is our first day of experiments, so we'll keep them a bit informal, but I do want everyone to concentrate. I won't ask you to work all the time, but when you *do* work, I ask that you give it your all."

She directed them into the front lab, where she installed Anna and Lewis at what looked like study carrels on either side of the room—study carrels with mysterious-looking equipment. Kaitlyn didn't hear all the instructions she gave them, but in a few minutes both Anna and Lewis seemed to be working, oblivious to anything else in the room.

"Gabriel says he's coming," Marisol announced from the door. "And the volunteers are here. I could only get two so early on Sunday morning."

The volunteers turned out to be Fawn, an extremely pretty blond girl in a motorized wheelchair, and Sid, a guy with a blue Mohawk and a ring in his nose. Very California, Kait thought approvingly. Marisol took him into the back lab.

Joyce gestured at Kait to sit down on a couch over by the window. "You'll be working with Fawn, but you'll have to share her with Rob," she said. "And I think we'll let him go first. So just relax."

Kaitlyn didn't mind—she was both excited and nervous about her own testing. What if she couldn't perform? She'd never been able to use her power on cue—except at Joyce's "vision screening," and then she hadn't *known* she was using her power.

"Now, Rob," Joyce said. She had attached a blood pressure gauge to one of Fawn's fingers. "We'll have six trials of five minutes each. What I'm going to ask you to do is to pull a slip of paper out of this box. If the slip says 'Raise,' I want you to try to raise Fawn's blood pressure. If it says 'Lower,' I want you to try to lower it. If it says 'No change,' I want you to do nothing. Understand?"

Rob looked from Fawn to Joyce, his brow wrinkled. "Yes, ma'am, but—"

"Call me Joyce, Rob. I'll be charting the results. In each case, don't tell anyone what the slip says, just do it." Joyce checked her watch, then nodded at the box. "Go ahead, pick."

Rob started to reach in the box, but then he dropped his hand. He knelt in front of the blond girl's wheelchair.

"Your legs give you much trouble?"

Fawn looked at Joyce quickly, then back at Rob. "I have MS—multiple sclerosis. I got it early. Sometimes I can walk, but it's pretty bad right now."

"Rob . . ." Joyce said.

Rob didn't seem to hear her. "Can you lift this foot here?"

"Not very high." The leg lifted slightly, fell.

"Rob," Joyce said. "Nobody expects you to . . . We can't *measure* this kind of thing."

"Excuse me, ma'am," Rob said softly, without looking

around. To Fawn: "How about this one? Can you lift it some?"

"Not as high as the other." The foot lifted and fell.

"That's just fine. Okay, now, you just hold still. You may feel some heat or some cold, but don't you worry about that." Rob reached forward to clasp the girl's bare ankle.

Joyce tilted her sleek blond head to look at the ceiling, then sighed and went to sit beside Kaitlyn.

"I suppose I should have known," she said, letting her hands with the watch and notebook fall on either side of her.

Kaitlyn was watching Rob.

His head was turned toward her, but he clearly wasn't seeing her. He seemed to be *listening* for something as his fingers moved nimbly over Fawn's ankle. As if looking at the ankle would only distract him.

Kaitlyn was fascinated by his face. Whatever she thought of boys in general, her artist's eye couldn't prevaricate. Words from a book she'd once read ran through her mind: "A beautiful, honest face with the eyes of a dreamer." And the stubborn jaw of a fighter, she added to herself, with an amused sideways glance at Joyce.

"How does that feel?" Rob asked Fawn.

"I . . . sort of tingly," she said, with a breathless, nervous laugh. "Oh!"

"Try to lift this foot again."

Fawn's sneaker came up—almost ten inches off the footrest.

"I did that!" she gasped. "No—*you* did that." She was staring at him with huge eyes full of wonder.

"You did it," Rob said, and smiled. He was breathing quickly. "Now we'll work on the other one."

Kaitlyn felt a stab of jealousy.

She'd never felt anything quite like it before—it was similar to the ache she'd gotten back in Ohio when she'd heard Marcy Huang planning parties. Just now, the way Rob was concentrating on Fawn—and the way Fawn was looking at Rob . . .

Joyce chuckled. "Same thing I saw at his school," she said to Kait in a low voice. "Every girl swooning when he goes by—and him not even knowing what's going on. That boy has no idea he's so sexy."

That's it, Kait realized. He has no clue. "But *why* doesn't he?" she blurted.

"Probably because of the same thing that gave him his talent," Joyce said. "The accident."

"What accident?"

"He didn't mention it? I'm sure he'll tell you all about it if you ask. He was hang gliding and he crashed. Broke most of his bones and ended up in a coma."

"Oh, my God," Kaitlyn said softly.

"They didn't expect him to live, but he did. When he woke up, he had his powers—but he also had some deficits. Like not knowing what girls are for."

Kaitlyn stared at her. "You're kidding."

"Nope." Joyce grinned. "He's pretty innocent about the world—in a lot of ways. He just doesn't see things quite the way other people do."

Kaitlyn shut her eyes. Of course, that explained why Rob casually reached up girls' skirts. It explained everything— except why just looking at him made her heart pound. And why just the thought of him lying in a coma hurt her. And why she had a very uncharitable desire to run over and physically drag him away from pretty Fawn right now.

There's a word for your condition, her mind told her snidely. It's called—

Shut up, Kaitlyn thought. But it was no use. She knew.

"That's enough for now," Rob was saying to Fawn. He sat back on his heels and wiped his forehead. "If we kept working on it every week, I think I could maybe help more. Do you want to do that?"

All Fawn said was, "Yes." But it was the *way* she said it, and the melty, awed way she looked into Rob's eyes, Kait thought. Fortunately, at that moment Joyce stood up.

"Rob, you might talk to *me* about arranging that," she said.

He turned and looked at her mildly. "I knew you'd want me to," he said.

Joyce muttered something under her breath. Then she said, "Right, we'll work something out. Why don't you take a break now, Rob? And, Fawn, if you're too tired for another experiment . . ."

"No, I feel *great*," Fawn said, not sappily but buoyantly. "I feel so strong—ready for anything."

"Energy transfer," Joyce murmured, taking off the blood pressure cuff. "We'll have to explore that." Then she looked up as the door connecting the front and back labs opened. "What is it, Marisol?"

"He is *not* cooperating," Marisol said. Gabriel was right behind her. He looked particularly gorgeous and somehow elegant—but his expression was one of cold contempt.

"Why not?" Joyce asked.

"You know why," Gabriel said. He seemed to sense Kait's eyes on him, and he gave her a long, deadly look.

Joyce put a hand to her forehead. "Right, let's go talk about it."

Rob reached out and caught her arm. "Ma'am—Joyce—I don't know if that's such a good idea. You want to be careful—"

"I'll handle this, Rob, please," Joyce said, in a voice that indicated she'd had enough. She went into the back lab, taking Marisol and Gabriel with her. The door shut.

Anna and Lewis were looking up from their study carrels. Even Fawn was staring.

Kaitlyn braced herself to look at Rob this close. "What'd you mean by that?" she said, her voice as casual as she could make it.

His gaze seemed to be turned inward. "I don't know—but I remember what happened at that center in Durham. *They* tried to make him do experiments, too." He shook his head. "I'll see y'all later," he said softly, and left. Kaitlyn was pleased that he didn't turn to look back at Fawn, and displeased that he didn't turn to look back at *her*.

A few minutes later Joyce returned, looking slightly frazzled. "Now, where were we? Kaitlyn, it's your turn."

Oh, not now, Kaitlyn thought. She felt raw and throbbing from her new discoveries about Rob—as if she'd had a layer of skin stripped off. She wanted to go off by herself somewhere and think.

Joyce was thumbing through a folder distractedly. "Informal; we'll keep this informal," she murmured. "Kaitlyn, I want you to sit down here." She guided Kaitlyn behind the folding screen, where there was a plush reclining chair. "In a minute I'm going to have you put on these headphones and this blindfold." It was a weird-looking blindfold, like goggles made of the two halves of a tennis ball.

"What's *that?*"

"Poor man's version of a Ganzfeld cocoon. I'm trying to get the money to set up a proper Ganzfeld room, with red lights and stereo sound and all. . . ."

"Red lights?"

"They help induce relaxation—but never mind. The point of Ganzfeld testing is to cut off your ordinary senses, so you can concentrate on the psychic ones. You can't see anything with the blindfold; you can't hear anything because the headphones fill your ears with white noise. It's supposed to help you be receptive to any images that come into your head."

"But images *don't* come into my head," Kait said. "They come into my hand."

"That's fine," Joyce said, and smiled. "Let them come—here's a pencil and paper on a clipboard. You don't need to see to draw; just let the pencil move as it wants to."

It sounded crazy to Kaitlyn, but Joyce was the expert. She sat down and put on the blindfold. Everything went dark.

"We'll try just one target image," Joyce said. "Fawn will be concentrating on a photograph of a certain object. You try and receive her thought."

"Sure," Kaitlyn muttered, and put on the headphones. A sound like a waterfall filled her ears. Must be white noise, she thought, leaning back in the chair.

She felt Joyce put the pencil in her hand and the clipboard in her lap.

Okay, relax.

It was actually rather easy. She knew no one could see her behind the screen—which was a good thing, because she must look pretty silly. She could just stretch out and let her thoughts drift. The darkness and the waterfall noise were like a slippery chute—there was nothing to hold on to. She felt herself sliding down . . . somewhere.

And she began to be afraid. The fear swept up and engulfed her before she knew what was happening. Her fingers clenched on the pencil.

Easy—calm down. Nothing to be scared of . . .

But she *was* scared. There was a terrible sinking in her stomach and she felt as if she were smothering.

Just let images come—but what if there were horrible images out there? Frightening things in the dark, just waiting to get into her mind . . . ?

Her hand began to cramp and itch.

Joyce had said to let the pencil move as it wanted to. But Kaitlyn didn't know if *she* wanted it to move.

Didn't matter. She had to draw. The pencil was moving.

Oh, God, and I have no idea what's coming out, she thought.

No idea—except that whatever it was, was scary. Formless darkness writhed in Kaitlyn's mind as she tried to picture whatever it was that the pencil was drawing.

I have to see it.

The tension in her muscles had become unbearable. With her left hand, Kaitlyn pulled the goggles and headphones off.

Her right hand was still moving, like a disembodied hand from a science fiction movie, without her mind having any idea of where it was going to go next. It didn't seem part of her. It was horrible.

And the drawing—the drawing was even more horrible. It was . . . grotesque.

The lines were a little wobbly, but the picture perfectly recognizable. It was her own face. Her face—with an extra eye in the forehead.

The eye had dark lashes all around, so it looked almost insectlike. It was wide and staring and unbelievably repulsive. Kaitlyn's left hand flew to her own forehead as if to make sure there was nothing there.

Only skin puckered with worry. She rubbed hard.

So much for remote vision. She'd bet anything Fawn wasn't out there concentrating on a picture like *this*.

Kaitlyn was about to sit up and tell Joyce that she'd ruined the experiment when the screaming began.

CHAPTER 6

It was very loud even though it seemed to be coming from far away. The rhythm sounded almost like a baby's crying—the frantic, desperate howls of an abandoned infant—but the voice was much deeper.

Kait dropped the clipboard and vaulted out of the chair. She darted around the folding screen.

Joyce was opening the door to the back lab. Everyone else was staring, apparently frozen. Kait dashed up behind Joyce—just as the screaming stopped.

"Calm down! Just calm down!" Marisol was saying. She was standing in front of the blue-Mohawk guy, who was cringing against the wall. His eyes were wild, his mouth loose and wet with saliva. He seemed to be crying now.

"How long?" Joyce said to Marisol, approaching the Mohawk guy with hands outstretched in an I-mean-no-harm gesture.

Marisol turned. "About forty-five seconds."

"Oh, my God," Joyce said.

"What happened?" Kaitlyn burst out. She couldn't stand to watch this college-age guy cry anymore. "What is going *on* here? What's wrong with him?"

"Kaitlyn, please," Joyce said in a harassed voice.

Kaitlyn looked around the room—and saw that the door to the steel room was opening. Gabriel stepped out with a sneer on his arrogant, handsome face.

"I warned you," he said coldly to Joyce's back.

"This volunteer is a psychic," Joyce said in a thin voice.

"Not psychic enough, obviously," Gabriel said.

"You don't care at all, do you?" a voice said from behind Kaitlyn. She felt herself start—she hadn't heard Rob walk up.

"Rob—" Joyce said, but just then the Mohawk guy made a movement as if to dash away, and she broke off, fully occupied in restraining him.

"I said, you really don't care," Rob was saying, stalking up to face Gabriel. To Kait he looked like a golden avenging angel—but she was worried about him. In contrast to Rob's light, Gabriel looked like dangerous darkness. For one thing, Gabriel had been in jail; if it came to a fight, Kaitlyn would bet he'd fight dirty. And for another, he'd obviously done *something* to that volunteer. He might do it to Rob.

"I didn't arrange this experiment," Gabriel was saying in a frightening voice.

"No, but you didn't stop it, either," Rob snapped.

"I warned them."

"You could have just said no."

"Why should I? I told them what might happen. After that, it's their problem."

"Well, now it's my problem, too."

They were snarling right in one another's faces. The air was thick and electric-feeling with tension. And Kaitlyn couldn't stand it any longer.

"Both of you—*just stop it,*" she exploded, reaching them with three long steps. "Yelling at each other doesn't help anything."

They went on glaring at each other.

"Rob," Kaitlyn said. Her heart was pounding. He looked so handsome, blazing with anger like this—and she could sense he was in danger.

Strangely, it wasn't Rob who responded to her. Gabriel turned his dark, cold gaze away from Rob's face to look at Kaitlyn. He gave her one of his disturbing smiles.

"Don't worry," he said. "I'm not going to kill him—yet. It would violate my parole."

Kaitlyn felt a chill as his gray eyes looked her up and down. She turned to Rob again.

"Please?"

"Okay," Rob said slowly. He took a long breath and she could feel the tension go out of his body. He stepped back.

Everyone seemed to feel the change in atmosphere and relax. Kaitlyn had almost forgotten about the volunteer in the last few minutes, but now she saw that Joyce and Marisol had coaxed him into a chair. He sat with his head bent nearly to his knees.

"Oh, man, what did you do to me?" he was muttering.

"What *did* you do to him?" Rob said to Gabriel. Kaitlyn wanted to know, too—she was *wild* to know—but she was afraid of another flare-up.

Instead, Gabriel just looked grim—almost bitter. "Maybe you'll find out someday," he said significantly, making it a threat.

It was then that Kaitlyn heard Lewis's hesitant voice calling from the front lab.

"Uh . . . Joyce, Mr. Zetes is here."

"Oh, God," Joyce said, straightening up.

Kaitlyn didn't blame her. All the experiments disrupted, everybody standing around, one volunteer practically writhing on the ground . . . It was a lot like getting a visit from the school principal when the class is in a total uproar.

Mr. Zetes was wearing a black coat again, and the two dogs were behind him.

"Problems?" he said to Joyce, who was quickly smoothing down her short blond hair.

"Just a slight one. Gabriel had some difficulties—"

"It looks as if that young man had some, too," Mr. Zetes

said dryly. He walked over to the Mohawk guy, looked down at him, then up at Joyce.

"I was going to call an ambulance," she said. "Marisol, would you—"

"There's no need," Mr. Zetes interrupted. "I'll take him in the car." He turned to look at Gabriel, Rob, and Kait, who were all standing by the steel room. "The rest of you young people can take a break," he said.

"Yes, go on. Testing is finished for today," Joyce said, still flustered. "Marisol, why don't you escort Fawn back home? And . . . make sure she's not upset about anything."

Marisol headed for the front lab without changing her sullen expression. Gabriel went, too, with the smooth, long steps of a wolf. Rob hesitated, looking at the Mohawk guy.

"Can I maybe help—"

"No, *thank you*, Rob. If you want some lunch, there are cold cuts in the fridge," Joyce said, in such a voice that Rob had to leave.

Kaitlyn followed, but she paused in the doorway as if trying to shut the door very quietly. It was sheer curiosity; she wanted to know if Mr. Zetes was going to yell at Joyce.

Instead, he said, "How long?"

"About forty-five seconds."

"Ah." It sounded almost appreciative. Kaitlyn got one glimpse of Mr. Zetes, tapping his cane thoughtfully on the ground, and then she had to shut the door.

Gabriel was already gone. Marisol and Fawn were leaving, Marisol looking sullen and Fawn looking back at Rob. Rob was chewing his lip, staring at the floor. Lewis was looking from one person to another. Anna was petting a white mouse she held in her hand.

"Where'd you get that?" Kaitlyn asked. She felt someone ought to say something.

"He was in my experiment. See? This box has different-numbered holes, and I'm supposed to make him go into one of them. Whichever number the monitor shows."

"There must be a sensor inside the hole to register whether you get it right," Lewis said, coming over.

Anna nodded, but she was looking past him. "Don't worry, Rob," she said. "Joyce and Mr. Zetes will take care of that guy. It'll be all right."

"Yeah, but can Mr. Z take care of *Gabriel?*" Lewis said. "That's the question."

Kaitlyn smiled in spite of herself. "Mr. Z?"

"Sure. 'Mr. Zetes' is too long."

"I just don't think he should be here," Rob said broodingly. "Gabriel. I think he's trouble."

"And *I* think I'm going to go crazy wondering what it is he *does*," Kaitlyn said. "But I don't think Joyce is going to tell us."

"Gabriel has a right to privacy, if he wants it," Anna said gently, putting the mouse in a wire cage. "*I* think we ought to do something to get our minds off it, since we have the afternoon off. We could go into town—or we could finish setting up the common room upstairs."

As always, just being around Anna calmed Kaitlyn down. Serenity drifted from the Native American girl and filled the room.

"Let's do the room," Kaitlyn said. "We can take lunch up there. I'll make sandwiches."

"I'll help," Rob said, and Kaitlyn's heart gave a startled leap.

What do I say, what do I *say?* she thought in the kitchen. Lewis and Anna had gone upstairs; she and Rob were alone.

At least her hands knew what to do. She was used to fixing meals for her dad, and now she spun the lids off mustard jars and stacked cold cuts efficiently. They were very Californian cold cuts: turkey baloney and chicken slices, low-fat salami, Alpine Lace cheese.

Rob worked just as efficiently—but he seemed abstracted, as if his mind were on other things.

Kaitlyn couldn't stand the silence. Almost at random, she said, "Sometimes I wonder if it's really a good idea to try and develop our powers. I mean, look at Gabriel."

She'd said it because she had a vague notion Rob would agree. But he shook his head vigorously and came out of his brown study.

"No, it *is* good—it's important for the world. What Gabriel needs is to develop some *control*—he's bad off for that. Or maybe he just doesn't want to control himself." Rob shook his head and slapped a piece of sprouted whole wheat bread on a sandwich. "But I think everybody ought to develop their talents. D'you realize most people have ESP?" He looked at Kait earnestly.

She shook her head. "I thought we were special."

"We've got more of it. But just about everybody has some. If everybody could work on it—don't you see? Things might start getting better. And they look pretty bad right now."

"You mean . . . for the world?"

He nodded. "People don't care much about each other. But, you know, when I channel energy I feel people's pain. If everybody could feel that, things would be different. There wouldn't be any murder or torture or stuff—because nobody would want to cause pain to anybody else."

Kaitlyn's heart had picked up. He'd "channeled energy" for her—did that mean he felt close to her?

But all she said, very gently, was, "Not everybody can be a healer."

"Everybody has some talent. Everybody could help in some way. When I get out of college I'd like to do the kind of work Joyce is doing—only try to get *everybody* involved in it. Everybody everywhere."

Kaitlyn was staggered by the vision. "You want to save the world?"

"Sure. I'd do my bit," he said, as if saying, *Sure, I'd do my bit for recycling.*

Dear God, Kait thought. I believe him.

There was something about this boy with the golden dreamer's eyes and the quiet voice that commanded her respect. A person like this, Kait thought, comes along only once in a very long time. A person like this can make a difference.

That was what she *thought*. What she felt was . . . was . . . well . . .

Anyway, there was no fighting against it anymore, she thought as they took the sandwiches upstairs.

All through the afternoon, which was spent moving furniture, arguing, and arranging things, Kait hugged her new knowledge to herself. It was both pleasure and pain, just as it was both a pleasure and painful to be able to watch Rob, to be in his company.

She would never have believed she could fall in love on one day's acquaintance.

But there it was. And every minute she was around Rob, the feeling grew stronger. She had trouble focusing on anything else when Rob was in the room, her heart began to beat hard when he looked at her, his voice made her shiver, and when he said her name . . .

By dinnertime, she was a basket case.

The strange thing was, now that she'd admitted it to herself, she wanted to talk about it. To explain to somebody else how she felt. To share it.

Anna, she thought.

When Anna went into their room to clean up before dinner, Kait followed her. She shut the door, then ducked into the bathroom and turned on the faucet.

Anna was sitting on her bed, brushing her long black hair. "What's that for?" she said, amused.

"Privacy," Kait said grimly. She sat down on her own bed, although she could hardly keep herself sitting still. "Anna—can I talk to you?"

"Of course you can."

Of course she could. Kaitlyn knew that suddenly. "It's so strange—back home I never had any friend I could really talk to. But I *know* I can talk to you. I just don't know how to start," she added explosively, discovering this.

Anna smiled, and Kaitlyn felt more peaceful, less agitated. "It wouldn't have anything to do with Rob, would it?"

"Oh, my God," Kaitlyn said, stiffening. "Is it that obvious? Do you think *he* knows?"

"No . . . but I'm a girl, remember? I notice things boys don't notice."

"Yes, well, that's the problem, isn't it?" Kaitlyn murmured, sitting back. She felt crushed suddenly. "I've got this feeling *he* isn't ever going to notice."

"I heard what Joyce said about him."

Kaitlyn was very glad—she wouldn't have to repeat the story, like gossip. "Then you know it's practically hopeless," she said.

"It's not hopeless. You just have to *get* him to notice you, that's all. He likes you; he just doesn't realize you're a girl."

"You think he likes me?"

"Of course he does. And you're beautiful—any normal guy wouldn't have any trouble seeing you're female. With Rob, you're just going to have to do something extra."

"Like take off my shirt?"

"I was thinking of something less extreme."

"I've *thought* of things," Kaitlyn said. "All afternoon I've been thinking of ways . . . well, like trying to get him into romantic situations. But I don't know if it's right. Isn't that like tricking him?"

Anna smiled—a very wise smile, Kait thought. "See that mask?" she said, nodding to the one on the wall. "That's Skauk, the Raven. He was my greatgrandfather's guardian spirit—and when the missionaries came along and gave my family the name 'White,' he was the one who stuck 'Raven' on, so we would always know who we were. Friends of Raven the Trickster."

Kaitlyn stared at the mask, with its long, blunt beak, in fascination.

"Raven was always doing things for his own good—but they turned out to be for everybody's good in the end. Like the time when he stole the sun."

Kaitlyn grinned, sensing a story. "When he what?"

"He stole the sun," Anna said gravely, only her eyes smiling. "Gray Eagle had the sun, but he hated people so much that he kept it hidden in his house, and everybody else lived in darkness. Raven wanted the sun for his own, but he knew Gray Eagle would never let him inside. So he turned himself into a snow white bird and tricked Gray Eagle's daughter into letting him in."

"*Tch,*" Kaitlyn said. Anna's eyes smiled.

"As soon as she did, Raven grabbed the sun and flew away—but Gray Eagle flew after him. Raven got so scared that he dropped the sun . . . and it landed in the sky, where it lit up the world for everybody."

"That's nice," Kaitlyn said, pleased.

"There're lots of stories about Raven. But the point is, sometimes a little trickery isn't so bad." Anna flashed Kait a dark-eyed glance. "And especially where boys are concerned, I think."

Kaitlyn stood up, feeling excitement churn inside her. "Then I'll do it! If I can think of something good."

"You can start with cleaning up a little," Anna said, laughing. "Right now he'll only notice you for the dirt on your nose."

Kaitlyn not only washed but changed her clothes and pulled her hair back with a gold barrette—but she didn't see that it made any difference in Rob's attitude at dinner. Dinner was novel mostly because Gabriel put in an appearance.

"He eats," Kaitlyn whispered to Anna under cover of passing the brown rice. "I was beginning to wonder."

After dinner, Gabriel vanished again. Lewis and Rob went into the common room, which they now called the study, although Kaitlyn didn't think there was much chance of anyone studying in it. Not with U2 on the CD player competing with a horror movie on the TV. It didn't seem to bother Anna, who curled up in the alcove with a book, but Kaitlyn wanted to get away.

She needed to be by herself because of Rob—and because school was tomorrow, her new school, her new chance. Her feelings were all mixed up, flying around in confusion and bumping into each other and ricocheting off even faster.

But most important, she needed to draw.

Not the ESP kind of drawing. Just regular drawing, which always helped smooth out her thoughts. She hadn't really drawn for two days.

That reminded her of something. The drawing she'd done in the lab—she'd just left it there, behind the folding screen. She should go pick it up sometime; she certainly didn't want anyone else to see it.

"I'll be back in a little while," she said to the others in the study, and then she stopped to be grateful a moment because everybody said good-bye as she left. That had always been one of her dreams, to say to a roomful of people, "I'm going" and have them all say good-bye.

The drawing wasn't in the lab. As she let herself out the back door, she hoped someone had thrown it away.

She took only her sketchbook and a couple of sticks of charcoal—it was too dark outside to really see colors. But there was enough moonlight to see trees, and the air was deliciously fresh and cold.

This is more like winter, she thought. Everything was silver and shadows. In back of the house a narrow dirt road sloped down to a stand of redwood trees. Kaitlyn followed it.

At the foot of the hill was a little, almost dry streambed, with a low concrete bridge crossing it. The road looked as if it were never used. Kaitlyn stood in the middle of the redwoods, breathing in the night and the tree smell.

What a wonderful place. The trees cut off the lights of the house, and not even U2 could penetrate this far. She felt quite alone.

She sat on a concrete curb with her sketch pad on her knees.

Although the moonlight was beautiful, the coolest kind of light imaginable, there wasn't really enough of it to draw properly. Oh, well, Kaitlyn thought, Joyce wants me to learn how to draw blind. With loose, fluid motions, she sketched in the shapes of some redwoods across the streambed. It was interesting to get only the shape and no detail.

What a peaceful place. She added a bush.

She was feeling much better already. She added a dark, sinuous line for the stream.

A night like this made you believe in magic. She started to add a few rocks—and then she heard a sound.

A thump. Like, Kaitlyn thought, freezing, someone falling out of a tree.

Or jumping.

Strange, how she knew right away it was human. Not an animal sound, and certainly nothing natural.

Someone was out here with her.

She looked around, moving only her head, keeping her body still. She had good eyes, artist's eyes, and when she'd walked down here she'd noticed the shape of the trees and bushes. She ought to be able to spot anything different.

But she couldn't. She couldn't see anything new, and she couldn't hear anything, either. Whoever was out there wasn't speaking.

That made it not funny. Not a joke. When somebody hides at night and doesn't let you know who they are—when you can *feel* eyes on you, but you don't know whose—that wasn't funny. Kaitlyn's hands felt cold and her throat felt very tight.

Just get up. Leave. *Now,* she thought.

She managed two steps up the hill and saw movement among the trees. It was a person, moving out from the cover of the redwoods.

Kaitlyn's body prepared to fight or flee—but not until she

saw who it was. She had to see the face before she could be released from paralysis.

The person came closer, feet crunching on dead leaves. Moonlight shone on his face, on slanting eyes and softly curling brown hair. It was the man who'd grabbed her in the airport.

He was wearing regular clothes now, not the red robe he'd worn before. And he was coming straight at her, very quickly.

CHAPTER 7

Fight, Kait decided. Or rather, her body decided it for her, seeming to feel instinctively that she'd never make it up that hill.

Her sketchbook was spiral-bound with heavy wire, and one end was slightly uncoiled—it had been poking her for weeks. Now she dropped the charcoal sticks and brought the book up, poised for attack.

Aim for the eyes, she thought.

She knew she should be screaming, but her throat was too constricted.

All this passed through her mind in the few seconds it took the stranger to reach her. Kaitlyn hadn't been in a fight since elementary school, but now her body seemed to know what to do. The stranger grabbed for her arm—Kaitlyn jerked it away.

Now, she thought, and lashed out with the sketchbook.

And it worked—the heavy wire caught him in the cheek, tearing a long bloody scratch.

Fierce triumph surged up in Kait. But the next instant the stranger had her wrist and was twisting it, trying to make her let go of the sketch pad. It hurt, and the pain freed her voice.

"Let go of me," she gasped. *"Let go!"*

He twisted harder. Blood was running down his cheek, black in the moonlight. Kaitlyn tried to kick, but he turned his body and her kicks glanced off harmlessly. He had both her arms now. He was pushing her down onto the sloping ground of the hill. He was winning.

Scream, her mind told her.

Kaitlyn sucked in a deep breath and screamed. But it was cut off almost before it started, by the stranger's hand.

"Shut up!" he said, in a furious whisper.

Kaitlyn stared up at him over his smothering hand, knowing her eyes were wide with fear. He was so strong, and so much heavier than she was—she couldn't move at all.

"You're so reckless—you never *think,*" the stranger hissed. The moon was behind him, so his face was in shadow—but she could feel his anger.

He's going to kill me. And I'll never even know why, a small, clear part of her mind said. The rest of her was engulfed in sheer black terror as his hand stayed over her mouth. It was getting very hard to breathe. . . .

Something reared up behind the stranger.

Kaitlyn's dazed mind couldn't tell at first what it was. Just a shape silhouetted against the moonlit sky. Then she saw it was a human shape, with something shining in its hand.

There was a movement quicker than Kait's eyes could follow, and the stranger on top of her was jerked backward slightly. The moonlight reflected off a knife blade.

"Let go of her," a clipped, harsh voice said, "or I'll cut your throat."

Gabriel? Kaitlyn thought in disbelief. But it was true, and now her panicked senses could interpret the scene in front of her. Gabriel was holding the stranger at knifepoint.

The stranger's hands lifted away from Kaitlyn. She drew in a gasping, wheezing breath.

"Now get up," Gabriel said. "Nice and easy. I'm in a bad mood tonight."

The stranger rose in one slow, coordinated motion, like a dancer. The knife stayed at his throat the whole time.

As soon as his weight was removed, Kaitlyn got her feet under her and took two scrambling steps up the hill. Adrenaline was still flooding over her in painful, useless waves. Her hands were shaking.

I should help Gabriel, she thought. No matter how tough he is, he's a kid, and that stranger's a man. A strong man.

"Want me to go back to the house and tell them?" she gasped, trying to make herself sound hard and competent.

"Why?" Gabriel said briefly. He made some movement and

the stranger went spinning, landing on his back on the ground.

"Now get out," he said, looking down at the supine figure. "And don't come back unless you're tired of living. If I see you around again, I'll forget I just did two years for murder."

A shock went through Kait. But she didn't have time to think—Gabriel was speaking again.

"I said, get out. Run. Show me a four-minute mile."

The stranger got up, not nearly as smoothly and gracefully as before. From what Kait could see of his expression, he was both furious and frightened.

"You're *both* so stupid—" he began.

"Run," Gabriel suggested, holding the knife as if ready to throw it.

The stranger turned and went, half running, half angrily stalking.

When the crunch of his footsteps had died, Kaitlyn looked at Gabriel, who was folding up the knife and putting it in his back pocket all in one practiced gesture.

Murder, she thought. He was in jail for murder.

What she said, rather unsteadily, was, "Thank you."

He glanced up at her briefly, and she could swear he was amused, as if he knew the difference between her thoughts and her words. "Who was he? An old boyfriend?" he asked.

"Don't be ridiculous," Kait snapped, and then wished she hadn't. One ought to be more polite to a murderer, especially when one was alone with him in the dark. "I don't know *who* he is," she added. "But he was at the airport when I came yesterday. He must have followed Joyce and me home."

Gabriel looked at her skeptically, then shrugged. "I don't think he'll come back." He started toward the house without turning to see if Kait was following.

Kaitlyn picked up her sketchbook and went after him.

"What happened?" Rob said, vaulting to his feet. He and Lewis and Anna were in the study—as was Joyce. Kaitlyn had looked for her on the first floor, then come up here.

Rob was staring from Kaitlyn, who was just realizing that she had bits of dead leaves and grass in her hair, to Gabriel, who was behind her. "What happened?" he repeated, in a more controlled but more frightening voice.

"What does it look like?" Gabriel taunted, at his very nastiest.

Rob started toward him, golden eyes blazing.

"No," Kaitlyn said. "Rob, don't. He didn't hurt me; he saved me."

She felt a surge of dizzy excitement—Rob was angry *for* her, protective. But she couldn't let him fight Gabriel.

"He saved you?" Rob said, with open scorn. He was on one side of the doorway, staring at Gabriel as if trying to bore holes in him. Gabriel was on the other side, almost lounging against the wall and looking devastatingly handsome. Kait was caught in between them.

She appealed to Joyce, who was rising from the study couch.

"It was that guy, the guy from the airport," she said. "He was out back." She explained what had happened, watching the alarm grow on Joyce's face.

"Jeez, we'd better call the police," Lewis said when she was done. He sounded more impressed than scared.

"He's right," Anna said, her dark eyes sober.

"Oh, sure, call them," Gabriel sneered. "I only just got paroled. They love to see people like me with switchblades."

Joyce grimaced. She squeezed her eyes shut and did some stretching exercises with her shoulders.

Kaitlyn's heart sank. Gabriel would be in trouble—he might even get sent back to jail. His part of the experiment would be ruined, and he might never learn to control his powers. All because he'd helped her.

Rob was suddenly looking quite cheerful. "Well, we've *got* to report it."

"Fine. Just give me ten minutes' start," Gabriel said through his teeth.

"Stop it, both of you," Kaitlyn said. Then she sighed. Being in love wasn't easy. She didn't want to make Rob unhappy, but she had no choice.

"I have an idea," she said hesitantly. "We could call the police, but not tell them Gabriel was involved. I'll just say I got away from the guy out there. Then nobody would get in trouble, but the police could do whatever they need to."

Rob's smile faded. Gabriel was still glaring. But Joyce opened her aquamarine eyes and beamed.

"Trust you, Kait," she said. "Now, where's a phone?"

Gabriel didn't stay to hear the call.

He went into his room and shut the door behind him. And then, tired but too restless to even sit down, he began to pace.

Images kept floating through his mind. Kaitlyn lying in the moonlight—with some maniac on top of her. What if he hadn't come along just then?

The maniac had been right about one thing—she *was* reckless. She shouldn't be *allowed* out alone at night. She didn't have the right instincts for danger, she wasn't tough enough to protect herself. . . .

So . . . what? his mind asked. So you're going to protect her?

Gabriel flashed one of his best disturbing smiles at nothing. Hardly.

He was going to keep away from her, was what he was going to do. She was a nuisance—and she was stuck on Kessler. Gabriel could see that, even if Kessler was too stupid.

Keep away from her. Yes. And he'd bet—he smiled again—that after what she'd seen tonight, she'd keep away from him.

Two hours later Kait was lying in bed, trying to calm down enough to go to sleep.

There had been a lot of fuss with the police, who'd gone

down into the backyard but had found nothing. They'd promised to have a cruiser patrol the area, and Joyce had told the kids to check the door locks and keep a close lookout for strangers from now on.

"And I don't want you going anywhere alone," she told Kait firmly. "Especially at night." Kait was happy to agree.

But now she couldn't sleep. It had all been too weird, too disturbing. Why would some cult guy from the airport follow her home? *Was* he some cult guy? If not, why had he been wearing the robes? A disguise? A stupid one.

What did he *want?*

And beneath all her other thoughts ran a continuous whispering thread. . . .

Gabriel was a murderer.

The others didn't know. Except Rob—Kaitlyn felt sure Rob knew. But even not knowing, they'd treated him pretty badly tonight. No one had said anything complimentary about him saving Kait. Lewis and Anna had kept their distance, as if they expected him to pull a switchblade on *them* at any minute, and Rob had watched him with steady, smoldering fury.

Rob—she *wouldn't* think about Rob now. She couldn't take the agitation.

Anna was breathing peacefully on the other side of the bedroom. Kaitlyn glanced at her, a motionless shape in the darkness, then very carefully and quietly got out of bed.

She shouldered into her robe and slipped noiselessly out the door.

The study was dim. Kait sat on the window seat in the alcove, her chin on her knees. Outside, a few lights shone through waving tree branches. Then she noticed that light was also shining through the curtains in Gabriel's room.

What she did then was born of sheer impulse. If she'd thought about it, she never would have gone through with it. But she didn't give herself time to think.

She jumped off the window seat and went to knock on his door.

A very quiet knocking, in case he was asleep with the light on. But after only an instant the door opened.

He was wearing a rather sleepy scowl.

"What?" he said ungallantly.

"Come into the study," Kaitlyn whispered.

The scowl disappeared, changing into a dazzling bared-teeth smile. "No, *you* come in *here*."

He was daring her, Kaitlyn realized. All right; great. She'd prove she trusted him.

Head very high, back straight, she swept by him. She sat down on the desk chair. She glanced around unobtrusively— the room was as nice as Lewis had said. Huge bed, matching furniture, *acres* of space. It seemed bare of personal possessions, though. Maybe Gabriel didn't have any.

Slowly, watching her, Gabriel sat down on the bed. He'd

left the door a little ajar. Kaitlyn, motivated by she didn't know what, got up and closed it.

"You're crazy, you know," Gabriel said unemotionally, as she resumed her seat.

"I wanted to say thank you," Kaitlyn said. *And that I'm not afraid of you,* she added silently. She still couldn't figure out what she felt about Gabriel—even whether she liked him or hated him.

But he had saved her from a very bad situation.

Gabriel didn't look gratified by the thanks. "And that's all?" he said mockingly.

"Of course."

"You're not just a little curious?" When Kaitlyn blinked at him, he leaned forward. His teeth were bared again. "You don't even want to know?"

Kaitlyn felt distaste pinching her features. "You mean . . . about . . ."

"The murder," Gabriel said, his dazzling grin getting nastier by the minute.

Fear uncoiled in Kaitlyn's stomach. He was right—she *was* crazy. What was she doing sitting here in his bedroom? Two days ago she wouldn't have sat in *any* guy's bedroom, and now she was chatting with a killer.

But Joyce wouldn't have brought him to the Institute if he was really dangerous, she thought. Joyce wouldn't take that risk.

Kaitlyn said slowly, "Was it really murder?" Then she looked straight up at Gabriel.

His expression changed as he met her eyes—as if she'd startled him. Then he seemed to regain his balance.

"*I* called it self-defense, but the judge didn't agree," he said. His eyes were now cold as ice.

Something inside Kaitlyn relaxed. "Self-defense," she said.

Gabriel looked at her for a long moment, then away. "Of course, the other one wasn't self-defense. The first one."

He's trying to shock you, Kaitlyn told herself.

He's succeeding, her mind whispered back.

"I'd better go," she said.

He was *very* fast. She was closer to the door, but before she could reach it, he was in front of her, blocking it.

"Oh, no," he said. "Don't you want to hear all about it?"

Those dark gray eyes were strange—almost fixed, as if he were looking through her. His expression was strange, too. As if he were covering unbearable tension with mockery and derision. Kaitlyn could see the glint of clenched teeth between his parted lips.

"Stop it, Gabriel," she said. "I'm going."

"Don't be shy."

"I'm not *shy*, you jerk," she snapped. "I'm just sick of you." She tried to push past him and he wouldn't let her. They tussled.

Kaitlyn found out very quickly how much stronger he was.

Stupid, *stupid,* she thought, trying to get a hand free to hit him. How had she gotten herself *into* this mess? Her heart was going like a trip-hammer, and her chest felt as if it would burst. She was going to have to scream—unless he stopped her. Choked her, maybe. Was that what he'd done to the others?

Maybe he'd used a knife. Maybe he cut them. Or maybe it had been something even worse. . . .

She and Gabriel had been struggling silently, their faces inches apart. Kaitlyn's mind was dark with imaginings of how he might have killed before.

And then . . .

And then it all stopped. Kaitlyn's fantasies were cut off as if somebody had slammed down a window in her mind. And all because of the look in Gabriel's eyes.

Grief. Guilt, too, plenty of that, but mainly grief. A kind Kaitlyn recognized, the kind that makes you nearly bite through your lip so you won't make a noise. The kind Kaitlyn could remember from when she was eight years old, when her mother died.

Gabriel, with his handsome, arrogant face, and his savage bared teeth, was trying to make the tears go away.

Kaitlyn stopped struggling with him, realizing in the moment she did that he hadn't hurt her. He'd been blocking her, restraining her, but he hadn't bruised her.

"Okay," she said, her voice loud in the silence. "So tell me, then."

It caught him off guard. Actually rocked him backward. For a moment he looked shocked—and vulnerable.

Then his face hardened. He was taking it as a challenge.

"I will," he snarled back. He let go of her and stepped away—a hunted, constrained movement. His chest was rising and falling quickly.

"You've all been wondering what I *do*," he said. "Haven't you?"

"Yes," Kait said. She moved cautiously away from the door. "Is that so surprising?"

"No." He laughed—a very bitter laugh. "It's what everyone wants to know. But when they find out, they don't like it." He turned and looked at her with mock bewilderment. "For some reason, they seem to be scared of me."

Kaitlyn didn't smile. "I know what it's like," she said flatly to the carpet. "When they're scared of you. When they can't look you in the eye and they kind of edge away when you get close . . ." She looked up at him.

Something flickered in his eyes; then he shook his head, turning away. "You don't know what it's like when they're so scared that they *hate* you. When they want to *kill* you because they're so scared that you'll . . ."

"That you'll what?"

"Read their minds. Steal their souls. Take your pick."

There was a silence. Ice crept along Kaitlyn's spine. She was bewildered—and afraid.

"Is that what you do?" she said, fighting to keep her voice above a whisper.

"No." The cold knot in Kaitlyn's stomach loosened slightly—until he turned around and looked at her with the calm gray eyes of a madman. "It's not as simple as that. Do you want to know how it works?"

Kaitlyn didn't move, didn't speak. She just looked at him.

He spoke precisely, as if giving a lecture. "Any time two minds make contact, there's a transfer of energy. That's what contact *is,* the transfer of a certain kind of energy. Back and forth, energy carrying information. You understand?"

Rob had talked about energy—channeling energy. But maybe that had been a different kind.

"Go on," Kaitlyn said.

"The problem is that some minds are stronger than others. More powerful. And if a strong mind contacts a weaker one— things can get out of control." He stopped, looking at the dark, curtained window.

"How?" Kaitlyn whispered. He didn't seem to hear her. "How can it get out of control, Gabriel?"

Still looking at the window, he said, "You know how water flows from a high place to a low place? Or how electricity keeps trying to find a ground for its force? Well, when two minds touch, energy flows. Back and forth. But the stronger mind always has more pull."

"Like a magnet?" Kaitlyn asked quietly. She'd never been

great at science, but she did know that—the bigger the magnet, the stronger it was.

"A magnet? Maybe at first. But if something happens—if things get off balance—it's more like a black hole. All the energy flows out of the weaker mind. The strong one drains it. Sucks it dry."

He was standing very still, every muscle rigid. His hands were shoved in his pockets, fingers clenched. And his gray eyes were so bleak and lonely that Kaitlyn was glad he wasn't looking at her.

She said, evenly, "You're a telepath."

"They called it something different. They called me a psychic vampire."

And I felt sorry for myself, Kaitlyn thought. Just because I couldn't help people, because my drawings were useless. But his gift makes him kill.

"Does it *have* to be that way?"

He flicked a glance at her, eyes narrowing. He'd heard the pity in her voice.

"Not if I keep the contact short. Or if the other mind is fairly strong."

Kaitlyn was remembering. *How long? About forty-five seconds. Oh, my God.*

And the Mohawk guy had come out screaming.

This volunteer is a psychic. Not psychic enough, obviously.

How strong did a mind need to be to hold up to Gabriel?

"Unfortunately," Gabriel said, still watching her with narrowed eyes, "even a little thing can upset the balance. It can happen before you know it."

Kaitlyn was afraid.

A bad thing to be around Gabriel. He saw it, sensed it. And it obviously triggered some instinct in him—to go for the throat.

He gave one of his wild, disturbing smiles. There was bright sickness in his eyes. "That's why I have to be so careful," he said. "I have to stay in control. Because if I lose control, things can happen."

Kaitlyn struggled to breathe evenly. He was moving closer to her, like a wolf scenting something it wanted. She forced herself not to cower, to look at him without flinching. She put steel into her neck.

"That was how it happened the first time," Gabriel told her. "There was a girl at that center in Durham. We liked each other. And we wanted to be together. But when we got close—something happened."

He was directly in front of her now. Kaitlyn felt her back flatten against the wall.

"I didn't mean it to happen. But I got emotional, you see. And that was dangerous. I wanted to be closer, and the next thing I knew, we were linking minds." He stopped, breathing quickly and lightly, then went on. "She was weak—and afraid. Are you afraid, Kaitlyn?"

CHAPTER 8

Lie, Kaitlyn thought. But she felt sure he could detect a lie. She also felt sure the truth might kill her.

Nothing to do but take the offensive.

"Do you want me to be? Is that what you want—for it all to happen again?"

A veil-like spiderweb seemed to fall over his gray eyes, taking out their dark brightness. He even pulled back a fraction.

Kaitlyn stayed on the attack, "I don't think you meant to hurt that girl. I think you loved her."

He stepped back even farther.

"What was her name?" Kaitlyn said.

To her surprise, he answered. "Iris. She was just a kid. We were both kids. We had no idea what we were doing."

"And she was there because she was psychic?"

His lip curled. "'Not psychic enough,'" he quoted, as if

giving Kait the answer she was expecting. Stark bitterness was in his eyes. "She didn't have enough . . . whatever. Life force. Bioenergy. Whatever it is that makes people psychic—and keeps them alive. That night at the center . . . by the time I was able to let go of her, she was just limp. Her face was white, blue-white. She was dead."

His chest heaved, and then he said deliberately, "No life. No energy left. I'd drained her dry."

Kaitlyn wasn't on the offensive any longer, and she couldn't hold his gaze. Her own chest felt as if there were a tight band around it. After a moment she said quietly, "You didn't do it on purpose."

"Didn't I?" he said. He seemed to have conquered whatever emotion had possessed him; he was breathing easily again. When Kait looked up, she saw his gray eyes were no longer bitter, or even shielded. They were . . . empty.

"The people at the center had a different idea," he went on. "When I realized she wasn't breathing, I called for help. And when they came and saw her—all blue like that—they thought the worst. They said I'd attacked her. They said I'd tried to force her, and when I couldn't, I killed her."

Kait felt a wash of pure, dizzying horror. She was glad there was a wall behind her; she let her weight rest on it, and only then realized she'd shut her eyes.

"I'm sorry," she whispered, opening them. Then, trying to find some comfort, she said, "Rob was right. What Joyce is doing *is* important for the world. We all need to learn how to control our powers."

Gabriel's face twisted. "You believe that country-boy stuff?" he said with utter contempt.

Kaitlyn was taken aback. "Why do you hate Rob so much?"

"Didn't you know? The golden boy was there, in Durham. They practically worshiped him—everything he did was right. And *he* was the one who figured out what had happened to Iris. He didn't know how I'd done it, but he knew her energy had been tapped, like blood if you cut an artery. They hunted me, you know. Like an animal. The center and the police and everyone." His voice was dispassionate.

But that wasn't Rob's fault, Kait thought. It *wasn't*. Aloud she said, "So you went on the run."

"Yeah. I was fourteen and stupid. Lucky for me, they were stupider. It took them a year to find me, and by then I was in California. In jail."

"For another murder," Kaitlyn said steadily.

"When the world is so stupid, you take your revenge, you know? People deserve it. Anybody that weak deserves it. The guy I killed tried to mess with me. He wanted to shoot me over the five dollars in my pocket. I got him first."

Revenge, Kaitlyn thought. She could picture the parts of the story Gabriel hadn't told. Him running away, not caring what happened to him, not caring what he did. Hating everything:

the universe, for giving him his power; the stupid weak people in the universe, for being so easy to kill; the center, for not teaching him how to control his gift—and himself. Especially himself.

And Rob, the symbol of someone who'd succeeded, whose powers brought only good. Who was in control. Who still *believed* in something.

"He's an idiot," Gabriel said, as if reading her thought. He did that too much; it bothered Kaitlyn. "Him and those other two, they're all idiots. But you have some common sense—or at least I thought you did."

"Thanks," Kait said dryly. "Why?"

"You see things. You know something's wrong here."

Kaitlyn was startled. "Something wrong? You mean, at the Institute?"

He gave her a look of knowing contempt. "I see. That's how you're going to play it."

"I'm not *playing* anything—"

He flashed a disturbing smile and turned, walking to the center of the room. "After all, if you leave, you don't stand much chance of getting him. Can't reel him in from Ohio."

Kaitlyn felt herself flush with anger.

It was over—the confidences, Gabriel's almost-decency, his letting down of walls. He was going to be as nasty and objectionable as possible now, just so she wouldn't get the wrong idea about him. Like that he was an okay person.

Well, I won't rise to it, Kaitlyn thought. I won't even dignify that with an answer. And however it sounds, he can't really *know* what Anna and I talked about behind closed doors.

She pushed herself off the wall and moved one step toward Gabriel. She said, very formally, "I'm sorry for what happened to you. It was all terrible. But I think that you should start thinking about what you can do to change things from now on."

Gabriel smiled silkily from behind his walls. "But what if I don't want to change things?"

Two minutes ago, Kaitlyn had been dizzy with sympathy for him. Now she wanted to kick him in the shins.

Boys, she thought.

"Good night, Gabriel," she said.

You jerk.

He widened his eyes. "Don't you want to stay? It's a big bed."

Kaitlyn didn't bother to answer that at all. She went out with her head very high, muttering words that would have shocked her father.

One thing was fortunate. For a while there, she'd felt quite close to Gabriel—and that could have meant trouble. Imagine her, Kaitlyn the cold, falling for not just one but *two* boys. But he'd taken care of that. He'd pushed her away, and she felt certain he wouldn't let her ever get close again.

No, thank God, she wasn't in any danger. She found Gabriel interesting—even, in a weird way, heartbreaking—and he was certainly gorgeous. But . . . well, anyone with the bad luck to fall in love with *him* would have to disembowel herself with a bamboo letter opener.

She wouldn't tell anyone what he'd told her about his power. That would be betraying a confidence. But she thought she might talk with Rob about him someday. It might change Rob's views, to know that Gabriel could feel regret.

Strangely, when Kait got back to bed, she fell asleep at once.

The next day Joyce took them to San Carlos High School. They were already registered for classes, and Kait was delighted to find that she shared sociology and British literature with Anna and Rob. In fact, she was delighted with everything. She'd never dreamed school could be like this.

It was different from Ohio. The campus itself was bigger, more sprawling, more open in design. Instead of one big building, there were lots of little ones, connected by covered paths. Ridiculous if it snowed—but it *never* snowed here. Never.

The buildings were more modern, too. Less wood, more plastic. Smaller rooms with more crowding. No brick, no peeling paint, no wheezing furnace.

The students seemed friendly—Rob's blond good looks had something to do with that, Kaitlyn thought. He was clearly a high-status, desirable boy, and he ate lunch with her and Anna and Lewis. Kait could see the glances other girls shot at their table.

Anna was clearly high-status, too—because she was beautiful, not at all nervous, and she didn't seem to care if anyone approached her. By the end of lunch, several girls had come by offering to show the newcomers around. They stayed to chat. One mentioned a party on Saturday.

Kait was very happy.

The thing she'd worried most about was explaining why she and the others were living together. She didn't want to tell these California girls anything about psychic powers and the Institute. She didn't want to be different at this school. She wanted to *fit in*.

But fortunately Lewis took care of that. Between snapping pictures of the girls, he grinned and said that a nice old man had given them a lot of money to go to school here. No one believed him, but it created an irresistible aura of mystery that enhanced their status even more.

At the end of the day, Kaitlyn walked out of art studio class feeling blissful. The art teacher had called her portfolio "impressive" and her style "fluid and arresting." All she wanted to make the world perfect was Rob.

Gabriel, of course, didn't associate with anyone, and ate lunch alone. Kaitlyn saw him several times that day, always away from people, always with his lip curled. He could have had tremendous status himself, she thought, because he looked so handsome and moody and dangerous, but he didn't seem to want it.

Marisol collected them after school in a silver-blue Ford van—all except Gabriel, who didn't show up at the pickup point. Kaitlyn thought about his parole and hoped he was on his way back to the Institute.

"Now for some testing," Joyce said when they got home.

That was fine with Kaitlyn. She was jubilant from her first day at school, and an afternoon of testing meant an afternoon with Rob. She still hadn't figured out a plan for helping him discover she was female, but it was always at the back of her mind. Maybe an opportunity would come up spontaneously.

But the first thing Joyce did was send Rob upstairs, saying she'd call him after she got the others settled.

"The REG is ready, Lewis," she added. She sat Lewis down at the same study carrel as before. This time Kait was bold enough to come up behind them.

"What is that thing?" she asked, looking at the machine in front of Lewis. It looked like a computer, but the monitor had a grid-marked screen with a wiggly green line running across the middle. Like a hospital monitor charting a patient's heartbeat.

"This is a random event generator," Joyce said. "It's a computer that only does one thing—it spits out random numbers. It's producing numbers right now, some positive, some negative, all completely random. That's what the green line is charting. Lewis's job is to make the line go up higher—to influence the machine to spit out more positive numbers than negative ones."

"You can do that?" Kait asked, looking at Lewis in surprise. "With your mind?"

"Yeah, that's what PK is. Mind over matter. This is actually a lot easier than making dice come up a certain number—but I can do that, too, sometimes."

"Stay away from Vegas, kid," Joyce said, rapping him on the head with her knuckles. "They'd shoot out your kneecaps."

She turned to Anna. "Right, you. Same as yesterday. I want you to tell that mouse which hole to go in."

Anna already had the white mouse out of its cage. "Come on, Mickey. Let's go make history."

"Right. Now, Kaitlyn," Joyce said. She nodded Kait toward the folding screen, where Marisol was wheeling up a machine on a cart. Kaitlyn eyed the dials and wires apprehensively.

"Don't be nervous. It's just an EEG machine," Joyce said. "An electroencephalograph. It records your brain waves."

"Oh, great."

"That isn't the part you're not going to like. You're going to really hate *this*." She held up what looked like a tube of toothpaste. "It's electrode cream, and it's murder to get out of your hair."

Kaitlyn sat in the reclining chair, resigned.

Marisol's thickly lashed brown eyes met Kait's only for the briefest of moments. Her full lips were curved in a bored, unchanging pout.

"This is just prep stuff to clean your skin," she said, squeezing a plastic bottle over a ball of cotton. She swabbed several places on Kaitlyn's head, forehead, and temples.

"Don't move your head." She dabbed some of the toothpaste on Kaitlyn's temple, then dabbed more on an electrode. Kaitlyn watched out of the corner of her eye as the wicked-looking little thing was stuck to her.

It didn't hurt. It tickled slightly. Kait shut her eyes and relaxed until Marisol finished wiring her up.

"Now, Medusa," Joyce said. "As I said, we're going to monitor your brain waves while you're doing your stuff. Brain wave levels change depending on what you're doing: Beta waves show you're attending to something, theta waves show you're drowsy. We're looking for alpha waves—the ones usually associated with psychic activity."

She saw Kaitlyn's expression and added, "Just try to ignore all this equipment, right? You'll be doing exactly the same thing as yesterday."

Kaitlyn looked sideways without moving her head, and saw Marisol bringing two strangers into the lab. New volunteers. Kaitlyn felt a sudden sharp twinge.

"Joyce, is one of those volunteers . . . for Gabriel?"

"I don't know where Gabriel is—although I'd like to," Joyce said grimly, handing Kait a pencil and clipboard. "Now relax, kiddo. No blindfold or earphones this time."

Kaitlyn shut her eyes again. She could hear some activity

on the other side of the folding screen—Joyce giving a photo to the volunteer.

"Right," Joyce said. "The subject is concentrating, Kait. You try and receive her thought."

It was only then that Kait discovered how anxious she was. Yesterday she hadn't known what to expect. Today she did know, and she was uneasy. Worried that she wouldn't be able to perform—and worried that she would.

She didn't feel like sliding down that mental chute into nothingness again. And if she did succeed . . . what if she drew something as grotesque as yesterday's picture?

Don't think about it. Take it easy. This is what you're *here* for, remember?

Don't you want to learn to control your power?

Kaitlyn gritted her teeth, then made a supreme effort to relax, to tune the world out. She could hear muted voices.

"Still beta waves on the EEC." That was Marisol.

"Give her time." That was Joyce.

Be calm, Kaitlyn thought. Ignore them. The chair's comfortable. You didn't get much sleep last night.

Slowly, gradually, she felt herself sink into drowsiness.

"Theta waves."

Blackness, falling . . .

"Alpha waves."

"Good!"

Kaitlyn's hand began to cramp and itch. But as she lifted

the pencil, eyes shut, she suddenly remembered yesterday's picture. Anxiety twisted in her stomach.

"Back to beta waves," Marisol said, as if announcing a death in the family.

Joyce peered around the screen. "Kaitlyn, what's wrong?"

"I don't know." Now Kait felt guilty as well as anxious. "I just can't focus."

"Hmm." Joyce seemed to hesitate, then she said, "Right, wait a sec," and disappeared.

She was back again quickly. "Shut your eyes, Kait."

Kaitlyn obeyed automatically. She felt a quick dab and then the touch of something cold on her forehead. Very cold.

"Now try again," Joyce said, and Kait heard her go.

Again Kait tried to relax. This time she felt the darkness swirl around her immediately. Then she had an odd sensation, a feeling of pressure in her head. Like an explosion building. And then—

—pictures. Images rushing in, almost with more force than Kaitlyn could stand.

"Alpha waves like crazy," a faraway voice said. Kaitlyn scarcely heard it.

Nothing like this had ever happened to her before—but she was too startled to be afraid. The pictures were kaleidoscopic, each passing in a flash almost before she could recognize it.

Gabriel. Something purple. Joyce—or someone like her.

Something purple and irregular. A doorway with someone standing in it. A bunch of purple round things. Something tall and white—a tower? A bunch of purple . . . grapes.

She could feel her hand moving, drawing small circles over and over on the paper. She couldn't help opening her eyes—and the instant she did, the images in her head vanished.

She'd drawn a bunch of grapes. Made sense. That was the picture she'd gotten most frequently.

Recklessly, ignoring the wires, she stood up and looked around the screen.

"What happened?" she demanded of Joyce. "I saw pictures in my head—what did you *do?*"

Joyce stood up quickly. "Just put on another electrode."

Kaitlyn put a hand to her forehead. It felt as if there was something between the electrode and the skin.

"Over your third eye," Marisol added stonily.

Joyce glanced back at her. Marisol's olive-skinned face was expressionless.

Kaitlyn had frozen. Her drawing yesterday . . . "What's—what's a third eye?"

"According to legend, it's the seat of all psychic power," Joyce said lightly. "It's in the center of your forehead, where the pineal gland is."

"But—but why would an electrode—"

"God, she's still in alpha waves," Marisol interrupted.

"Time to get you unwired," Joyce said briskly. She began pulling electrodes off. Kaitlyn felt the forehead one go, but Joyce's hands moved so quickly, she didn't see what became of it.

"By the way, what did you get?" Joyce asked, taking the clipboard from her. "Oh, *terrific,*" she cried. "Oh, look at this, everybody!"

The warmth in her voice made Kaitlyn forget what she'd been upset about.

"I don't believe it—you got the target picture exactly, Kait! *Exactly,* down to the number of grapes on the bunch."

Anna and Lewis were crowding around. The volunteer, a tall girl with night-dark skin, showed Kait the photo she was holding. It was a bunch of grapes—and Kait's own drawing might have been traced directly from it.

"That's impressive," a warm, drawling voice said from behind Kaitlyn. She felt her heart pick up speed.

"I think it was an accident," she told Rob, turning.

"No accident," Joyce said. "Good concentration. And a good volunteer; we'll have to have you back."

Rob was looking at Kaitlyn's face, his golden eyes darkening. "Are you okay? You look kind of tired."

"Actually—this is so strange—I just got a headache." Kait put her fingers to the center of her forehead, where pain like an ice pick had suddenly begun jabbing. "Oh—I guess I didn't get enough sleep last night. . . ."

"I think she needs a break," Rob said.

"Of course," Joyce said at once. "Why don't you go upstairs and lie down, Kait? We're done here."

Kait was wobbly on her feet.

"I'll help," Rob said. "Hold on to me."

It was the perfect opportunity; better than any plan or trick Kaitlyn could have thought up. And it was *useless,* because all at once her head hurt so badly that she only wanted to lie down and go to sleep.

The pain came in throbbing waves. Rob had to lead her into her bedroom because she couldn't see straight.

"Lie down," he said, and turned off the bedside lamp.

Kaitlyn eased down, then felt the mattress give under Rob's weight beside her. She didn't open her eyes. She couldn't; even the diffuse afternoon light from the window hurt.

"It sounds like a migraine," Rob said. "Is the pain all on one side?"

"It's here. In the middle," Kaitlyn whispered, indicating the spot. Now she was feeling waves of nausea. Oh, *wonderful.* How romantic.

"Here?" Rob said, sounding surprised. His fingers on her forehead were blessedly cool. Strange; they'd been warm last time.

"Yes," Kaitlyn whispered wretchedly. "I'll be all right. Just go away." And now, to top everything off, she'd told the boy she loved to get lost.

Rob ignored the suggestion. "Kait, I was wrong. It's not

a migraine; it's not even an ordinary headache. I think you're sick from burning energy too fast—psychic energy. You've run yourself dry."

Kaitlyn managed a feeble "So?"

"So—I can help you. If you'll let me."

For some reason, that frightened Kaitlyn. But a stab of agony made up her mind. "All right . . ."

"Good. Now, relax, Kaitlyn." Rob's voice was soft but commanding. "It may feel strange at first, but don't fight it. I have to find an open transfer point. . . ."

Cool, deft fingers touched either side of Kaitlyn's neck, paused for a moment as if searching for something. Then lifted, not finding it. They moved to probe delicately at the tender area behind the jaw. "No . . ." Rob murmured.

Kaitlyn felt her hand gently taken. Rob's thumb centered on her palm, his index finger directly opposite it on the back of her hand. Again he seemed to be searching for something, moving his fingers minutely. Almost like a nurse feeling for a vein before taking blood.

"No."

Rob shifted. "Let's try this—move that way a little." Kaitlyn followed his urging and scooted toward the side of the bed. She opened her eyes automatically—and then quickly shut them in alarm. Rob was bending over her, his face very close. Suddenly a pounding heart added to her pain.

"What . . . ?" she gasped.

"This is just one of the most direct ways to transfer energy," he said simply. "You need a lot."

His lack of embarrassment or self-consciousness saved her. Kaitlyn kept her eyes shut and held still as he put his forehead to hers. Their lips were almost touching.

"Got it," he murmured. His mouth actually brushed hers, but he didn't seem to notice. "Now . . . think about where it hurts. Concentrate on the place."

A minute ago she hadn't been able to think about anything else. But now . . . Kaitlyn's awareness was flooded with *him*. She didn't want to move or breathe. She could sense his entire body, even though only his forehead was touching her. Third eye to third eye, she thought dizzily.

Then, all at once, a new sensation rushed in and drove out all thought of anything physical. It was so new that she didn't have any way to classify it.

It wasn't like sight, or touch, or taste, but Kaitlyn's fogged brain tried to interpret it that way. If it had been sight, it would have been millions of sparkling lights that glowed and glittered like jewels. A dynamic, changing pattern of multicolored sparks, twinkles, and flares.

If it had been touch, it might have been pressure—not an uncomfortable pressure, but one that swept away all the pain of her headache. Like a river rushing through her mind, clearing out everything stagnant and clotted and decayed.

If it had been taste, it would have been like fresh, pure

water—water she drank greedily, like an exhausted runner whose mouth has been full of choking dust.

It was electrifying—overwhelming. It didn't simply take away the pain. It filled her with life.

Kaitlyn never knew how long she lay drinking in the life-giving energy. But some time later, she realized that Rob was slowly sitting up. She opened her eyes.

They looked at each other.

"I . . . thank you," Kaitlyn said, barely above a whisper.

She expected him to smile and nod. Instead he blinked. It was the first time she'd seen him at a loss for words.

And then, as they looked at each other, a simple thing happened. Neither of them looked away. With ordinary friends you always look away after a moment—or you speak.

But Rob didn't speak and he didn't look away.

The air between them seemed to shimmer.

CHAPTER 9

It was as if Rob were seeing her for the first time. More than that—it was as if he were seeing a *girl* for the first time. He looked astonished and wondering, like a person who had never heard music before suddenly catching a few notes of a beautiful melody on the wind. Catching it and wanting desperately to follow it.

His expression was that of someone on the brink of the greatest discovery of his life.

"Kaitlyn?" he whispered, and his voice was awed and questioning and almost frightened.

Kaitlyn couldn't speak. They were both on the threshold of something so big—so *transforming*—that it terrified her. It would change everything, forever. But she *wanted* it. She wanted it to happen.

The whole universe seemed to be hushed and waiting, breath held.

But Rob didn't move. He was on the brink of discovery—but not there yet.

He needs help, Kaitlyn thought. He still doesn't understand what's going on.

It was up to her to show him, to help him take that first step—if she wanted to. And she did. Kaitlyn suddenly felt calm and clear. She saw in her mind what was going to happen, like a picture already finished.

She would cradle his face with her hands and kiss him—very softly. And Rob would look at her with such surprise. So completely innocent—but not stupid. Rob wasn't slow to catch on. After she kissed him the second time, the astonishment would turn to dawning wonder. His golden eyes would start smoldering the way they did when he was angry . . . but for a very different reason.

Then he'd put his arms around her, and kiss her—so lightly—and the energy, the healing energy, would flow between them. And everything would be wonderful.

Breath held, Kaitlyn reached up to touch Rob's face, seeing her own graceful artist's fingers on his jaw. Even that little contact sent sparks dancing up her palm. It all seemed so simple and natural—as if she knew what to do without thinking. As if she'd always known, in some wise place inside.

Imagine it—Kaitlyn the cold, knowing what to do, feeling so sure. It was all about to happen.

Then voices broke into her reverie. Laughing, ordinary

voices that didn't belong at all to the beautiful new world Kaitlyn was inhabiting. She looked up in confusion.

Lewis and Anna were just outside the door. Gabriel was behind them.

"Hey, Kait," Lewis began cheerfully. And then, seeing her face, "Uh, oops."

Anna's dark eyes were stricken and apologetic. "We didn't mean to interrupt," she said, grabbing Lewis's shoulder as if to propel him away.

"A little therapeutic touch in the dark?" Gabriel asked blandly.

Sick dismay swept through Kaitlyn. The discovery, the wonder, in Rob's face was shattered. It had been so fragile, something that was about to be born rather than something that already existed—and now it was gone. Snatched away, leaving only Rob's usual kindness and concern. His affection for Anna and Lewis.

And his hatred for Gabriel.

"Kait had a headache," he said, standing up to face Gabriel directly. "If it's any of your business."

"She seems to be better now," Gabriel observed, looking around him at Kaitlyn. Kaitlyn glared at him with deadly heat.

"It would help if people would leave me alone," she said.

"We were just going," Anna said, her eyes telegraphing her contrition to Kaitlyn. "Come on, Lewis."

"That's right," Rob said, and then, to Kait's utter frustration and disbelief, he walked out the door himself. "Want me to close this?" he asked.

If it had been a ploy to make sure Gabriel and the others stayed away, Kaitlyn would have understood. But it wasn't. Rob had reverted completely. The only emotion she could see in his golden eyes now was brotherly affection.

And there was no way to get through to him, no way to change things back. At least for today, it was over.

She didn't know who to be angry with—Gabriel and the others or Rob himself. She might just kill Rob—but she loved him more than ever.

"Yes, please close the door," she said.

When they were all gone, Kaitlyn lay on her bed, watching as cool violet twilight replaced the warm light of afternoon. The room became shadowy, mysterious. She shut her eyes.

A sound alerted her—a sound like paper rustling. Sitting up quickly, she stared around the room. There it was, something white glimmering out of the shadows, creeping in under the door. No, not creeping—being *pushed.*

Kaitlyn quietly got off the bed and padded to the door. Yellow light from the hallway was shining through the crack beneath the door—and the paper was still moving. She ignored it, grabbed the doorknob, and yanked the door open.

Marisol was kneeling on the hallway floor.

The older girl's chin jerked up, and for a moment her brown eyes met Kaitlyn's. They looked shocked and surly. Then she was on her feet and heading for the stairs.

"Oh, no, you don't!" Fired by all the emotions of the past afternoon, Kait pounced. Frustration, excitement, and fury gave her the strength to seize Marisol and spin her around.

"What were you doing pushing stuff under my door? What *is* that?" Kaitlyn demanded, pointing to the piece of folded paper lying on the threshold. Marisol just tossed her hair out of her eyes and looked defiant.

Kaitlyn let go of her long enough to pick up the paper, then blocked her as she headed for the stairway again.

"This is my picture!" It was the one Kait had done yesterday, the one of her own face with the extra eye, the one she'd left on the lab floor.

Except that now it had writing on it.

Scrawled across the bottom in heavy black pen were the words: WATCH OUT. THIS COULD HAPPEN TO YOU.

"Another joke?" Kaitlyn said grimly, drawing herself up.

Marisol, who was several inches taller, just looked down at her with smoldering brown eyes. Kaitlyn, reckless of the consequences, grabbed Marisol's arm and *shook* her.

"Why are you trying to scare me? Is it because you hate psychics?"

Marisol laughed shortly.

"Do you want me to go *away?* Is it . . . oh, I don't know, some jealousy thing or something?" Kaitlyn was desperately groping for a reason that made sense.

Marisol pressed her full lips together.

"Okay, fine," Kaitlyn said, her voice slightly shaky. "I guess I'll just have to go and ask Joyce."

She got halfway to the stairs before Marisol spoke.

"Joyce can't help you. She doesn't know what's really going on. She wasn't around for the pilot study—but I was."

"What's a pilot study?" Kaitlyn asked, without turning.

"Never mind. The point is, you won't get help from Joyce. All she cares about is getting her experiments done, getting her name in the journals. She's blind to what's really happening. That's why Zetes hired her."

"But what does this thing *mean?*" Kaitlyn asked, shaking the paper.

Silence. Kaitlyn turned around. More silence.

"God, you're dumb," Marisol said at last. "Don't you remember the experiment today? Didn't you wonder at all how you got that picture of the grapes?"

Kaitlyn remembered that kaleidoscopic flood of images. "I assume because I'm psychic," she said, but she could hear the stiff defensiveness in her own voice.

"If you were *really* psychic, you'd figure out why you're here. And then you'd be on the next plane home."

Kaitlyn had had it with innuendo. "What are you *talking*

about? Why can't you say something straight instead of all this secret stuff?" she almost shouted. "Unless you don't really have anything to say—"

Marisol had flinched at the volume of Kaitlyn's voice—and now she suddenly shoved past her, elbowing Kait hard in the arm. As she reached the stairway, she glanced back and snapped, "I came up to tell you you're late for dinner."

Kaitlyn sagged against the wall.

This had been the most confusing roller coaster of a day . . . and Marisol seemed to be *crazy*, that was all. Except that didn't explain what had happened during Kait's experiment. When Joyce had put that "electrode" on Kaitlyn's forehead . . .

Over my third eye, Kait thought. She looked at the now crumpled paper. The extra eye in the picture stared up at her grotesquely, as if trying to tell her something.

I've got to talk to somebody. I can't deal with this alone. I need *help*.

The decision made her feel better. Kaitlyn wadded the paper up and stuck it in her pocket. Then she hurried down the stairs to dinner.

"What's it got to do with me?" Gabriel said, flicking the paper back toward Kaitlyn. He was lying on his bed reading a magazine about cars—expensive cars. "It's not my problem."

Kaitlyn caught the paper in midair. It had taken a great deal of control to come here. She probably wouldn't have done it except that she couldn't face Rob alone just now, and Anna had been on the phone with her family since dinner.

Grimly Kaitlyn held on to her precarious calm.

"If there's anything to what Marisol is saying, then it's *everybody's* problem," she told Gabriel tightly. "And *you* were the one who said that there was something wrong here."

Gabriel shrugged. "What if I did?"

Kaitlyn felt like screaming. "You really think something's wrong—but you don't care about finding *out?* You wouldn't want to *do* anything about it?"

A faint smile touched Gabriel's lips. "Of course I'm going to do something. I'm going to do what I do best."

Kaitlyn saw it coming, but couldn't avoid feeding him the straight line. Feeling like Sergeant Joe Friday at the end of a scene, she rapped out, "And what's that?"

"Taking care of myself," Gabriel said smugly. His dark eyes were full of wicked delight at having the last word.

Kaitlyn didn't bother to hide her disgust as she left.

Outside his door, she leaned against the wall again. Lewis was in the study playing Primal Scream's newest CD at tooth-vibrating levels. Anna was still in the bedroom on the phone. And as for Rob . . .

"Did the headache come back?"

Kaitlyn whirled, somehow feeling cornered against the wall. Why didn't she ever hear Rob coming?

"No," she said. "I'm fine. At least . . . No, I *am* fine." She couldn't deal with Rob right now, she really couldn't. She was afraid for him—afraid of what she might do to him if she got the chance. It seemed equally likely that she'd kiss him or kill him.

"What's that?" he said, and the next thing Kait knew, he was taking the paper out of her hand. She tried to snatch it back, but he was too fast.

"That's nothing—I mean—"

Rob smoothed the paper, glanced at it, then looked up at her sharply. "Did *you* draw this?"

"Yes . . . but I didn't do the writing. I don't—Oh, it's all so confusing." Kaitlyn had come to the end of her resources. She was tired of fighting, of pushing, of badgering people. She was *tired*.

"Come on," Rob said gently. The hand that cupped her elbow was gentle, too, but irresistible. He guided her without hesitation to the one room on the second floor that wasn't occupied—the bedroom he and Lewis shared.

"Now, tell me all about it." He sat beside her on the bed, as naturally as if he were her brother, as close as that. And with as little ulterior motive. It was agonizing—and wonderful at the same time.

And his eyes—he was looking at her with those grave golden eyes, extraordinary eyes. *Wise* eyes.

I can trust him, Kait thought. No matter what else happens between us, I can trust him.

"It's Marisol," she said, and then she was telling him everything. About waking up that first night to find Marisol in her room, about the strange things Marisol had said. *Watch out or get out. This place is different than you think.* About Marisol claiming it was all a joke the next morning. About the experiment today, and how the pictures had come into her mind—after Joyce put the cold thing on her forehead. About Marisol pushing the drawing under her door.

"And then I tried to get her to explain—but all she talked about was some pilot study, and how if I knew why I was *really* here, I would be on the next plane home. And how Joyce didn't know what was really going on, either."

She stopped. She half expected Rob to laugh, but he didn't. He was frowning, looking puzzled and intent.

"If Joyce doesn't know what's going on, then who does?"

"I guess Mr. Zetes. But, Rob, it's all so crazy."

Rob's mouth tightened. "Maybe," he said under his breath. "But I wondered about him. . . ."

"That first day? The speech about us psychics being so superior and following different laws?"

Rob nodded. Kaitlyn was meeting his eyes without self-consciousness now, as grim as he was. He believed her, and that made this whole thing much more serious than before. This was *business.*

"And why he brought Gabriel here," Rob said.

"Yes," Kaitlyn said slowly. Someday she really would have to talk to Rob about Gabriel—but not now. "But what does it all add up to?"

"I don't know." Rob looked at the drawing again. "But I know we have to find out. We have to talk to Joyce."

Kaitlyn swallowed. It had been a lot easier to threaten to tell Joyce in the heat of anger than it was to consider going to her now. But of course, Rob was right.

"Let's do it," she said.

Joyce's room was off the little wood-paneled hallway under the stairs that led to the front lab. It had originally been a solarium, a glass-enclosed porch. Not only that, but the French-door entrance was so large that anyone in the living room or foyer could see straight in. Only Joyce, Kait thought, could live in a room like this without any privacy. It probably had something to do with the fact that Joyce *always* looked good, whether she was doing business in a tailored suit or lounging in layered pink sweats—like tonight.

"Hi, guys," she said, looking up from a laptop computer. Light from her bedside lamp reflected off the glass walls.

Kaitlyn sat gingerly on the bed, and Rob pulled up the desk chair. He was still holding the drawing.

Joyce looked from one of them to the other. "Why so serious?"

Kaitlyn took a deep breath at the same time as Rob said, "We need to talk to you."

"Yes?"

Kait and Rob exchanged glances. Then Kaitlyn burst out, "It's about Marisol."

Joyce's eyebrows lifted toward her sleek blond hair. "Yes?"

"She's been saying things to Kaitlyn," Rob said. "Weird things, about the Institute being dangerous. And she wrote . . . this . . . on a drawing Kaitlyn did."

Still looking puzzled, Joyce took the paper, scanned it. Kait felt her stomach knot. She had stopped breathing completely.

When Joyce threw back her head, Kait thought for a moment she was going to scream. Instead, she burst into laughter.

Peals of laughter, musical and uncontrollable. After a minute she calmed down into snorts, but when she looked at Kaitlyn and Rob, she went off again.

Kaitlyn felt her own mouth stretch into a smile, but it was the polite, unhappy smile of someone waiting to be let in on a joke. At last Joyce collapsed against the mounded pillows, wiping tears from her eyes.

"I'm sorry . . . it's not really funny. It's just . . . it's her medication. She must not be taking it."

"Marisol takes medication?" Rob asked.

"Yes. And she's fine when she *does* take it; it's just that sometimes she forgets or decides she doesn't need it, and then . . . well. You see." Joyce waved the paper. "I suppose she means it symbolically. She's always been a little worried about psychics misusing their powers." Joyce turned to Kaitlyn, obviously struggling not to grin. "You didn't take her *literally*, I hope?"

Kaitlyn wanted to drop through the floor.

How could she have been so stupid? Of course, it had all been a terrible mistake—she should have realized that. And now she'd blundered in on Marisol's emotional problems, or mental problems, or whatever.

"I'm sorry," she gasped.

Joyce waved a hand, biting her lip to keep from laughing. "Oh, look."

"No, I'm really sorry. It was just—it was kind of spooky, and I didn't understand. . . . I *thought* there must be some simple explanation, but . . ." Kaitlyn took a breath. "Oh, God, I hope we haven't gotten her into trouble."

"No—but maybe I should let Mr. Zetes in on this," Joyce said, sobering. "He was the one who recruited her; she was actually hired before I was. I think she's a friend of his daughter's."

Mr. Zetes had a daughter? She must be pretty old, Kaitlyn thought. It was surprising she would have a friend as young as Marisol.

"Anyway, don't worry about it," Joyce said. "I'll talk to Marisol about her meds tomorrow and get everything straightened out. By the way, Kait, when did you draw this?"

"Oh—yesterday, during the remote viewing experiment. I dropped it when I heard that guy with the Mohawk screaming."

"How is that guy?" Rob asked softly. He was looking at Joyce with steady golden eyes.

"He's fine," Joyce said, and Kaitlyn thought she sounded slightly defensive. "The hospital gave him a tranquilizer and released him."

"Because," Rob went on, "I still think you should be careful with Ga—"

"Yes, right. I'm going to change the protocol with Gabriel's experiment." Joyce's tone closed the subject and she glanced at her clock.

"I'm so embarrassed," Kaitlyn said as she and Rob walked back up the stairs.

"Why? After what Marisol did, you had every right to ask what was going on."

It was true, but Kait still felt that somehow she should have realized. She should have more faith in Mr. Zetes, who, after all, had paid a lot of money to give the five of them a new life. She should have *known* that Marisol was having paranoid delusions.

The new life felt a bit lonely as Kait and Rob parted in the hallway. It was maddening to have him say good night so cheerfully, as if he *enjoyed* being her big brother. As if being anything else had never crossed his mind—which, in his view, it probably hadn't. He seemed to have wiped the entire incident this afternoon out of his consciousness.

Anna sat up as Kaitlyn came in the bedroom. "Where've you been?"

"Downstairs." Kaitlyn wanted to talk to Anna, but she was

very, very tired. She fumbled in a drawer for her nightgown. "I think I'll go to sleep early—do you mind?"

"Of course not. You're probably still sick," Anna said, instantly solicitous.

Just before falling asleep, Kaitlyn murmured, "Anna? Do you know what a pilot study is?"

"I think it's a kind of practice experiment—you do it first, before the real experiment. Like a pilot episode for a TV show comes first."

"Oh. Thanks." Kaitlyn was too sleepy to say more. But it occurred to her that maybe Marisol had told the truth about one thing. Marisol had claimed to have been "around for the pilot study," and Joyce had said that Marisol had been recruited before *her*.

The rest was nonsense, though. Like the idea that Joyce had put something weird on her forehead—God, she was glad Rob hadn't mentioned that to Joyce. Joyce would have thought Kaitlyn needed medication, too.

And Rob . . . But she wouldn't think about Rob now. She'd deal with him tomorrow.

All that night she had strange dreams. In one she was on a windswept peninsula, looking out over a cold gray ocean. In another she was with Marisol and a group of strangers. All of them had eyes in their foreheads. Marisol smirked and said, "Think you're so smart? You're growing one, too. The seed's been planted." Then Gabriel appeared and said,

"We've got to look out for ourselves. You see what can happen otherwise?"

Kaitlyn did see. Rob had fallen into a deep crevasse and he was shouting for help. Kaitlyn reached out to him, but Gabriel pulled her back, and Rob's voice kept echoing. . . .

All at once she was awake. The room was full of pale morning light, and the shouting was real.

CHAPTER 10

The shouts were distant and muffled, but unmistakably hysterical. The clock said 6:15 A.M.

Gabriel, Kait thought wildly, jumping out of bed. What has he done now?

Anna was up, too, her long black hair loose. Her eyes were alert, but not panicked. "What is it?"

"I don't know!"

She and Kait spilled out into the hallway without bothering to put on robes. Rob was just emerging from his room, wearing a tattered pair of pajama bottoms. Kait felt a surge of relief that he wasn't the one doing the shouting.

"It's coming from downstairs," he said.

He took the stairs two at a time, with Kait and Anna right behind him. Kait could hear words in the shouting now.

"Help! God! Somebody help! Quick!"

"It's Lewis!" she said.

The three of them swung around through the dining room and into the kitchen. The shouting stopped.

"Oh, *no*," Anna said.

Lewis was standing by the kitchen sink, panting. There was a sort of heap at his feet, a heap with mahogany-colored hair at one end.

Marisol.

"What happened?" Kait gasped. Lewis just shook his head. Rob had dropped to his knees at once, and was gently turning Marisol over. A trembling started in Kait's legs as she saw the face. Under her olive complexion, Marisol looked chalky. Even her lips were pale. Her eyes were open a little, showing slits of white eyeball.

"Did you call nine-one-one?" Anna asked quietly.

"It's no use," Lewis said in a strangled voice. He was braced against the sink for support, looking down. His face, normally sweet and impish, was drawn with horror. "She's dead. I know she's dead."

Waves of chills swept over Kaitlyn. What Rob was moving was now Marisol's *body*, not Marisol. That one word, "dead," made all the difference. Suddenly Kait didn't want to touch . . . *it*. The body.

She knelt by it anyway, and put a hand on its—Marisol's— chest. Then she jumped a little.

"I think she's breathing."

"She's not dead," Rob said positively. His eyes were shut,

his fingers at Marisol's temples. "Her life force is really low, but she's alive. I'm going to try to help." He stopped talking and sat still, his face lined with concentration.

In the background, Kait could hear Anna calling 911.

"What *happened*, Lewis?" she demanded again.

"She had a sort of . . . It looked like a seizure. I came down early because I was hungry, and she was in here cutting up grape-fruits, and I said hi, and she was kind of crabby, and then all of a sudden she fell down." Lewis swallowed and blinked rapidly. "I tried to pick her up, but she just kept jerking and shaking. And then she stopped moving. I thought she was dead."

Medication, Kait thought. If Marisol had been on medica-tion for seizures—and she stopped taking it . . . Or for diabe-tes. Could diabetes give you seizures?

"Where's Joyce?" she said, getting up suddenly. It was the first question she should have asked. Joyce was always down here before the kids, drinking mugs of black coffee and helping Marisol make breakfast.

"Here's a note on the fridge," Anna said. Underneath a magnet shaped like a strawberry was a note in spiky, casual handwriting.

Marisol—

Coffee filters you bought ystdy wrong kind. I'm going to exchange. Start

*bkfst-cut 3 grapefruit, make muffins.
Muff mix in blue bowl in fridge. Where
did you put receipt?*

-J

"She's at the store," Kait said, and at that moment heard the front door open.

"Joyce!" She and Lewis shouted it together. Kaitlyn rushed to the dining room entrance. "Joyce, something's happened to Marisol!"

Joyce came running. When she saw Marisol on the floor, she dumped her ecological cloth grocery bag on the counter, where several apples and a box of coffee filters spilled out.

"Oh, my God—what happened?" she said sharply. "Is she breathing all right?" Her hands flew from Marisol's wrist to her neck, searching for a pulse.

Rob didn't answer. He was sitting lotus style by Marisol's head, eyes shut, fingers on her temples. Early sun slanted in the east window and shone on his tanned shoulders.

"I think she's breathing okay now," Lewis whispered. "He said he would try to help her."

Joyce looked hard at Rob, then the strain in her face eased. "Good," she said.

"Is she epileptic?" Kaitlyn asked softly but urgently. "Because Lewis said she had a seizure."

"What? No." Joyce spoke absently. "Oh—you mean the medication? No, it's for something else entirely; he said a psychiatrist prescribed it. God knows, maybe she took an overdose. I never even got to talk to her about it."

"I know. We saw your note," Kait began. "But—"

"Listen—sirens," Anna said.

After that, things happened very quickly. Kait and Anna ran to the front door to wave down the paramedics. Just as the rescue van arrived, a black limousine pulled up behind it. Mr. Zetes got out.

And then there was a lot of confusion. Mr. Z was walking very quickly, despite his cane—and the paramedics were rushing inside with equipment—and the rottweilers were barking—and Kait was behind everyone, trying to see into the kitchen. The noise was deafening.

"Get those dogs out!" one of the paramedics shouted.

Mr. Zetes snapped an order and the dogs backed into the dining room.

"Clear this room!" another paramedic said. She was pulling at Rob, trying to get him away from Marisol. Rob was resisting.

Then Mr. Zetes spoke, in a voice that quieted everyone. "All you young people—go upstairs. You, too, Rob. We'll let the professionals take care of this."

"Sir, she's barely hanging on—" Rob began, his voice thick with worry.

"Move!" the pulling paramedic shouted. Rob moved.

On her way up the stairs, Kait came face-to-face with Gabriel, who was coming down.

"They don't want us," she said. "Go back up. How come it took you so long, anyway?"

"I never get up until seven," Gabriel murmured, backing up. He was fully dressed.

"Didn't you hear the yelling?"

"It was hard to ignore, but I managed."

Rob glared at him as he passed. Gabriel returned it with a derisive look that started with Rob's bare feet and ended with Rob's tousled head.

"We can see from the study window," Lewis said, and they all followed him into the alcove—except Gabriel, who went to one of the other windows.

In a few moments the paramedics came out with a stretcher. Lewis's hand made a slight movement toward his camera, which was lying on the window seat. Then it dropped to his side again.

They all watched as the stretcher was loaded into the back of the paramedics' van. Kait felt both frightened and strangely remorseful. Marisol's face had looked so small among all the big rescue workers and the equipment.

"I hope she's all right. She's got to be all right," she said, and then she sat down on the window seat. Her legs were very shaky.

Anna sat down and put an arm around her. "At least Joyce is going, too," she said in her quiet, gentle voice. A little of her calm penetrated Kaitlyn, like a cool wind blowing. Below, Joyce climbed into the van and it pulled out. The black limo stayed.

Rob was leaning against the window glass, one knee on the seat beside Kait. He was completely unselfconscious about his lack of dress.

"Mr. Z sure does have bad luck," he said softly. "Every time he comes here, he finds trouble."

The cool wind blowing through Kaitlyn turned cold. She looked quickly at Rob. "What are you saying?"

"Nothing," he said, still gazing out the window. "It's just too bad for him, that's all."

Lewis and Anna looked puzzled. Kait stared down at the black limousine, feeling an uneasy stirring in her stomach.

After a while, Mr. Zetes called them down to go to school. Nobody wanted breakfast. Kait didn't want to go to school, either, but Mr. Zetes didn't ask her opinion. He escorted them out to the limousine and ordered the driver to take them.

"Oh, God, I left my sociology book," Kait said when they reached the corner. The limousine, instead of turning around, backed up.

Kait ran up the porch steps and yanked the door open, conscious of the five people waiting on her in the car. She burst inside—and then stopped in middash. Mr. Z's two rottweilers were running toward her, toenails clacking and skidding on the hardwood floor. A terrible baying struck her with the force of a physical blow.

Kaitlyn had never been afraid of a dog in her life—but these weren't dogs, they were salivating monsters whose barking made the ceiling ring. She could see their pink and black gums.

She looked around desperately for a weapon—and saw Mr. Zetes.

He was standing in the little hallway just in front of Joyce's room. The strange thing was that Kaitlyn hadn't seen him arrive—and she was sure he hadn't been there when she burst in. She'd been looking in that direction, because that was where the dogs had come from.

Even stranger, she would have sworn that no door had opened or closed over there. The door to the front lab, just behind him, was shut. So were the French doors to his left— the ones that opened on Joyce's room.

But there *wasn't* any other door—to Mr. Z's right was only a solid wall that supported the staircase. So he *had* to have come from the lab or Joyce's room.

Kait saw his mouth move, and the dogs shut up. He gave her a courtly nod, his piercing dark eyes on her face.

"I forgot my sociology book," Kaitlyn said unsteadily. Her pulse was hammering, and for some reason she felt as if she were being caught in a lie.

148

"I see. Run up and get it," was all he said, but he waited until she came downstairs with it, and saw her out the door.

The drawing came, appropriately, during art studio class.

Kaitlyn had been thinking about Mr. Zetes all day, and had made the interesting discovery that it's quite possible to be miserable during lunch even though important people are being nice to you. Several cheerleaders and three or four attractive guys had sat down to talk to her group—but it didn't matter. However Kaitlyn tried to listen to them, her mind kept drifting to Mr. Zetes standing in that cul-de-sac of a hallway. Like a magician appearing in a sealed cabinet.

In art class, Kaitlyn was supposed to be doing a project for her portfolio—that important collection of pictures that might get her college credit next year—but she couldn't focus. The busy, creative classroom around her was only a blur and a hum.

Almost mesmerized, she flipped to a blank page in her sketchbook and reached for her oil pastels.

She loved pastels because they made it so easy to get what she saw from her eyes to the paper. They were quick, fluid, vigorous—free. For a normal picture, she would start by rapidly sketching the major shapes, then layering on detail. But for the *other* kind of picture, the kind she didn't control . . .

She watched her hand dot tiny strokes of carmine and crimson lake in a rectangular shape. A tall rectangle. Around the rectangle, strokes of Van Dyke brown and burnt umber. The close dots of the browns gradually formed a shimmering pattern, with whorls and lines like wood grain.

Her hand hesitated over the box of pastels—what color next? After a moment she picked up black.

Black strokes clustered heavily inside the rectangle, forming a shape. A human silhouette, with broad shoulders and body lines that swept straight down. Like a coat. A man in a coat.

Kaitlyn sat back and looked at the drawing.

She recognized it. It was one of the images she'd seen in that visionary mosaic yesterday—the doorway. Only now she could see the full picture.

A man in a coat in front of the rectangle of an open door. The red of the doorway gave an impression of energy around him. Framing the door was wood—wood paneling.

The solid wall across from Joyce's door was wood-paneled.

"Nice broken color technique," a voice above her said. "Do you need a squirt of fixative?"

Kaitlyn shook her head and the teacher moved on.

The limousine picked them up after school. Joyce was still at the hospital, Mr. Zetes told them when they got home. Marisol was still unconscious. There wouldn't be any testing today.

Kait waited until everyone had drifted upstairs, and then quietly, one by one, she began to gather them. "We've got to talk. In the study," she said. Anna, Lewis, and Rob all came at once. Gabriel came when she stuck her head in his room and hissed at him.

When they were together in the study, she shut the door and turned the TV on. Then she showed them the picture and told them what she'd seen that morning.

"So you think, like . . . what? There's really a door there?" Lewis asked. "But what does that *mean?* I mean, so what?"

Kaitlyn looked at Rob, whose eyes were dark, dark gold.

"There's more," she said, and she told Anna and Lewis what she'd told Rob and Gabriel the night before. All of it, about Marisol's warnings and the strange things that had been happening.

When she was through, there was no sound except the blaring of a music video on TV.

Anna sat with her head slightly tilted, her long braid falling into her lap, her eyes faraway and sad. Lewis rubbed his nose, forehead puckered. Rob's face was set, his fists resting on his knees. Kaitlyn herself gripped the sides of her sketchbook tensely.

Gabriel was sitting back with one knee hooked over the arm of the couch. He was playing with a quarter, flipping it over and catching it. He seemed completely unconcerned.

Finally Anna said, "*Something's* going on. Any one of those things—like what Marisol said, or the cold thing on your forehead—any one of them could be explained. But when you put them all together, something's . . ."

"Amiss," Rob supplied.

"Amiss," Anna said.

Lewis's face cleared. "But look. If you think there's a door down there, why don't we just go down and *see?*"

"We can't," Anna said. "Mr. Z's in the living room, and so are the dogs."

"He's got to leave sometime," Rob said.

Lewis squirmed. "Look—you're really saying that the Institute is, like, evil? You really think so?" He turned to Rob. "I thought you loved this place, the whole idea of it."

Gabriel snorted. Rob ignored him. "I do love the idea of it," he said. "But the reality . . . I've just got a bad feeling about it. And Kait does, too."

Everyone looked at Kait, who hesitated. "I don't know about feelings," she said finally, looking down at the picture of a door. "I don't even know whether to trust my drawings. But there's only one way to find out about this one."

It took them half an hour to plan the burglary. Actually, it only took five minutes to do the planning. The other twenty-five were spent trying to force Gabriel to help.

"No, thanks. Include me out," he said.

"You wouldn't have to go inside," Kaitlyn said through her teeth. "All you need to do is sit in the alcove and watch for cars coming in the driveway."

Gabriel shook his head.

Anna tried gentle reasoning with him; Lewis tried bribery. None of it worked.

At last Rob stood up with an exclamation of disgust and turned toward the door. "Stop catering to him. He's afraid. It doesn't matter; we can do it without him."

Gabriel's eyes went hard. "Afraid?"

Rob barely glanced back at him. "Yeah."

Gabriel stood up. "Care to say that again?"

This time Rob turned. He stood face-to-face with Gabriel and their eyes locked, silently fighting it out.

Kaitlyn watched them both without breathing. Thinking again that they were so different, such opposites. Rob all gold, radiant energy, his waving hair tousled, his eyes blazing. And Gabriel darkness, his skin paler than usual, his hair looking black in contrast. His eyes bottomless and cold.

Like the sun and a black hole, side by side, Kait thought. In that moment the image was etched into her mind, a picture she would never draw. It was too frightening.

Once again, she was afraid for Rob. She knew what Gabriel could do—with or without a knife. If they started fighting . . .

"I'm going downstairs," she said abruptly. "To ask Mr. Z if we can order a pizza."

Everyone looked at her, startled. Then Kait saw understanding flash in Anna's eyes.

"That's a good idea. I'm sure nobody wants to cook dinner," Anna said, standing and gently taking Rob's elbow. She nudged Lewis with her foot.

"Uh, fine with me," Lewis said, putting his baseball cap on backward. He was still looking at Gabriel.

Slowly, to Kaitlyn's great relief, the two combatants broke their locked stare and stepped away from each other. Rob submitted to Anna's gentle tugging. Kaitlyn made sure he got out the door.

Then she looked back at Gabriel.

His eyes were still dark as black holes, but his mouth was mocking and sardonic. "You can put it off, but it's going to happen someday," he said. Before Kaitlyn could defiantly ask *what* was going to happen, he added, "I'll watch for cars up here. But that's all. I won't risk my neck to help you. If something goes wrong, you're on your own."

Kaitlyn shrugged. "I've always been on my own," she said, and went downstairs to order pizza.

Mr. Zetes didn't leave until eleven o'clock. Kaitlyn was afraid to have the group stay downstairs with him after dinner, afraid that one of them might give something away. They sat in the study, pretending to do homework, and all the time listening for a sign that Mr. Z was going.

When he finally did go, he called them to the staircase and said that Joyce would undoubtedly be coming soon.

"But you won't be alone until then. I'll leave Prince and Baron," he said.

Kaitlyn studied his face, wondering how much he suspected they suspected. Were those dark eyes fierce or just acute? Was there the shadow of a grim smile on his lips?

He can't *know* anything, she thought.

Acting for all she was worth, she said, "Oh, thank you, Mr. Zetes."

When the front door shut behind him, Kaitlyn looked at Anna, who looked back helplessly.

"Prince and Baron?" Kait said.

Anna sighed, fingering the end of her black braid. In anyone else it would have been a nervous gesture. "I don't know. I *will* try, but they look very hard to influence."

"You'd better go if you're going," Gabriel said curtly.

"You just go hide—I mean *stand guard*—in the dark," Rob said. Kaitlyn grabbed his wrist and dragged him a step or two down the stairs. Dearly as she loved Rob, there were times when she wanted to bash his head in.

Gabriel retreated into the darkened study, his handsome face inscrutable.

"You first, Anna," Kaitlyn said. Anna walked down the stairs, so slowly and gracefully that she might have been drifting. Rob and Kait followed, with Lewis behind.

"Careful. Easy," Anna said as she reached the bottom. A low growl sounded from somewhere behind the staircase.

One dog was in the paneled hallway, Kaitlyn saw as they rounded the corner. The other was in the darkened living room, almost blending into the shadows. Both were watching Anna intently.

"Easy," Anna breathed, and that was the last word she said.

She stood perfectly still, looking at the dog in the living room, her left hand raised toward the dog in the hallway, the way you'd gesture to a person to wait.

The growl died away. Anna's upraised hand slowly closed, as if she'd caught something in her fist. She turned, smoothly and without haste, to look at the dog in the hallway.

"Look out!" Rob yelled, jumping forward.

In absolute silence, with its lips peeled back and the hair on its back bristling, the dog in the living room was stalking toward Anna.

CHAPTER 11

Everything happened too quickly for Kaitlyn to take in. She only knew that she grabbed desperately for Rob's arm to hold him back, thinking that only Anna could deal with the dog, and anyone else was likely to distract her. And then Anna was holding up her hand in a commanding gesture—*stop*—but the dog was still coming. Moving eerily, as if on oiled machinery, every tooth showing.

"No!" Anna said sharply, and added some words in a language Kaitlyn didn't know. "Hwhee, Sokwa! Brother Wolf—go to sleep! It's not hunting time now. Rest and sleep."

Then, without showing the slightest sign of fear, she reached for the snarling muzzle. She locked one hand over it, grabbing the hair at the dog's neck with the other. Her eyes gazed straight into the animal's, unflinching and unwavering.

"I'm the pack leader here," she said clearly. "This is not your territory. I am dominant." Kaitlyn had the feeling that the words were only part of the communication. Something unspoken was passing between the graceful girl and the animal.

And the dog was responding. His lips slid down to cover his teeth again. The hair on his back flattened. More—his entire back flattened, drooped, until his belly almost touched the floor. His tail tucked between his legs. His eyes shifted. His entire attitude was one of submission.

Anna held out a hand to the other dog, which moved toward her slowly, tail down, almost crawling on its elbows. She clamped a hand over its muzzle, clearly establishing dominance.

Rob's eyebrows were up. "How long can you sustain that?"

"I don't know," Anna said without turning. "I'll try to keep them right here—but you guys had better work fast." She tilted her head and, still looking at the dogs, began chanting something softly. Kaitlyn didn't understand the words, but the rhythm was soothing. The dogs seemed mesmerized, cringing a little, pushing at her gently with their noses.

"Let's go," Rob said.

The paneling in the hallway was dark—walnut or mahogany, Kaitlyn thought vaguely. She and Rob both scanned it intently, while Lewis squinted doubtfully.

"There," she said, pointing to the middle panel. "That looks like a crack, doesn't it? It could be the top of a door."

"That means there must be a release somewhere around here," Rob said, running his fingers over the smooth wood and into the grooves between panels. "But we'll probably never find it by accident. You may have to push more than one place, and do it in a certain sequence or something."

"Okay, Lewis," Kait said. "Do your stuff."

Lewis edged between them, muttering, "But I don't know what *to* do. I don't know anything about secret doors."

"You don't know exactly what you're doing when you use PK on the random number machine, either, do you?" Kaitlyn demanded. "So how do you manage that?"

"I just kind of . . . nudge at the thing with my mind. It's not conscious. I just nudge and see what happens, and if something works, I keep doing it."

"Like biofeedback," Rob said. "People don't know *how* they slow down their heart rate, but they do."

"Well, nudge this panel and see what happens," Kait told Lewis. "We've got to find that door—if there is a door."

Lewis began, stroking the panel lightly with outspread fingers. Every so often he would stop and push on the wood, his entire body tense. Kaitlyn knew he was pushing with his mind, too.

"Come on, where are you?" he muttered. "Open, open."

Something clicked.

"Got it!" Lewis said, sounding more astonished than triumphant.

Kaitlyn stared, her knees going weak.

There *was* a door. Or a passage, anyway. The middle panel had recessed and slid smoothly behind the panel on the left. There was a gaping hole in the formerly solid wall.

It looked just like Kaitlyn's drawing, except that there was no figure in the doorway. There were only stairs leading downward, faintly illuminated by half-covered reddish lights at foot level. They seemed to have been activated by the door opening.

Lewis breathed one word. "Jeeeeeez."

"Why is it so dark?" Kait murmured. "Why not put some real lights in?"

Rob nodded toward the French doors to Joyce's room just opposite. "Maybe because *she's* there. This way, you could walk into this place without being seen, even at night."

Kaitlyn frowned, then shrugged. There was no time to wonder about it. "Lewis, you stay up here. If Gabriel yells that he sees lights coming up the driveway, tell us. We'll come up fast, and you can close the door."

"*If* I can close the door," Lewis said. "It's like trying to learn how to wiggle your ears—you don't know how until you do it." But he stationed himself by the panel like a resolute soldier.

"I'll go first," Rob said, and began cautiously making his way down the stairs. Kaitlyn followed, wishing that she'd brought a flashlight. She didn't at all like this journey into red-hazed dimness—although the lights illuminated the steps themselves, they showed nothing around them. The stairway seemed suspended in an abyss.

"Here's the bottom," Rob said. "It feels like another hall-way—wait, here's a switch."

Light blossomed, cool, greenish fluorescent light. They were in a short hallway. The only door was at the end.

"We may need Lewis again," Kaitlyn said, but the door opened when Rob turned the handle.

Kaitlyn didn't know what she expected to see, but it certainly wasn't what she saw. An ordinary office, with a corner desk and a computer and filing cabinets. After the sliding panel and the dark staircase, it was something of a letdown.

She looked at Rob. "You don't think . . . I mean, what if we're completely wrong here? What if he just has a hidden room because he's eccentric? It's possible."

"Anything's possible," Rob said, so shortly that she knew he wondered, too. He went to the filing cabinet and pulled out a drawer with a sliding rattle.

The sound made Kaitlyn's skin jump. If they *were* wrong, they had no business poking into things.

Defiantly she went over to the desk and thumbed through some papers from the letter tray. They were business letters, mostly from important-sounding people, addressed to Mr. Zetes. They all seemed to be photocopies, duplicates. Big deal.

"You know what?" she asked grimly, still pawing. "I just realized. If Mr. Z *was* trying to hide something, he'd never hide it *here*. Why should he? He's got to have better places. He's got a *house*, doesn't he? He's got a *corporation*, somewhere—"

"Kaitlyn."

"Well?"

"I think you should look at this." Rob was holding a file from the cabinet. There was a photograph of Kait clipped on the jacket, and in bold letters: KAITLYN BRADY FAIRCHILD, PROJECT BLACK LIGHTNING.

"What's Project Black Lightning?"

"I don't know. There's a file like that for each of us. Inside there's just a bunch of papers—all kinds of information. Did you know they have your birth certificate?"

"The lawyers told Dad they needed stuff. . . . What's that?"

"A graph about your testing, I think." Rob's tanned finger traced the bottom axis. "Look, this is dated yesterday. It says *First Testing with*—and then there's a word I can't read."

"First testing with something," Kaitlyn repeated slowly. She touched her forehead. "But what does it mean?"

Rob shook his head. "There's another set of files here, with other names." He held up a file jacket with a photo of a smiling girl with dark brown hair. It was labeled SABRINA JESSICA GALLO, BLACK LIGHTNING PILOT STUDY.

Running diagonally across the label, in thick red ink, the word TERMINATED was scrawled.

Kaitlyn and Rob looked at each other.

"Which was terminated?" Kait breathed. "The study or the girl?"

Silently, with one impulse, they turned back to their search.

"Okay, I've got a letter," Kait said after a moment. "It's from the Honorable Susan Baldwin—a judge. It says, 'Enclosed is a list of potential clients who might be interested in the project.' *The project*." Kaitlyn's eyes scanned down the list. "'Max Lawrence—up for sentencing May first. TRI-Tech, Inc.—settlement conference with Clifford Electronics Limited, June twenty-fourth.' It's all like that, names and trial dates and stuff."

"Here's another file," Rob said. "It's hard to figure out, but I think it's an old grant from NASA. Yeah, a grant from NASA for half a million, back in eighty-six. For"—he paused and read carefully—"investigation into the feasibility of the development of psychoactive weaponry.'"

"What of the what?" Kaitlyn said hopelessly. "Psycho-*what?*"

Rob's eyes were dark gold and bleak.

"I don't know what it all adds up to. But it's not good. There's a *lot* Mr. Z didn't tell us."

"'This place is different than you think,'" Kaitlyn quoted. "And there *was* a pilot study before us—so Marisol told the truth. But what happened to those kids? What happened to Sabrina?"

"And what's going to happen to—" Rob broke off. "Did you hear that? A noise up there?"

Kaitlyn listened, but she didn't hear anything.

Upstairs, Gabriel was seething.

The whole plan was stupid, of course. Why did they want to go meddling in what was obviously not their business? The time to worry about Zetes was when he was trying to *do* something to you, not before. Then fight—kill him, if necessary. He was only an old man. But why ruin what had so far proved to be a very comfortable deal?

It was all *his* idea, Gabriel felt sure. Kessler's. Rob the Virtuous probably felt there was something unspiritual about coming into so much money. He had to wreck it somehow.

And Kaitlyn was just as bad these days. Completely under Kessler's spell. Why should Gabriel care about her, a girl who was in love with a guy he hated? A girl who only disturbed him . . .

A girl with hair like fire and witch eyes, his mind whispered.

A girl who hounded him, badgered him . . .

Who challenges you, his mind whispered. Who could be your equal.

A girl who interfered with him, trying to get inside his guard . . .

Whose spirit is like yours.

Oh, shut up, Gabriel told his brain, and stared broodingly into the darkness beyond the study window.

The street in front of the Institute was silent and deserted. Naturally, it was midnight—and here in the suburbs that meant everyone was tucked nice and snug in their beds.

Nevertheless, Gabriel felt uneasy. Little sounds seemed to be nagging at his subconscious. Cars on the streets behind the Institute, probably.

Cars . . . Suddenly Gabriel stiffened. Eyes narrowed, he listened for a moment, then he left the alcove.

Nothing out the west window of the study. With the silent

steps of a housebreaker he headed for the back of the house, to Rob and Lewis's bedroom. He looked out the back window, the one facing north.

And there it was. The limo. It had obviously come up the narrow dirt road in back. Now the only question was whether Zetes was just about to get out, or—

Directly beneath him, in the kitchen, Gabriel heard a door open.

The back door, he thought. And those idiots downstairs are all waiting for him to come from the front.

There wasn't any time to go down and warn them—and Zetes would hear a shout.

Gabriel's lip curled. Tough. Kaitlyn knew the truth. He'd told her he wouldn't risk his neck for her. Not that there was anything he could do anyway, except . . .

He shook his head slightly. Not that. In the darkened window his reflected eyes were cold and hard.

Below, the kitchen door slammed.

No, he told himself. He wouldn't. He wouldn't . . .

On the bottom of the letter tray was a scribbled page like something you might doodle while on the telephone. Kaitlyn could make out the scrawled words "Operation Lightning Strike" and "psychic strike team."

"This is weird—" she began. She never finished the sentence because *it* hit her.

Just what *it* was, she couldn't tell at first. Like Rob's healing transfusion of energy, it wasn't something you could see or
hear or taste. But while Rob's energy flow had been wonderful,
invigorating, an intense pleasure, this was like being hit by a
runaway train. Kaitlyn had the feeling of being violated.

And while it didn't trigger any of her normal senses, it
mimicked them. Kaitlyn smelled roses. She felt a burning in
her head—a painful searing that built until a light like one
of Lewis's flashbulbs went off in her brain. Then, through the
explosion, she heard a voice.

Gabriel's voice.

Get out of there! He just came in the back door!

For a moment Kait stood paralyzed. Knowing that Gabriel
could communicate directly with her mind was very different
from *feeling* it. Her first reaction was that she was hallucinat-
ing; it was impossible.

Rob was gasping. "God. He's a telepath."

*Shut up, Kessler. Move. Do something. You're about to get
caught.*

Kaitlyn felt another wave of astonishment. The communication was two-way—Gabriel could hear Rob. Then some
primitive instinct within her awoke and shoved all speculation
aside. This wasn't the time to think—it was time to *act*.

She threw the letters back in the tray and slid the drawers
of the file cabinet shut. Then she had an idea and she tried
to do something she'd never done before. She tried to send

a thought. She didn't know *how* to send one, but she tried, concentrating on the burning-roses sensation in her head. *Gabriel—can you hear me? You need to tell Anna he's here. Tell her to hang on to the dogs until—*

I can hear you, Kaitlyn. It's Anna. The answer was lighter, calmer, than Gabriel's communication. It was a lot like Anna's speaking voice.

Kaitlyn realized something. Not only could she hear Anna, but she had a sense of where Anna was, and what Anna was doing. It was as if she could feel Anna's presence. And Lewis's . . .

Lewis, shut the panel, she thought. *And then get upstairs. Anna, let the dogs go as soon as he does.*

And what are you going to do? Lewis asked. Kait could sense that he was working on the panel.

Hide, Rob said briefly, turning off the fluorescent lights in the hallway and the office.

Although it seemed like hours since the explosion in Kaitlyn's mind, she knew it was only a few seconds. This strange telepathy might be very, very disconcerting, but it was an extraordinarily efficient way to communicate.

I've got the panel shut. I'm going upstairs, Lewis said.

I'm letting the dogs go—quick, Lewis! Come on! Anna's voice sharpened, and Kait felt a surge of urgency from her.

What's happening? Kait demanded.

Wait—I think it's all right. Yes. Now what Kait felt from

Anna was relief. *He was coming around through the dining room just as we went up the stairs, but I don't think he saw us. He was looking down at the dogs.*

You two had better get into bed. He might come upstairs, Rob said. Kaitlyn turned toward him in the dark. It was fascinating—his silent mental voice sounded just like his ordinary voice, but more so. It was more honest, it seemed to carry more of *him* in it. Right now it was full of quiet concern for Anna and Lewis.

"Or he might come down here," Rob's real voice whispered to Kait. "Come on."

He took her hand. How he could navigate in the dark was beyond her, but he guided them both to the corner desk.

"Get under it," he whispered. "The file cabinets block off the view from the door."

Kaitlyn found herself squeezing into a very tight place.

And then they waited. There was nothing else to do. Kaitlyn's heart was beating violently, seeming loud in the quietness. Her hand in Rob's was slick. Sitting still was much harder than moving and talking had been.

Another fear had gripped her. This was Gabriel's power, right? The one that had killed Iris, the girl in Durham; that had driven the Mohawk volunteer crazy after forty-five seconds. How long had Gabriel kept their minds linked up tonight? And how much longer before he started to suck *their* brains out?

It has to get unstable, she reminded herself. *That's what he said. He can control it if he keeps the contact short.*

She was still afraid. Even though Gabriel hadn't said anything since the beginning, she could *feel* him out there. A strong presence, surrounded by smooth, hard walls. He was keeping them all in contact. And every second that ticked by made the contact more dangerous.

Beside her, Rob stiffened. *Listen,* he said.

Kaitlyn heard. A sliding, rattling sound. The panel.

I don't think that's Lewis, Rob said.

It's not. I'm in bed, Lewis said.

Anna's mental voice was clear and purposeful. *Do you want us to do anything, Kait?*

Kait took a deep breath, then sent the thought, *No, just sit tight. We'll be fine.* At the same time she felt Rob squeeze her hand. There were some things that could be said without even telepathy. She and Rob both knew that they wouldn't be fine—but she couldn't think of any way for Anna to help.

Light suddenly showed in a diffuse fan pattern on the office floor. Mr. Zetes had turned on the fluorescents in the hallway.

Please don't let him come in. Please don't let him come in, Kaitlyn thought. Then she tried to stop thinking, in case the others could hear her panic.

The office door was opening, light spilling in.

Beneath the desk, Kaitlyn buried her face in Rob's shoulder, trying to keep absolutely still. If he didn't actually *come* in—if he only looked in . . .

More light. Mr. Z had turned on the office switch. Now he

had only to step beyond the file cabinets to see them.

I wonder if we'll be terminated, Kait thought. Like Sabrina. Like Marisol. She wanted to jump out and get it over with, to confront Mr. Zetes. They were lost anyway. The only thing that kept her from moving was Rob's arm around her.

Upstairs, she heard a wild clamor. An explosion of barking and baying.

What is it? she thought.

Gabriel's voice, cool sarcasm underlaid with heated anger, came back. *I've riled the dogs a little. I figure that should bring him up.*

Kaitlyn held her breath. There was a pause, then the lights in the office went off and the door shut. A minute later the light in the hallway went off, too—and then she heard a rattle.

She sagged against Rob. He squeezed her with both arms and she clung back, even though it was really too warm for clinging.

Above, the barking went on and on. Then, gradually, it faded as if getting more distant.

Gabriel's voice came again. *He's taking them out to the limo. I don't think he's coming back, but Joyce might be—any minute now.*

Lewis, Rob said, *get us out of here.*

Ten minutes later, they were all upstairs in the study.

It was perfectly dark except for the moonlight coming in the window. They could barely see each other, but that didn't matter. They could *feel* each other.

Kaitlyn had never been so aware of other people in her life. She knew where each of them was; she had a vague sense of what each was doing. It was as if they were not quite separate creatures—isolated and yet attached somehow.

Like insects caught in a huge web, she thought. Tied together by almost invisible threads. Every pull on the strands lets you know someone else is moving. Her artist's mind gave her an image: the five of them hanging trapped, spread-eagled, and the silken strands between them humming with power.

"Nice picture. But I don't want to be trapped in a web with you," Lewis said mildly.

"And I don't want to have you reading my thoughts," Kaitlyn told him. "That was private."

How am I . . . "I mean, how am I supposed to tell?" Lewis asked, changing from mental voice to ordinary voice in mid-sentence.

"Nobody likes it," Rob said. "Switch it off, Gabriel."

There was a silence which Kaitlyn sensed with both mind and ears.

Everyone turned to look at Gabriel. He looked back with cold defiance.

"Fine," he said. "Just tell me how."

CHAPTER 12

Kaitlyn stared into the darkness where Gabriel was sitting. *What do you mean?* Rob asked, deadly quiet. He didn't even seem to notice he wasn't speaking out loud.

"What have you done before?" Anna put in quickly. "I mean, how does it stop, usually?"

Gabriel turned to her. "Usually? When people drop dead or start screaming."

There was another blank silence, then a sudden gabble of voices, both mental and otherwise.

Are you saying it's going to kill us?—that was Lewis.

"Just a minute; let's all stay calm."—Anna.

I think you'd better start explaining, buddy!—Rob.

Gabriel sat for a moment, and Kait had the feeling of raised hackles and bared teeth from him—like one of the rottweilers. Then, slowly and coldly, he began to explain.

It was the story he'd told Kaitlyn about his powers: about how Iris, the girl in Durham, had died, about his escape afterward, about the man who'd tried to kill him, the man he'd killed instead. He told it without emotion—but Kaitlyn could feel the emotion that was suppressed behind the wall. They all could—and Kaitlyn could tell that, too.

I hate this as much as you do, Gabriel finished. *The last thing I want is to see what's in your helpless little minds. But if I knew how to control it, I wouldn't be here.*

He feels more trapped than anyone else. Like a spider caught in its own web, Anna commented, and Kaitlyn wondered if it was meant to be a shared insight, or if Anna was just thinking it.

"But then why did you do it to *us* tonight?" Rob demanded. Kait could feel the bewilderment emanating from him. Direct contact with Gabriel's mind had shaken his view of Gabriel as a selfish, ruthless killer—Kaitlyn could tell that. Which was funny, she thought, because the image of a selfish, ruthless killer was exactly what Gabriel was trying so hard to project right now. "If you knew you couldn't control it, why did you use telepathy on us?" Rob said angrily.

Because I couldn't think of any other way to save your useless necks! Gabriel's reply had the force of a knockout blow.

Rob sat back.

"There probably *wasn't* another way," Kaitlyn said judiciously. "Mr. Zetes was just about to walk in on us when the dogs started barking. What did you do to them, by the way?"

Threw a shoe at them.

At those *dogs? Jeeeez,* Lewis said.

Gabriel seemed to give a mental shrug. *I figured he'd have to come up and see what was going on. Then he couldn't get them to shut up, so he finally had to take them outside.*

"Look," Anna broke in, "maybe we shouldn't be using this thing so much. Maybe it'll go away sooner if we all just ignore it."

"It'll go away when we go to sleep," Gabriel said flatly— but aloud, Kaitlyn noticed.

"Are you sure?" Lewis asked.

"Yes."

Kaitlyn decided not to mention that Gabriel didn't *feel* as sure as he sounded.

"We really should go to sleep, anyway," she said. It was only now, when all the panic and excitement were over, that she could begin to realize how tired she was. She was stiff from tension and from sitting under that desk. And her mind was exhausted from trying to take in everything that had gone on today. From Marisol's seizure, to Mr. Zetes appearing by the hidden door, to her drawing in art class, to the burglary—so much had happened that her brain was simply giving up.

"But you didn't tell us what was down there behind the panel," Lewis said. "Did you find *anything?*"

"We found plenty, all bad," Rob said. "But Kaitlyn's right. We can talk about it tomorrow."

Kaitlyn could feel Anna biting her lip on questions, judging that it was wiser to wait. She could feel Lewis sighing. But it was all muffled by an enormous sense of weariness—even of dizziness, of illness. She wasn't just feeling her own fatigue, she realized. Gabriel was on the verge of collapse. He was—

Rob, she said urgently.

Rob was already moving. In trying to stand up, Gabriel had staggered and fallen to his knees. Kaitlyn helped Rob put him back on the couch.

"He's bad off—like you when you burned up so much energy yesterday, Kait," Rob told her. He was holding Gabriel's arm—and Gabriel was resisting feebly.

"I don't burn energy doing this. I take energy," he said.

"Well, you burned something this time," Rob said. "Maybe because you were connecting so many people. Anyway . . ." Kaitlyn could hear him take a deep breath—and sense him getting a better grip on Gabriel's arm. "Anyway, maybe I can help you. Let me—"

"No!" Gabriel shouted. "Let go of me."

"But you need energy. I can—"

I said, let go! Once again, the thought itself was an attack. Kaitlyn winced and everyone backed up a little—everyone except Rob. He stood his ground.

Lewis said weakly, "I think he's got enough energy right now."

Gabriel's attention was still on Rob. "I don't need anything from anyone," he snarled, trying to pull out of Rob's grip. "Especially not from you."

"Gabriel, listen—" Kait began. But Gabriel wasn't in a mood to listen. She could feel waves of defensive, destructive fury beating at her like the icy battering of a storm.

I don't need any of you. This doesn't change anything, so don't think it does. By tomorrow it'll be gone—and until then, just leave me alone!

Rob hesitated, then released Gabriel's arm. "Whatever you want," he said almost gently. He stepped back.

Now, Kaitlyn thought, comes the interesting part. Whether Gabriel can make it to his room on his own or not.

He did. Not very steadily, but belligerently. Not needing words to send the message that they'd all better keep away.

The door to the large bedroom shut hard behind him. Kaitlyn could still feel his presence on the other side, but it was a feeling of walls, of spiky barriers. She herself used to have walls like that.

"Poor guy," Lewis muttered.

"I think we'd all better go to bed," Anna suggested.

They did. Kaitlyn's clock said 2:52 A.M. She wondered vaguely how they were going to make it to school tomorrow, and then exhaustion overcame her.

The last thing she remembered, as her defenses lowered

in sleep, was thinking, *By the way, Gabriel, thanks. For risking your own neck.*

She got only nasty images of icy walls and locked doors as an answer.

She was dreaming, and it was the old dream about the peninsula— the rocky peninsula and the ocean and the cold wind. Kaitlyn shivered in the spray. The sky was so dark with clouds that she couldn't tell if it was day or evening. A single, lonely gull circled over the water.

What a desolate place, she thought.

"Kaitlyn!"

Oh, yes, Kaitlyn remembered. The voice calling my name; that was in my first dream, too. And now I turn around and there's no one there.

Feeling resigned, she turned. And started.

Rob was climbing down the rocks. His gold-blond hair was flecked with spray and there was damp sand on his pajama bottoms.

"I don't think you're supposed to be here," Kaitlyn told him with the confused directness of dreams.

"I don't *want* to be here. It's freezing," Rob said, hopping and slapping his bare arms with his hands.

"Well, you should have worn more sensible clothes."

"I'm freezing, too," a third voice said. Kaitlyn looked.

Lewis and Anna were behind her, both looking chilled and windswept. "Whose dream is this, anyway?" Lewis added.

"This is a very strange place," Anna said, gazing around with dark, thoughtful eyes. Then she said, "Gabriel—are you all right?"

Gabriel was standing a little way down the peninsula, his arms folded. Kaitlyn felt that this dream was getting crowded— and ridiculous. "It's funny—" she began.

I don't think it's funny, and I'm not going to play. Gabriel's voice said in her head.

. . . if it was a dream.

Suddenly Kaitlyn was very much in doubt.

"Are you *really* here?" she asked Gabriel. He just looked at her coldly, with eyes the color of the ocean around them.

Kaitlyn turned to the others. "Look, you guys, I've had this dream before—but not with all of *you* in it. But is it really you, or am I just dreaming you?"

"You're not dreaming *me*," Lewis said. "I think I'm dreaming you."

Rob ignored him and shook his head at Kait. "There's no way for me to prove I'm real—not until tomorrow."

Strangely, that convinced Kait. Or maybe it was just the nearness of Rob, the way her pulse quickened when she looked at him, the certainty that her mind couldn't be making up anything this vivid.

"So now we're sharing *dreams?*" she asked edgily.

"It must be the telepathic link. That web of yours," said Anna.

"If Kaitlyn's had the dream before, it's *her* fault," said Lewis. "Isn't it? And where are we, anyway?"

Kaitlyn looked up and down the narrow spit of land. "I don't have a clue. I've only had this dream a couple of times before, and it never lasted this long."

"Can't you dream us somewhere warmer?" Lewis asked, teeth chattering.

Kaitlyn didn't know how. This dream didn't *feel* like a dream exactly—or, rather, she felt much more like the waking Kaitlyn than the fuzzy Kaitlyn who moved semiconsciously through dreams.

Anna, who seemed least affected by the cold, was kneeling near the edge of the water. "This is strange," she said. "You see these piles of stones everywhere?"

It was something Kaitlyn hadn't noticed before. The peninsula was bordered with rocks, most of which looked as if they had just washed up. But some of the rocks were gathered into stacks, piled one on top of another to form whimsical towers. Some rocks had their long axis up and down, some were placed horizontally. Some of the towers looked a bit like buildings or figures.

"Who did it?" Lewis asked, aiming a kick at a pile.

"Hey, don't," Rob said, blocking the kick.

Anna stood up. "He's right," she told Lewis. "Don't spoil things. They're not ours."

They're not anyone's. This is just a dream, Gabriel said, throwing a look more chilling than the wind at them.

"If it's *just* a dream, how come you're still in it?" Rob asked.

Gabriel turned away silently.

Kaitlyn knew one thing: This particular dream had gone on *much* longer than any of the others. And they might not really be here, but Rob's skin was covered with gooseflesh. They needed to find shelter.

"There must be somewhere to go," she said. Where the peninsula joined the land, there was a very wet and rocky beach. Above that, a stony bank, and then trees. Tall fir trees that formed a dark and uninviting thicket.

On the other side, water . . . and across the water, a lonely cliff, bare in some places, black with forest in others. There was no sign of human habitation, except—

"What's that?" she said. "That white thing."

She could scarcely make it out in the dimness, but it looked like a white house on the distant cliff. She had no idea how one might get to it.

"It's useless," she murmured, and at the same moment a surge of warmth swept over her. How strange—everything was getting cloudy. She was suddenly aware that while she was standing on the rocky peninsula, she was also lying down . . . lying down in bed. . . .

For a moment it seemed as if she could choose where she wanted to be.

Bed, she thought firmly. *That other place is too cold.*

And then she was turning over, and she *was* in bed, pulling up the covers. Her brain was too foggy to think of calling to the others, of finding out if it really had been a shared dream. She just wanted to sleep.

The next morning she woke up to: *Oh, no.*

Lewis? she thought hazily.

Hi, Kaitlyn. Hi. Rob.

G'way, Lewis. I'm sleeping, Rob said indistinctly. Only, of course, he didn't say it, not with his voice. He was in his own bedroom, and so was Lewis. Kait could *feel* them there.

She looked up over hummocks of sheets and blankets, to see Anna looking at her from the other bed. Anna looked flushed with sleep, sweet, and resigned.

Hi. Anna. Kaitlyn said, feeling somewhat resigned herself.

Hi, Kait.

Hi, Anna, Lewis said chirpily.

And good night, John-boy! Gabriel shouted from across the house. *Shut the hell up, all of you!*

Anna and Kaitlyn shared a look. *He's crabby when he wakes up,* Kaitlyn observed.

All boys are, Anna told her serenely. *At least he seems to have got his strength back.*

I thought, Rob said, his mental voice seeming more awake, *that you said it would be gone by this morning.*

Thunderous silence from Gabriel.

We might as well get dressed, Kaitlyn said at last when the silence went on. *It's almost seven.*

She found that if she concentrated on herself, the others receded into the background—which was just as well, she thought as she showered and dressed. There were some things you *needed* to be alone for.

But no matter what she did, they were there. Lurking around the edges of her mind like friends just within earshot and shouting range. Paying attention to any one of them brought that one closer.

Except Gabriel, who seemed to have locked himself off in a corner. Paying attention to him was like bouncing off the smoothness of his steely walls.

It wasn't until she was dressed that Kaitlyn remembered her dream.

"Anna—last night—did you dream anything in particular?"

Anna looked up from beneath the glistening raven's wing of her dark hair. "You mean about that place by the ocean?" she said, brushing vigorously. She seemed quite undisturbed.

Kaitlyn sat down. "Then it was real. I mean, you were really there." *You guys were all in my dream,* she added silently, so the others could hear it.

Well, it's not really that surprising, is it? Rob asked from his room. *If our minds are linked telepathically, and one of us has a dream, maybe the others get dragged in.*

Kaitlyn shook her head. *There's more to it than that,* she told Rob—but what more, she didn't know. Just then Lewis interrupted anyway, from the stairway.

Hey, I think Joyce is home! I hear somebody in the kitchen. Come on down!

All thoughts of the dream vanished. Kaitlyn and Anna ran out and met Rob on their way to the staircase.

"Joyce!" Lewis was saying when they got to the kitchen. He was also saying *Joyce!* but Joyce didn't seem to notice.

"Are you all right?" Kaitlyn asked. Joyce looked very pale, and there were huge dark circles under her eyes. She looked . . . young, somehow, like a kid with a short haircut that's turned out wrong.

Kaitlyn swallowed, but couldn't manage the next words. Anna said them for her. "Is Marisol . . . ?"

Joyce put down a box of Shredded Wheat as if it were heavy. "Marisol is . . . stable." Then her adult control seemed to desert her and she blurted, lips trembling, "She's in a coma."

"Oh, God," Kaitlyn whispered.

"The doctors are watching her. I stayed with her family at the hospital last night, but I didn't get to see her." Joyce fished in her purse, found a tissue, and blew her nose. She picked up the Shredded Wheat box and looked at it blankly.

"Now, you just let go of that and sit down," Rob said gently. "We'll take care of everything."

"That's right," Kaitlyn said, glad for the guidance. She herself felt sick and terrified. But *doing* something made her feel better, and in a few minutes they had Joyce sitting at the kitchen table, with Anna stroking her hand, Kaitlyn making coffee, and Rob and Lewis setting out bowls and spoons.

"It's all so confusing," Joyce said, wiping her eyes and crumpling the tissue in her fist. "Marisol's family didn't know she was on medication. They didn't even know she'd been seeing a psychiatrist. I had to tell them."

Kaitlyn looked at Rob, who, shielded by the pantry door, returned the look with grim significance. Then, carefully measuring scoops of ground coffee, she asked Joyce, "Who told *you* she was seeing a shrink?"

"Who? Mr. Zetes." Joyce passed a hand over her forehead. "By the way, he said you kids behaved really well last night. Went to bed early and all."

Anna smiled. "We're not children." She was the only one who could talk; the others were all engaged in a torrent of silent communication.

I knew it, Kaitlyn was telling Rob. *Joyce doesn't know anything about Marisol except what comes from Mr. Z. Don't you remember—when I asked about Marisol's medication, she told me, "He said a psychiatrist prescribed it." It was Mr. Zetes who told her that. For all we know, Marisol wasn't on any medication at all.*

Rob's face was tight. *And now she's in a coma because—*

Because she knew too much about what was going on here. What was really going on, Kait finished.

Which you guys still haven't told us, Lewis reminded her. *But look, why don't we tell* Joyce *what's going on? I mean, what's going on with us. She might know how this telepathy thing works—*

NO!

The thought came like a clap of thunder from upstairs. Kaitlyn involuntarily glanced upward.

Gabriel's mental voice was icily furious. *We can't tell anyone— and especially not Joyce.*

"Why not?" Lewis said. It took Kaitlyn a moment to realize he'd said it aloud. Anna was casting alarmed glances from the table.

"Uh, anybody want sugar or Equal or anything on their cereal?" Rob interjected. *Lewis, be careful!* he added silently.

"Sugar," Lewis said, subdued. *But why can't we tell Joyce? Don't you trust her?* he added in what came across as a mental stage whisper.

"Equal," Kaitlyn said, to Rob. *I do trust her—I think. I don't believe she knows anything—*

You idiot! You can't trust anyone, Gabriel snarled from upstairs. The volume of his thoughts was giving Kaitlyn a headache.

Looking pained, Rob and Lewis sat down at the table. Kaitlyn poured Joyce a cup of coffee and joined them. The spoken and unspoken conversations formed an eerie counterpoint to each other.

I hate to say this, but I think he's right, Rob said silently, when the echoes of Gabriel's forceful message had died. *I want to trust Joyce, too—but she tells Mr. Zetes everything. She told him about Marisol and look what happened.*

"Everything's going to be all right," Anna told Joyce. *She's very upset over Marisol. That's genuine,* she told the others.

She's an adult, Gabriel said flatly. *You can't trust any adult, ever.*

And if she's innocent, she could get hurt, Rob added.

"If there's anything we can do to help Marisol, let us know," Kaitlyn said to Joyce. *All right. We won't tell her,* she conceded. *But we need to get information about telepathy from somewhere. And we need to talk about what Rob and I found in that hidden room.*

Rob nodded, and covered it with a violent spasm of coughing. *We'd better meet at school—alone. Otherwise talking like this is going to drive me crazy.*

Kaitlyn felt agreement from everywhere, except upstairs.

That means you, too, Gabriel, Rob said grimly. *You're the one who started this. You're going to be there, boy.*

Aloud he said, "Could somebody pass that orange juice, please?"

CHAPTER 13

They met at lunch, and Kaitlyn and Rob told about everything they'd found in Mr. Zetes's hidden office below the stairs. Anna and Lewis were as puzzled as Kait had been over the various files and papers.

"Psychoactive weaponry," Gabriel said, seeming to relish the words. By unanimous agreement they were all talking out loud, and Kaitlyn couldn't tell what Gabriel was thinking behind his barriers.

"Do you know what it means?" Rob asked. His attitude toward Gabriel had changed overnight. There was a new tolerance in him—and a new combativeness. Kaitlyn had the slightly alarmed feeling that he meant to push and challenge Gabriel whenever he thought it was good for Gabriel.

"Well, psychoactive should be obvious even to a moron," Gabriel said. "It means something activated by psychics."

As opposed to something activated by psychos?

"Lewis!" Kaitlyn, Anna, and Rob all said. Gabriel contented himself with a withering look.

"I couldn't help it. I'm sorry. I'm not saying anything, see?" Lewis took a desperate chug of milk.

"Something . . . activated . . . by psychic power," Gabriel repeated coldly, one eye on Lewis. When there was no interruption, he turned to Rob. "Do I have to explain weaponry, or can you manage that alone?"

Rob leaned forward. "Why . . . would NASA . . . want him . . . to develop weaponry?"

Kaitlyn slammed a fork on the table between them to get their attention. "Maybe NASA didn't want him to actually develop it—but to find out if somebody *else* could be developing it. Eighty-six was the year the *Challenger* shuttlecraft exploded, right? Well, what if NASA thought the explosion was, like, sabotage? *Psychic* sabotage?"

"Sabotage by who?" Rob asked quietly.

"I don't know—the old Soviet Union? Somebody else who didn't want the space program to go ahead? If you got psychics to develop PK that could work over really long distances, you could have them throw switches in the shuttlecraft while they were sitting here on earth. I know it's not a nice idea, but it's possible."

"We're not dealing with nice people," Anna said.

"Look, what about all the other things in that room?"

Lewis asked. "The pilot study stuff, and the letter from the judge—"

"Forget it. All of it," Gabriel said sharply, and when several people turned to protest, he added, *Forget it! We've got something else to worry about first. Understand?*

Kaitlyn nodded slowly. "You're right. If this . . . web . . . that connects us gets unstable . . ."

"Even if it doesn't, we've got to get rid of it," Gabriel said brutally. "And the only place to get information about telepathy— *hard* information, in detail—is the Institute."

"That's right, Joyce has a bunch of books and journals and things in the lab," Lewis said. "But she's going to think it's weird that we're suddenly interested."

"Not if we go now," Gabriel said. "She's probably asleep."

"She *might* be asleep," Kaitlyn said cautiously. "And she might not be—and Mr. Zetes might be there. . . ."

"And pigs might fly. We'll never find out unless we go see." Gabriel stood, as if everything were decided.

Jeez, he's sure active all of a sudden. Now that he's got a stake in things.

"Lewis," Kaitlyn said mildly. But Lewis was right.

Joyce was asleep, with the French doors to her room wide open. Kaitlyn glanced at Rob, and what otherwise would have been just a meaningful look took on words.

Too bad, she told him. *I was hoping we might get a chance to go back into that hidden room—but it's too risky. She'd hear us.*

He nodded. *It would have been too risky anyway. Those doors are mostly glass—and if she woke up, she'd be looking straight out at that panel.*

Lewis was screwing his face into an unaccustomed frown. *I thought we were supposed to be talking out loud.*

Not when we're standing outside Joyce's door, Kaitlyn said. *This thing is useful when we need to be quiet.* She moved stealthily away.

They found Gabriel already in the front lab, kneeling by a bookcase, scanning the journals inside. Kaitlyn went to help him.

"There are more bookcases in the back," Anna said, and she and Lewis went through the door. Rob joined Kaitlyn. He didn't need to say anything—she could feel his watchful protectiveness. He meant to keep an eye on her when Gabriel was around.

There's no need, Kaitlyn thought, and then wondered if anyone had heard her. Oh, she didn't *like* this—this *exposure.* Not being sure if your own thoughts were private. She reached crossly for a book.

We've got to get rid of this thing.

On either side of her, Rob and Gabriel were radiating agreement.

They looked for what seemed like hours. Kaitlyn scanned journals with names like *Journal of the American Society for Psychical Research* and *Research in Parapsychology.* Some were translations of foreign journals with tongue-twisting names like *Sdelovaci Technika.*

There were articles about telepathy, thought projection, suggestibility. But nothing that looked remotely helpful to their situation.

At last, when Kaitlyn was beginning to worry that Joyce *had* to wake up soon, Anna called excitedly from the other room.

People, I've found something!

They all hurried to the back lab and gathered around her.

"'On stability in telepathic linkage as a function of equilibrium in self-sustaining geometric constructs,'" she said, holding a journal with a red cover. "It's about groups in telepathic links—groups like *us*."

"What on earth is a self-sustaining geometric construct?" Kaitlyn asked, very calmly.

Anna flashed a smile. "It's a web. You said it yourself, Kaitlyn—we're like five points that are joined to form a geometrical shape. And the point is that it's *stable*—that's what this article is saying. Two minds connected aren't stable. Three or four minds connected aren't stable. But five minds connected are. They form a—a sort of stable shape, and the whole thing stays in balance after that. That's why we're still linked."

Rob glanced at Gabriel. "So it's your fault. You shouldn't have connected all five of us."

Gabriel ignored him, reaching for the journal. "What I want to know is how to get *un*connected."

"I'm getting there," Anna said, holding it away from him. "I haven't read that part yet, but it's got a section here about how to disrupt the stability and break the connection." Her eyes scanned down the page as she continued to hold the journal away from Gabriel.

The others waited impatiently.

"This says that it's all theoretical, that nobody's ever really gotten five minds linked together. . . . Wait . . . then it says that some *larger* groups may be stable, too. . . . Okay, here. Got it." Anna began to read aloud. "'Breaking the link would be harder than initiating it, would require a far greater amount of power. . . .' But wait, it says there *is* one certain way of breaking it—" Anna stopped abruptly, eyes fixed on the page. Kaitlyn could feel her shock and dismay.

"What?" Gabriel demanded. "What does it say?"

Anna looked up at him. "It says the only certain way of breaking the connection is for one of the group to die."

Everyone stared at her, stunned. There was no sound, either mental or vocal.

"You mean," Lewis said shakily, at last, "that the web won't kill us—but that the only way to get rid of it is for one of us to *be* killed?"

Anna shook her head—not a negative, merely a helpless gesture. "That's what the article says. But—it's only a theory. Nobody can really know—"

Gabriel snatched the journal from her. He read rapidly, then stood for a moment very still. Then, with a furious gesture, he threw the journal at a wall.

"It's permanent," he said flatly, turning to stare at the wall himself.

Kaitlyn shivered. His anger frightened her, and it mixed with her own feelings of shock and fear.

In a lot of ways she'd enjoyed the connection. It was interesting, exciting. Different. But to *never* be able to break it . . . to know you'd be stuck in a web until one of them died . . .

My whole life has changed, she thought. Forever. Something . . . irrevocable . . . has happened, and there's no way to undo it.

I will never be alone, unconnected, again.

"At least we know it's not going to kill any of us," Anna said in a quiet voice.

Kaitlyn said slowly, "Like you said, that article might be wrong. There might be some other way to break it—we can read other books, other journals, and see."

"There is a way. There *has* to be," Gabriel said, in a cracked, almost unrecognizable voice.

He's the most desperate of all of us, Kait realized with something like dispassion. He can't stand being this close— having us all this close to him.

Until we find it, you all stay away from me, Gabriel's mental voice said, as if in answer to Kaitlyn's thought. Had he heard her?

"Meanwhile," Rob said in a quiet, level voice, "we might work on learning how to control it—"

Just stay away! Gabriel shouted, and he strode out of the room.

Lewis, Anna, Rob, and Kaitlyn were left staring after him.

"Why's he so mad at *us?*" Lewis asked. "If it's anyone's fault, it's his."

Rob smiled faintly. "That's why he's mad," he said in a dry voice. "He doesn't like being wrong."

"It's more than that," Kaitlyn said. "He helped us—and look where it got him. So it just confirms what he thought in the first place, that you should never help."

There was another silence, while everyone just stood. We still haven't taken it all in, Kaitlyn thought. We're in shock.

Then she gave herself a mental shake. "Those bookcases look pretty bad. We'd better clean things up quick. We can look for other articles about breaking the web later, when we know Joyce won't be around."

They straightened the books and the rows of plastic journal holders in both labs. It was as she was putting on the final touches that Kaitlyn found another article that intrigued her.

Someone had marked the page with a red plastic Post-it flag. The title was simply "Chi and Crystals."

You guys? What's chi? she asked, scarcely aware that she wasn't asking it out loud.

"It's a Chinese word for your life energy," Lewis said, coming to her. "It flows all through your body in different channels, sort of like blood—or electricity. Everybody has it, and psychics have more of it."

"So chi is what Rob channels?" Kaitlyn said.

"That's one name for it," Rob said. "At the other center they told me lots of others—like in India they call it *prana,* and the ancient Egyptians used to call it *sekhem.* It's all the same thing. All living things have it."

"Well, according to this article, crystals store it," Kaitlyn said.

Rob frowned. "Crystals aren't alive. . . ."

"I know, but this says that theoretically a crystalline structure could store it up, kind of like a charged battery," Kaitlyn said. She was still looking at the article thoughtfully. Something was tugging at her, whispering significance, demanding that she pay attention to it. But she didn't know *what.*

The article looked as if it had been read a lot. . . .

"She's up," Rob said. Kaitlyn could hear it, too—water running in the single downstairs bathroom. Joyce was awake and washing.

Anna checked her watch. *It's three-thirty. We can just tell her that we walked home from school.*

Kaitlyn nodded and she felt agreement from the others. She straightened her back, kept her head high, and went to face Joyce.

The week that followed was hectic. There was school to go to during the days, and testing with Joyce in the afternoons. Any leisure time was filled with two things: trying to find a way to break the web, and trying to find out more about Mr. Zetes's plans. The problem was that they didn't make much progress with either.

They didn't get into the hidden room again. Although Kait and Rob waited for a chance, Joyce never left the Institute again and she slept with her doors open.

Kaitlyn lived in a perpetual state of astonishment and nervousness. It was hard to be constantly on her guard with Joyce, to keep from talking about the only two things that were now important in her life. But somehow she managed it—they all managed it.

Marisol remained in a coma. No one outside her family was allowed to visit her, but Joyce called every day. Every day the news was the same: no change.

Mr. Zetes visited the Institute several times, always unexpectedly. They kept their secrets from him, too—or at least, Kaitlyn was pretty sure they did. Occasionally, when she saw Mr. Z's penetrating dark eyes lingering on Gabriel, she wondered.

Gabriel himself was . . . disturbing. Disturbed. Not taking things well.

For Kaitlyn, even though this new intimacy was strange and terrifying, it was exciting, too. She'd never been so close to other people in her life. The sparkling enthusiasm of Lewis's thoughts—the cool serenity of Anna's—that was *good*. And the closeness to Rob was almost painful delight.

But for Gabriel, it was all torture. He spent every minute of his free time reading journals and books, trying to find a way to break the web. He convinced Joyce he was simply interested in researching his talent, and she was delighted. She let him go to the library and get more books, more journals.

He didn't find anything helpful. And every day he didn't, he withdrew further from the others. He learned how to wall himself off telepathically so that Kaitlyn could barely sense his presence.

We're trying to leave you alone, she told him. And it was true, they were, because they were all worried. Gabriel seemed to be getting wound tighter and tighter, like something waiting to explode.

On Tuesday, one week after the web was established, Joyce tested Kaitlyn with the EEG machine again.

Kaitlyn had been waiting for this. *I think she's going to do it,* she told Rob. They had gotten pretty good at sending messages to specific people.

I can come in any time you want, he said. *But what do you want me to do—just try to watch her?*

Kaitlyn debated as she followed Joyce's instructions to sit down and close her eyes. *No—if there's anything she doesn't want you to see, she won't let you watch. Could you make a distraction when I tell you to? It only needs to last a minute.*

Yes, Rob said simply.

Now that Marisol wasn't there to help, Joyce had stopped

testing Gabriel at all, and usually sent Rob and a volunteer to the back lab while the other three did their testing in the front. Rob was there now with Fawn, the girl who had MS. Kaitlyn could feel him waiting, alert and vigilant.

"Right; you know how to do this," Joyce said, sticking a final electrode in place—in the center of Kaitlyn's forehead. Over her third eye. "I'll concentrate on the picture. You relax."

Kait murmured something, concentrating on the feel of that single electrode. Cold. It was definitely colder than all the others, and her forehead had a prickling feeling.

When she relaxed, letting her mind fall into darkness, she knew what to expect.

It came. First the feeling of incredible pressure behind her forehead. It turned into a feeling of inflation, like a balloon being blown up. Then came the pictures.

They flashed through her mind with bewildering speed, and she could only recognize a few. She saw roses and a horse. She saw Mr. Zetes in front of the hidden doorway again. She saw a white house with a caramel-colored face in the window.

And—unexpectedly—she heard voices.

Anna's voice: *Kait—I can't think—what's happening?*

Lewis's: *Jeeeeeeeez.*

Rob's: *Just hang on, everybody.*

At the same time, to Kait's astonishment, she could clearly hear Gabriel. *What the hell is this? What are you trying to do?*

She forced herself to ignore the distracting pictures. *Gabriel, where are you?*

Just coming up on Exmoor Street.

Kaitlyn was amazed. Exmoor Street was blocks away from the Institute. They'd found that their telepathy fell off sharply with distance, and anything more than a block was too far for clear communication.

But Gabriel was clear now—painfully clear.

I'll explain later, Kait told him. *Just try to deal with it for a few minutes.* Then she told Rob, *Now.*

Immediately she heard a thud, and then Fawn's voice shouting. "Joyce! Oh, please—Rob's hurt!"

Kaitlyn remained perfectly still, eyes shut. She heard a rustle on the other side of the screen, then Anna's voice saying, *She's going. She's in the back lab now.*

Kaitlyn opened her eyes, reaching up to her forehead. The little electrode came away easily, but something remained behind. She could feel it with her fingertips, something stuck to her skin by the electrode cream.

Carefully, her heart beating violently, she peeled it off.

When she looked at it, pinched between thumb and forefinger, she got a shock of disappointment. It wasn't anything after all—just a lump of white electrode cream. Then her fingernails scraped at it and she saw that beneath the coating of paste was something hard. It was white, too, or translucent, which made it difficult to see. It was about the size and shape of her little fingernail, and quite smooth and flat.

It looked like crystal.

All this time she could hear faint voices in the other room. Now Rob said, *Watch out, Joyce is standing up.*

Quickly Kaitlyn stuck the small crystal back onto her forehead. She jammed the electrode on over it, praying they both would stay.

She's coming back, Lewis reported.

Here she is, Anna said.

Kait rubbed the telltale paste from her fingers onto her jeans. She picked up the pencil and clipboard and began to draw. It didn't matter what. She sketched a rose.

The folding screen was moved. "Kaitlyn, I'm going to unhook you," Joyce said in a rapid, harassed voice. "Rob's completely collapsed—I think he's overdone things with that girl. Anna, Lewis, can you help get him to the couch here? I want him to lie down for a while."

Kaitlyn held still, fingers curled because she was guiltily aware that there was still electrode cream under her fingernails. She was relieved that Joyce didn't seem to notice anything peculiar about the forehead electrode. What *Kaitlyn* noticed, though, was that after taking that one off, Joyce's hand went quickly to her shirt pocket. As if palming something and putting it away.

Rob, you okay? Kaitlyn asked, as Lewis and Anna helped him in, and Joyce turned to settle him on the couch.

She got the mental impression of a wink. *Just fine. Did you see anything?*

A crystal, Kait told him. *We need to talk about this, try to figure it all out.*

Rob said, *Sure thing. Just as soon as she lets me get up.*

"Before you go, what did you draw?" Joyce asked, looking up as Kait headed for the door.

Kaitlyn got the clipboard and showed her the rose picture.

"Oh, well—better luck next time. It was supposed to be a horse. I'm sorry we had to interrupt your testing."

"It doesn't matter." Kaitlyn said. "I'm going upstairs to get this electrode stuff out of my hair." Silently she added, *We'd better meet before dinner.*

She went upstairs. She wanted to think, but somehow her head seemed cloudy, her thoughts slow.

Rob's voice came to her. *Kaitlyn—are you feeling okay?*

Kaitlyn started to answer, and then *realized* just how she was feeling. *Oh, Rob, I'm stupid. I forgot what happened to me last time she did this.*

She could sense revelation and sympathy from Lewis and Anna, but Rob put it into words. *A headache.*

A bad one, Kaitlyn admitted. *It's coming on fast and getting worse.*

Rob's frustration was almost palpable. *And I'm stuck down here with Joyce fussing over me.*

It doesn't matter, Kait told him quickly. *You're supposed to be in a collapse, so stay collapsed. Don't do anything to make her suspicious.*

To distract herself, she looked out the window, squinting against the mild light. And then she saw something that made her heart jump into her throat.

Instantly there was an answering wave of alarm from downstairs. *What, what?* Lewis said. *What's wrong?*

It's nothing, Kaitlyn said. *Don't worry. I've just got to check something out.* It was the first time she'd tried to deceive the others, but she wanted a moment to think alone. She pulled away from them mentally, knowing they'd respect that. It was like turning your back in a crowded room: the only kind of privacy any of them had now.

She hesitated by the window, looking out at the black limousine parked on the narrow dirt road—and the two figures beside it. One was tall, white-haired, wearing a greatcoat. The other lithe, dark-haired, wearing a red pullover.

Mr. Zetes and Gabriel. Talking in a place where no one could hear them.

CHAPTER 14

Kaitlyn hurried downstairs and slipped out the back door.

Quietly, she told herself as she made her way down the hill behind the Institute. Quietly and carefully. She kept to the blurred shadows of the redwood trees, creeping up on her prey.

She got close enough that she could hear Gabriel and Mr. Zetes talking. She knelt behind a bush, looking at them cautiously through the prickly winter-green foliage.

It gave her a grim satisfaction to realize that Gabriel's wall-building could have some drawbacks. He'd barricaded himself from the rest of them so efficiently that he didn't sense her a few yards away. Fortunately, Mr. Zetes's dogs didn't seem to be around to spot her, either.

Shamelessly eavesdropping, Kaitlyn strained her ears.

One dread pounded inside her, sharper than her headache.

She had a terrible fear that they were talking about the web.

In a way, she wouldn't be surprised. The strain on Gabriel had been growing every day. He was desperate, and desperate people look for desperate cures.

But if he'd betrayed them, if he'd gone to Mr. Zetes behind their backs . . .

As she listened, though, her heartbeat calmed a little. It didn't seem to be that kind of conversation. Mr. Zetes seemed to be stroking Gabriel's ego, complimenting Gabriel in a vague and extravagant way. Like somebody buttering up a fraternity pledge, Kaitlyn thought. It reminded her of the speech Mr. Zetes had given the first day at the Institute.

"I know how you must feel," he was saying. "Repressed, hemmed in by society—forced into this *ordinariness*. This *mediocrity.*" Mr. Zetes gestured around him, and Kaitlyn instinctively scrunched lower behind her bush. "While all the time your spirit feels caged."

That's nasty, Kaitlyn thought. Talking about cages to someone just out of a boys' prison . . . that's *low*.

"Alienated. Alone," Mr. Zetes continued, and Kait allowed herself a grin. She knew for a fact that one thing Gabriel was *not* feeling these days was alone.

Mr. Zetes seemed to sense that he was off the mark, too, because he went back to harping on the repressed and caged bit. He was manipulating Gabriel; that was clear enough. But why? Kaitlyn thought. She could barely feel Rob, Lewis, and

Anna from here, and she didn't dare try to get in touch with them. It would certainly alert Gabriel, and she wanted to find out what was going on.

"Society itself will someday realize the injustice that's been done to you. It will realize that extraordinary people must be allowed a certain liberty, a certain freedom. They must follow their own paths, without being caged by laws made for ordinary individuals."

Kaitlyn didn't like the expression on Gabriel's face, or the dim feelings she could sense from him behind his walls. He looked . . . *smug*, self-important. As if he were taking all this crap seriously.

It's the strain, Kaitlyn thought. He's so sick of us that he's gone right round the bend.

"I think we should continue this discussion at my house," Mr. Zetes was saying now. "Why don't you come up with me this evening? There's so much we have to talk about."

Horrified, Kaitlyn saw that Gabriel was shrugging. Accepting. "I've been wanting to get away," he said. "In fact, I'd do just about anything to get out of here."

"We might as well go from here," Mr. Zetes said. "I was going to pay a visit to the Institute, but I'm sure Joyce can carry on without me."

Alarm flashed down Kaitlyn's nerves and her heart thumped. Gabriel was getting in the car. They were going to leave right *now*—and there was no time to do anything.

Only one thing. She stood up, trying to look bold and casual at once, and to think clearly despite the pain in her head.

"Take me, too," she said.

Two heads snapped around to look at her. Gabriel had paused with one foot inside the limousine. Both he and Mr. Zetes looked very startled, but in an instant Mr. Zetes's expression had changed to fierce, pitiless scrutiny.

"I've been listening," Kaitlyn said, since this was obvious. "I just came down to—to think, and I saw you, and I listened."

Gabriel's eyes were dark with fury—he was taking it as another invasion of his privacy. "You little—"

"Different rules for extraordinary people," Kaitlyn told him imperiously, standing her ground. "Society shouldn't cage me in." It was the best she could do trying to remember the gibberish Mr. Z had been spouting.

And it seemed to soften Mr. Z's fierce expression. His grim old lips curved a little. "So you agree with that," he said.

"I agree with freedom," Kaitlyn said. "There're times when I feel just like a bird hitting a pane of glass—and then flying back a little and hitting it again—because I just want to get *out*."

It was the truth, in a way. She *had* felt like that—back in Ohio. And the ring of truth seemed to convince Mr. Zetes.

"I often thought you might be the second one to come around," he murmured, as if to himself. Then he looked back at her.

"I should very much like to talk to you, my dear," he said,

and there was a tone of formality, of *finality,* in his voice. As if the simple words were part of some ceremony. "And I'm sure Gabriel will be delighted to have you along."

He made a courteous gesture toward the limo.

Gabriel was gazing at Kaitlyn darkly, looking unconvinced and not at all delighted to have her. But as she slowly got into the car, he shrugged coldly. "Oh, sure."

"Shouldn't we go to the Institute first?" Kaitlyn asked, as Mr. Zetes got in and the limousine began to move, backing up smoothly toward the bridge. "I could change my clothes. . . ."

"Oh, you'll find things quite informal at my home," Mr. Zetes said, and smiled.

They were getting farther away from the purple house every second. *Rob,* Kaitlyn thought, and then with more force. *Rob! Rob!*

She got only a distant sense of mental activity as an answer. Like hearing a muffled voice, but being totally unable to make out the words.

Gabriel, help me, she thought, deliberately turning her face away, looking out the limousine window. It frightened her to be using telepathy with Mr. Zetes in the car, but she didn't have a choice. She sent the thought directly at Gabriel, jarring through his walls. *We need to tell Rob and the others where we're going.*

Gabriel's response was maddeningly indifferent. *Why?*

Because we're going off with a nut who could have anything in mind for us, that's why! Don't you remember Marisol? Now, just help me! I can't get through to them!

Again Gabriel seemed completely unaffected by her urgency. *If he were going to put us in a coma like Marisol, he would hardly need to take us to San Francisco,* he said contemptuously. *And besides, it's too late now. We're too far away.*

He was right. Kaitlyn glared out the window, trying not to let her tension show in her body.

Nobody asked you to come and invite yourself along, Gabriel told her, and she could feel the genuine coldness behind his words. The resentment and anger. *If you don't like it, that's your own fault.*

He hates me, Kaitlyn thought bleakly, putting up walls of her own. She wasn't as good at it as he was, but she tried. Right now, she didn't want to share anything with him.

It was getting dark, the swift chilly darkness of a winter evening. And every mile the limousine went north was taking her farther and farther away from Rob and the Institute, and closer to she didn't know what.

By the time they reached San Francisco, it was fully dark, and the city lights twinkled and gleamed in skyscraper shapes. The city seemed vaguely menacing to Kaitlyn—maybe because it was so beautiful, so charming and cheerful-looking. As if it were decked out for a holiday. She felt there had to be something beneath that lovely, smiling facade.

They didn't stay in the city. The limo headed toward dark hills decorated with strings of white jewels. Kaitlyn was surprised at how quickly the tall buildings were left behind, at how soon they were passing streets of quiet houses. And then the houses began to be farther and farther apart. They were driving through trees, with only an occasional light to show a human habitation. The limousine turned up a private driveway. "Nice little shack," Gabriel said as they pulled up in front of a mansion. Kaitlyn didn't like his voice at all. It was mocking, but dry and conspiratorial, as if Mr. Zetes would appreciate the joke. As if Gabriel and Mr. Zetes shared something.

Something *I* don't share, Kaitlyn thought. But she tried to put the same tone in her own voice. "Really nice."

Under heavy eyelids, Gabriel gave her a glance of derisive scorn.

"That's all for tonight," Mr. Zetes told the chauffeur as they got out. "You can go home."

It gave Kaitlyn a tearing sensation to watch the limousine cruise away. Not that she'd ever said more than "hello" to the driver, but he was her last connection with . . . well, normal human beings. She was alone now, with Mr. Zetes and a Gabriel who seemed to resent her very existence.

"I live very simply, you see," Mr. Zetes was saying, walking up the columned path to the front door. "No servants, not even the chauffeur. But I manage."

Prince and Baron, the two rottweilers, came bounding

up as he opened the door. They calmed at a glance from Mr. Zetes, but followed closely behind him as he and his visitors walked through the house. Just another thing to make Kaitlyn nervous and unhappy.

Mr. Zetes took off his coat and hung it on a stand. Underneath he was wearing an immaculate, rather old-fashioned suit. With real gold cuff links, Kait thought.

The inside of the house was as impressive as the outside. Marble and glass. Thick, velvety carpets and polished, gleaming wood. Cathedral ceilings. All sorts of foreign and obviously expensive carvings and vases. Kaitlyn supposed they were art, but she found some of them repulsive.

Gabriel was looking around him with a certain expression— one it took her a moment to categorize. It was . . . it was the way he'd been looking at the magazine with the expensive cars. Not greedy; greed was too loose and unformed. This expression had *purpose;* it was sharp and focused.

Acquisitive, Kaitlyn thought. That was it. As if he's planning to *acquire* all this. As if he's determined to.

Mr. Zetes was smiling.

I should look like that, too, Kaitlyn thought, and she tried to stamp an expression of narrow-eyed longing on her own face. All she wanted was to fool Mr. Zetes until he let them go home. At the beginning she'd had some idea about finding things out about Mr. Zetes—but not anymore. Now she was just hoping to live through whatever was coming and get back to the Institute.

"This is my study," Mr. Zetes said, ushering them into a room deep in the large house. "I spend a great deal of time here. Why don't you sit down?"

The study was walnut-paneled and darkly furnished, with leather chairs that creaked when you sat on them. On the walls were gold-framed pictures of horses and what looked like fox hunts. The curtains were a deep, lightless red, and the lamps all had rust-colored shades. There was a bust of some old-fashioned-looking man on the mantelpiece and a black statue of a foreign-looking woman on the floor.

Kaitlyn didn't like any of it.

But Gabriel did, she could tell. He leaned back in his chair, looking around appreciatively. It must be a guy thing, Kaitlyn thought. This whole place is so masculine, and so . . . Again, she had trouble finding a word. The closest she could come was *old money.*

She supposed she could see why Gabriel, used to living on the road or in a cell with one bunk and a metal toilet, might like that.

The dogs lay down on the floor. Mr. Zetes went over to the bar—there was a full bar, with bottles and silver trays and crystal decanters—and began pouring something. "May I offer you a brandy?"

My God, Kaitlyn thought.

Gabriel smiled. "Sure."

Gabriel! Kaitlyn said. Gabriel ignored her completely, as if she were a fly buzzing around the perimeter of the room.

"Nothing for me, thanks," she said, trying not to sound as frightened as she felt. Mr. Zetes was coming back with only two glasses, anyway—she didn't think he'd even meant to include her in the offer.

He sat down behind the desk and sipped golden liquid out of a ballooning glass. Gabriel sat back in his chair and did the same. Kaitlyn began to feel like a butterfly in a spider's web.

Mr. Zetes himself seemed more aristocratic and imposing than ever, more like an earl. Someone important, someone who ought to be listened to. This whole study was designed to convey that impression, Kaitlyn realized. It was a sort of shrine that drew your attention to the figure behind the large, carved desk. The figure with the immaculate suit and the real gold cuff links and the benevolent white head.

The atmosphere was beginning to get to her, she realized.

"I'm so glad we're able to have this talk," Mr. Zetes said, and his voice went with the atmosphere. It was both soothing and authoritative. The voice of a man who Knew Best. "I could see right away at the Institute that you were the two with the most potential. I knew that you'd outstrip the others very quickly. You both have so much more capacity for understanding, so much more sophistication."

Sophisticated? Me? Kaitlyn thought. But a part of her, a tiny part, was flattered. She'd been more sophisticated than other kids in Thoroughfare, she knew that. Because while all they'd been thinking about was cheerleading or football games, she'd been thinking about the world. About how to get out into the world.

"You can conceive of . . . shall we say, broader horizons," Mr. Zetes was saying, as if he'd followed her train of thought. It was enough to bring Kait up short, to make her look at him in alarm. But his piercing old eyes were smiling, bland, and he was going on. "You are people of vision, like myself," he said. He smiled.

"Like myself."

Something in the repetition made Kaitlyn very nervous.

It's coming, she realized. Whatever it is. He's been building up to something, and here it is.

There was a long silence in the room. Mr. Zetes was gazing at his desk, smiling faintly, as if lost in thought. Gabriel was sipping his drink, eyes narrowed but on the floor. He seemed lost in thought, too. Kaitlyn was too uneasy to speak or move. Her heart had begun a slow, relentless hammering.

The silence had begun to be terrible, when Gabriel raised his head. He looked Mr. Zetes in the eyes, smiled faintly, and said, "And just what is your vision?"

Mr. Zetes glanced toward Kaitlyn—a mere formality. He seemed to assume that Gabriel spoke for both of them.

When he started talking again, it was in a dreadful tone of

complicity. As if they *all* shared a secret. As if some agreement had already been reached.

"The scholarship is only the beginning, of course. But naturally you realize that already. The two of you have such . . . enormous potential . . . that with the right training, you could set your own price."

Again Gabriel gave that faint smile. "And the right training is . . . ?"

"I think it's time to show you that." He put his empty glass down. "Come with me."

He stood and turned to the walnut-paneled wall of the study. As he reached out to touch it, Kaitlyn threw Gabriel a startled glance—but he wasn't looking at her. His entire attention seemed fixed on Mr. Zetes.

The panel slid back. Kaitlyn saw a black rectangle for one instant, and then a reddish glow flicked on as if activated automatically. Mr. Zetes's form was silhouetted against it.

My picture! Kaitlyn thought.

It wasn't, exactly. Mr. Zetes wasn't wearing a coat, for one thing, and the red light wasn't as bright. Her picture had been more a symbol than an actual rendition—but she recognized it anyway.

"Right this way," Mr. Zetes said, turning to them almost with a flourish. He expected them to be surprised, undoubtedly, but Kaitlyn couldn't work herself up to pretending. And when Gabriel entered the gaping rectangle and started down the stairway, she realized she couldn't protest, either. It was too late for that. Mr. Zetes was looking at her, and the dogs were on their feet and right behind her.

She had no choice. She followed Gabriel.

This stairway was longer than the one at the Institute, and it led to a hallway with many doors and several branching corridors. A whole underground complex, Kaitlyn realized. Mr. Zetes was taking them to the very end.

"This is . . . a very special room," he told them, pausing before a set of double doors. "Few people have seen it. I want you to see it now."

He opened one of the doors, then turned toward them and stopped where he was, gesturing them in, watching their faces. In the greenish fluorescent light of the hallway his skin took on an unhealthy chalky tone and his eyes seemed to glitter.

Kaitlyn's flesh began to creep. She knew, suddenly and without question, that whatever was in there was terrible.

Gabriel was going in. Mr. Zetes was watching her with those glittering eyes in a corpselike face.

She didn't have a choice.

The room was startling in its whiteness. All Kaitlyn could think at first was that it was exactly what she'd imagined the laboratories at the Institute would be like. White walls, white tile, everything gleaming and immaculate and sterile. Lots of unfamiliar machinery around the edges, including one huge metal-mesh cage.

But that was all incidental. Once Kaitlyn was able to focus on anything, she focused on the thing in the center of the room—and then she forgot everything else.

It was . . . what? A stone plant? A sculpture? A model space-ship? She didn't know, but she couldn't look away from it. It drew the eye inevitably and then held it fast, the way some very beautiful paintings do—except that it wasn't beautiful. It was hideous.

And it reminded Kaitlyn of something.

It was towering, milky, semitranslucent—and that should have given her a clue. But she couldn't get over her first impression that it was some horrible parody of a plant, even when she realized that it couldn't be.

It was covered with—things. Parasites, Kait thought wildly. Then all at once she realized that they were growths, smaller crystals sprouting from a giant parent. They stuck out in all directions like the rays of a star, or some giant Christmas decoration. But the effect wasn't festive—it was somehow obscene.

"Oh, God—what *is* it?" Kaitlyn whispered.

Mr. Zetes smiled.

"You feel its power," he said approvingly. "Good. You're quite correct; it can be terrible. But it also can be very useful."

He walked over to the . . . thing . . . and stood beside it, the dogs padding at his heels. When he looked at it, Kaitlyn saw that his eyes were admiring—and acquisitive.

"It's a very ancient crystal," he said, "and if I told you where it came from, you wouldn't believe me. But it will amaze you, I promise. It can provide energy beyond anything you've ever imagined."

"This is the training you were talking about?" Gabriel asked.

"This is the means of training," Mr. Zetes said softly, almost absently. He was still looking at the crystal. "The means of sharpening your powers, increasing them. It has to be done gradually to avoid damage, but we have time."

"*That* thing can increase our powers?" Gabriel said with scorn and disbelief.

"Crystals can store psychic energy," Kaitlyn said in a small voice. It sounded small and distant even to her. She had the feeling of someone who'd walked into a nightmare.

Mr. Zetes was looking at her. "You know that?" he said.

"I . . . heard it somewhere."

He nodded, but his eyes lingered on her as he said, "You two have the potential—this crystal has the power to develop that potential. And I have . . ." He stopped, as if thinking how to phrase something.

"What do you have?" Gabriel said.

Mr. Zetes smiled. "The contacts," he replied. "The . . . clients, if you will. I can find people who are willing to pay considerable amounts for your services. Amounts that will climb as your powers are honed, of course."

Clients, Kaitlyn thought. That letter—the letter from Judge Baldwin. A list of potential clients.

"You want to hire us out?" she blurted before she could stop herself. "Like—like—" She was too overwrought to think of an analogy.

Gabriel could think of one. "Like assassins," he suggested. His voice chilled Kaitlyn—because it wasn't at all outraged or indignant. He sounded quite calm—thoughtful, even.

"Not at all," Mr. Zetes said. "I think there would be very few assassinations involved. But there are a number of business situations in which your talents would be invaluable. Corporate espionage—industrial sabotage—influence of witnesses at certain trials. No, I would prefer to call you a psychic strike team, available for handling all sorts of situations."

A strike team. Project Black Lightning, Kaitlyn thought. The words scribbled on that piece of paper. He wanted to turn them into a paranormal dirty tricks team.

"I hadn't meant to explain all this to you so quickly," Mr. Zetes was going on. "But the truth is that something has come up. You remember Marisol Diaz, of course. Well, there has been a bit of a problem with Marisol's family. Several of them have become . . . unexpectedly difficult. Suspicious. I'm afraid that money has little influence on them. I need to quiet them some other way."

There was a pause. Kaitlyn couldn't say anything because she felt as if she were choking, and Gabriel simply looked sardonic.

"I thought we weren't assassins," he said.

Mr. Zetes looked pained. "I don't need them killed. Just quieted. If you can do it some other way, I'm very happy."

Kaitlyn managed to get words through the blockage in her throat. "You did it to Marisol," she said. "You put her in the coma."

"I had to," Mr. Zetes said. "She had become quite unstable. Thank you for bringing that to my attention, incidentally— if you hadn't mentioned it to Joyce, I wouldn't have realized so soon. Marisol had been with me for several years, and I thought she understood what we were doing."

"The pilot study," Kaitlyn said.

"Yes, she told you about that, didn't she? It was a very great pity. I didn't know then that only the strongest minds, the most gifted psychics, could stand contact with one of the great crystals. I gathered six of the best I could find locally—but it was a terrible disaster. Afterward I realized that I would have to expand my search—cover the whole nation—if I wanted to find students who could tolerate the training."

"But what happened to *them?*" Kaitlyn burst out. "To the ones in the pilot study—"

"Oh, it was a dreadful waste," Mr. Zetes said, as if repeating something she should have gotten the first time. "Very good minds, some of them. Genuine talent. To see that reduced to idiocy and madness is very sad."

Kaitlyn couldn't answer. The hair on her arms and the back of her neck was standing up. Tears had sprung to her eyes.

"Marisol, now—I did think she understood, but in the end she proved otherwise. She was a good worker in the beginning. The problem was that she knew too much to be simply bribed, and she was too temperamental to be controlled by fear. I really had no other choice." He sighed. "My real mistake was to use drugs instead of the crystal. I thought a seizure might be very effective—but instead of dying, she wound up in the hospital, and now her family is posing a problem. It's really very difficult."

He might look like an earl—but he was insane, Kaitlyn thought. Truly insane, insane enough that he didn't realize how insane all this would sound to sane people. She looked at Gabriel—and felt a shock that sent chills up from her feet.

CHAPTER 15

Because Gabriel didn't look as if he found it insane. Slightly distasteful, maybe, but not crazy. In fact, there was something like agreement in his face, as if Mr. Z were talking about doing something unpleasant but necessary.

"But we can take care of that problem," Mr. Zetes said, looking up and speaking more briskly. "And once it's over, we can get to our real work. Always assuming you're interested, of course?"

His voice had a note of gentle inquiry, and he looked from Gabriel to Kaitlyn, waiting for an answer. Again Kaitlyn felt a shock of disbelief. Those dark, piercing eyes of his looked so acute—how could he not realize what she was feeling? How could he look at her as if he expected agreement?

She had exploded into speech before she knew what was happening. All the fear, all the fury, all the disgust and horror, that had been building inside her burst out.

"You're *insane,*" she said. "You're completely insane, don't you know that? Everything that you've said is completely *insane.* How can you talk about people being reduced to idiots as if—as if—" She was degenerating into sobs and incoherence. "And *Marisol,*" she gasped. "How could you do that to *her?* And what you want to turn us all into—you're just completely, totally *crazy.* You're *evil.*"

She was having hysterics, she supposed. Raving. Shouting as if shouting were going to do any good. But she couldn't stop herself.

Mr. Zetes seemed less surprised than she did. Displeased, certainly, but not astonished. "Evil?" he said, frowning. "I'm afraid that's a very emotional and inexact word. Many things seem evil that are, in a higher sense, good."

"You don't *have* any higher sense," Kaitlyn shouted. "You don't care about anything except what you can get out of us."

Mr. Zetes was shaking his head. "I'm afraid I can't waste time in arguing now—but I honestly hope you'll see reason eventually. I think you will, in time, if I keep you here long enough." He turned to Gabriel. "Now—"

Then Kaitlyn did something she realized was stupid even as she was doing it. But her anger at Mr. Zetes's insufferable smugness, his indifference to her words, drove her beyond any caution.

"You won't get any of the others to join you," she said. "Not any of them back home. Rob wouldn't even *listen* to it.

And if I don't come back, they'll know something's wrong. They already know about the hidden room there at the Institute. And they're linked, we're all linked telepathically. All five of us. And—"

"*What?*" Mr. Zetes said. For the first time, a real emotion was showing on his face. Astonishment—and anger. He looked at Gabriel sharply. "What?"

"We are, aren't we?" Kaitlyn demanded. "Tell him, Gabriel." *And tell him he's crazy, because you know he is. You know he is!*

"It's something that happened," Gabriel told Mr. Zetes. "It was an accident. I didn't know it would become permanent. If I had"—he glanced at Kaitlyn—"it never *would* have happened."

"But this is—You're telling me that the five of you are involved in a stable telepathic link? But don't you realize . . . ?" Mr. Zetes broke off. There was plenty of emotion in his face now, Kaitlyn noted. It was dark with blood and fury. "Don't you realize that you're useless within a linked group like that?"

Gabriel said nothing. Through their connection, Kaitlyn could feel that he was as angry as Mr. Zetes.

"I was counting on you," Mr. Zetes said. "I *need* you to help me take care of the Diaz problem. If that isn't controlled . . ." He stopped. Kaitlyn could see he was making a great effort to get hold of himself. And, after a moment or two, he apparently succeeded. He sighed, and the fury drained out of his face.

"There's no help for it now," he said. "It's a very great pity. You don't know how much work is wasted." He looked at Kaitlyn. "I had great hopes for you."

Then he said, "Prince, back."

Kaitlyn had almost forgotten about the dogs—but now one came straight for her, hair bristling, teeth showing to the gums. It was completely silent, which only made it scarier.

Involuntarily Kaitlyn took a step backward—and the dog kept coming. As it reached her, she stepped back again and again—and then she realized what was happening. She was standing inside the metal cage.

Mr. Zetes had gone over to a kind of console across the room. He pressed a button and the door to the cage slid shut.

"I told you," Kaitlyn said tensely. "If you keep me here, they'll know—"

Mr. Zetes interrupted as if he didn't notice her speaking. Turning to Gabriel, he said, "Kill her."

Shock washed over Kaitlyn like an icy bath—and again and again. She'd realized, all at once, just *how* stupid she'd been. The cold reality of her situation left her unable to breathe. Unable to think.

"Don't worry; it's just a Faraday cage," Mr. Zetes was telling Gabriel. "It's built to keep out normal electromagnetic waves, but it's quite transparent to your power. It's like the steel room at the Institute, and you projected easily through that."

Gabriel was silent. His stony expression told Kaitlyn

nothing, and she couldn't feel anything from him through the web. Maybe she was just numb.

"Go on," Mr. Zetes said. He was beginning to look impatient. "Believe me, there's no other alternative. If there were, I would save myself the work of getting another subject like her—but there's no choice. The link has to be broken. The only way to break it is to kill one of the five of you."

Gabriel's chest rose and fell with a sudden deep breath. "The link has to be broken," he repeated, grimly. Kaitlyn did feel something then. She felt that he meant it.

"Then go on," Mr. Zetes said. "It's unfortunate, but it has to be done. It's not as if it's the first time you've killed." He glanced at Kaitlyn. "Have you heard about that? Drains his victims' life energy dry. An extraordinary power." There was a kind of macabre satisfaction in his face.

Then it turned to impatience again. "Gabriel, you know what the rewards will be with me. You can literally have anything you want, in time. Money, power—your rightful position in the world. But you must cooperate. You must prove yourself."

Gabriel stood like a statue. Except for that one sentence, he hadn't said a word. Something artistic in Kaitlyn's brain watched him with mad clarity, thinking about how really beautiful his face was in repose. He looked a bit like his namesake, like an angel carved in white marble. Except for his eyes, which were definitely not an angel's eyes. They were dark and fathomless— and right now rather pitiless. Cold as a black hole.

One could very easily imagine an assassin having eyes like that.

Then something like sadness entered them. Because he's sorry to have to kill me? Kaitlyn wondered.

She felt nothing at all through the telepathic web. It was like being connected to a glacier.

"Go on," Mr. Zetes said.

Gabriel glanced at Kaitlyn, then at the white-haired man.

"I'd rather kill you," he said conversationally, to Mr. Zetes.

Kaitlyn didn't get it at first. She thought he might just be stating a preference, rather than refusing.

Mr. Zetes, though, looked unamused. Forbidding. He put one hand behind him.

"If you're not for me, you're against me, Gabriel," he said. "If you won't cooperate, I'll have to treat you as an enemy yourself."

"I don't think you'll have time," Gabriel said, and took a step toward him.

Kaitlyn grabbed at the metal mesh of her cage. Her numbed brain was finally getting things together. She wanted to laugh hysterically—but it didn't seem right.

Don't kill him, she thought wildly to Gabriel. *Don't really kill him—he's crazy, don't you see? And we've got to do things—police, an institution—but we can't actually kill people.*

Gabriel tossed her the briefest of glances. "*You're* the one who's crazy," he said. "If anybody ever deserved it, it's him. Not that your idea didn't have its points," he added to Mr. Zetes. "Especially in the rewards department."

Mr. Zetes's eyes shifted from Kaitlyn to Gabriel during this exchange. They narrowed, and he nodded slightly.

Kaitlyn was waiting for some sign of fear. It didn't come. Mr. Zetes seemed calm, even resigned.

"You won't change your mind?" he asked Gabriel.

Gabriel took another step toward him. "Good night," he said.

Mr. Zetes brought his hand from behind his back, and Kaitlyn saw that he was holding a dark and very modern, very nasty-looking gun.

"Baron, Prince—guard," he said. And then he added, "If you make a move now, these dogs will jump up and tear out your throat. And then there's the gun—I've always been a very good shot. Do you think you can dispose of all three of us with a knife before we can kill you?"

Gabriel laughed—a very disquieting sound. Although his back was to Kaitlyn now, she knew that he was giving Mr. Zetes his most dazzling, disturbing smile. "I don't need a knife," he said.

Mr. Zetes shook his head, gently and disparagingly. "There's something I'm afraid you haven't realized. Joyce hasn't tested you since you formed this . . . unfortunate linkage, has she?"

"So what?"

"If she had, you would have discovered by now that it's quite difficult for a telepath who is already in a stable link to reach outside that link. Nearly impossible, I believe. In other words, young man, except for communications within your group of five, you've lost your power."

Kait could feel the disbelief surging in Gabriel. His walls were lowered now, his attention was focused elsewhere. Then she felt something like the drawing back of the ocean just before a tsunami—a sort of gathering in Gabriel's mind. She braced herself—and felt him unleash it.

Or try to. The wave, instead of crashing down on Mr. Zetes, seemed to crash around her and Gabriel instead.

It was true. He couldn't link with anyone else. Not to communicate with them—and not to harm them.

"And now, if you'll sit down in that chair," Mr. Zetes said.

Kaitlyn's eyes shifted to the chair. She'd barely noticed it before. It stood on the opposite side of the room from the door, and it looked frighteningly high-tech. It was made of metal.

With the gun in front of him and a dog on either side, Gabriel backed up to the chair. He sat.

Mr. Zetes went over and made some quick movements, stooping once. When he stood, Kaitlyn realized that Gabriel was now restrained in the chair by metal cuffs at his wrists and ankles.

Then Mr. Zetes stepped behind the chair. Two winglike

devices swung forward. In another instant, Gabriel's head was held motionless by a device that looked as if it were meant for brain surgery.

"The crystal can do more than just amplify power," Mr. Zetes said. "It can cause excruciating pain—even madness. Of course, that was what happened with the pilot study." He stepped back. "Are you quite comfortable?" he asked.

Kaitlyn was remembering the pain that had resulted from being in contact with a tiny shard of the crystal, a piece the size of her fingernail.

Mr. Zetes went over to the towering thing with the jagged growths in the center of the room. For the first time, Kaitlyn realized that the metal stand that supported it was mobile. The entire structure, though obviously heavy, could be moved.

Very carefully and delicately, Mr. Zetes was bringing the crystal to Gabriel. Tipping it slightly. Adjusting it. Until one of the jagged terminals, one of the growths, was resting against Gabriel's forehead.

In direct contact with the third eye.

"It will take a while for it to build. Now I'm going to leave the room," Mr. Zetes said. "In an hour or so I'll come back— and by then I think you might have changed your mind."

He walked out. The dogs went with him.

Kaitlyn was alone with Gabriel—but there was absolutely nothing she could do.

She looked wildly at the door of the metal cage, pulled at

it with the strength of desperation. She only succeeded in cutting her fingers. It took her about two minutes to discover that there was no way she could affect it, with fists or feet or the weight of her body.

"Don't bother," Gabriel said. The strain in his voice frightened her into going over to look at him.

He was completely immobile, his face white as paper. And now that Kaitlyn was still, she could feel his pain through the web.

He was trying to hold it back, to close himself—and the pain—off from her. But even what little got through to her was terrible.

The pressure behind the forehead—like what she had experienced with the crystal Joyce had used, but indescribably worse. As if something alive were swelling there, trying to get out. And the heat—like a blowtorch directed against that spot. And the sheer black agony—

Kaitlyn's knees gave out. She found herself half lying on the floor of the cage.

Then she pulled herself up to a sitting position.

Oh, Gabriel . . .

Leave me alone.

"I'm sorry," she whispered, saying it and sending it at once. *I'm so sorry. . . .*

Just leave me alone! I don't need you. . . .

Kaitlyn couldn't leave him alone. She was locked into it with him, sharing the waves of agony that kept building. She could feel them break over her, spread out infinitely around her. Spreading, swelling . . . to include all of them. All five who shared the web.

Kaitlyn! a distant voice shouted.

The connection was shaky, tenuous. But Kaitlyn recognized Rob.

It wasn't just pain. It was power. The crystal was feeding Gabriel power.

Rob—can you hear me? Lewis, Anna—can you hear me?

Kaitlyn, what's happening? Where are you?

It's them, Gabriel! We've got them! It's them! For a minute, despite the screaming of her nerves, Kaitlyn was simply delirious with joy.

We might lose them any second, Gabriel said. But Kaitlyn could feel what he felt—there were no walls between them now. The crystal had annihilated those. And his relief and joy were as strong as hers.

Rob, we're in Mr. Zetes's house. You've got to find out somehow where that is—and fast. Kaitlyn told them about the study, and the panel. *It might be closed again, but Lewis can open it. But you have to hurry, Rob—come quick.*

If you want to find us alive, Gabriel added. Kaitlyn was amazed that he was even speaking coherently. She knew that he was taking the worst of the pain himself. She felt a surge of admiration for him.

Keep it to yourself, witch, he told her.

It was an endearment, she realized. *Witch.* She supposed she'd better learn to like it.

You could have told Mr. Zetes you'd think about killing me. You could have bought yourself time, she said.

I don't bargain with people like him.

Kaitlyn, through the waves of pain that were starting to be tinged with crimson and carmine, felt an intense pride and triumph. *You see?* she thought to Rob. *Mr. Zetes was wrong about all of us. You see how wrong?*

But Rob wasn't there anymore. The connection had been too fragile—or now the pain was wiping everything out.

She leaned against the metal cage, dimly feeling its coolness. *Hang on,* she thought. *Hang on. Hang on. He's coming.*

She didn't know if she was saying it to Gabriel or to herself, but he answered. *You believe that?*

It roused her a little. *Of course,* she said. *I know he is. And so do you.*

It's dangerous. He's risking his own neck by coming here, Gabriel said.

You know he's coming, Kaitlyn said, able to say it with perfect assurance because she could *feel* it, directly.

"Rob the Virtuous," Gabriel said, aloud. He made a contemptuous sound like a snort—which was marred because he almost immediately gasped in pain.

Kaitlyn could never really remember the time that passed after that. It wasn't time to her, so much as a series of terrible, endless waves that eventually turned brilliant, bursting red and white like molten rock. She had no means of keeping track of them, and no consciousness of anything but them. She was alone with the waves of colored agony, thrown about by them like a swimmer caught in a riptide.

Alone—except for Gabriel. He was there, always connected. They were both being thrown around by the pain, dimly aware of each other. Kaitlyn didn't think it did Gabriel much good to know she was there, but she was glad of his presence.

It seemed a very long time, centuries maybe, but at last she sensed another presence in the maelstrom that was her world.

Kaitlyn—Gabriel. Can you hear us now? Kaitlyn! Gabriel!

Rob. Her own response was so weak and faltering, so small in the huge waves, that she didn't think he would hear it.

Thank God! Kait, we're here. We're in the house. Everything is going to be all right—Joyce is with us. She's on our side. She didn't know anything about what he was doing. We're coming to help you, Kait.

There was a near frenzy to Rob's words. Emotion—an emotion Kait had never sensed from him before. But she couldn't think now. Too much pain.

She lost awareness until she felt a presence very close.

Rob. She dragged herself up. The room was both too bright and strangely gray and dim. Alternating, like lightning. Rob was there, golden as an avenging angel, somehow coming between her and the pain. And Lewis was there, and Anna, both crying. And Joyce, her sleek blond hair all ruffled like a dandelion. They were running toward the crystal, although Kaitlyn saw their movements as discontinuous, as if under a strobe lamp.

And then—like a light switch being turned off—the pain was gone.

It left echoes, of course, and normally Kaitlyn would have found even the echoes unbearable. But it was so different from the actual pain that she felt wonderful. Able to think again, able to breathe. Able to see.

She saw that Joyce had pulled the terminal of the crystal away from Gabriel. His forehead was bleeding freely, the skin torn. He must have moved his head somehow, in spite of the metal restraints. The blood ran down his face in streams, as if he were crying.

He'd hate that, Kaitlyn thought. But Gabriel wasn't awake to be hating it. She realized now that it was some time since she'd felt any sort of communication from him, even a scream. He was unconscious.

The door of the Faraday cage was opening. Rob was beside her. Rob was holding her.

Are you all right? Oh, God, Kait, I thought I might lose you.

There it was again. The new emotion. The one that felt almost like pain, but was different.

Kaitlyn looked up into Rob's eyes.

I didn't know, he said. *I didn't realize how much I had to lose.*

It was like being transported back to the afternoon when he'd looked at her with awe and wonder, on the brink of a discovery that would change both their lives. Except that now he wasn't just on the brink. The full discovery was in those golden eyes, shining with terrible clarity. A pure light that was almost impossible to look at.

It would have been like losing me, like losing my own soul, Rob said, but it wasn't really like him saying it to her, it was as if he were simply realizing these things himself. *And now it's like finding my soul again. The other half of me.*

Kaitlyn felt it again, the universe around her hushed and waiting, enclosing the two of them. This time, though, there was a trembling joy to the hush, a *certainty.* They weren't on the threshold anymore. They were passing through. Everything being said between them, without spoken words or even words of the mind. It was simply as if their souls were mingling, joining in an embrace that wasn't quite the web and wasn't quite Rob's healing power, although it had elements of both.

It was beyond all that. It was a union, a *togetherness,* that Kaitlyn had never dreamed of.

I'm with you. I belong to you.

I'm a part of you. I will be forever.

Kaitlyn didn't even know which of them was speaking. The feelings were in both of them.

We were born for this.

He was holding her hands, she was holding his. She could

feel the power flowing between them, the energy like millions of sparkling lights, like fresh, cleansing water, like music, like stars. But she felt she was healing him as much as he was healing her. Giving him back what the accident had taken from him, the part of him that had been missing.

And then it was all so simple and natural. As if they both knew what to do without thinking—as if they'd always known what to do.

She tilted her face up, he bent down.

His lips touched hers.

In a minute they were exchanging the softest, most innocent kisses imaginable.

Kait had *never* thought that kissing a boy would be like this.

Not even Rob. She'd thought that kissing Rob would be wonderful. But this wasn't like something physical at all. It was simply like falling into the color of Rob's eyes. It was like falling endlessly into sunlight and gold.

Born for each other. For this.

A long sunlit wave, a wave of gold, came and carried them away.

Dimly, gradually, Kaitlyn was aware of a loud sound. A loud *vocal* sound.

"I said, I'm sorry to interrupt you, but really. Rob, there's something to do here!"

It was Joyce, sounding sadly unmusical after the lovely

voices Kaitlyn had been hearing. Joyce was looking at them, impatient and worried, and the tears on Anna's face were still wet. It had only been a minute or so since they'd all come in.

Impossible, of course. Kaitlyn in her heart knew it had been hours, but that was *real* time, soul time, and not the time that was ticking away on this dreary planet. She and Rob had been floating around for hours, but it had only taken a minute *here*.

Rob disengaged himself, letting go of Kaitlyn's hands. A small parting, but a hard one. Kaitlyn's fingers curled, empty.

"I'm sorry. I think I can help Gabriel," Rob said. He got up, took a step, then turned back to Kait. He knelt down by her again. *I forgot to say, I love you.*

Kaitlyn gave a half-gasping laugh. As if *that* needed to be said. "You go help Gabriel," she whispered.

"No, I need both of you," Joyce was saying. "And *quickly.* You can't solve this with energy channeling, Rob—he needs to be brought back from wherever he is. I need all four of you to get in contact with the crystal."

That broke through the lingering gold haze in Kaitlyn's vision. *"What?"* she said, standing up. She noticed dimly that she felt good, physically. Strong. Healing power *had* flowed between her and Rob.

"I need you all to get in contact with the crystal," Joyce said patiently. "And Gabriel, too—"

"No!"

"It's the only way, Kaitlyn."

"You saw what it did!"

"This time it will only be for a moment. But I need *all* of you to touch the crystal, everyone who's in the link. Now, for God's sake, hurry. Don't you realize that Mr. Zetes may be back at any minute?"

Kaitlyn staggered as she made her way out of the cage. To let the crystal touch Gabriel again—impossible. It couldn't be done, it was too cruel. And the crystal was *evil;* Kaitlyn knew that. . . .

But Joyce said it was the only way.

Kaitlyn looked at Joyce, who looked back with clear aquamarine eyes. Eyes that looked anguished but earnest.

"Don't you want to save him, Kait?"

Kaitlyn's hand began to itch and cramp.

She needed to draw—but there wasn't any time. No time. And nothing to draw with. Not a pen or paper in this entire sterile lab.

"*Please* trust me, everyone. Come on, Lewis. Just get your hand ready to touch it. When I say *now,* grab a terminal."

Lewis took a deep breath and then nodded. He held his hand ready.

"Anna? Good. Thank you. Rob?"

Rob looked at Kaitlyn.

If she could draw . . . But she couldn't. Looking back at Rob, Kaitlyn made a helpless motion that ended with a nod.

"We'd better do it," she whispered.

Joyce shut her eyes and sighed in relief. "Good. Now, I'll get behind Gabriel. When I say *now*, I'll move him in contact. Each of you grab a terminal and hold on, right?"

Kaitlyn could vaguely sense the others agreeing. She herself was moving to stand in front of the crystal, one hand outstretched. But her mind was whirring with frantic speed.

I can't draw . . . not with my hands. But the power's not in my hands. It's in my head, in my mind. If I could draw in my mind . . .

CHAPTER 16

Even as Kaitlyn thought it, she was doing it. Desperately visualizing oil pastels, her favorite, sweeps of color. *First I'd take lemon yellow, fluffy sweeps, with dashes of palest ocher. Then curves of flesh tint—and two small pools of light blue and Veronese green, dotted together.*

All right! What is it? Step back! Step back and look.

In her mind, she stepped back, and the sweeps and dots made a picture. Joyce. Unmistakably Joyce.

Then gray. Curves and lines of gray. A shape—a glass. With flesh tones holding it—Joyce holding a glass.

"Everyone ready?" Joyce said.

Kaitlyn didn't move, didn't open her eyes. She was concentrating on the next part of the picture. *Rich olive-hued flesh, with a mass of burnt umber and deep madder for hair. The brown and red went together to make mahogany.*

Marisol. A picture of Joyce and Marisol. And Joyce was holding out to Marisol a glass—

"I've got his head," Joyce said. "And—*now*—"

Kaitlyn's scream, both mental and verbal, cut through the words. *"Don't do it! Don't do it! She's with him—Mr. Zetes!"*

In the split second that followed, she wondered if she might be wrong. Joyce might have given Marisol something unknowingly—but the picture hadn't said that. It might not even be a picture of a real event, but for once, the *meaning* was clear to Kaitlyn. And the meaning was one of menace and danger. It felt to her the way the picture of the old witch giving Snow White a poisoned apple had felt to Kaitlyn the child.

And, even as Kaitlyn opened her eyes, she saw that she *hadn't* been wrong. Joyce had thrust Gabriel's head against the crystal and was holding it, and her face had an expression that Kaitlyn had never seen before. A look of twisted, bestial fury.

She knew all the time. She was in on everything, Kaitlyn thought, sickened. She could feel the shock and pain of the others—especially Rob. But her shout had reached them in time. Not one of them had touched the crystal.

Except Gabriel—Gabriel, who was now being roused from unconsciousness by the white-hot lightning bolts of pain.

Kaitlyn started to move—to tear Joyce away from Gabriel. Rob started at the same moment she did. But before they could get there, the doors burst open and chaos exploded on them.

It was Mr. Zetes—and the dogs. Something knocked into Kaitlyn with the force of a speeding truck and she fell. A dog was ripping at her. Mr. Zetes had the gun.

Still holding Gabriel against the crystal, Joyce was shouting. "I'll break the link! I'll break it!"

Rob was fighting the other dog. Anna was trying to pull the animal off him, her own calls to it lost in the clamor.

"There's an easier way to break it! Only one of them needs to die!" Mr. Zetes shouted. He was aiming the gun at Lewis.

And this is how it ends, a part of Kaitlyn's mind thought, curiously detached. None of them could help Lewis. None of them could do anything before Mr. Zetes could shoot.

She seemed to sense the old man's finger tightening on the trigger. At the same time she saw the room as one large picture, every detail etching itself into her mind as if with the burst of a flashbulb. Rob and Anna tangled with the rottweiler, Lewis standing in almost comical horror, Joyce's twisted face over the face of Gabriel, whose cheeks were masked in blood and who was just opening his eyes . . .

She felt Gabriel's awakening at the same instant, felt his pain—and his fury. Someone was hurting him. Someone was threatening a member of his web.

Gabriel lashed out.

Mr. Zetes had said that a telepath in a stable link couldn't reach outside that link—but Gabriel was now connected to a source of unthinkable power. His mind blazed out like the flare of a supernova—in four directions. With absolute precision and deadly force, he sent a torrent of fire through Mr. Zetes and Joyce and the two dogs.

Kaitlyn felt the dim shadows of it through the web, the reverberations of what Gabriel had unleashed on them. It knocked her flat.

Mr. Zetes fell without firing a shot. Behind Gabriel, Joyce hit the wall. The dog tearing Kaitlyn's arm spasmed as if it had been electrocuted and was still.

Then Gabriel stopped it. He had sagged back from the crystal, collapsing. The entire room was silent and motionless.

Let's get out of here, Rob gasped.

Kaitlyn was never sure how they got out of the house. Rob was the main force in moving them. He practically carried Gabriel. She and Anna and Lewis helped each other. There was a long time of stumbling and dragging and finally they were on grass.

Grass cool with dew. It felt wonderful. Kaitlyn rested against it gratefully, as if she'd just staggered out of a fire.

At last Lewis whispered thickly, "Are they dead?"

The dogs are, I think, Anna said. Kaitlyn agreed, but didn't mention that she'd seen blood coming out the eyes and nose and ears of the one on top of her.

But Mr. Zetes and Joyce—I don't know, Anna finished. *I think they might be alive.*

"And so Joyce didn't want to save Gabriel," Lewis said.

"She wanted to break the web somehow," Kaitlyn said, not surprised to find her voice hoarse. "Even if it killed us. Gabriel wasn't any good to them linked to us. . . . Don't ask why. I'll explain everything later."

"But Joyce was bad," Lewis said sadly. The simple innocence of the statement caught Kait—and did something to her.

Joyce was bad. She'd been against them, ready to use them, the whole time. Marisol had been wrong; Joyce had clearly known everything. She'd known about the big crystal and had had no hesitation about using it. She must have known all about the hidden room, too.

"God," Kaitlyn whispered. "How could I have been so dumb? It was probably *her* room—everything was copies, remember, Rob? Duplicates. Mr. Zetes had his stuff here, and she had hers in the Institute."

"Kaitlyn," Rob whispered, and there was both pain and tenderness in his voice, although he couldn't reach her since he was cradling Gabriel. "Don't. It's not worth it."

Kaitlyn looked at him in surprise—and realized she was crying. Thick streams of tears. She put a hand to her cheek and touched the wetness. As soon as she did, she felt something swell up in her chest.

And then she was sobbing, huge sobs, the kind she hadn't cried since she was eight years old.

Anna held her. *Leave her alone,* she told Rob. *She deserves to cry. We all do.*

The shaking sobs passed quickly, and Kaitlyn began to feel better.

Gabriel was stirring.

"This time," Rob told him, "you don't have any choice. You're half-dead—and we can't stay here. You *have* to take help." He added, silently, where it would mean more, *You saved my life a little while ago. There's only one way I can repay that.*

Gabriel blinked. He looked terrible—the blood and the pain had distorted his handsome face. But he managed a trace of the old arrogance as he whispered, "Only because I can't stop you."

Kaitlyn stopped sniffling and smiled. *It's not much good to talk like that when all your walls are down,* she told him. Then she added, *I like you this way. Walls can be very bad things.*

Gabriel ignored her, which was all he could do at the moment.

Now Rob was touching Gabriel with gentle, irresistible fingers, and Kaitlyn could feel strength flowing into Gabriel. Through Rob's healing points, through the telepathic web. She put her hand on Rob's and added her own strength, letting Rob take her energy and channel it into Gabriel. Lewis and Anna crowded close and touched Rob's hand, too, adding their contribution. All four of them, linked tightly, willing life and energy into Gabriel.

Kaitlyn could sense his need and his fear—which rapidly turned into astonishment. He'd never felt energy freely given before, she realized. Now she knew what he was feeling and she could feel it with him—the sparkling lights, the pure water, the refreshment. The awakening from half-sleep into real, vivid life.

She could feel astonishment and joy from Anna and Lewis, too.

And I never believed them about kundalini rising, Lewis said. *Jeeeez, was I wrong.*

About what? Anna asked, laughing in her mind.

Kundalini—old Chinese health concept. Relating to chi, you know. Remind me to tell you about it sometime.

Anna, still laughing, said, *I will.*

When they were all feeling ready to ride tigers and fight elephants bare-handed, Rob lifted his hands.

"That's enough," he said, and then added gently, "We really shouldn't stay here. I think Anna was right, and that Joyce and Mr. Zetes are alive. We need to keep moving."

"But where?" Kaitlyn said. She could stand, she found; she could even move easily.

Gabriel was on his feet, too. "Well, out of San Francisco for a start," he said, wiping his face with his dew-wet shirt. Even in the simple act of standing up he had pulled away from them all a little, mentally.

It's only to be expected, Kaitlyn told herself. Don't be disappointed. He needs his space.

"Well, of course, out of San Francisco. But then—where? Home?"

Even as she said it, she knew she couldn't go. If Mr. Zetes and Joyce survived, they would come after her. Kaitlyn knew about them now—Kaitlyn was a danger in the way that Marisol had been a danger. They'd want to have Kaitlyn . . . quieted.

And as much as Kaitlyn adored her father, she knew him very well. He was loving, impractical—vague. Happiest in his own small world, singing and doing odd jobs. What protection could he offer her? He wouldn't even be able to understand her story, much less help her deal with it.

In fact, she'd probably be putting *him* in danger by going home. Nothing would be easier than for Joyce and Mr. Zetes to find her there. And once they found her, she'd be dead— along with anyone else who had heard her story.

Kaitlyn didn't have the least doubt that Mr. Zetes had ways to get people killed. He had contacts. He had clients. He would find a way.

Looking around at the others, she could see them reaching the same conclusion about their own families. She could feel their dawning bewilderment.

"But then . . . where do we go?" Lewis said, in a croaking whisper.

"We have to do something to stop them. Not just Mr. Zetes and Joyce, but whoever else is involved. There must be others— like that judge. We have to find a way to stop them all."

Kaitlyn felt her breath snatched away. She looked at Rob.

Yes, she loved him, but really . . . really, she'd just been thinking about how to keep herself and her friends safe. That was going to be hard enough.

"If we don't stop them," Rob said, turning and looking directly at her, "then they'll do it again. They'll try again, with some other group of kids."

Rob was counting on her. Trusting her. And of course, he was right.

"It's true," Kaitlyn said quietly. "We can't let that happen."

"I agree," Anna chimed in softly.

There was a pause, and then Lewis said, "Oh, jeez . . . Count me in."

They all looked at Gabriel.

"I don't even have a home," he said mockingly. "All I know is that I'm not going back into a lockup cell."

"Then come with us," Rob said.

"You don't even know where you're going."

Kaitlyn said, "I might."

Everyone looked quickly at her.

"It's just an idea," she said. "I don't even know exactly why it's come into my head . . . but do you remember that dream, the one we were all in together?"

There were nods.

"Well, what if . . . what if the place in the dream was a real place? When I think about it, I get this sort of feeling that it might be. Does anybody else?"

Everyone looked doubtful, except Anna, who looked thoughtful.

"You know," she said, "I had the same feeling while I was there—in the dream, I mean. That beach felt real. It was a lot like the beaches where I live, up North. It felt almost . . . familiar. And that white house—"

"Wait," Kaitlyn said. "The house. The white house." Her brain was whirring again. She'd seen a white house somewhere else. In her mind this afternoon—could it only be this afternoon?—when Joyce had tested her with the shard of crystal.

She'd never drawn that picture—it had disappeared in a flash. But now she suddenly felt she might be able to reach it again.

Don't think—draw. Draw with your mind. Let your mind go.

Whether it was the recent contact with the great crystal, or simply desperation, she'd never know. But her mind began to draw, sketching with easy, fluid strokes. Vigorous clean strokes. She didn't even have to think about what colors to use. They simply appeared before her, shimmering, in a picture that was completed in a few heartbeats.

A white house, yes. With red roses growing at the door. A lonely house, but an eerily beautiful one. And a face in the window—a caramel-colored face, with slanting eyes and softly curling brown hair.

The man who'd attacked her—but *had* he attacked her? He'd grabbed her and tried to talk with her when she was waiting to meet Joyce. He'd grabbed her in the backyard of the Institute—and she'd hit him. And then he'd called her reckless and told her she never *thought*.

She was thinking now. Whoever he was, he had been in the house in her dream. And he had showed her a picture of a rose garden, with a crystal in the fountain.

She hadn't recognized it as a crystal then. But when she'd seen the big crystal, that monstrosity that Mr. Zetes had owned, she'd almost remembered.

The crystal in the rose garden hadn't looked . . . perverted. It had been clean and clear, with no obscene growths sprouting out. It had looked . . . pure.

So what did it all add up to? Kaitlyn didn't know, but she took a deep breath and tried to explain it to the others.

When she was done, there was a silence.

"So we're following our dreams," Gabriel said with mock sentimentality, his lip still slightly curled.

The words pleased Kait somehow. "Yes," she said, and smiled at him. "And we'll see where they take us."

"Wherever it is, we're going together," Rob said.

Kaitlyn looked at him. She was cold and battered and she knew that the danger was just beginning. And they had no clear idea of which way to travel and even less idea of *how* to travel.

But somehow it didn't matter. They were all alive, and all together. And when she looked into Rob's golden eyes, she knew that it was going to be all right.

THE POSSESSED

For Rosemary Schmitt,
with thanks for all her good wishes
and support

CHAPTER 1

"Hurry!" Kaitlyn gasped as she reached the top of the staircase. And she added with her mind, in case it might make more of an impression that way: *Hurry.*

From four different directions she felt acknowledgment, and an urgency just as strong as her own. Felt it with a sense that wasn't one of the ordinary five, but that was like seeing music or tasting color.

Telepathy was strange.

But sometimes comforting. Right now Kait was grateful for Rob's presence in her mind. It burned with a strong golden glow that warmed and steadied her. She could sense him in the next room, working fast but without panic, flipping through drawers and stuffing jeans and socks into a canvas bag.

They were leaving the Institute.

Not exactly the way they'd intended to, when they'd come to be part of a year-long psychic research project. Kaitlyn had expected to leave the Zetes Institute next spring with a band playing, a college scholarship under her arm, and her father looking on proudly. Instead, she was scrambling in the middle of the night to get her belongings together and get out before Mr. Zetes caught up with them.

Mr. Zetes, the head of the Institute, the one who wanted to turn them into psychic weapons and sell them to the highest bidder.

Only maybe now he just wanted them dead. Because they'd found out what he was up to and fought back and beaten him. Impossible as that might sound, with all Mr. Z's power, they'd *won*. They'd left him knocked out cold in the secret rooms of his San Francisco mansion.

When he woke up he was going to be mad enough to kill.

"What are you taking?" Anna asked, and her usually calm voice had a hurried sound.

"I don't know. Clothes—warm clothes, I guess. We don't know where we'll be sleeping at night." Kait repeated the last thought mentally, so Rob and Lewis and Gabriel could hear. *Warm clothes, everybody!*

A mental voice answered her, sharp as a knife and cool as midnight. *And money,* it said. *Take all the money you can get your hands on.*

"Always practical, Gabriel," Kaitlyn murmured and stuffed her purse into a duffel bag, recklessly piling jeans and sweaters and underwear on top of it. She took her lucky hundred dollar bill out of a jewelry box on the dresser and jammed it in her pocket.

"What else?" she said aloud. She found herself grabbing crazy things: a velvet cap with gold embroidery, a necklace that had been her mother's, the paperback mystery she'd been reading. Finally she jammed in her smallest sketchbook and the plastic box that held her oil pastels and colored pencils. She *couldn't* leave without her art kit—she'd rather go naked.

And her drawings weren't just recreation; they were far more important than that. They were how she told the future.

Hurry, quick, she thought.

Anna was hesitating, looking at a carved wooden mask on the wall. It was Raven, the totem of Anna's family, and it was much too big to take with them.

"Anna . . ."

"I know." Anna touched the blunt beak of the mask once with graceful fingers, then turned from it. She smiled at Kaitlyn, her dark eyes serene over high cheekbones. "Let's go."

"Wait—soap." Kait dashed into the bathroom and snagged a bar of Ivory, catching a glimpse of herself in the mirror. Nothing like as serene as Anna—her long red hair was in elf-locks, her cheeks were flushed, and the strange blue rings in her eyes were burning smokily. She looked like a feverish witch.

"Okay," Rob said as they all met in the hall. "Everybody ready?"

Kaitlyn looked at them, at the four people who'd become

closer to her than she would have imagined any people could be.

Rob Kessler, all warmth and color, gold-blond hair and golden eyes. Gabriel Wolfe, arrogant and handsome, like a drawing done in black and white. Anna Eva Whiteraven, her expression gentle even under pressure. Lewis Chao with his almond-shaped eyes glittering with anxiety, slapping a baseball cap onto smooth black hair.

Thanks to Gabriel's power going out of control, they were linked by a telepathic web. None of them would ever be alone again—unless they could find a way to break the link.

"I want to get something from downstairs," Gabriel was saying.

"Me, too," Rob said, "and I need Lewis to help. All right, let's get moving. You all right, Kait?"

"Just breathless," Kaitlyn said. Her heart was pounding, and there was a shakiness in every limb that made her not want to stand still.

Rob reached to take her duffel bag with the ruthless courtesy of his North Carolina lineage. For just an instant their hands touched; his strong fingers wrapped around hers.

It'll be all right, he told her in a swift private communication meant for no one else.

The feeling that flooded Kaitlyn was almost painful. For God's sake, not *now,* she thought and ignored the sparks that swarmed where he'd touched her skin.

"Be careful, you—healer," she said and started down the stairs.

Lewis kept glancing over his shoulder. "My computer," he mourned softly. "My stereo, my TV set . . ."

"Why don't you go back and get them?" Gabriel asked nastily. "What could be more inconspicuous?"

"Keep *moving*," Rob ordered. At the bottom of the stairs he said, "Lewis, come with me."

Kait followed them. "What are you doing?"

"Getting the files," Rob said grimly. "Okay, Lewis, open that panel."

Of course, Kaitlyn thought. Mr. Zetes's files, the ones he kept in the hidden room here under the stairway. They were full of all kinds of information, most of it cryptic, some of it undoubtedly incriminating.

"But what can we *do* with them? Who can we show them to?"

"I don't know," Rob said. "But I want them anyway. They *prove* what he's been up to."

Lewis was running sensitive fingertips over the dark paneling on the wall. Kaitlyn could feel what he was doing, trying to locate the spring release with his mind. "It's not easy to perform on demand like this," he muttered, but then there was a click and the panel slid back.

"Mind over matter," Rob said, grinning.

Hurry, Kaitlyn told him sharply.

She didn't wait to see him start down into the dimly lit hallway behind the door. She took her duffel bag into the front laboratory where Anna was opening a wire cage.

"Go on," she was saying. "Go on, Georgie Mouse, go on, Sally Mouse . . ." She knelt to hold the cage by the open side door.

"You're letting them out?"

"I'm *sending* them away, telling them to find a field. I don't know what Mr. Z will do to them," Anna said. "I don't even trust Joyce anymore." Joyce Piper was the parapsychologist who actually ran the Institute for Mr. Zetes, the one who'd recruited Kaitlyn. Even now, Kaitlyn couldn't think about her without feeling a twinge of betrayal.

"Okay, but *hurry.* We don't have time to waste," she said and moved restlessly back into the hallway. Lewis was tugging at his baseball cap nervously.

Gabriel, in the small bedroom beyond, was going through Joyce's purse.

Gabriel! Kait said. She could feel her shock reverberating in the telepathic web, and she tried to muffle it.

He merely slanted her an ironic glance. "We need money."

"But you can't—"

"Why not?" he said. His gray eyes were so dark they looked almost black.

"Because it isn't . . . it's not . . ." Kaitlyn could feel herself sagging. "It's wrong," she said finally.

Gabriel didn't admit to concepts like "wrong."

"Joyce is our enemy," he said shortly. "If it wasn't for her, we wouldn't be running away in the middle of the night in the first place. It's necessary—and you know it, don't you, Kait?"

It was dangerous to look into Gabriel's eyes for more than an instant. Kaitlyn turned away without answering, then turned back to hiss, "All right, but don't take any credit cards. They can trace those. And don't let Rob know, or he'll go ballistic. And *hurry.*"

That one word had begun to pound relentlessly in her brain: hurry, hurry, hurry. Faster than a heartbeat. She had a feeling—no, a certainty—that every second they stayed here was too long.

A premonition? But she didn't have that kind of premonition. It was only by drawing that she could get an image of the future.

Hurry. Hurry. Hurry.

Trust yourself, she thought suddenly. Go with your feelings.

"Gabriel," she said abruptly, "we've got to leave now." She added in an urgent mental shout, *Lewis, Rob, Anna—we have to leave! Right now, this second! Something's going to happen—I don't know what, but we've got to get out of here—*

"Take it easy." She felt Gabriel's hand on her arm and only then realized how agitated she was. As soon as she'd spoken her feelings out loud, she'd realized how strong they were, how urgent.

"I'm all right, but Gabriel, we've got to go. . . ."

He looked into her eyes briefly and nodded. "If you feel like that—come on."

In the hallway Rob was hurrying out of the open panel with an armful of file folders. Anna was emerging from the lab.

"What's wrong? Is someone coming?" Rob asked.

"I don't know, I just know we have to hurry—"

"We'll take Joyce's car," Gabriel said.

Rob hesitated, then nodded. "Come on, out the back door." He hustled Lewis and Anna ahead of him. Kaitlyn followed right on his heels, feeling she couldn't move fast enough.

"We'll just use the car to get out of the area," Rob was saying, when a wave of adrenaline broke over Kaitlyn. It left a metallic taste of fear in her mouth.

Behind her the front door burst open.

CHAPTER 2

Kaitlyn looked back.

Mr. Zetes.

Light from the porch shone behind him so he appeared as a dark silhouette, but somehow Kait could still see his face. When she'd first come to the Institute a week ago, she'd thought that Mr. Z was a handsome, aristocratic old gentleman—like Little Lord Fauntleroy's grandfather. Now she knew the truth, and the leonine head with its shock of white hair appeared completely evil to her. Those piercing dark eyes seemed to burn like—

Like a demon's, Kaitlyn thought. Except he's not a demon, just an insane genius, and we've got to get *out* of here. . . .

They were all paralyzed. Even Gabriel, who was in front of Kaitlyn now that she had turned around, closer to Mr. Zetes. Something about the man stopped them all dead, drained the will out of them.

They were held by pure fear.

Don't look at him, Rob's voice said in Kaitlyn's mind, but it was faint and distant. The terror reverberating in the web was much stronger.

"Come here," Mr. Zetes said. His voice was strong and rich and utterly commanding. He stepped forward and Kaitlyn could see him more clearly in the living room lights. There was blood in his thick white hair and on his starched shirt collar. Gabriel's mental attack had done that, knocked him out, made him bleed. But Gabriel was exhausted now. . . .

As if he were part of the web and could hear her thoughts, Mr. Zetes said, "You're all tired. I don't think you can use your powers any further tonight. Why don't we sit down and talk together?"

Kait had been too frightened to speak, but this struck fire in her. "We don't have anything to talk about," she said caustically.

"Your futures," Mr. Zetes said. "Your lives. I realize that I was too harsh earlier tonight. It was a shock to find you'd gotten yourselves into a permanent telepathic link. But I still think we can work together. We'll find another way to break the link—"

"You mean besides killing one of us?" Kaitlyn snarled.

Don't stick around and argue with him, Gabriel said, his cold mental voice cutting through the thrumming fear in the web. *You four go—start heading for the back door. I'll keep him here.*

"No," Kaitlyn said aloud, before she could help it. Even in

the middle of this danger, she felt a wash of emotion. Gabriel, who'd always claimed he didn't care about anybody, was risking himself to protect them. . . .

And he was moving now, putting himself directly between her and Mr. Zetes. Once she could no longer see Mr. Zetes's face, she felt her paralysis break.

But we can't leave you, she told Gabriel. *You nearly died once tonight already—*

Gabriel didn't glance back. His posture was wolflike, his attention fixed on Mr. Zetes. *Kessler, get them out. I'll handle the old man.*

But Rob's mental voice was sharp. *No! None of us can stay. Don't you see, he wants to keep us here—and we haven't seen Joyce yet.*

The instant he said it, Kaitlyn knew he was right. It was a trap.

"Come on!" she shouted, both mentally and aloud—but even as she was shouting it, a shape appeared in the kitchen doorway beside her. Hands grabbed for her.

"Let me go!"

Kait found herself kicking and screaming. Other shouts hurt her ears. All she could see was the venomous, twisted face in front of her.

Joyce Piper's sleek blond hair was plastered flat to her head with sweat and blood. Dried rivulets ran down her cheeks. Her aquamarine eyes were full of heated poison, and her lips were drawn back.

Oh, God, she wants to kill me; she really wants to kill me. I trusted her and she's crazy, she's as crazy as Mr. Zetes is—

Hands were pulling her away from Joyce, shoving her toward the back of the house. Rob's voice rose over the background shouting.

"Run, Kaitlyn! Go! Everybody run!"

Looking back, Kaitlyn had a brief glimpse of Rob and Gabriel grappling with Joyce, of Mr. Zetes coming toward them, his face suffused with fury. Then she was running, with Lewis and Anna jostling around her. She didn't realize she still had her duffel bag until she got to the back door and had to put it down to undo the locks.

She yanked the door open—and there was Mr. Zetes's chauffeur. Looking immovable as a mountain, blocking the way.

Get him!

Kaitlyn wasn't sure who shouted it, but she and Anna and Lewis were all moving at once. It was as if they suddenly had only one mind, divided into three bodies. Lewis put his head down and ran at the man's stomach; Kait swung her duffel bag at his face; Anna slammed a foot into his shin. He toppled over and they ran on, stampeding toward the green convertible in the driveway.

It was Joyce's car, the car they'd taken from Mr. Zetes's mansion to get back to the Institute. The keys were still inside.

"Get in the back," Kaitlyn told Lewis and Anna, throwing

her duffel bag into the backseat. *Rob! Gabriel! Get out here! Come on; we're ready for you!*

She twisted the key in the ignition, yanked at the gearshift, and turned the wheel hard. She wasn't a very good driver—she hadn't had much practice back in Ohio—but now she sent gravel flying as she swung the convertible in a tight arc on the driveway.

"Headlights—" Lewis gasped. Kait reached down blindly and wrenched a dial. The blaze of light illuminated the chauffeur, who was on his feet again in front of them.

Kaitlyn headed right toward him.

She could hear yelling, but everything seemed to be happening in slow motion. The chauffeur's mouth was open. For endless seconds the car kept getting closer and closer to him, and then suddenly he was diving sideways. He got out of the way just as Rob and Gabriel burst through the back door.

Get in! Kait hit the brake, jolting the car. Rob and Gabriel scrambled in, climbing over Lewis and Anna. Kaitlyn didn't wait for them to untangle themselves; she put her foot on the accelerator and pressed—hard.

Go, she was thinking—or maybe it was somebody else thinking it, she couldn't tell. *Go, go, go, go.*

Tires squealed as she reached the street, turned, and sped away from the purple house that was the Zetes Institute for Psychic Research.

It was a great relief to be moving this fast. She overshot

stop signs, shrieked around corners. She didn't know where she was going, just that she had to get as far away as possible.

"Kait." It was Rob's voice. Rob was in the front seat beside her, an armful of folders clutched to his chest. He put a hand on her arm. *Kait.*

Kaitlyn was breathing hard and shivering—a fine all-over tremor. She'd reached El Camino Real, the main street in San Carlos. She ran a red light.

Kait, ease up. We got away. It's all right. His fingers tightened on her arm, and he repeated, "It's all right."

Kaitlyn felt her breath come out more slowly. She was able to ease her grip on the steering wheel. "Are you guys okay?"

"Yeah," Rob said. "Gabriel knocked them out again. They're both lying unconscious in the lab." He turned to look into the backseat. "Nice going."

"Oh, glad you thought so," Gabriel said in a voice as cold as Rob's had been warm. But through the web, Kaitlyn could feel Gabriel's desperate tiredness.

She sensed a rush of concern from Rob and knew he felt it, too. "Look," he said, "you're wiped out. Do you want me to—"

No, Gabriel said flatly.

Kaitlyn's heart sank. Just an hour or so ago Gabriel had been willing to accept Rob's help—all their help. Back at the mansion he'd let Rob use his healing power, let him channel energy from the rest of them to save Gabriel's life. Gabriel had come to trust all of them, when he'd never trusted anyone before. They'd actually gotten through to him, broken down the walls. And now . . .

Gabriel was reverting again. Shutting them out, pretending he wasn't part of them. And there was nothing they could do about it.

Kaitlyn gave it a try anyway. Sometimes Gabriel seemed to . . . respect her more than the others, or at least he listened to her opinions more. "You've got to keep your strength up," she began lightly, trying to catch his eye in the rearview mirror.

He cut her off with a terse, *Leave me alone.*

Kait got an image of walls, high walls with nasty spikes sticking out of them. Gabriel trying to cover his vulnerability. She knew what he wouldn't verbalize, that he didn't want to be indebted to Rob ever again.

Anna's quiet voice broke into her thoughts. "Where are we going?"

"I don't know." It was a good question and Kait's heart started pounding again. "You guys, where *can* we go?"

She could sense consternation all around her. None of them except Lewis was familiar with the San Francisco area.

"Well—jeeez," Lewis said. "Okay, we don't want to go into the city, right? My parents live up in Pacific Heights, but—"

"But that's the first place Mr. Z will look," Rob said. "No, we agreed before, we can't go to our parents. We'll only get them in trouble, too."

"The truth is," Gabriel began, "we don't know *where* we're going—"

"It doesn't matter," Kaitlyn interrupted him. "It doesn't matter where we're going eventually. What we need to figure out is what to do *now*. It's two A.M. and it's dark and it's cold and Mr. Zetes is going to be after us . . ."

"You're right about that," Gabriel said. "And he'll have the police after us, too, when he wakes up from being knocked out. We're in a stolen car."

"Then we'd better get away from San Carlos fast," Lewis said, alarm sharpening his voice. "There's Highway 101, Kait. Get on it going north."

Kaitlyn clenched her teeth and got on the freeway, which was a big one, five lanes in each direction. She knew the others must be aware of how nervous she was, but no one mentioned it.

"Now, let's see . . . we don't want to go to San Francisco. . . . Okay, take the San Mateo bridge there, and when you get across, go on 880 north. That's the East Bay; you know, Hayward and Oakland."

The bridge started out wide but narrowed to a ribbon of concrete that seemed to barely clear dark water. In a few minutes they were cruising up another freeway.

"Good job," Rob said softly, and Kaitlyn felt a flash of warmth. "Now, don't speed too much; we don't want to draw attention to ourselves."

Kaitlyn nodded and kept the red hand of the speedometer quivering just below sixty miles per hour. They hadn't been driving two minutes before Lewis said, "Uh-oh."

"What 'uh-oh?'" Kaitlyn asked tightly.

"There's a car behind us with antlers," Anna said.

"Antlers?"

"Police light bar," Lewis said. His voice was thin.

Rob stayed calm. "Don't panic. They won't pull you over for going three miles over the speed limit, and Mr. Z probably isn't even awake yet. . . ."

Lights sprang to life on the roof of the car behind Kaitlyn. Blue and yellow flashing lights.

Kaitlyn's stomach plunged as if she'd stepped into an elevator. Her heart had begun a sick pounding.

"Can we panic now?" Lewis gasped. "I thought you said Mr. Z wouldn't be awake yet."

"We forgot," Anna said. "He had plenty of time to call the police and report the car stolen back at the mansion. When he *first* woke up."

Kait had a wild impulse to run. She'd run from the police a time or two back in Ohio, mainly when they wanted her to make some prediction about a case they were working on. But that had been on foot, out in the farmland that surrounded Thoroughfare—and she hadn't been a criminal then.

Now she was in a stolen car, and she'd just helped assault three grown-ups.

And you've got me *in the car, and I'm violating my parole,* Gabriel's voice said in her mind. *Remember? I'm not supposed to leave the Institute except to go to school.*

"Oh, God," Kaitlyn said aloud. She gripped the wheel with palms that were slick with sweat. The need to run, to jam on the accelerator and get *out* of here, was swelling in her like a balloon.

"No," Rob said urgently. "We won't be able to get away from them, and the last thing we want is a high-speed chase."

"Then what do we do, Rob?" Anna asked.

"Pull over." Rob looked at Kait. "Pull over and we'll talk to them. I'll show them *this*." He hefted the files. "And if they take us to the police station, I'll show it to everyone there."

Kaitlyn felt a surge of incredulity from Gabriel. "Are you joking? How naive are you, Kessler? Do you think anybody is going to believe five kids—especially any cop—" He broke off. When he spoke again, it was in a different voice, taut and yet somehow expressionless. "Fine. Pull over, Kait."

Walls. Kait could feel Gabriel's walls go up, but she had more critical things to think about. She took the next exit off the freeway and the flashing blue and yellow lights followed her.

She went quite a way down the street before she could make herself slow and stop. The police car glided up behind her like a shark and stopped, too.

Kaitlyn was breathing hard. "Okay, you guys . . ."

"I'll do the talking," Rob said, and Kait was grateful. She watched in the rearview mirror as a figure got out of the cruiser. There was only one officer, a policeman.

With numb fingers, Kaitlyn rolled down the window. The policeman bent down a bit. He had a neat dark mustache and a very solid-looking chin.

"Driver's license," he said, and Rob, leaning over Kait, said, "Excuse me." And then Kait felt it.

A pulling-back, like the ocean gathering for a tsunami. It came from the backseat. Before she could move or say anything, Gabriel struck.

Dark power shot out of him toward the policeman, a wave of crashing, destructive mental energy. The policeman made a sound like a hurt animal and dropped his notebook, clapping his hands to his head.

"No!" Rob shouted. "Gabriel, stop!"

Kaitlyn could only feel the echoes of the attack through the web, but it was blinding her, making her sick. Dimly she saw the policeman fall to his knees. Anna was gasping. Lewis was whimpering.

Gabriel, stop! Rob roared in a voice to cut through all the confusion. *You'll kill him. Stop!*

I have to help him, Kaitlyn thought. We can't become murderers . . . I have to help. . . .

It took a tremendous effort of will to turn around, to focus on Gabriel's mind. She wanted to shield herself from the terrible power still pouring out of Gabriel. Instead, she opened herself to it, trying to break through to him.

Gabriel, you're not a killer, not anymore, she told him. *Please stop. Please stop.*

She had a sense of wavering, and then the black torrent eased. It seemed to flow back into Gabriel, where it disappeared without a trace.

Trembling, Kaitlyn leaned her head against the seat back. There was absolute silence in the car.

Then Rob erupted. "*Why?* Why did you *do* that?"

"Because he would never have listened to us. Nobody's going to listen, Kessler. Nobody's on our side. We've got to *fight* if we want to live. But you don't know anything about that, do you?"

"I'll show *you* something about it—"

"Stop it!" Kaitlyn shouted, grabbing Rob, who was lunging at Gabriel. "Shut up, both of you. We don't have time to fight—we've got to get out of here, now." She fumbled with the door handle and flung the door open, dragging her duffel bag behind her.

The policeman was lying still now, but to Kaitlyn's relief he was breathing.

Who knows if his mind's okay, though, she thought. Gabriel's power could drive people into screaming insanity.

The others were scrambling out of the car. Lewis was

ghastly pale in the police car's headlights, and Anna's dark eyes were huge—owl eyes. When Rob knelt by the policeman, Kaitlyn could feel the tension in his body.

Rob passed a hand over the policeman's chest. "I think he'll be all right—"

"Then let's *go*," Kaitlyn said, casting a desperate look around and pulling at him. "Before somebody sees us, before they send more police . . ."

"Take his badge first," Gabriel suggested nastily, and that got Rob on his feet. And then something seemed to break in all of them simultaneously, and they were running away from the deserted police car.

At first Kaitlyn didn't care where she was running. Gabriel was in the lead, and she blindly followed his twists and turns onto side streets. Eventually, though, when a stabbing pain in her side slowed her down to a walk, she began to notice her surroundings.

Oh, God, where *are* we?

"It's not Mister Rogers' neighborhood," Lewis muttered and jammed his baseball cap on backward.

It was the most eerie and menacing street Kait had ever seen. The gas station they were passing was derelict: no glass in the windows, no gas pumps. So was the station across the road. The Dairy Belle snack shop was enclosed by a very solid-looking chain-link fence—a fence that had barbed wire on the top.

Beyond the Dairy Belle was a liquor store with a flickering yellow sign and iron bars in front of the glass windows. It was open and several men stood in the doorway. Kaitlyn saw one of them look across the street—directly at her.

She couldn't see his face, but she saw teeth flash in a grin. The man elbowed one of his companions, then took a step toward the street.

CHAPTER 3

Kaitlyn froze, her legs suddenly refusing to move. Rob moved up beside her, put an arm around her, urging her on. "Anna, come here," he said quietly, and Anna obeyed without a word. Lewis crowded up close.

The man across the street had stopped, but he was still watching them.

"Just go on walking," Rob said. "Don't look back." There was calm conviction in his voice, and the arm around Kait's shoulders was hard with muscle.

Gabriel turned around to sneer. "What's the matter, Kessler? Scared?"

I'm scared, Kaitlyn told him, before Rob could respond. She could feel Rob's anger—he and Gabriel were spoiling for a fight. *I'm scared of this place, and I don't want to stay here all night.*

"Well, why didn't you say so?" Gabriel nodded down the

street. "Let's go there, where the factories are. We'll find some place to hole up where the cops won't find us."

They crossed railroad tracks, passed huge warehouses and yards full of trucks. Kaitlyn kept glancing behind her nervously, but the only sign of life here was the white smoke billowing out of the Granny Goose factory's smokestacks.

"Here," Gabriel said abruptly. It was a vacant lot, fenced and barb-wired like everything else around here. A sign inside read:

SALE LEASE 4+ ACRES

APPROX. 180,000 SQ. FEET

PACIFIC AMERICAN GROUP

Gabriel was standing by a gate in the fence, and Kaitlyn saw that the barbed wire on top of the gate was squashed flat. "Give me a sweater or something," he said. Kaitlyn took off her ski jacket, and Gabriel spread it over the flattened barbed wire.

"Now climb."

In another minute they were inside the lot, and Kait had her jacket back—now dotted with perforations. She didn't care; all she wanted to do was huddle down like a duckling in some place where nothing could get her.

The lot was a good place. A huge rampart of dirt clods

screened the middle of it off from the street. Kaitlyn stumbled over to a corner where two walls of dirt met and collapsed against it. The adrenaline that had fueled her for the last eight or nine hours had run out, leaving every muscle like jelly.

"I'm so tired," she whispered.

"We all are," Rob said, sitting beside her. "Come on, Gabriel, get down before somebody sees you. You're half dead."

Right, Kaitlyn thought. Gabriel had been exhausted before knocking out the policeman, and now he was almost shaking with fatigue.

He stayed on his feet for a moment, just to prove that he wasn't listening to Rob, then sat down. He sat across from the rest of them, keeping his distance.

Lewis and Anna, though, scooted in close to Kaitlyn. She shut her eyes and leaned back, glad of their closeness, and of Rob. Rob's warm, solid body seemed to radiate protectiveness. He won't let anyone hurt me, she thought foggily.

No. I won't, Rob's voice in her mind said, and she felt immersed in gold. An amber glow that warmed her and even fed her, somehow, pouring radiance into her. Like cuddling up with a sun, she thought.

I'm so tired. . . .

She opened her eyes. "Are we going to sleep here?"

"I think we'd better," Rob said, his voice dragging. "But maybe one of us should stay up—you know, to keep watch in case somebody comes."

"I'll watch," Gabriel said briefly.

"No." Kaitlyn was appalled. "You need sleep more than any of us. . . ."

Not sleep. The thought was so fleeting, so faint, that Kaitlyn wasn't sure if she'd really heard it or not. Gabriel was the best at screening his thoughts from the rest of them. Right now Kaitlyn could sense nothing from him in the web, except that he was drained. And that he was adamant.

"Go ahead, Gabriel, suit yourself," Rob was saying grimly.

Kaitlyn was too tired to argue with either of them. She'd never imagined that she could sleep outdoors like this, sitting on the bare ground with nothing over her head. But it had been the longest night of her life—and the *worst*—and the dirt wall behind her felt amazingly comfortable. Anna was pressed up against her on one side and Rob on the other. The March night was mild and her ski jacket kept her warm. She felt—almost safe.

Kaitlyn's eyes closed.

Now I know what it's like to be homeless, she thought. Uprooted, out in the world, adrift. Heck, I *am* homeless.

"What city are we in?" she mumbled, feeling somehow that this was important.

"Oakland, I guess," Lewis muttered back. "Hear the planes? We must be near the airport."

Kaitlyn could hear a plane, and crickets, and distant

traffic—but they all seemed to be fading into a feature-less hum. In a few moments she stopped thinking and was dreaming instead.

Gabriel waited until all four of them were asleep—fast asleep—and then he stood up.

He supposed he was putting them in danger by leaving. Well, he couldn't help it—and if Kessler couldn't protect his girl, that was his own lookout.

It had become painfully obvious that Kaitlyn was Kessler's girl now. Fine. Gabriel didn't want her anyway. He should be grateful to Rob the Golden Boy for saving him—because a girl like that could trap you, could get under your skin and change you. And this particular girl, with hair like autumn fire and skin like cream and the eyes of a witch, had already shown that she wanted to change *him*.

Almost succeeded, too, Gabriel thought as he picked his way through the scraggly brush poking its way between dirt clods. She'd gotten him in a state to accept help from Kessler, of all people.

Never again.

Gabriel reached the fence and boosted himself over it, clearing the barbed wire. When he came down, his knees almost buckled.

He was weak. Weak in a way he'd never been before. And

there was a feeling inside him—a *hunger*. A burned-out feeling, as if a fire had passed over him, leaving him blackened and parched. Like cracked earth thirsty for summer rain.

He'd never felt like this before. And part of him, a small part that sat back from the rest of his mind and sometimes whispered judgment, said that there was something dangerous about feeling this way. Something *wrong*.

Ignore it, Gabriel thought. He made his legs move down the uneven sidewalk, tightening muscles so they wouldn't shake. He wasn't afraid of this kind of neighborhood—it was his native environment—but he knew better than to show weakness here. The weak got picked off in a place like this.

He was looking for someone else weak.

The whispering part of his mind twinged at that.

Ignore it, Gabriel thought again.

The liquor store was up ahead. Beside it was a long brick wall decorated with the remains of tattered posters and notices. Men stood against the wall, or sat on crates in front of it.

Men—and one woman. Not a beauty. She was skin and bones, with hollow eyes and unhealthy hair. A tattoo of a unicorn covered the calf of one leg.

Now there was irony. A unicorn, the symbol of innocence, virginity.

Better this scrawny ratbag than the innocent witch back in the lot, he thought, and flashed his most brilliant, disturbing smile at nothing.

That thought demolished the last of his hesitation. It had to be someone. He'd rather it be this bit of human garbage than Kaitlyn.

The burned, parched feeling was overwhelming him. He was a scorching void, an empty black hole. A starving wolf.

The woman turned toward him. She looked startled for a moment, then smiled in appreciation, her eyes on his face.

Think I'm handsome? Good, that makes it easy, Gabriel thought, smiling back.

He put his hand on her shoulder.

The ocean hissed and spat among the rocks. The sky was an uneasy color, more metallic violet or grayed lavender than real gray, Kaitlyn thought. She was standing on a narrow rocky peninsula. On either side of her was the ocean. Ahead the peninsula stretched out like a bony finger into the water.

A strange place. A strange and lonely place . . .

"Oh, no. Here *again?*" Lewis said from just behind her. Kait turned to see him—and Rob and Anna, as well. She smiled. The first time she'd found them in her dream she'd been confused and almost angry. Now she didn't mind; she was glad of the company.

"At least it's not so cold this time," Anna said. She looked as if she fit into this wild place where nature seemed to rule without human interference. The wind blew her long dark hair behind her.

"No, and we should be *glad* to be here," Rob said, his voice full of suppressed excitement. He was scanning the horizon alertly. "This is where we're *going,* remember—if we can find it."

"No," Kait said. "*That's* where we're going." She pointed across the water to a distant shore where a cliff rose, black with thick-growing trees. Among the trees, shining in the eerie light, was a single white house.

It was the white house Kaitlyn had seen in a vision at the Institute. The one in the photograph shown to her by a lynx-eyed man with caramel-colored skin. She knew nothing about the man except that he was an enemy of Mr. Zetes, and nothing about the house except that it was connected to the man.

"But it's our only chance," she said aloud. The others were looking at her, and she went on, "We don't know who they are, but they're the only people who even have a chance to help us against Mr. Z. We don't have any choice but to try and find them."

"And maybe they can help us with"—Lewis changed to telepathic speech in midsentence—*this thing. Maybe they'll know how to break the link.*

Anna spoke quietly. "You know what the research says. One of us has to die."

"Maybe they can find some way around that."

Kaitlyn said nothing, but she knew they all felt the same way. The web that tied them together had brought them very close, and there were some wonderful things about it. But all the same, in the back of her mind there was always the pounding insistence that it *had* to be broken. They couldn't live the rest of their lives like this, welded together this way. They *couldn't*. . . .

"We'll find the answers when we get there," Rob said. "Meanwhile, we'd better look around. Examine everything about this place. There must be some clue as to where it *is*."

"Let's walk up there," Kait suggested, nodding toward the end of the peninsula. "I'd like to get as close to that house as possible."

They kept a close watch as they walked. "Same old ocean," Lewis said. "And back there"—he gestured behind them—"same old beach with trees. If I had my camera we could get a photo to compare to other things. Like, you know, pictures in books or travel brochures."

"There's just not enough to distinguish it from other beaches," Kaitlyn said. "Except—look, does it seem to you that there are more waves on the right side?"

"It does," Rob said. "That's weird. I wonder what would cause it?"

"And then there are these," said Anna. She dropped to one knee beside a pile of rocks, some long and thin, some nearly square. They were stacked like a child's blocks, but much more whimsically, forming an irregular tower that had appendages sticking out at intervals—like airplane wings.

The piles were all over the peninsula, resting on the huge

boulders that lined either side. They ranged from small to gargantuan. Some, to Kaitlyn's eye, looked like crude depictions of people or animals.

"I have the feeling I should *know* this," Anna said, her hands framing the stack, not quite touching it. "It should have some meaning to me." Her face was troubled, her full lips pinched, her eyes clouded.

"Never mind," Rob said. "Keep walking and maybe it'll come to you. Is it a place you've seen before?"

Anna shook her head slowly. "I don't *think* I've seen it. And yet it's *familiar*—and it's north, I'm sure of that. North of California."

"So we look at all the beaches north of California?" Lewis muttered, with unaccustomed bleakness. He kicked at a rock pile.

"Don't!" Anna said quickly—with unaccustomed sharpness. Lewis ducked his head.

At the end of the peninsula Kait tilted her face to the wind. It felt good and it was exhilarating to have the ocean crashing around her on three sides, but they still weren't much closer to the white house.

"Who's giving us these dreams, anyway?" Lewis asked from a little way behind her. "I mean, do you think it's *them,* in that house? Do you think they're in there now?"

"Let's ask," Rob said, and without warning he cupped his hands around his mouth and shouted across the water. "Hey, you! You out there! Who are you?"

Kaitlyn's heart jolted at the first bellow. But the shout had a *good* sound, a sound to combat the ghostly violet sky and the vast stretch of moving water. This was a big place, and big sounds fit here.

She cupped her own hands around her mouth. "Whooo are yoooou?" she shouted, sending her voice across the ocean as if she really expected someone in the white house to hear.

"That's it," Anna said, and she threw her head back and gave a long-drawn-out cry that sent gooseflesh up Kait's spine. "Whooo are yoooou? Where are weeee?"

Lewis joined in. "Thiiiis suuucks! Talk to us! Can't you be a little clearer?"

Kaitlyn choked on laughter, but kept calling. The racket caused a pair of gulls to soar upward, alarmed.

And then, amidst their own clamor, came an answer.

It was louder than their shouting voices, but it was a breathless whisper nevertheless. As if, Kaitlyn thought suddenly, a thousand people were whispering at once, almost in chorus but not quite. A thousand people crowded around you in a small, echoing room.

It shut them all up immediately. Kait stared wide-eyed at Rob, who had grasped her shoulder in an automatic impulse to protect her.

"Griffin's Pit! Griffin's Pit! Griffin's Pit!" the urgent whispers said.

Kaitlyn's lips formed the word "What?" but no sound came out. The cacophony of sound was beating at her from all sides. She could see Lewis grimace. Anna had her hands to her head.

"Griffin's Pit Griffin's Pit Griffin's Pit . . ."

Rob, it hurts. . . .

Then wake up, Kaitlyn! It's your dream; you have to wake up!

She couldn't. But she could see that the pounding noise was hurting Rob, too. His face was tense, his golden eyes dark.

"GriffinsPitGriffinsPitGriffinsPit—"

Kaitlyn gave a jerk and the peninsula disappeared.

She was staring into the night sky. A lopsided moon was dipping toward the horizon. A single airplane roared slowly among the stars, red lights winking.

Rob was stirring beside her, Anna and Lewis sitting up.

"Everybody all right?" Kaitlyn said anxiously.

Rob smiled. "You did it."

"I guess. And we got our answer—I guess." She rubbed at her forehead.

"Maybe that's why they didn't try to communicate in words before," Anna said. "Maybe they knew it would hurt us. And what they were saying wasn't too clear, anyway."

"Griffin's Pit," Kaitlyn said. "It sounds—ominous."

Lewis wrinkled his nose. "Griffin's—*what? Oh,* you mean Whippin' Bit."

"*I* heard something like 'Wyvern's Bit,'" Anna put in. "But that doesn't make much sense."

"Neither does Whiff and Spit," Rob said. "Unless it's some kind of combination perfume and tobacco factory. . . ."

"C'mon down to the Whiff and Spit; snuff it up and cough it out," Lewis chanted, giving it a catchy rhythm. "But, look, if none of us heard the same thing, it means we're back where we started."

"Wrong," Rob said and twisted Lewis's cap down over his eyes. He grinned; Kaitlyn could tell he was in a good mood. "We know there's somebody out there, and they're trying to talk to us. Maybe they'll get better. Maybe we'll get lucky. Anyway, we have a direction to go—north. And we know what to look for—a beach like that. The search is on!"

His enthusiasm was infectious. His smile, the lights dancing in his golden eyes—all infectious, Kaitlyn thought.

Kaitlyn had a feeling—wild, inappropriate, but consuming—of hope. All her life she'd wanted to belong somewhere, wanted it with a deep-down, gut-wrenching ache. And she'd always had the strange conviction that she *did* belong somewhere. That there was a place where she fit in perfectly—if only she could find it.

Since Gabriel had locked them into the web, she'd found *people* to belong to. Whether she wanted it or not, she was bonded for life to her four mind-mates. And now—well, maybe the dream was calling them to a *place* to belong. The place she'd sensed in the back of her mind all along, the place where all her questions would be answered and she would understand who she really was and what she was supposed to do with her life.

She smiled at Rob. "The search is on." She scooted closer to him, knee to knee, and added in a private message, *And I love you.*

Strange coincidence, Rob's voice said in her mind.

Amazing how he could make her feel. Safe in a vacant lot, warm in the middle of the night. Just being this close to him, being able to touch his thoughts and feel his presence, was comforting—and dizzying.

I like being close to you, too, he said. *The closer I get, the closer I want to get.*

Kaitlyn was floating, drowning in the gold of Rob's eyes. She began, *I wish we could be like this forever—*

She was cut off. Anna, who had been sitting with her chin on her knees, now suddenly raised her head.

"Wait a minute—where's Gabriel?"

Kait had forgotten about him. Now she realized that the rampart of earth across from them was deserted.

"He must have gone to check on something," Lewis said hopefully.

"Or maybe he's gone for good," Rob said—and there was a sort of grim hope in his voice, too.

"Sorry. No deal." A shower of earth fell from the dirt wall, and Gabriel appeared, wearing a rather chilling smile.

And he looked—well. Refreshed. Not tired anymore.

Kaitlyn felt the shadow of alarm. She brushed it away before anyone else could notice it. Of *course* Gabriel was all right. There was nothing wrong with him looking so . . . rejuvenated. He'd had a chance to rest, that was all.

"It's getting light," Gabriel was saying. "I checked around; there's no activity out there: no cops, nothing. If we're going to get out, now's the time."

"Okay," Rob said. "But first, sit down a minute. We have to figure out what the plan is, what we're doing next. And we have to tell you what happened to us tonight."

"Something happened?" Gabriel looked around sharply. "I was—only gone for a few minutes."

"It wasn't anything real; it was a dream," Kaitlyn said, and she tried to quash her alarm again. That hesitation between "I was" and "only gone for a few minutes"—Gabriel was lying. She couldn't feel it in the web, but she knew.

Where had he been?

Rob was telling him about the dream. Gabriel listened to the whole story, looking amused and slightly contemptuous.

"If that's where you really think you're going, I don't care," he said when Rob finished. His handsome lip was curled. "All I care about is getting away from the California Youth Authority."

"Okay," said Rob. "Now, we ought to take stock—what have we got with us here? What're our assets?" He gave a rueful grin.

"'Fraid I don't have anything but my wallet and these files."

For the first time Kait consciously realized that neither Rob nor Gabriel had their duffel bags with them. Lost in the fight with Mr. Zetes, she guessed.

"I've got my bag," she said. "And a hundred dollars in my pocket"—she checked to make sure—"and maybe fifteen in my purse."

"I've got *my* bag," Lewis said. "But I don't think any of my clothes are going to fit either of you guys." He eyed Rob and Gabriel doubtfully—they were both several inches taller than he was. "And about forty dollars."

"I've only got a few dollars in change," Anna said. "And my bag of clothes."

"And I've got—oh, twelve-fifty," Rob said, flipping through his wallet.

"Jeez, only a hundred and fifty-something—remind me never to run away with you guys again," Lewis said.

"It's not even enough to buy bus tickets—and then we have to eat," Rob said. "And it's not as if we have just one destination—we've got to *look* for the place, so we don't really know where we're going. Gabriel, how much—"

Gabriel had been shifting where he sat, noticeably impatient. "I've got about ninety dollars," he said shortly—without, Kait noticed, mentioning that he'd gotten it from Joyce's purse. "But we don't need bus tickets," he added. "I've taken care of it. We've got transportation."

"Huh?"

Gabriel shrugged and stood, brushing crumbs of dirt off his clothes. "I've got us a car. I hotwired it and it's ready. So if you're finished talking . . ."

Kaitlyn leaned her head into her hands. "Oh, God."

She could *feel* the golden-white blaze of anger beside her. And now Rob was standing, moving up to get right in Gabriel's face. He was absolutely furious.

"You did *what?*" he said.

CHAPTER 4

Gabriel gave one of his wildest smiles. "I stole us a car. What about it?"

"What about it? It's *wrong*, that's what. We are not going around stealing people's cars."

"We stole Joyce's," Gabriel said musically and mockingly.

"Joyce was trying to *kill* us. That makes it—not right, maybe, but justifiable." He got even closer to Gabriel and said with deadly anger, emphasizing each word, "There is *no* justification for stealing things from innocent people."

Gabriel was clearly enjoying himself, relaxed but ready for action any minute. He wanted to fight, Kaitlyn realized—he was dying for it. Almost as if he were feeding off the blazing energy Rob radiated. "What's *your* idea, country boy? How do we get out of here?" he said.

"I don't know, but we don't steal. It's wrong. That's all." And for Rob, it *was* all, Kaitlyn knew. It was that simple for him.

She was chewing her lips, uneasily aware that it wasn't so simple for her. Half of her was impressed that Gabriel had gotten a car, and she had a sneaking feeling she'd be happy to ride away in it if she weren't nervous that they'd get caught. A car would be something to hold on to, an anchor against the uprooted, drifting feeling of being homeless.

But Rob would never go for it. Dear Rob. Dear honorable Rob, who was completely and utterly pigheaded and who could be the most exasperating boy on earth. Who was now glaring at Gabriel challengingly.

Gabriel bared his teeth in response. "And what about the old man? You don't think he's going to give up, do you? He'll have the police after us—and maybe other people. He has a lot of friends, a lot of connections."

It was true. Kaitlyn remembered the papers she had seen in Mr. Z's hidden room. There had been letters from judges, CEOs of big companies, people in the government. Lists of names of important people.

"We need to get out of here—*now*," Gabriel said. "And that means we need transportation." His eyes were locked on Rob's. Neither of them willing to give in.

They're going to fight, Kaitlyn thought, and she looked at Anna in despair. Anna had paused in the middle of brushing the dark and shining raven wing of her hair. She looked back worriedly at Kait.

We've got to stop them, she said.

I know, Kait thought back. *But how?*

Come up with another solution.

Kaitlyn couldn't think of another solution—and then it came to her.

Marisol, she thought.

Marisol. The research assistant back at the Institute. She'd been with Mr. Zetes even before Joyce, and she'd known about his plans. She'd tried to warn Kaitlyn—and Mr. Z had put her in a coma for it.

Kait said it aloud, with mounting excitement. "Marisol!"

It broke into Rob and Gabriel's stareout. "What?" Rob said.

Kaitlyn scrambled to her feet. "Don't you see—if anybody would help us, if anybody would believe us—and we're in *Oakland.* I'm sure Joyce said she was from Oakland."

"Kait, calm down. What are you—"

"I'm saying we should go to Marisol's *family.* They live here in Oakland. We could probably walk. And they might help us, Rob. They might understand this whole horrible thing."

The others were staring at Kait—but it was a good staring, full of dawning wonder.

"You know, they might, at that," Rob said.

"Marisol may even have told them something about it—maybe not in detail, but she might have given hints. She liked to give hints," Kait said, remembering. "And they've got to be upset over what happened. Their daughter's fine, a little moody but perfectly healthy—and then one day she falls down in a coma. Don't you think they'd have their suspicions?"

"It depends," Gabriel said. He looked dark and cold—cheated of his confrontation. "If she was taking drugs—"

"*Joyce* said she was taking drugs. And personally, I'm not inclined to trust anything Joyce said—are you?" Kaitlyn tilted her chin at him and to her surprise got a flash of amusement from the gray, chill eyes.

"Anyway, it's the best chance we've got," Lewis said. Always quick to see the bright side of things, he was smiling now, his dark eyes sparkling. "It's someplace to go—and maybe they'll *feed* us."

Anna twisted her hair into a long tail and stood gracefully, and Kaitlyn realized it was settled. Two minutes later they were walking down the sidewalk, looking for a phone book. Kaitlyn felt unkempt and empty—she hadn't eaten since lunch yesterday—but surprisingly fit.

The street was deserted, now, and although the fenced-in buildings were just as decrepit, the whole place looked a little safer. Lewis was cheerful enough to pull out his camera and take a picture.

"For posterity," he said.

"Maybe it's better not to look like a tourist," Anna suggested in her gentle voice.

"If anybody comes near us I'll take care of them," said

Gabriel. His thoughts were still black with jagged red streaks—leftover from his fight with Rob.

Kait looked at him. "You know, I was meaning to ask you. Mr. Z said you couldn't link with another mind once you were in a stable link with us—but you linked with that policeman, and with Mr. Z and Joyce earlier."

Gabriel shrugged. "The old man was wrong," he said briefly.

Again, Kaitlyn felt a whisper of anxiety in her blood. Gabriel was hiding something from all of them. Only Gabriel, she thought, could manage that so easily in the web.

And despite his barriers, she could sense something—strange—in him. Something that had changed in the last night.

The crystal, she thought. Mr. Zetes had forced Gabriel into contact with a giant crystal, a monstrosity of jagged edges that housed unthinkable psychic power.

What if it had done something to Gabriel? Something . . . permanent?

"Gabriel," she said abruptly, "how's your forehead?"

He put his fingers to it quickly, then, deliberately, dropped his hand to his side. "Fine," he said. "Why?"

"I just wanted to look at it." Before he could stop her, she reached up herself, brushing his dark hair aside. And there on his forehead she could see it, shadowy on the pale skin. Not the kind of scab she would have expected from the cut the crystal had given him. It looked more like a scar or a birthmark—a crescent-shaped dimness.

"Right over your third eye," Kaitlyn said involuntarily, just as Gabriel grabbed her wrist in a bruising grip. She and he had both stopped dead. He stared at her, and there was something frightening in his gray gaze. Something menacing and alien that she'd never seen before.

The third eye—the seat of psychic power. And Gabriel's powers had been greater ever since his contact with the crystal. . . .

He'd always been the strongest of all of them, psychically. It scared Kait to think what he might become if he got any stronger.

"What's *wrong* with you guys?" Lewis was demanding. The others were far ahead. Rob was walking back toward them, his brows drawn together.

Then Anna, who was farthest down the street, called, "I see a phone!"

Gabriel released Kait's wrist, almost throwing it, and started toward Anna briskly.

Leave it alone, Kaitlyn told herself. For now. For now, concentrate on surviving.

They found Marisol's name among a flood of Diazes in the phone book. Lewis wasn't familiar with Ironwood Boulevard, the street where she lived, but they studied a map at a gas station.

It was almost nine-thirty before they arrived, and Kaitlyn was hot, dusty, and starving. It was what Lewis called a pueblo house, a fake adobe house covered with pinky-brown stucco. No one answered the doorbell.

"They're not home," Kaitlyn said in despair. "I was stupid. They're at the hospital with Marisol; Joyce said they went every day."

"We'll wait. Or come back," Rob said firmly, his resolution and his temper undisturbed. They were heading toward the shade of the garage when a boy, a little older than they were, came around from the back of the house.

He had no shirt and his thin, sinewy body looked tough. Kait would never have dared approach him on the street. But he also had curly hair that shone in the morning light like mahogany, and a full, rather sullen mouth.

In other words, thought Kaitlyn, he looks like Marisol.

For several heartbeats they all just stared at each other, the boy obviously resenting these intruders on his property, ready to fight them off. Rob and Gabriel were reacting by bristling. Then Kaitlyn stepped forward impulsively.

"Don't think we're crazy," she said. "But we're friends of Marisol's and we've run away from Mr. Zetes and we don't know where else to go. We've been on the road since last night and it took us hours to walk here. And—well, we thought you might help us."

The boy stared harder, through narrowed eyes that had long, dark lashes. Finally he said slowly, "Friends of Marisol's?"

"Yes," Kaitlyn said firmly, tucking away in her mind all the memories of how Marisol had snubbed her and terrorized her. That didn't matter now.

The boy looked each of them over, his expression sour. Just when Kaitlyn was convinced he was going to tell them to go away, he jerked his chin toward the house.

"Come on in. I'm Tony. Marisol's brother."

At the door he asked casually, "You a *bruja?* A witch?" He was looking at her eyes.

"No. I can do—things. I draw pictures and eventually they come true."

He nodded, still casual. Kaitlyn was vastly grateful that he seemed to believe her. He accepted the idea of psychic powers without surprise.

And despite his surly looks, he was—thoughtful. Generous. One minute after they were in the house he rubbed his chin, cast a sideways glance at Lewis, and muttered, "You been on the road, huh? You guys hungry? I was going to eat breakfast."

A lie, Kaitlyn thought. He must have seen how Lewis was sniffing at a lingering aroma of eggs and bacon. She warmed to him immediately.

"There's a lot of stuff people brought over when Marisol got sick," he said, leading them into the kitchen. From the refrigerator he pulled out a giant baking dish full of what looked like corn husks and a smaller one full of noodles. "Tamales," he said hefting the big one. He put down the small one. "And chow mein."

Fifteen minutes later they were all seated around the big kitchen table, and Kait was finishing up the story of their flight from the Institute. She told how Joyce had recruited them, how they'd come to California, how Marisol had warned them that things at the Institute weren't what they seemed, and how Mr. Zetes had finally revealed himself last night.

"He's completely evil," she said finally and looked at Tony uncertainly. But again he seemed unsurprised, merely grunting. Rob had his pile of folders and papers ready as proof, but it didn't seem necessary.

Staring down into a tamale, Kaitlyn asked the others, *Now how do we tell him Mr. Zetes put his sister in a coma?*

From every one of them—except Gabriel—she felt discomfort. Gabriel was toying with his food, apparently not interested in eating. He sat a little away from the rest of them, as usual, and looked as if he were farther away mentally.

Anna spoke up. "How is Marisol?"

"The same. The doctors say she's always going to be the same."

"We're sorry," Lewis said, wiggling his fork inside a corn husk.

"Did you ever think," Rob said quietly, "that there was anything—strange—about what happened to her?"

Tony looked at him directly. "Everything was strange. Marisol didn't take drugs. I heard some stuff last week about how she was supposed to be on medication—but it wasn't true."

"Joyce Piper told *us* she was on medication. She told us Marisol was seeing a psychiatrist. . . ." Rob's voice trailed off, because Tony was shaking his head vigorously. "Not true?"

"She saw a shrink once or twice last year, because of the really weird stuff that was going on. That was when she worked at Zetes's house. He had some sick people there—for a study, Marisol said."

"The pilot study? You know about that?" Kaitlyn leaned forward eagerly. "Marisol mentioned it—a study with other psychics like the one Mr. Zetes was doing with us."

Rob was sorting through the folders, pulling out one Kaitlyn had seen before. It was a file jacket with a photo of a brown-haired girl labeled SABRINA JESSICA GALLO, BLACK LIGHTNING STUDY.

Scrawled across the label in thick red ink was the word TERMINATED.

Tony was nodding. "Bri Gallo. She was one of them. I think they had six all together. They were into some really bizarre crap. Sick. Zetes had this mental domination over them."

He shifted, seemed to consider, then said, "I'll tell you a story. There was a guy who worked with Marisol, another assistant. He didn't like the boss, thought Zetes was crazy. He used to fight, you know? Talk back. Show up late. And finally he decided he was going to talk to a newspaper about what was going on at that house. He told Marisol that one night. She said the next morning when she saw him, he was—different. He didn't talk back anymore, and he sure didn't talk about any newspapers. He just did his work like he was sleepwalking. Like somebody *enbrujado*—under a spell."

"A spell?" Kait wondered. "Or drugs?"

"Stranger than drugs. He kept on working there, and he kept on getting paler and sleepier. Marisol said he had this blank look, like he was there but his soul wasn't." Tony glanced toward the hallway where a large candle burned in a niche beneath a statue of the Virgin Mary. Simply and unemotionally he said, "I think Boss Zetes works black magic."

Kaitlyn glanced at Rob, who was listening intently, his eyes amber-brown and grim. He met her gaze and said silently, *It's as good a word as any for what he does with that crystal. And maybe Mr. Z does have some mental powers we don't know about.*

Aloud, Kaitlyn said, "He used drugs on Marisol. Joyce Piper gave her something—I don't know what, but I saw it in a vision."

At first Tony seemed not to have heard. He said, "I told her to get out. A long time ago. But she was ambitious, you know? She made money, she bought a car, she was going to get her own place. She said she could handle things."

Kaitlyn, who had always been poor, could understand that.

"She did try to get out in the end," Rob said. "Or at least to get us out. And that was why Mr. Z had to stop her."

Tony grabbed a kitchen knife and slammed it into the wooden table.

Kait's heart almost jumped out of her body. Anna froze, her dark owl eyes on Tony's face. Lewis winced, and Rob frowned.

Gabriel, his eyes on the quivering knife handle, smiled.

"Lo siento," Tony muttered. "I'm sorry. But he shouldn't have done that to Marisol."

Almost without thinking, Kaitlyn put her hand on his. Back in Ohio she would have laughed at the idea. She'd hated boys, loud, smelly, interfering boys. But she understood exactly what Tony was feeling.

"Rob wants to stop him—Mr. Zetes," she said. "And we have this idea that if we can get to this certain place, we might get help. There are people there who act like they're against the Institute."

"Can those people help Marisol?"

Kaitlyn had to be honest. "I don't know. But if you want, we'll ask them. I promise."

Tony nodded. He took his hand from under Kaitlyn's and wiped his eye absently.

"We're not even sure who they are," Rob said. "We think they live somewhere up north, and we have an idea of what the location looks like. We figure it may take us a while to find them, and we'll be on the road all that time. The only problem is that we don't know how to get there."

"No," Gabriel broke sarcastically, speaking for the first time since they'd arrived. "That's not the only problem. The other problem is that we're broke. And stranded."

Tony looked at him, then smiled. It was a crooked smile, but genuine, as if he liked Gabriel's directness.

"We thought we might talk to your parents," Kaitlyn said delicately. "If we go to our own parents they'll find us, you see. And our parents wouldn't understand."

Tony shook his head. He stared out the window into a neat backyard as if thinking. At last he said, "Don't wait for my parents. It'll only upset them."

"But—"

"Come on outside."

Kaitlyn and the others exchanged looks. The web was as blank with surprise as their faces. They followed.

The backyard was filled with dormant rosebushes. There was an extension of the driveway behind an iron gate. On the driveway was a silver-blue van.

"Hey, that's the van from the Institute," Lewis said.

Tony had stopped and was regarding it with folded arms. He shook his head. "No, it's Marisol's. It was hers. It is hers." He stood for a moment, shaking his head as if trying to figure this out, then turned abruptly to Kait. "You take it."

"*What?*"

"I'll get some stuff—sleeping bags and things. We've got an old tent in the garage."

Kaitlyn was overwhelmed. "But—"

"You need stuff for a trip, right? Otherwise you're going to die out there. You're never going to make it." He shook off

Kaitlyn's reaching hand and backed up, but he met her eyes. His voice was almost a growl. "And you're going to fight *him,* the bastard that hurt Marisol. Nobody else is. Nobody else *can,* because you need magic to fight magic. You take the van."

His eyes were Marisol's eyes, too, Kaitlyn realized. Rich brown almost the color of his hair. She could feel her own eyes filling, but she held his gaze. "Thank you," she said softly.

And we'll do whatever we can to get them to help Marisol, she thought. She knew the others could hear her, but it was really a private promise.

"We better get you out of here before my mom gets back," Tony said. He took Rob and Lewis into the garage. Kait, Anna, and Gabriel examined the van.

"It's perfect," Kaitlyn whispered, looking around the inside. She'd ridden in it before, to and from school, but she'd never really *looked* at it. To her eyes now, there seemed to be square miles of room. There were two bucket seats in front and two long bench seats in back, with lots of space between them.

There still seemed to be miles of room once Tony piled in blankets, sleeping bags, and pillows. Riches untold, Kaitlyn thought, fingering a thick down-filled comforter. He even took Gabriel and Rob back into the house and lent them spare clothes. Finally he put groceries from the refrigerator into a paper bag.

"It won't last long with five of you, but it's something," he said.

"Thank you," Kait said again as they got ready to leave. Rob was in the driver's seat; Gabriel in the other front bucket seat. Anna and Lewis were in the bench seat behind them. Kaitlyn had ended up in the rear bench seat—too far from Rob, but no matter. They'd change places later.

"You just get Zetes, right?" Tony said, then slid the door of the van shut.

We're going to try, Kaitlyn thought. She waved as Rob backed out of the driveway.

"Keep going down this street and I'll tell you how to get back on Highway 880," Lewis said. He was studying a map of California that Tony had supplied. When they were on the highway, he changed it for a map of the United States.

"Well, we've got clothes, we've got food, and we've got sleeping gear. And we certainly have transport," Rob said, settling back in his bucket seat and running a caressing hand over the steering wheel. "Now—exactly where are we going?"

CHAPTER 5

"Let's just get out of California as fast as possible," Gabriel said. Rob wouldn't agree.

"We ought to think about this before we just start driving blindly. We're looking for a beach, right? There are a lot of beaches in California—"

"But we *know* it's not in California," Kait interrupted. "Anna and I know that. We're sure." In front of her, Anna was nodding.

"And we've got to get *out* of this state," Gabriel said. "This is where the cops will be looking for us. Once we're in Oregon we can relax a little."

Kaitlyn was afraid Rob would argue just for the sake of arguing with Gabriel—she wasn't sure how things stood between them just now—but he just shrugged and said, "Okay, then," peaceably.

Lewis rattled the map. "The fastest way is to go up Interstate 5," he said. "I'll tell you how to get there. We still won't make it to Oregon before dark."

"We can change drivers every few hours," Kaitlyn said. "Oh, and everybody, try and look like you're on a field trip or something, at least until one o'clock or so. People might think it's strange for a bunch of teenagers to be riding around in a van during school hours."

The country kept changing as they drove. At first it was beige and flat, with scrubby grass and an occasional gray-purple bush beside the road. As they got farther north it became more hilly, with trees that were either bare or dusty green. Kait watched it all with an artist's eye and eventually picked up her sketchpad.

It felt like a long while since she'd had time to draw. It had only been twenty-four hours, since yesterday's art studio class— but her entire life of yesterday felt years away. The oil pastels spread smoothly onto the fine-toothed paper, and Kaitlyn felt herself relax. She needed this.

She blocked out the shape of the distant hills with side strokes of the pastel stick, catching an impression of them before the scene changed. That's what she liked about pastels—you could work fast on a burst of inspiration. She filled the hills in with loose, vigorous strokes, and the picture was done in minutes.

That was practice. Now turn the page. Reach for cool colors—pale blue and icy mauve. Maybe acid green and blue-purple, too.

A picture was coming alive under her fingers without her conscious intent.

Kaitlyn was used to letting her fingers go at moments like this, while her mind simply drifted. Right now her mind had drifted to thoughts of Gabriel.

She was going to have to talk with him, and soon. As soon as she could find any privacy. Something serious was wrong. She had to find out what it was. . . .

With a shock Kaitlyn recognized what she'd drawn on the sketch pad.

Gabriel. Not the stark black-and-white portrait she'd always imagined, but a form arising out of a dense network of colored lines. It was unmistakably Gabriel . . .

. . . and in the center of his forehead, blazing with cold blue brilliance, was a third eye.

It seemed to glare at her balefully, and Kaitlyn suddenly felt faint. As if she were about to fall into the picture.

She jerked back, and the sensation disappeared, but chills ran down her neck.

Stop it, she told herself. There was nothing strange about a picture of the third eye. Gabriel was psychic, wasn't he? And this just a metaphor showing he was. She'd drawn a picture of herself with a third eye once.

The reassurances didn't reassure. Kaitlyn knew in her bones that the drawing foretold something evil.

Kait, what's wrong?

Rob's voice in her head. Kaitlyn looked up from the maze of colors to see that everyone was looking at her. Gabriel had turned around in the front, and Lewis and Anna were looking over the back of their seat. She could see Rob's worried eyes in the rearview mirror.

While she'd been drawing she'd forgotten about the web, hadn't even felt the presence of the others. And she could tell from their confusion that they hadn't heard *her* thoughts, either, just gotten a general sense that she was upset.

Interesting, one part of her mind said. So drawing is a way to screen my thoughts. Or maybe it's just concentrating.

Meanwhile, the rest of her mind was answering Rob.

It's nothing. Just a drawing.

She felt Rob's alarm. "A precognition?" he said aloud.

"No—I don't know." It was horribly impossible to lie in the web. "Whatever it is, I don't want to talk about it now."

She didn't, either. Not with Gabriel sitting there hearing every word, not with Lewis and Anna looking on. Gabriel would be furious at the violation of his privacy, and the others might panic. No, Kaitlyn had to talk to him alone about this first.

She could feel frustration from Rob—he could tell she was hiding something, but not *what*. Anna's clear dark eyes were questioning.

Time to change the subject. "Shouldn't we stop and switch drivers?" she said.

Lewis grinned. "Let's wait a couple of exits and stop at the

Olive Pit. There was a sign back there advertising free samples."

"This must be olive country," Kait said, glad of a distraction. "I keep seeing groves of olive trees."

She kept talking until they stopped, and then there was the complexity of selecting olive samples—chili olives and Cajun olives and Texas olives and Deep South olives—and by the time they all got back into the van everyone seemed to have forgotten their questions.

Gabriel drove. Rob sat in the rear with Kaitlyn, who leaned against him.

"You all right?" he said, too softly for the others to hear.

Kaitlyn nodded, avoiding his golden eyes. She didn't *want* to have any secrets from Rob, but she was afraid to upset the precarious balance between him and Gabriel.

"Just tired," she said. She didn't feel like drawing anymore, not even when a huge and beautiful mountain appeared before them in the distance. Its single peak was white with snow, accented by black ridges of rock.

"Mount Shasta," Lewis said.

They passed rolling hills and crossed riverbeds, mostly dry. The motion and the sound of the van was lulling. Kait's head drooped onto Rob's shoulder and her eyes shut.

She woke with a start and a shiver. How strange—it was *cold* suddenly. Icy cold, as if she'd stepped into a restaurant freezer.

She looked around, dazed with sleep. Mount Shasta was

behind them, glowing like a huge watermelon jewel in the sunset. The sky was murky mauve.

In the front bench seat Anna's black head was lifting. "Gabriel, turn down the air conditioning!" she pleaded.

"It's not on."

"But it's *cold*," Kait said and was caught by another shiver.

Shivering himself, Rob wrapped his arms around her. "It sure is," he said. "We haven't gone *that* far north—is it usually like this, Lewis?"

Lewis didn't answer. Kait saw Anna look at him curiously, and at the same time realized she could sense nothing from him in the web.

"Is he asleep?" she asked Anna.

"His eyes are open."

Kaitlyn's heart rate seemed to quicken. *Lewis?* she thought, sending the word to him.

Nothing.

"What's happening?" she said aloud as Rob let go of her to lean around the front seat and look into Lewis's face. She had a bad feeling—a very bad feeling. Something was *strange*. The air wasn't just cold, it was full of electricity. And there was a smell, a smell like a sewer drain.

And a sound. Kaitlyn heard it suddenly over the soft roar of the van's engine. A sharp, sweet sound, one note, as if somebody had run a wet finger around the rim of a crystal goblet. It hung in the air.

"What the *hell* is going on?" Rob demanded. He was shaking Lewis. At the same moment Gabriel snarled from the front, "What are you guys *doing* back there?"

"We're not doing anything," Kait called—just as Lewis jumped up and dived for the empty bucket seat beside Gabriel.

His hands grabbed and beat at the air. His body slammed into Gabriel, who cursed and wrestled with the steering wheel. The van swerved.

"Get out of here! Get him out of here!" Gabriel shouted. "I can't see—"

Rob twisted in behind Lewis, trying to pull him back. The van kept swerving and skidding as Lewis's elbows hit Gabriel. Kaitlyn clung to the seat in front of her, frozen.

"Come *on!*" Rob yelled. *Lewis, come on back! There's nothing there!*

Lewis kept on fighting, and then all at once he went limp, and like a cork popping out of a bottle, he shot backward with Rob. They both crashed into Anna, who yelped. Then they fell in a tangle on the floor.

"Hey—what's the matter? You getting fresh or something?" Lewis said. "Let go of me."

It was an ordinary, complaining voice. Lewis was disentangling himself, looking mildly bewildered but absolutely normal.

Rob sat up and stared at him.

Gabriel had finally gotten the van on course again. He shot

a glare over his shoulder. "You crazy jerk," he said. "What'd you think you were doing?"

"Me? I wasn't doing anything. Rob was grabbing me." Lewis looked around at all of them, his round face honestly puzzled.

"Lewis—you really don't remember?" Kaitlyn asked. She could tell by his expression, by his presence in the web that he didn't. "You jumped up and started beating on something in that seat," she said, nodding. "Only there was nothing there."

"Oh . . ." A sort of light was dawning on Lewis's face. Then his expression turned sheepish. "I guess—I was dreaming, you know? I don't really remember the dream, but I thought I saw somebody sitting there. A kind of whitish shape—a person. And I knew I had to get it. . . ." His voice trailed off. He gave another look around and hunched his shoulders apologetically.

"A dream," Gabriel said in disgust. "Next time keep your dreams to yourself."

A dream? Kaitlyn thought. No. It didn't make sense; it couldn't be the whole explanation. Why should Lewis suddenly start having dreams that made him attack things? And what about the cold—it had disappeared as quickly as it had come; the air felt fine now. And the drain smell, and that sound . . .

We're all tired, Anna's gentle voice said in her head, reminding her that she hadn't been trying to shield her thoughts. *Not just tired but exhausted. And we've been under so much stress—it could come out in strange ways.*

"We could all have been dreaming a little," Rob said with a laugh.

"I suppose," Kaitlyn said. She tried to put any further doubts out of her mind—for now, at least. Lewis obviously believed his own story, and Anna and Rob believed him because he believed it. There was no point in harping on it.

We'll wait and see what happens, she told herself. She settled back on the seat, and Rob returned to sit by her again. The light was fading in a way that made her want to check if she was wearing sunglasses. To the west and in front of them were huge flaming hot cherry clouds.

"Should we stop?" Rob asked, peering at his watch in the dimness.

Gabriel turned the van's headlights on. "We're still in California. We can stop when we get to Oregon."

The sky went gray and then black. Ghost trucks with dazzling headlights came and went on the other side of the highway. It was nearly eight o'clock when they reached a sign saying WELCOME TO OREGON.

They drove on until they found a rest stop and then ate dinner sitting on the cool dark grass outside the van. Dinner was peanut butter sandwiches and one apple apiece, drawn from the grocery bag Tony had given them. Dessert was some cherry cough drops Lewis had found in the glove compartment and the last of the Cajun olive samples.

"We can stay here tonight," Rob said, looking around the

almost-deserted rest stop. There were few cars on the highway nearby. "Nobody will bother us."

Kait found she'd brought toothpaste but no toothbrush. In the women's rest room she rubbed her teeth with a corner of a cotton shirt she'd packed. They all wanted to go to bed early.

"But *how?*" Kaitlyn said when she got back, confronted at last with the logistics of five of them sleeping in the van. Suddenly there no longer seemed to be acres of room. "Where do we all *fit?*"

"The rear seat reclines," Rob said. He and Lewis had the back of the van open and were fiddling with the bench seats. "See, it folds back into a flat bed. That's room for two people there. Somebody else can sleep on the other bench seat, and then the two bucket seats in front recline."

"I'll take one of those," Lewis said. "Unless somebody wants to share the back . . . ?" He looked from Anna to Kait hopefully.

"The girls can have the back," Rob said.

Anna's dark eyes were laughing. "Oh, no . . . I think you and Kaitlyn should have the back. I'll sleep on the other bench."

"And *I'll* sleep outside," Gabriel said shortly, leaning in from the front and yanking a sleeping bag out of the pile.

Daggers and broken glass, that was what Kait felt from him through the web. She and Rob hadn't even *agreed* yet, although she knew they would. She liked to sleep close to Rob, it felt safe. And she knew Rob liked to have her close, because then he didn't worry about her as much.

"It's just convenience," she began, but Gabriel cut her off with a look. He seemed pale and tense under the van's interior lights.

"Look, I don't think it's such a good idea, sleeping outside," Rob said in a mild voice. Gabriel gave him the look, too.

"I can take care of myself," he said and showed his teeth.

He left the van. Kaitlyn helped Rob spread out blankets automatically, trying to screen her thoughts from the others. She still hadn't had a chance to speak to Gabriel privately. She was going to have to *make* a chance, and soon.

Sleeping in the back of the van was cramped and a little stuffy—like sleeping in a compartment on a train, Kaitlyn guessed. But she didn't really mind being crowded in with Rob. He was warm and nice to hang on to. Comfortingly solid.

It was the first time they had been alone together—and Kaitlyn was so tired her eyelids felt like lead weights. There were no golden sparks at his touch now, just a steady shining light that seemed to pour reassurance into her.

"I love you," she murmured sleepily, and they kissed. A sweet kiss that made her cling to him afterward.

I love you, Rob thought back. His thought carried the essence of *him* with it—pure Rob. Warm as sunlight, with an underlying hint of strength that made Kait think of lions basking in the savanna. Rob had a fine stubborn temper of his own, but he cared too much about other people to let it rule him.

And he didn't care who heard him say he loved her. A vocal whisper would have been much more private than telepathy. Distantly Kaitlyn could feel tolerant amusement laced with envy from Lewis and peaceful approval from Anna—but from outside the van, from Gabriel, a wave of dark repudiation. Bitterness. An anger that frightened her.

He feels that he's been cheated of something, she thought, even as she clung harder to Rob. But that's not right; I never led him on. . . .

We've got to find a way to break this link, Rob said stiffly. *It's all right when you want it, but having people spying on your thoughts when you don't want—*

"Rob, don't annoy him," Kait whispered. Rob was broadcasting loud and clear, and Gabriel was getting angrier by the minute. The two of them together were like flint and iron—sparking off each other at every opportunity.

I've said from the beginning that we've got to get rid of it, Gabriel said from outside. *And I know of one certain way, at least.*

He meant for one of them to die. It had come to that, Gabriel threatening them again, acting as if he hated them all.

"Leave it alone," Kaitlyn hissed before Rob could answer. "Oh, *please,* Rob, just leave it; I'm so tired." To her surprise she felt on the verge of tears.

Rob immediately gave up the argument, mentally turning his back on Gabriel. *We'll find a way to break it—another way,* he promised Kaitlyn. *The people in the white house will help us. And if they don't, I'll find a way.*

"Yes," Kaitlyn murmured, her eyes shutting. Rob was holding her close, and she believed him, as she'd believed in him from the beginning. She couldn't help it; Rob *made* you believe.

"Go to sleep, Kait," he whispered, and Kaitlyn sank into the darkness fearlessly.

As long as you're with me I'm not afraid, she thought.

The last thing she heard before sleep was a distant whisper from Anna. "I wonder if we'll dream again?"

Gabriel twisted inside the sleeping bag. There was nothing but grass underneath him, but he felt as if he were lying on roots— or bones.

Ghoulish thought. The bones of the dead beneath him. Maybe the bones of his personal dead, the ones he'd dispatched himself. That would be poetic justice, at least.

Though he wouldn't have admitted it to anyone, Gabriel believed in justice.

Not that he regretted having killed the guy in Stockton. The one who'd been ready to shoot him over the five crumpled dollar bills in his jeans pocket. He was quite happy to have sent that particular home boy to hell.

But that had been his second murder. The first had been unintentional—the product of what happened when a strong mind came in contact with a weaker one. He'd been strong, and Iris—sweet Iris—had been weak. Fragile as a little white mouse, delicate as a flower. Her life energy had poured into him as if one of her arteries had been cut. And he—

—hadn't been able to stop it.

Not until it was over and she was lying limp and motionless in his arms. Her face blue-white. Her lips parted.

Gabriel found that he was lying rigid, staring straight up into the endless darkness of the night sky. His hands were clenched into fists and he was sweating.

I'd die if it would bring her back, he thought with sudden clarity. I'd change places with her. I belong in hell with home boy, but Iris belongs here.

It was strange, but he couldn't really remember her face anymore. He could remember loving her, but not what she'd looked like alive, except that her gaze had been wide-open and defenseless, like a deer's.

And he couldn't take her place. Things weren't that *simple* in the universe; he wasn't going to get off that easy. No, his part was to lie here on grass that felt like bones and think about the new murders, the ones that he was going to commit, inevitably, in the future.

There wasn't any other way for him.

The girl in Oakland—that scrawny ratbag with the tattoo—

he hadn't killed her, quite. He'd left her in an alley with her life force almost drained, but still flowing. She'd live.

But tonight . . . the need was stronger. Gabriel hadn't expected that. He'd been feeling it for hours, the parched, cracked-earth sensation, and by now it was almost unbearable. It was all he could do not to rip into Kessler, who was a constant beacon of energy, radiating it like a lighthouse or one of those stars that flared regularly. The temptation was almost unendurable, especially when Kessler was being annoying, which was almost always.

No. He couldn't touch any of his own group. Aside from the fact that it would blow his secret, it was—impolite. Impolitic. Uncivil.

And wrong, the distant part of his mind whispered.

Shut up, Gabriel told it.

He was out of his sleeping bag in one lithe twist.

Since Rob the Wonder Boy was off limits, he would have to go hunting elsewhere. Through the web, Gabriel could feel the deep sleep of his mind-mates; through the windows of the van he saw nothing. Nobody was going to miss him.

He looked around under the stars for someone to quench his thirst.

CHAPTER 6

The people were leaning over her. The first thing Kait noticed was that they looked like pencil drawings—monochrome, all the color sucked out. The second thing was that they were evil.

She didn't know how she knew that, but it was clear. Clearer than the faces of the people. It wasn't that they didn't have features, but the features seemed blurred, as if they were moving back and forth thousands of times a second, or as if something about them had affected Kait's sight.

Aliens, she thought wildly. Little gray people from flying saucers. And then: Lewis's white shape.

Kaitlyn's heart began pounding with deep sick thuds that seemed to choke off her breath.

She wanted to scream, but that was impossible. She didn't even know if she were awake or asleep, but she was paralyzed.

If I could move—if I could just move I could tell. I could make them go away. . . .

What she wanted to do was to kick upward with her legs and lash out with her arms to see if the visions were solid. But she couldn't even lift her knee. The things were leaning over her from all sides. There was a strange property about them—when Kaitlyn looked at any one of them, it seemed to be rushing toward her, but the group stayed in the same place. They were *looking* at her. Staring with a fixed blank gaze that was worse than any malevolence. And they seemed to be bending farther down, coming closer . . .

With a violent jerk Kaitlyn managed to lift her arm. At least, it felt like a violent jerk to her, but what she saw was her arm rising feebly and almost dreamily toward the figures. It brushed through one monochrome leaning face, and she felt a shock of coldness on the skin.

Refrigerated air . . .

The figures were gone.

Kait lay on her back, blinking. Her eyes were open now, and she thought they'd been open the whole while—but how could she tell? She was staring into darkness as black as the blackness behind closed lids. The only thing she could see was the faint shape of her arm waving in the cold air.

Cold—the air was definitely cold. And there had been a sudden drop in temperature just before Lewis saw *his* vision.

I don't believe it was a dream, Kaitlyn thought. Or not an ordinary dream.

But then, what? A premonition? She didn't have premonitions that way, and Lewis didn't have them at all. Lewis had psychokinesis, PK, the power to move objects with his mind.

Whatever it had been, it had left her with a terrible sick feeling. There was a—a *running* in her middle, a hot restless feeling that made it agony to lie still. She felt cramped and her eyes ached and her whole body was vibrating with adrenaline.

Rob was lying peacefully beside her, his breathing even. Deeply asleep. Kaitlyn hated to wake him; he needed the rest. Lewis and Anna were sleeping soundly, too—she could feel that through the web.

And Gabriel outside? Kait sent her mind searching, doing something she couldn't have described to an outsider. It was like wondering how your foot was feeling, concentrating your attention on a particular part of yourself in a particular location. Somehow she could wonder how Gabriel was doing, and then feel . . .

. . . that he wasn't there, she realized with a shock. Not outside the van where he had been before. She could sense him dimly—somewhere else—but she couldn't locate him exactly, and she couldn't tell what he was doing.

Fine. *Good.* With sudden determination Kaitlyn inched her legs up, pulling the blanket off her by degrees. Just as slowly, she sat up and then stood, crouching, edging sideways to the door in the middle of the van.

She passed Anna, curled neatly on her short bench, black hair swathing her face. Lewis's bucket seat was reclined so far she had to reach under it to get the door open. But finally, with a clank, the door slid back.

Kaitlyn could feel everyone stir, then settle again. She dropped lightly out of the van and shut the door as quietly as she could.

Now. She was going to find Gabriel. Her nervous energy would be put to good use—she was going to *talk* to him, confront him about the strangeness she'd felt inside him, about what he'd been doing when he'd left them all last night. It was the perfect opportunity; with the others asleep, they'd have complete privacy. And if Gabriel didn't like it—tough. Kaitlyn was wound up and ready for a fight herself.

She turned from the van and looked around the rest stop. Aside from the lighted bulk of the rest rooms, everything was dark. There were only three cars to be seen—a battered Volkswagen Bug, a lowslung Chevy, and a white Cadillac.

And no Gabriel. Kaitlyn couldn't get a location on him. She peered into the darkness behind and in front of her, then shrugged and started walking.

He was here *somewhere.* Just walled off so she couldn't feel him. As if he lived in a private fortress. Well, she'd explain differently to him; he was *part* of them, and he couldn't keep denying it.

And he shouldn't be wandering around alone like this in the dark. Kait passed the Bug and the Chevy, noting absently that Oregon license plates had pictures of mountains on them. She passed the Cadillac, which was parked under the last street-light, and hesitated on the brink of the darkness beyond.

That way . . . she had an urge to go that way. An instinct. If there was one thing Kait had learned recently, it was to trust her instincts—but it was lonely-looking out there, lit only by a half-full moon just beginning to rise.

Bracing herself, she began to move cautiously forward, stepping off the sidewalk onto grass. The ground curved down, leading toward a lonely clump of trees—Kait could see their upper branches against the lighter black of the night sky.

It was very quiet, and Kaitlyn's skin was prickling, tiny hairs lifting. Well, that wasn't surprising: Oregon was cooler than California. It was just the night air.

But where *was* Gabriel? Kaitlyn was moving blindly toward the trees, but it wasn't like Gabriel to go sit under a tree. Maybe instinct had been wrong this time.

All right, she'd go just down to that first tree—she could see it fairly well now that her eyes were adjusting to the darkness—and then she'd turn back. She was far enough from the van that she could only feel Rob and Lewis and Anna very dimly, and she knew that communication would be impossible.

I'm truly alone, she thought. The only way any of us can be alone now, by getting out of range of the others. Maybe that's why Gabriel's been wandering off at night; I could understand that. Simply to get some distance.

She almost had herself convinced by the time she got to the tree.

What she found there she discovered with all her senses at once. Her ears picked up some slight sound of movement and the hiss of a ragged breath. Her eyes made out a shape half concealed behind the tree. And her psychic senses felt a disturbance in the web—a *shimmering,* as if she'd stepped near a charged field.

All the same, she could hardly make herself believe what she was witnessing. Heart beating madly, she stepped closer, moving around the tree. The shape—in the moonlight it looked like a romantic painting of Romeo and Juliet, a kneeling boy holding a limp girl in his arms. But the sound, the quick panting breath—that was more like an animal.

What she felt through the web was animalistic, too. It was hunger.

Please, no, Kaitlyn thought. She'd begun to shake, an uncontrollable trembling that started in her legs and went everywhere. Please, God, I don't want to see this. . . .

But then the kneeling boy raised his head, and there was no way to deny it anymore.

Gabriel. It was Gabriel and he was holding a girl who looked unconscious or dead, and when he looked up, it was straight into Kaitlyn's eyes.

She could see the shock on his face—and in the web she felt a shattering. A crashing-down of walls as the barriers he'd been holding around himself collapsed. She'd taken him off guard, and suddenly she could feel—everything.

Everything he was going through. Everything he was experiencing at that moment.

"Gabriel—" she gasped aloud.

Hunger, she got back. She could feel it pounding at her. Hunger and desperation. An intolerable, agonizing pain—and the promise of relief in the girl he was holding. A girl who wasn't dead, Kaitlyn realized, but comatose and bursting with life energy. What Lewis called *chi.*

"Gabriel," Kaitlyn said again. Her legs were wobbling; they weren't going to support her much longer. She was overwhelmed by the need she felt—*his* need.

"Get away," Gabriel said hoarsely.

She was surprised he could talk. There wasn't much rationality in his presence in the web. What Kait felt there seemed less like Gabriel than some shark or starving wolf. A desperate, merciless hunter ready to make his kill.

Run, something inside Kaitlyn said. He's about to kill, and it could be you as easily as that girl. Be smart and *run* . . .

"Gabriel, listen to me. I won't hurt you." Kaitlyn got the words out raggedly, on separate breaths, but she managed to hold her hands out toward him almost steadily. "Gabriel, I understand—I can *feel* what you need. But there has to be another way."

"Get *out* of here," Gabriel snarled.

Ignoring the terrified sickness in her stomach, Kaitlyn took a step toward him. Think, she was telling herself frantically. Think, be rational—because *he* certainly isn't.

Gabriel's lips peeled back from his teeth, and he jerked the girl to him. As if protecting his prey from an intruder. "Don't come any closer," he hissed.

"It's energy, isn't it?" Kaitlyn didn't dare take another step, so she dropped to her knees instead. She was at Gabriel's level now, and she could see that his eyes were like two windows opening on darkness. "It's life energy you need. I can feel that. I can feel how much it hurts—"

"You can't feel anything! Get out before you really do get hurt!" It was a tortured cry, but almost instantly afterward Gabriel stilled. A deathly calm spread over his face, and his eyes went like black ice. Kaitlyn could feel his purposefulness in the web.

Without looking at her, ignoring her completely, he turned his attention to the girl in his arms. The girl had soft curly hair—dark blond or light brown, Kaitlyn thought. She looked almost peaceful. Gabriel had undoubtedly stunned her with his mind somehow.

Now he turned her head to one side, pushing the disordered curls off the back of her neck. Kaitlyn watched in horror, frozen by the cool deliberation of his movements.

"Right here," Gabriel whispered, and he touched the nape

of the girl's neck, a point at the upper part of the spine, just between vertebrae. "This is the transfer point. The best place to take energy. You can stay and watch if you want."

His voice was like an Arctic wind, and his presence in the web like ice. He was looking at the girl's neck with cold hunger, eyes narrowed, lips skinned back a little.

And then, as Kaitlyn watched, he bent to put his lips to the girl's skin.

"No!"

Kait didn't know what she was going to do until she did it. But suddenly she was moving, she was throwing herself across the little distance to Gabriel. She was putting her hands between the girl and him—one hand on the girl's neck, the other on Gabriel's face. She felt his lips, and then the brush of teeth.

Keep out of this! Gabriel's mental shout was so powerful it sent shockwaves through Kaitlyn. But she hung on.

Give her to me! he shouted. Kaitlyn's vision was red; she could see nothing, feel nothing, but the all-encompassing fury of Gabriel's hunger. He was a snarling, clawing animal now— and she was fighting him.

And losing. She was weaker, both physically and psychically, and he was utterly ruthless. He was tearing the girl away from her, his mind a black hole ready to consume. . . .

No, Gabriel, Kaitlyn thought—and she kissed him.

That was the result, anyway, of her sudden darting movement. She'd meant for a different contact—forehead

to forehead, the way Rob had touched her to channel healing energy once. But at the touch of his lips against hers she
felt a shock of a different sort and it was an instant before
she could pull back to get the position right.

She'd shocked Gabriel, too—shocked him into stillness.
He seemed too astonished to fight her or jerk away. He simply
sat, paralyzed, as Kaitlyn shut her eyes, and, gripping his shoulders, thrust her forehead against his.

Oh.

That simple contact, skin to skin, third eye to third eye,
brought the biggest shock of all. A jolt that went through Kait
like lightning—as if two ends of electric wiring had touched,
sending a violent current coursing through.

Oh, she thought. *Oh* . . .

It was frightening—terrifying in its power. And for the first
instant it hurt. She felt a tearing in her body, in her bloodstream—
as if something was being pulled out of her. A vital pain at the
roots of her being. Dimly, with some part of her mind that could
still think, she remembered what Gabriel had said once. That
people were afraid he would steal their souls. That was what this
felt like.

And yet, at the same time, it was compelling. It swept
her along with it, helpless to resist. It demanded that she sur-
render. . . .

You wanted to help him, the part of Kait that could still
think said. So help him. *Give.* Give what he needs.

Kaitlyn felt a wrenching—and then a bursting. It was as if some barrier in her had been broken, ripping under pressure. She trembled violently—and felt herself *give.*

It still hurt, but in a new way. A strange way that was almost pleasure. Like the release of something painful, blocked . . . backed-up.

Kait had received psychic energy before, taking Rob's healing power when she'd been drained and exhausted. But she'd never given it, not on this scale. Now she felt a torrent of energy flowing from her into Gabriel, like a flood of golden sparks. And she could feel him responding, drinking in the energy greedily, gratefully. The darkness inside him, the black hole, being lit up by the gold.

Life, Kaitlyn thought dizzily. It's life I'm giving him really. He needs this or he'll die.

And then: Is this how healers feel? Oh, no wonder Rob likes doing it. There's nothing like it, nothing . . . especially if you *want* to help.

For the most part, though, she couldn't think at all. She simply *experienced,* feeling Gabriel's hunger gradually being sated, the burning need in him slowly cooling as it was met. And feeling his amazement, his wonder.

He was less of an animal now, and more Gabriel. The Gabriel who had tried to protect her from the pain of Mr. Zetes's great crystal, the Gabriel who'd had tears in his eyes when he spoke of his past. Kaitlyn realized suddenly that she'd gotten behind his walls again. She was seeing, touching, the Gabriel that was kept hidden from the world.

It's different—like this. The thought was almost a whisper, but it shook Kaitlyn with its strength. Its—intensity. She could feel the astonished gratitude behind it, and something like awe. *Different . . . when I took energy before—when I took it last night—it wasn't like this.*

And because Gabriel's mind was open to her, Kait knew what he meant. She could *see* the girl from last night, the one with the straggly hair and the unicorn tattoo. And she could taste the girl's fear, her anguish and aversion.

She was unwilling, Kaitlyn told Gabriel. *You forced her; she didn't want to help you. I do.*

Why?

One word, with the force of a blow behind it. Kaitlyn felt Gabriel's hands tighten on her shoulders as he projected the thought. She hadn't been aware of her physical body for some time, but now she realized that she and Gabriel were clinging to each other, still in contact at the transfer point. The curly-haired girl, the new victim, had fallen or been shoved aside.

Why? Gabriel repeated, almost brutally, demanding an answer.

Because I care about you! Kaitlyn shot back. The violence of the first channeling of energy was gone, but she could still feel it flowing from herself to him. And she could feel, in some distant way, an approaching dizziness, a weakness. She ignored it. *Because I care what happens to you, because I—*

Abruptly, with no warning at all, Gabriel pulled away. Whatever Kaitlyn had been about to say was lost.

The jolt of broken contact was almost as bad as the moment of initiation. Kaitlyn's eyes flew open. She could see the world again, but she felt blind. Blind and horribly alone. Even feeling Gabriel in the web was nothing to the intimacy of direct energy transfer.

Gabriel . . .

"It's enough," he said, speaking instead of returning her thought. She could feel him trying to gather his walls again. "I'm all right now. You did what you meant to do."

"Gabriel," Kaitlyn said. There was a terrible wistfulness inside her. Without thinking, she raised a hand to touch his face.

Gabriel flinched back.

Hurt and loss flooded over Kait. She clamped her lips together.

"Don't," Gabriel said. Then he looked away, shaking his head. "I'm not trying to hurt you, damn it!" he said sharply. "It's just—don't you realize how dangerous that was? I could have drained you. I could have killed you." He turned back and looked directly into her eyes again, with a sudden fierceness that frightened Kaitlyn. *"I could have killed you,"* he repeated with vicious emphasis.

"You didn't. I feel fine." The dizziness had gone, or never come. She looked steadily at Gabriel. In the moonlight his eyes were as black as his hair, and his pale face was almost supernaturally beautiful. "I'm psychic, so I have more of the energy than normal people. Obviously I've got enough to spare."

"It was still a risk. And if you touch me, there's the risk I'll take more."

"But you're all right now. You said so, and I can feel it, too. You don't need more; you're all right."

There was a pause and Gabriel's eyes dropped. Then, slowly, almost grudgingly, he said, "Yes." Kaitlyn could feel him trying to think, could sense his confusion. "And—I'm grateful," he said at last. He said it awkwardly, as if he hadn't had much practice, but when he lifted his eyes again she saw that he meant it. She could feel it, too, a childlike, marveling gratitude that was totally at odds with those chiseled features and grim mouth.

Kait's throat tightened. It was all she could do not to reach out to him again. Instead she said, as dispassionately as she could manage, "Gabriel, was it the crystal?"

"What?" He looked away from her again, as if realizing he'd revealed too much.

"You weren't like this before. You didn't *need* energy, not before Mr. Zetes hooked you up with that crystal. But now you've got a mark on your forehead, and you've changed—"

"Into a real psychic vampire." Gabriel laughed shortly. "That's what the people at the research center in Durham said—but they didn't know, did they? Nobody can know what the reality is like."

"That isn't what I was going to say. I was going to say that you'd changed, and I'd noticed it before tonight. I think you've become—more powerful. You can link up with minds outside the web, and before you couldn't."

Gabriel was rubbing his forehead absently but roughly. "I suppose it had to be the crystal," he said. "Who knows, maybe that's what it's for. Maybe it's what Zetes wanted, all of us slaves to this—need."

The idea took Kaitlyn's breath away. She'd been thinking of it as some side effect, something that had happened accidentally because the crystal had burned too much of Gabriel's energy. But the idea that anyone would do this deliberately—would make someone like this on *purpose* . . .

"It's nauseating, isn't it?" Gabriel said conversationally. "What I've become is nauseating. And I'm afraid it's permanent, or at least I don't see any reason why it shouldn't be."

He'd seen her horror and was hurt by it. Kait tried to think of some way to make him feel better, and settled on brisk normalcy.

"Well, at least we have a way of dealing with it," she said. "For now, we'd better get this girl back to where she came from, don't you think? And then we should go and tell Rob. He'll want to help and he may even be able to think—"

She broke off with a gasp. She'd been getting to her feet, but now Gabriel hauled her back down again with one powerful yank.

Kaitlyn found herself looking into eyes that were black and glittering with menacing fury.

CHAPTER 7

"No," Gabriel snarled. "We will not tell Rob—*anything*."

Kaitlyn was bewildered. "But—the others have to know—"

"They don't have to know. They're not my *keepers*."

"Gabriel, they'll *want* to know. They care about you, too. And Rob may be able to help you."

"I don't want his help."

It was said flatly, and with absolute finality. Kaitlyn realized that on this issue Gabriel was inflexible, and there was no use in arguing.

He went on anyway, just in case she needed convincing. "Of course, I can't stop *you* from telling them," he said, releasing her arm and giving a sudden disarming smile. "But if you do I'm afraid I'll have to leave this little expedition . . . and our group . . . permanently."

Kaitlyn rubbed her arm. "All right, Gabriel. I get the

point. And," she added with sudden conviction, "I'll still help you. But you've got to *let* me help. You've got to tell me when you're feeling—like you did tonight. You've got to come to me, instead of wandering around looking for girls to attack."

Gabriel's expression was suddenly bleak. "Maybe I don't want your help, either," he said stonily. Then he burst out, "How long do you think you can keep this up? This *donation?* Even a psychic doesn't have endless energy. What if you get weak?"

That's why I wanted to tell Rob, Kaitlyn thought, but she knew better than to start debating again. She simply said, "We'll deal with that when we come to it." She tried to hide the flicker of unease inside her. What *would* they do—if Gabriel had one of these fits and she was too weak to help him? He'd kill an ordinary person, drain him dry.

Think about it later, she decided. And then pulled out the old hope, the one that had been comforting her since they'd left the Institute.

"Maybe the people in the white house can help," she said. "Maybe they'll know a way to cure you—undo what the crystal did."

"If it was the crystal," Gabriel said. With a faint self-mocking smile he added, "It seems to me that we're expecting a lot from these people in the white house."

That's because we don't have any other hope. Kaitlyn didn't say it, but she knew Gabriel understood. She and Gabriel sometimes understood each other too well.

"Let's get this girl back. What car did she come from?" she asked, turning away from those ironic dark gray eyes.

They put the girl back in the Cadillac. According to Gabriel, she'd been alone, which was fortunate. Nobody would have noticed she was missing, or called the police. And Gabriel said that she'd never seen him—he'd come up behind her and put her to sleep with one touch of his mind.

"I seem to be developing new talents by the hour," he said and smiled.

Kaitlyn wasn't amused, but she had to admit to some relief. The girl would just think she'd fallen asleep and would drive away never knowing what had happened to her. Or at least that was what Kait hoped.

"You'd better get in the van with the rest of us," she said. "You need *sleep*."

Gabriel didn't object. A few minutes later he was settling down in the other bucket seat, while Kait was creeping into the back of the van again.

I need sleep, too, she thought, snuggling in beside Rob's warm body with a feeling of gratitude. And, please, please, I don't want any more dreams.

When Kaitlyn woke again, it was daylight. Rob was sitting up, and all around her were the noises of people stirring and yawning.

"How is everybody?" Rob asked. His blond hair was tousled

and he looked terribly young, Kaitlyn thought. Young and vulnerable when you compared his sleepy golden eyes to the dark gray ones she'd seen last night. . . .

"Kinked up," Lewis moaned from the front. He was wriggling his shoulders. Kaitlyn had a few kinks herself, and she saw that Gabriel was stretching cautiously.

"You'll be fine," Anna said and got up. She opened the side door and jumped lightly out, with no sign of stiffness.

"I feel like I swallowed a fuzz ball," Rob said, running his tongue over his teeth. "Does anybody—"

Oh, my God. What is it?

The exclamation came from outside the van, from Anna. The four inside immediately broke off what they were doing and started for the door.

What's wrong, Anna? Kaitlyn thought even before she got out.

I've never seen anything like it.

Anna's grave dark eyes were wide, fixed on the van itself. Kaitlyn turned and looked, but at first couldn't quite grasp what she was seeing. It looked almost *beautiful* at first.

The entire van was swathed with glittering ribbons—as if someone had painted stripes of shining stuff all over it, even over the windows. In the crisp morning light the stripes took on rainbow colors. There were hundreds of the bands, crossing and recrossing.

And yet it wasn't beautiful, really. It evoked a feeling of

revulsion in Kait. When she looked closely at one of the stripes, she saw it was tacky . . . slimy, almost. Like . . . like *mucus* . . .

"Slug trails!" Rob said and pulled Kaitlyn away from the van.

Kaitlyn's stomach lurched. She was glad she hadn't eaten more for dinner last night. "Slug trails—but it *can't* be," Gabriel said, sounding angry. "Look around you—there's no sign of a trail anywhere but on the van."

It was true. Kaitlyn swallowed and said, "I've never seen a slug big enough to leave a trail like *that.*"

"I have, in *Planet of the Giant Gastropods,*" Lewis said.

"I have, too, in my backyard," Anna said. She nodded when the others looked at her. "I'm serious. In Puget Sound there are slugs that big, banana slugs. Some people eat them."

"Thank you for sharing that with us," Kaitlyn whispered, stomach lurching again.

Gabriel still looked angry. "How did they get there?" he demanded, as if Anna had put them there personally. "And why aren't there any on those cars?" He pointed toward a gray Buick parked nearby, and the middle-aged couple in the Buick looked at him curiously.

"Leave her alone. She doesn't know," Rob said before Anna could answer.

"Do *you?*"

Rob slanted a dangerous golden glare at Gabriel and started to shake his head. Then he stopped and looked thoughtful. He turned to the van again, frowning.

"It could be—"

"What?" Kaitlyn asked.

Rob shook his head slowly. In the early sunlight he looked like a ruffled golden angel. "Oh, nothing," he said and shrugged.

Kait had the feeling that he was suppressing something, and the next minute he gave her a half-laughing look, as if to say she wasn't the only one who could hide things in the web.

A nasty *stubborn* angel, Kait thought, and Rob grinned.

"Come on, let's get out of this place," he said, turning to the others, who were looking displeased. "It's just slug stuff. Let's find a car wash."

Until that moment Kaitlyn had forgotten her dream about the colorless people. The episode with Gabriel had swamped it, somehow, driving it back into her subconscious. But now, suddenly, she remembered, and she looked at the van sharply.

"Heads up!" Lewis hissed before she could say anything. "It's the law!"

A police car was cruising into the rest stop. Kaitlyn's heart gave one thump, and then she was following the others in a quick but orderly retreat into the van.

Just keep your heads down and stay calm, Rob told them. *Pretend you're talking to each other.*

"A lot of good that's going to do," Gabriel said acidly.

The police car drove past them. Kait couldn't help glancing sideways at it. A uniformed woman in the passenger seat

344

glanced up at the same moment, and for an instant their eyes met.

Kaitlyn's breath stopped. She only hoped her face was as utterly blank as her mind felt. If that policewoman saw her terror . . .

The car cruised on.

Kait could feel her pulse in her throat. *Somebody start driving,* she thought. *Fast but casual.* Rob was already sliding into the driver's seat.

Kaitlyn was still terrified the police car would turn around, or follow them when they left. But it didn't. It seemed to have stopped at the other end of the rest stop.

Where the white Cadillac was, Kait's mind supplied, and she tried to squash the thought and the memories it evoked instantly. She didn't dare look at Gabriel or let herself wonder if the curly haired girl *had* remembered something after all.

"Don't be scared," Lewis said when they were once again on Highway 5. He'd felt her turmoil even if he didn't know the reason. "We're okay now."

Kaitlyn gave him a watery smile.

They found a do-it-yourself car wash in a town called Grants Pass, and Kaitlyn disbursed ninety-nine cents from their funds to buy paper towels. She also paid for breakfast burritos and coffee at a McDonald's, since none of them could face peanut butter this early in the morning.

"And now we should cut over to the coast," Rob said when

they were done eating. They'd washed themselves as well as the car at the car wash, a novel experience that Kait wasn't sure she wanted to repeat.

"Well, you have two choices," said Lewis, who had by default become the Keeper of the Map. "There's a road that goes through the Siskiyou National Forest, and then a little north of that there's a regular highway."

After a short discussion they decided on the highway. As Anna said, the white house might be surrounded by trees, but it wasn't in a landlocked forest. It was someplace where the ocean came between two wooded arms of land.

"Some place called Griffin's Pit," Lewis said, his eyes crinkling as he looked at Kait.

"We might try looking that up in a library somewhere," Rob said, steering the van back to the freeway. "That and all the other variations we can think of."

"Maybe we'll just *find* the place first," Kaitlyn said wistfully.

But at Coos Bay, where the highway finally reached the coast, she slumped and shook her head.

"Not north enough," she said and glanced at Anna for confirmation.

Anna was nodding resignedly. They all stood around the van, staring down at the ocean. It was vast and blue and sparkling—and *wrong*. Not at all like the water they'd seen in the dream.

"It's way too civilized," Anna said. She pointed to a large

freighter loaded with logs that was passing through the bay entrance. "See that? It's putting junk in the water—oil or gasoline or something—and the water we saw wasn't *like* that. It wasn't traveled like this. It felt clean."

"Felt clean," Gabriel repeated, almost sneering.

"Yes," Kaitlyn said. "It did. And look at those sand dunes. Did anybody see sand in the dream?"

"No." Rob sighed. "Okay, back in the van. Yukon ho."

"Can't we eat first?" Lewis pleaded. It had taken them until noon to get to the bay.

"Eat while we drive," Rob said. In the van Kaitlyn made and passed out peanut butter sandwiches.

They chewed on them apathetically, looking out the windows. The view as they drove north up the Oregon coast was not inspiring.

"Sand," Lewis said after half an hour. "I never knew there was so much sand in the world."

The dunes seemed endless. They were huge and rolling, sometimes blocking off the view of the ocean. In places they were hundreds of feet high.

"How horrible," Kaitlyn said suddenly. In the sand she could see distant trees—buried trees. Only the top third of their trunks emerged from the dune, standing but quite dead. It was as if the dunes had swallowed a forest . . . and digested it.

"Jeez, there's even vultures circling," Lewis said, eyeing a large bird.

"That's an osprey," Anna said almost unkindly.

Kait glanced at her, then sat back, relapsing into silence. She felt depressed, and she didn't know if it was the dunes, the prospect of endless traveling to an unknown destination, or the peanut butter sandwiches.

Everyone else was silent, too. There was a heavy feeling to the air. Oppressive. Laced with something Kaitlyn couldn't quite put her finger on. . . .

"Oh, come on," she said, half aloud. "Cheer up, everybody. This is only our second day." She groped in her mind for an interesting topic to distract them. After a moment she found one, not only interesting but slightly dangerous. Oh, well, nothing ventured, nothing gained.

"So, Lewis, about this *chi* stuff," she said. He glanced at her lethargically. "So, I was wondering, how much can somebody afford to lose before they get sick?"

She could see Gabriel stiffen in the front passenger seat.

"Um," Lewis said. "It depends. Some people have a lot— they generate it all the time. If you're healthy you do that, and it just kind of flows freely inside you, without any blocks. Through strange channels."

Kaitlyn laughed. "Through what?"

"Strange channels. Really. That's what my grandfather called some of the arteries the *chi* runs through. He was a master of *chi gong*—that's the art of manipulating *chi*, kind of like what Rob does when he heals."

Gabriel by now was deliberately *not* looking at Kait, all the while willing her fiercely to shut up. Unable to send a reassuring message, Kaitlyn ignored him.

"So it's sort of like blood," she said to Lewis. "And if you lose it, you manufacture more."

"In the Middle Ages people thought blood *was* the life energy," Rob said from the driver's seat. "They thought some people had too much—that's what they had in mind when they bled you with leeches. They thought if they could drain some of the extra blood off, it would relieve the pressure; help you produce better, clearer blood afterward. But of course they were wrong—about blood."

He looked over his shoulder as he said it, and Kait thought his glance encompassed Gabriel as well as her. Alarm shot through her. Rob wasn't stupid. What if he'd guessed . . . ?

Gabriel was radiating cold fury.

"Well, that's interesting," Kait gabbled. She now wanted to find a boring topic to make them all forget this. Even silence would be fine—but Rob was speaking again.

"Some people think that's how the legends of vampires started," he said. "With psychics that drained their victims of life energy, *sekhem, chi,* whatever you want to call it. Later the stories got twisted and people called it blood."

Kaitlyn sat frozen. It wasn't just what Rob was saying, it was the *way* he was saying it. His disgust and loathing filled the web.

"I've heard legends about that, too," Anna said, and her repugnance was equally clear. "About evil shamans who live by stealing power from others."

"That's sick," said Lewis. "If a *chi gong* master did that, he'd be ostracized. It completely violates the Tao."

Their abhorrence was reverberating in the web, shuddering over Kaitlyn in waves. Very distantly she could sense Gabriel's stony presence.

No wonder he didn't want them to know, she thought, knowing that no one else could sense her through the all-pervading horror and aversion. None of them can understand. They just think it's awful.

She wished she could tell Gabriel she was sorry, but Gabriel was looking out the window, his shoulders tense.

To Kaitlyn's vast relief, Lewis changed the subject. "And of course there are the people whose energy fields are too *strong,*" he said with a sly look at Rob. "You know, the people you agree with even when you don't know why. The ones that put you under a spell with their charisma—their energy just knocks you out."

Rob's eyes in the rearview mirror were innocent. "If I see somebody like that I'll tell you," he said. "Sounds dangerous."

"It is. You can find yourself fighting evil magicians just because some nut thought it was a good idea."

There was an edge to Lewis's voice that showed the remark wasn't entirely benign. Kaitlyn was glad they weren't talking about vampires anymore, but discouraged when everyone lapsed into silence again.

Something's wrong with us, she thought, and shivered.

The silence lasted for endless miles up the coast. The dunes ran out eventually and were replaced by black basalt headlands that plunged down to the sea. Huge waves crashed around strange rocks rising like monoliths out of the water.

At one point they passed a deep fissure in the cliffs, where the pounding sea had whipped the water into a froth like cream.

"Devil's Churn," Lewis said sepulchrally, raising his head from the map.

"Looks like it," Kaitlyn said. She meant to sound light-hearted, but somehow it came out grim.

Silence again. They passed offshore islands, but these were inhabited only by gulls and other birds. No trees, no white house. Kaitlyn shivered again.

"We're never going to find it," Lewis said.

This was so unlike him that Kait felt only surprise, but Anna turned sharply. "I wish you wouldn't be so pessimistic. Or if you have to be, I wish you'd keep your opinions to yourself!"

Kaitlyn's jaw dropped. The next moment she felt a rush of protective anger. "You don't have to be so nasty to him," she told Anna heatedly. "Just because you're so—so *stoic* all the time. . . ." She stopped and almost bit her tongue. What had made her say that?

Hurt flashed in Anna's dark eyes. Lewis scowled. "I can fight my own battles," he said. "You're always jumping in."

"Yes, she's a real little do-gooder," Gabriel said from the front.

Rage exploded in Kaitlyn. "And you're a cold-blooded *snake!*" she shouted. Gabriel gave her a brilliant, unsettling smile.

"She got that one right, anyway," Rob said. The van was swerving erratically. Rob was looking at Gabriel rather than at the road. "And you shut up, Lewis, if you know what's good for you."

"I think you're all horrible," Anna gasped. She seemed on the verge of tears. "And I've *had* it, all right? You can let me off here because I'm not going with you any farther."

Tires squealed as Rob hit the brakes. A horn blared behind them.

"Fine," Rob said. "Get out."

CHAPTER 8

"**G**o on," Rob said curtly. "Don't keep us all waiting."

The horn blared again behind them.

Anna rose without any of her usual grace. Her movements were jerky, full of repressed energy. She snatched up her duffel bag and began to fumble with the door handle.

Kait sat stiffly, her shoulders tense, her head high. Her heart was pounding with defensive fury. *Let* Anna go if she wanted. It just showed she'd never cared for the rest of them in the first place.

Ridiculous.

The thought came out of nowhere, like a tiny glint of light in her mind, there and gone in an instant. It was enough to shock Kaitlyn into some kind of sense.

Ridiculous—of course Anna cared for the rest of them. Anna cared about everything, from the earth itself to the animals she loved to just about any person that crossed her path.

But then why was Kait so *angry* with her? Kait could feel all the physical symptoms. The pounding heart, the shortness of breath—the flushed face and tight feeling at her temples. More, there was a wild need to *move* in her muscles, like the desire to hit something.

Physical symptoms. It was another glint, surfacing from Kaitlyn's subconscious. And suddenly she understood.

"Anna, wait. *Wait,*" she said just as Anna wrestled the door open. She tried to make her voice calm, when it kept wanting to come out panicked or seething.

Anna stopped but didn't turn.

"Don't you see—everybody, don't you *see?*" Kaitlyn looked around at the others. "This isn't real. We're all upset, but we're not really upset at each other. We're just *feeling* angry, so our minds think there must be a reason to *be* angry."

"It's just nerves, I suppose," Gabriel sneered. His lip was curled and his gray eyes were savage. "We couldn't possibly really hate each other."

"No! I don't know what it is, but—" Kaitlyn broke off, realizing that in addition to all the other physical symptoms she was shivering. It was *cold* in the van, colder than could be explained by the open door. And there was a strange odor in her nostrils, a sewer stench.

"Do you smell that? It's the same thing I smelled yesterday when Lewis did his sleepwalking bit. And it's cold like yesterday, too." Kaitlyn could see confusion mingling with the anger in the faces around her, and she turned to the one person she trusted absolutely.

Rob, she said fervently, *please listen. I know it's hard because you* feel *like you're angry, but just try. Something's going on.*

Slowly Rob's face cleared. The smoldering fury went out of his amber-colored eyes, leaving them golden and somewhat bewildered. He blinked and put a hand to his forehead.

"You're right," he said. "It's like that psychology experiment—give someone an injection of adrenaline, and then put them in a room with someone acting angry. The first person gets angry, too, but it's not real anger. It's been *induced.*"

"Someone's doing that to us," Kaitlyn said.

"But how?" Lewis demanded. He sounded scoffing, but not as exasperated as before. "Nobody's given us any injections."

"Long distance," Rob said. "It's a psychic attack."

His voice was flat and positive. His eyes had gone dark gold. Outside, the blaring horn had given way to several horns sounding continuously.

"Shut the door, Anna," Rob said quietly. "I'll find a place to pull over. There's something I ought to have told you before."

Anna slid the door shut. A few minutes later they had pulled over by the roadside and Rob was looking at the rest of them soberly.

"I should have mentioned it this morning," he said. "But I wasn't sure, and I didn't see any point in you all worrying.

Those slug tracks . . . well, back at Durham I heard stories about people waking up to find those around their house. Slime trails or sometimes footprints of people or animals. They almost always went along with nightmares—people having terrible dreams the night before."

Nightmares. Now Kaitlyn remembered. "I had a terrible dream last night," she said. "There were all these people leaning over me. Gray people—they looked like pencil sketches. And it was cold—just the way it was a few minutes ago." She looked at Rob. "But what *is* it?"

"They said all those things were signs of a psychic attack."

"A psychic attack," Gabriel repeated, but his tone was less sarcastic than it had been.

"The stories were that dark psychics could do things even over long distances. They could visualize you and use PK, telepathy, even astral projection." His troubled eyes turned back to Kait. "Those gray people you saw—I've heard that astral projections are colorless."

"Astral projections as in letting your mind do the walking? Leaving your body behind?" Lewis asked, cocking an eyebrow. The atmosphere had changed; the web was no longer quivering with animosity. Kait thought that everyone looked like themselves again.

Rob was nodding. "That's it. And I've heard that psychic attacks can make you weak or nervous—even make you think you're going crazy."

"I thought *I* was going crazy just now," Anna said. Her eyes were large and bright with unshed tears. "I'm sorry, everybody."

"I'm sorry, too," Kaitlyn said. She and Anna looked at each other a moment and then simultaneously reached forward to hug each other.

"Sure, everybody's sorry," Gabriel said impatiently. "But we've got more important things to think about. A psychic attack means one thing—we've been found."

"Mr. Zetes," Rob said.

"Who else? But the question is, who's he gotten to do it? What psychics are attacking?"

Kaitlyn tried to visualize the faces in her dream. It was impossible. The features had been too blurred.

"Mr. Z had a lot of contacts," Rob said wearily. "Obviously he's found some new friends."

Anna was shaking her head. "But how can he have found such powerful ones so fast? I mean, *we* couldn't do what they're doing, and we're supposed to be the best."

"The best of our age group," Rob began, but Kaitlyn said, "The crystal."

Understanding flared immediately in Gabriel's eyes. "That's it. The crystal is amplifying their power."

"But it's *dangerous*," Kaitlyn started, and then she shut up at an ominous glance from Gabriel.

Intent on his own thoughts, Rob didn't seem to notice.

"Obviously, they don't care about the danger, and while they're using the crystal they're much stronger than we are. The point is that we've got to be prepared. They're not finished with us—and the attacks will probably get worse. We've got to be ready for anything."

"Yeah, but ready how?" asked Lewis. "What can you do against that kind of attack?"

Rob shrugged. "At the Durham Center I heard people talk about envisioning light—protective light. The problem is that I never really listened. I don't know how you do it."

Kaitlyn let out her breath and sat back. The others were doing the same, and a sense of apprehension ran through the web. Apprehension—and vulnerability.

There was a long silence.

"Well, I suppose we'd better get back on the road," Kait said finally. "It's no good sitting around and thinking about it."

"Just everybody be on the lookout for anything unusual," Rob said.

But nothing unusual happened on the rest of the drive. Anna took the wheel and they resumed their beach-scanning, agree-ing that nothing on the Oregon coast looked like the place in their dreams. The rock was too black—volcanic, apparently—and the water too open.

"And it's still not north enough," Kait said.

They stopped that night at a little town called Cannon Beach, just below the Washington border. It was already dark by the time Anna pulled the van into a quiet street that dead-ended on the beach.

"This may not be legal, but I don't think anybody's going to bother us," she said. "For that matter, I've hardly seen anybody around here."

"It's a resort town," Rob said. "And this is off season."

It certainly seemed like off season to Kaitlyn. The sky was clouding over, and it was cold and windy outside.

"I saw a little store back there on the main street," she said. "We've got to buy something for dinner—we ate the last of the bread and peanut butter for lunch."

"I'll go," Anna said. "I don't mind the cold."

Rob nodded. "I'll go with you."

It was only once they were gone that Kait wished Lewis had gone, too. She was getting worried about Gabriel.

He seemed tense and distant, staring out the window into the dark. In the web Kaitlyn could feel only coldness and a sense of walls—as if he were living in a castle of ice.

He put the highest walls up when he had the most to hide, Kaitlyn knew. Right now she was worried that he was suffering—and that he wouldn't come to her for help.

And she'd noticed something else. He was still sitting in the front passenger seat. The rest of them had changed places every so often, but Gabriel always stuck to the front.

I wonder, Kait thought, if it could have anything to do with the fact that *I* always stick to the back.

She was getting fairly good at screening her thoughts when she concentrated. Neither Lewis nor Gabriel seemed to have heard that.

Rob and Anna returned windblown and laughing, clutching paper bags to their chests.

"We splurged," Rob said. "Microwave hot dogs—they're still pretty hot—and Nachos and potato chips."

"And Oreos," Anna said, puffing back wisps of black hair that had blown in her face.

Lewis grinned as he unwrapped a hot dog. "Pure junk food. Joyce would die."

Kaitlyn glanced at him, and for a moment everyone stilled. We still can't really believe it, Kait thought. We all *know* Joyce betrayed us, but we can't accept it. How could anyone put on an act the way she did?

"She was so—*alive*," Anna said. "Effervescent. Energetic. I liked her from the minute I saw her."

"And she used that," Gabriel snarled. "She was recruiting us; making us like her was just a technique."

So tense, Kaitlyn thought. He's incredibly on edge. She watched Gabriel tearing into a hot dog almost savagely, and worry shifted in her stomach.

"Really hits the spot, doesn't it?" she said. Her eyes were on Gabriel, and she tried to keep her presence in the web completely neutral. She added casually, "But maybe it's not enough."

"We got two for everybody and a couple of extras," Anna

said, following Kait's gaze to Gabriel. "You can have one of the extras, Gabriel."

He waved her off impatiently. His gray eyes, fixed on Kaitlyn, were full of angry warning.

"Just trying to be helpful," Kaitlyn said. She leaned close to Gabriel to fish a potato chip out of the bag and added in a low voice, "I wish you'd let me."

You can help by leaving me alone.

The thought was swift and brutal—and meant only for her. Kaitlyn could tell that none of the others had heard it. Trust Gabriel to have perfected the art of private communication.

So he wasn't going to come to her. He needed to, she was sure of that now. His face seemed even paler than usual, almost chalky, and there was a repressed violence to his movements. As if he were under some terrible internal pressure, and in danger of flying apart at any minute.

But he was stubborn, and that meant he wouldn't come. Gabriel didn't know how to ask for help, he only knew how to take.

Never mind, Kaitlyn thought, watching him surreptitiously. I'm stubborn, too. And I'm *damned* if I'm going to let you kill yourself—or anybody else.

Gabriel waited until they were all asleep.

Kaitlyn had been the last to succumb, fighting even the warmth they'd produced by running the van's heaters before they bedded down. He'd felt the red-gold shimmer of her thoughts running on when all the others were still and silent. She was trying to outwait him.

But it didn't work. Gabriel could be patient when he had to be.

When even Kaitlyn's thoughts had faded into a humming blank, Gabriel quietly sat up in the driver's seat and opened the door beside him. He slid out and had the door shut again almost before anyone could stir. Then he waited a moment, his senses focused on the inside of the van.

Still asleep. Good.

The wind out here was bitterly cold. Not the sort of night for any sensible person to be out wandering. That was a problem, and Gabriel thought about it as he trudged through the dry, loose sand above the high tide line.

Then he looked up. There were cottages and duplexes on the beach, as well as motel units. And some of them must be occupied.

He tried to dredge up a killing smile, but he couldn't quite manage. Breaking and entering was one crime he'd never committed before. Somehow it seemed different from picking a victim at random off the streets.

But the other choice was Kaitlyn.

This time the killing smile came easily. It was a smile for himself, and full of self-mockery. Because Kaitlyn was the obvious choice—the girl was warm and willing and definitely pleasant to link up with. Her life energy encased her in a scintillating ruby glow; her mind was a place of blue pools and blazing meteors. He'd been tempted all day by the aura that surrounded her like a charged field.

It had been all he could do not to plunge into that halo and drink it in gulps. Find a transfer point and fix on to it like a leech. He'd needed her desperately.

Only a complete fool would have turned down her help when it was freely offered.

Fighting his way through crumbling sand while the wind lashed around him like a lost spirit, Gabriel smiled.

Then he began to trudge toward one of the cottages that had a light in the window.

Kait woke up and cursed herself.

She'd been absolutely determined not to fall asleep. And now Gabriel was gone, of course. She could feel his absence.

How could she have been so *stupid?*

She'd had practice, now, in disentangling herself from Rob and slipping away soundlessly.

Kait almost yelped as she stepped away from the van and into the wind. She should have brought a jacket—but it was no use thinking about that now. Head bent, arms wrapped around herself, she cast her thoughts wide.

She'd had practice now in searching for Gabriel, too. He was good at concealing himself, but she knew what to look for. In only a moment she had found it—a faraway sense of glittering ice. Like a blue-white spark on the edge of her mind. Kait turned her body toward it and started walking.

It was rough going. The wind blew sheets of sand away from her. When the moon came out, it showed particles whisking through the air like ghosts. It also showed a gigantic rock shaped like a haystack rearing out of the ocean, where no rock had any business being.

A spooky place. Kaitlyn tried not to think about psychic attacks and Mr. Zetes. She was crazy to have come out here alone, of course—but what else could she do?

The wind smelled of saltwater. From her left came the soft-but-loud crashing of waves. Kait swerved to avoid driftwood and then turned sharply, heading for a cluster of cottages. There. Gabriel was very close; she could feel it.

The next moment she saw him; a dark silhouette against a lighted window. Alarm spurted through her. That window— she knew what he was doing loitering around a cottage. What if he'd already . . .

Gabriel!

The call was involuntary, wrung out of her by panic. Kaitlyn's heart thumped before she realized that Rob and the others were out of range.

Gabriel wasn't. His head whipped around.

What are you doing here?

What are you *doing?* she countered. *What have you done, Gabriel?*

She saw him hesitate, then saw him abandon the cottage window abruptly and come striding toward her. She walked to meet him, and he pulled her into the shelter of a carport.

"Can't I take a walk without being followed?" he said venomously.

Kaitlyn gave herself a moment before answering. She was trying to smooth her hair, which the wind had turned into a mane of elf-locks and fine tangles. And she needed to catch her breath.

At last she looked at him. A streetlight outside illuminated half his face, leaving the other half in shadow. Kaitlyn could see enough. His skin looked tight, as if it had been stretched over his bones. There were black circles under his eyes. And there was something about his expression . . . the way he stared at her, eyes narrowed, lips drawn back a little as he breathed quickly.

Gabriel was on the breaking point. And, no, he hadn't gotten into that cottage yet.

"Is that what you were doing?" she said. "Taking a walk?"

"Yes." His lips drew back a little farther. His eyes had turned defiant—he was going to brazen this out. "I need to get away from the rest of you once in a while. There's only so much of Kessler's mind I can stand."

"So you just wanted some privacy." She took a step toward

him. "And you decided now was the time for a little stroll."

With startling suddenness he flashed his most dazzling smile. "Exactly."

Kait took another step. The smile disappeared as suddenly as it had come, leaving his mouth grim. "In the middle of the night. In the freezing cold."

He looked dangerous now. Dark and dangerous as a wolf on the hunt. "That's right, Kait. Now be a good girl and go back to the van."

Kaitlyn moved again, close enough that she could feel his warmth—and he could feel hers. She could feel the instant tension in his body, could see his eyes darken. She could hear his breath become uneven.

"I've never been a good girl. Ask anybody back home—they said I have an attitude problem. So you were just hanging around that cottage by accident."

He took the sudden change in subject without blinking, but when he spoke it was through clenched teeth. "What else would I be doing?"

"I thought"—Kaitlyn tilted her head back to look up at him—"that you might need something."

"I don't need anything from anyone!"

She'd accomplished something astonishing just then—she'd made Gabriel give way before her. He'd retreated, stepping back until the concrete wall behind him stopped him.

Kait didn't give him a chance to regroup. She knew the risk

of what she was doing. Gabriel was on the verge of snapping—
and he was capable of violence. But she wouldn't let herself think
about the danger; she could only think about the shining tor-
ment in Gabriel's eyes.

She moved to him again, this time so close that they were
touching. Carefully, deliberately, she put her hands on his
chest. She could feel the running-stag clamor of his heart.

Then she looked up at him, her face inches from his.

"I think you're lying," she whispered.

CHAPTER 9

S omething in Gabriel's eyes fractured. It was like watching gray agate shatter into pieces.

He caught Kaitlyn by the shoulder. His other hand clamped in her hair, twisting her head to the side.

Black terror washed over Kait, but she didn't move. Her fingers tightened on the sleeves of Gabriel's borrowed shirt.

Then she felt his lips on the back of her neck.

The first sensation was a piercing, as if a single sharp tooth had penetrated at the upper part of her spine, just below her neck.

Vampires, Kait thought dazedly. She knew Gabriel was just opening a transfer point, but it felt as if he had punctured her skin. She could easily see how the legends about vampires had started.

The next instant the sharp pain had gone, replaced by a *tugging*, as if something inside her was being plucked up by the roots. She felt her own momentary resistance—like the earth clinging to a handful of weeds being pulled. And then a giving, a yielding. As if the weeds had come free in the pulling hand.

Energy fountained out of the open wound in a narrow stream. Kaitlyn felt a flare of heat—and pleasure.

All right. It's going to be all right, she thought, scarcely knowing whether she was speaking to herself or Gabriel. The experience itself was frightening—it was like working with high-voltage electricity. But she refused to be afraid on other grounds.

I trust you, Gabriel, she thought.

She could feel the energy pouring into him, and once again she felt his gratitude, his appreciation. His relief as his need was met.

I trust you.

The energy was still flowing steadily, and Kait had a sense of cleansing. Her entire body felt light and airy, as if her feet weren't touching the ground. She relaxed in Gabriel's arms, letting him support her.

Thank you.

The thought wasn't Kaitlyn's, and no one else was in range—so it had to be Gabriel. But it didn't sound like Gabriel. There was no anger, no mockery. It was the free and joyous communication of a happy child.

Then, all at once, the current streaming between them was broken. Gabriel released her and lifted his head.

Dizzy, Kaitlyn clung to him for a moment, hearing her own breath slowing.

"No more," Gabriel said. He was breathless, too, but calm. The starving emptiness inside him filled—at least partly.

Then he said, "Kait . . ."

Kaitlyn made herself let go of him. She stepped back, keeping her eyes down.

"Are—are you sure it's enough? You'll be okay now?" She spoke because sharing thoughts was too intimate.

It had occurred to her—finally—that she was courting another kind of danger here. Being this close to Gabriel, *giving* to him, and feeling his joy and gratification—it had bound them together in a way even the web could not match. It had brought down Gabriel's walls . . . again.

And that was unfair, because on her part it was just caring. It's not like what I feel for Rob, she told herself. It isn't—love. . . .

She could sense Gabriel looking at her. Then she felt an indefinable change in him, a mental straightening of shoulders.

"We need to get back," he said. His voice was short and he ignored her question.

Kait looked up. "Gabriel—"

"Before we're missed." Gabriel turned away and started out into the night.

But he waited for her after a few steps, and he stayed close as they made their way across the beach. Kaitlyn said nothing as they walked. She couldn't think of anything that wouldn't make matters worse.

As soon as they got within sight of the van, she saw that something was wrong.

The van should have been dark inside, but each window was glowing. For one instant Kait thought the others had turned on the dome light, and then she thought of fire. But the glow was too bright for the dome light and too cool for fire. And it had a strange opaque quality about it—almost like a phosphorescent mist.

Fear, icy and visceral, gripped at Kaitlyn.

"What is it?" she whispered.

Gabriel pushed her back. "Stay here."

He ran to the van, and Kait followed, scrambling up behind him when he opened the door. Instantly the trip-hammer beating of her heart seemed to double.

She could see the mist clearly now. And she could see Lewis in the front passenger seat and Anna curled on the first bench seat. They were both asleep—but not peacefully.

Lewis's face was twisted into a grimace, and he was moving his arms and legs jerkily as if trying to escape from something. Anna's long black hair hid her face, but she was writhing, one hand a claw.

"Anna!" Kaitlyn grasped her shoulder and shook her. Anna made a moaning sound, but didn't wake up.

"Rob!" Kaitlyn turned to him. He was lying on his back, thrashing helplessly. His eyes were shut, his expression one of agony. Kaitlyn shook him, too, calling his name mentally. Nothing helped.

She looked over to see how Gabriel was doing with Lewis—and froze.

The gray people were here.

She could see them hanging in the air between her and Gabriel. Lewis's seat cut right through one of them.

"It's an attack!" Gabriel shouted.

Kait was reeling. She felt giddy and confused, almost as if she might faint. It was the web, she realized—she was picking up the sensations of the three dreamers.

Oh, God—she had to do something fast, before she and Gabriel collapsed, too.

"Visualize light!" she shouted to Gabriel. "Remember what Rob said? You defend against psychic attacks by envisioning light!"

Gabriel turned his gray eyes on her. "Fine—just tell me how. And what *kind* of light?"

"I don't know." Panic was rioting inside Kaitlyn. "Just think about light—picture it all around us. Make it—a golden light."

She wasn't quite sure why she'd picked gold. Maybe because the mist was a sort of silvery-green. Or maybe because she always thought of gold as Rob's color.

Pressing her hands to her eyes, Kaitlyn began to envision light. Pure golden light surrounding all of them in the van. As an artist, she found it easy to hold the picture in her mind.

Like this, she thought to Gabriel and sent him the image. The next moment he was helping her, his conviction adding to hers. She felt she could actually *see* the light now; if she opened her eyes it would be there.

It's working, Gabriel told her.

It was. Kait's giddiness was fading, and for the first time since entering the van she felt warmth. The mist had been as cold as the outdoors.

It slipped away now, like an oppressive blanket sliding off Kait. Still visualizing the golden light, she opened her eyes.

The sleepers had quieted. The last traces of the mist were vanishing, curling in on themselves and disappearing. The gray people were still hanging in air.

The next instant they had vanished, too, but not before Kaitlyn got a strange impression. For just a moment she had looked into one of those gray faces—and recognized it. It seemed *familiar,* although she couldn't put her finger on why.

Then the thought was driven out of her mind as she realized that Rob was stirring. He groaned and blinked, dragging himself to a sitting position.

"What—? Kaitlyn—?"

"Psychic attack," Kaitlyn told him calmly and precisely. "When we got back the whole van was filled with mist and you wouldn't wake up. We got rid of it by visualizing light. Oh, Rob, I was so scared." Abruptly her knees folded and she sat down on the floor.

Anna was sitting up, too, and Lewis was moaning.

"Are you guys okay?" Kaitlyn asked shakily, from the floor.

Rob clenched one hand in his unruly blond hair. "I had the most terrible nightmare. . . ." Then he looked at Kait and said, "'When we got back?'"

Kaitlyn's mind went blank, which was probably a good thing. She was too shaken to summon a lie. But behind her Gabriel said smoothly, "Kait had to go to the bathroom, and she didn't want to go alone. I escorted her."

It was a good story. Rob and Anna had found a public rest room down the beach. But Kaitlyn felt little triumph when Rob nodded, accepting it. "Very gallant of you," he said wryly.

"We also saved you," Gabriel added pointedly. "Who knows what that mist was going to do?"

"Yes." Rob's face sobered. He tugged at his hair a moment and then looked up at Gabriel. "Thank you," he said, and his voice was frank and full of genuine emotion.

Gabriel turned away.

There was an awkward moment, and then Anna spoke up.

"Look, why don't you two explain just exactly how you 'visualized light,'" she said. "That way we'll know what to do if they attack again."

"And then maybe we can go back to *sleep*," Lewis added.

Kait explained without much help from Gabriel. By the time she finished she was yawning hugely and her eyes were watering.

They settled down to sleep prepared for the worst, but nothing else happened that night, and Kaitlyn had no dreams.

She woke in the morning to Rob's mental exclamation. She hurried out of the van to find him and Anna bent over, staring at the ground beside the van.

The asphalt was covered with a thin layer of sand blown from the beach. In that sand, all around the van, were delicate tracks and footprints.

"They're animal tracks," Anna said. "You see these? These are the tracks of a raccoon." She pointed to a footprint three inches long, with five long splayed toes, each ending in a claw. "And these are from a fox." She moved her finger to a series of delicate four-toed marks.

"And those oval ones are from an unshod horse, and the little ones are from a rat," Anna finished. Then she looked up at Kait.

Kaitlyn didn't even bother saying, "But *all* of those animals couldn't have been here last night." She remembered very well what Rob had said yesterday—sometimes victims of a psychic attack found the footprints of people or animals.

"Great," she muttered. "I have the feeling we should get out of here."

Rob stood up, brushing sand from his hands. "I agree."

It wasn't quite so easy, though, since the van picked that morning to be obstreperous. Rob and Lewis fiddled with the engine but could find nothing wrong, and in the end it started.

"I'll drive for a while," Anna said. She'd been sitting in the driver's seat, starting the engine when Rob told her to. "Just tell me where to go."

"Stay on 101 and we'll head into Washington," Lewis instructed. "But maybe we'd better stop at a McDonald's for breakfast first."

Kaitlyn wasn't sorry to say goodbye to the black basaltic Oregon coast. Gabriel had been edgy and silent all morning and she was beginning to wonder if what she'd done on the beach last night had been a mistake. She knew she would have to catch him sometime and talk it out, and the idea sent humming bees and butterflies into her stomach.

Please let us find the white house soon, she thought. And then, with a twinge, realized that Gabriel had been right. She *was* expecting a lot of the people in the white house. And what if they couldn't solve all the problems she was bringing them?

Kait shook her head, then turned to look at the dismal, slate-gray day outside.

They passed stands of what Anna said were alder trees, which from a distance looked like big pink clouds. The alder branches were mostly bare, but there were a few reddish leaves hanging on each twig, which gave the stand an overall reddish cast.

By the side of the road were little kiosks which held huge bunches of daffodils, yellow as spring. Signs on the kiosks said $1.00 A BUNCH, but there was no one to take the money. It's the honor system, Kaitlyn thought. She longed for the pure gold of the daffodils, but she knew they couldn't spare the money.

Doesn't matter, she thought. I'll draw instead. She opened her kit and pulled out aureolin yellow, one of her favorite colors. In a few minutes she was drawing, glancing up only occasionally as they crossed a high bridge over the Columbia River. A sign proclaimed:

WELCOME TO WASHINGTON

THE EVERGREEN STATE

"You're home, Anna," Rob said.

"Not yet. It's a long way to Puget Sound if we're sticking to the coast," Anna replied, but Kaitlyn could tell from her voice that she was smiling.

"And we may not get there," Lewis put in. "We may find the white house first."

"Well, it's not here," Gabriel said shortly. "Look at the water."

The left side of the road, which dipped down to the ocean,

was lined with large brown rocks and boulders. Nothing like the gray rocks in the dream.

Kaitlyn opened her mouth to say something—and her hand began to cramp.

A sort of itching cramp, a *need* that had her picking up a pastel stick before she knew what she was doing. She knew what the sensations meant. Her gift was kicking in. Whatever she drew now would be not just a picture but a premonition.

Cool gray and burnt umber, steel and cloud blue. Kaitlyn watched her hand dotting and stroking the colors on, with no idea of what image was forming. All she knew was that it needed a touch of sepia here—and just two round circles of scarlet lake in the center.

When it was finished, she stared at it, feeling a strange creeping between her shoulderblades.

A goat. She'd drawn a *goat,* of all things. It was standing in what looked like a river of silvery-gray, surrounded by cloudy surrealistic fog. But that wasn't what frightened Kait. It was the eyes.

The goat's eyes were the only dash of color in the drawing. They were the color of burning coals, and they seemed to be looking straight out of the picture at Kaitlyn.

Rob's quiet voice made her jump. "What is it, Kait? And don't say 'nothing' this time—I know there's something wrong."

Mutely Kaitlyn held out the picture to him. He studied it, brows drawing together. His lips were a straight line.

"Do you have any idea what it means?" he asked.

Kaitlyn rubbed pastel dust between her fingers. "No. But then I never do—until it happens. All I know is that somewhere, somehow, I'm going to see that goat."

"Maybe it's symbolic," suggested Lewis, who was leaning over the back of the other bench seat to look.

Kaitlyn shrugged and said, "Maybe." She had a nagging sense of guilt—what good was a gift that gave you this kind of premonition? She had produced the picture; she ought to be able to tell what it meant. Maybe if she concentrated . . .

She thought about it while they passed beaches of packed sand and mudflats—none of them like the white house terrain—and while they got lunch at a Red Apple Market. But all the concentration brought was a headache and a feeling of wanting to *do* something, something physical, to let off tension.

"I'll drive now," she said as they left the market.

Rob glanced at her. "Are you sure? You hate driving."

"Yes, but it's only fair," Kaitlyn said. "You've all taken a turn."

Driving the van wasn't as hard as she'd thought it would be. It was less responsive than Joyce's convertible, but the single-lane road was almost deserted and easy to follow.

After a while, though, it began to rain. It started with cat's-paw splatters that made a pleasant sound, but it got worse and worse. Soon it was raining violently—huge sheets that turned the windshield opaque in between sweeps of the wipers. As if someone were throwing buckets of silvery paint against the glass.

"Maybe someone else should drive now," Gabriel said from the bench seat behind Kaitlyn. He'd relinquished the front passenger seat when Kait had taken the wheel—as Kait had suspected he would.

She glanced at Rob, who'd taken the vacated seat. If it had been Rob's suggestion, she might have acquiesced. But Gabriel had a mocking, goading way of saying things that made you want to do just the opposite.

"I'm fine," she said shortly. "I think the rain is easing up."

"She's fine," Rob agreed, giving her one of his slow infectious smiles. "She can cope."

And then, of course, Kaitlyn was stuck with it. Tongue pressed against her front teeth, she peered into the rain and did her best to prove Rob right. The road straightened out and she drove faster, trying to demonstrate casual competence.

When it happened, it happened very suddenly. Later, Kaitlyn would wonder if it might have changed anything if Rob had been driving. But she didn't really think so. Nobody could have coped with what appeared on that narrow road.

Kait was almost convinced of her own competence when she saw the shape in the road. It was directly in her path but far enough ahead to avoid.

A gray shape. A low horned shape—a goat.

If Kaitlyn hadn't seen it before, she might not have recognized it—there was so little time. But she knew every line of that goat; she'd stared at it for hours this morning. It was exactly like her picture, down to the red eyes. They seemed to blaze at her, the only wink of color in the gray and rainy landscape.

Silver, some part of her mind thought wildly. The silvery-gray river hadn't been a river at all but a road. And the fog had been the rain-vapor rising from the ground.

But most of her mind wasn't thinking at all, it was just reacting. *Brakes,* it told her.

Kait's foot hit the brakes, pressing and releasing the way her driver's ed teacher had advised for bad weather.

Nothing happened.

Her foot slammed down in utter defiance of the driver's ed teacher. And again, nothing happened. The van didn't skid; it didn't slow in the least.

The goat was dead ahead. There was no time to scream, no time even to think. No time to pay attention to the sudden clamor in the web as the others realized that something was wrong.

Kaitlyn wrenched at the steering wheel. The van swerved and careered to the left, into the opposite lane. She got a flash of trees getting close very fast.

Turn right! Swerve back!

Kait wasn't sure whose thought it was, but she was already obeying. The van swung right—too far.

I'm going off the road, she thought with a curious calm.

Then everything was confusion.

Kaitlyn could never really remember what happened next, except that it was awful. Trees whipped by. Branches hit the windshield. There was an impact—shocking—but it didn't seem to slow them.

Then the van seemed to leap and go rocketing downward.

Kaitlyn had a sense of being rattled around like a pea in a tin can. She could hear screaming—she thought it might be her own voice. And then there was another impact and everything went dark.

CHAPTER 10

Kaitlyn could hear water—a musical gurgling sound. It was soothing and part of her wanted to listen to it and rest.

But she couldn't. There was something . . . someone she had to worry about. Someone . . . *Rob*.

Not just Rob. The others. Something terrible had happened and she had to make sure they were all right.

Strangely, she wasn't sure just what had happened.

All she knew was that it had been awful. She had to piece together just what the awful thing might have been from what she could see around her.

Opening her eyes, she found that she was in Marisol's van. The van wasn't moving and it wasn't on the road anymore. Through the windshield she could see trees, their branches dripping with green moss. Stretching in front of her she could see water. A creek.

For the first time, she realized that there was water around her feet.

Idiot! There was an accident!

As soon as she thought it, she looked over to Rob. He was blinking, trying to undo his seat belt, seeming as dazed as she felt.

Rob, are you okay? Instinctively Kait used the most intimate form of speech.

Rob nodded, still looking stupefied. There was a cut on his forehead. "Yeah—are you?"

"I'm sorry; I'm so sorry. . . ." If pressed, Kaitlyn couldn't have said what she was apologizing about. She only knew that she'd done something dreadful.

Forget sorry. We have to get out of here, Gabriel said.

Kaitlyn twisted to look behind her. "Are you guys all right? Is anybody hurt?"

"We're okay—I think," Lewis said. He and Anna were getting up. They didn't seem to be injured, but their faces were drained of color and their eyes stared wildly.

"Help me get this open," Gabriel said sharply, wrenching at the side door.

It took all three of them to get the door open, and then Kait and Rob had to crawl over the center console of the van to go out the same way. Jumping out of the van, Kaitlyn landed in water so cold it took her breath away. With Rob's help, she waded painfully over irregular stones to the bank.

From here she could see what had happened to the van. They'd gone off the road, hit a few trees, and then plunged down a steep embankment into the creek. Kaitlyn supposed it was lucky they'd finished right side up. The silver-blue van was dented and battered—the right front fender a mass of twisted metal.

"I'm sorry," she whispered. She now remembered what she had to be sorry for. She was doubly guilty—she'd lost control of the van and she'd failed to interpret her own drawing, the drawing that might have warned her.

"Don't worry, Kait," Rob said gently, putting his arms around her. But then he winced.

"Oh, Rob, your head—there's a terrible cut." He put a hand to it. "Not that bad." But he squatted down on the fern-covered embankment. Rain dripped from the trees around him.

"We should wash it," Anna said. "We've got water, but we need some cloth—"

"My duffel bag!" Kaitlyn started into the water, but Gabriel held her back, seizing her arm ungently.

"That's dangerous, you idiot," he said. His gray eyes were hard.

"But I *need* it," Kaitlyn said. She felt that she could stop the shaking inside her if she just had something to *do,* some action to perform.

Gabriel's mouth twisted. "For God's sake—oh, all *right.*

You stay here." Letting go of her so roughly it was almost a push, he turned and waded to the van. A moment later he was splashing back, holding not only Kait's bag, but Anna's, which contained the files Rob had taken from the hidden room.

"Thank you," Kaitlyn said, trying to look him in the eye.

"The blankets and sleeping bags are all soaked," Gabriel said briefly. "Not worth saving—we'll never dry them out in this weather."

Anna used a T-shirt of Kaitlyn's to wash Rob's cut and staunch the bleeding. Then she said, "Hold this, Kait," and went hiking up the embankment. She returned with a handful of something green.

"Hemlock needles," she said. "They're good for burns; maybe they'll help a cut, too." She applied them to Rob's head.

Lewis had been staring around at the dripping trees, twirling his baseball hat on one finger. Now he said abruptly, "Look, what happened? Did we skid or—"

"It was my fault," Kaitlyn said.

"No, it wasn't," Rob said stubbornly. The T-shirt bandage Anna had made hung over one eye, giving him the rakish look of a pirate. "There was a goat in the road."

Lewis stopped twirling his hat. "A goat."

"Yes. A gray goat . . ." Rob's voice trailed off and he looked at Kaitlyn. "Gray," he said. "Colorless, really."

Kaitlyn stared at him, then shut her eyes. "Oh."

Anna said, "You think it was an apparition? Like the gray people?"

"Of course it was," Kaitlyn said. She'd been so shaken by the accident that she'd forgotten what had happened just before. "I'm so stupid—it had red eyes. Like some sort of demon. And—oh, Rob!" She opened her eyes. "The brakes didn't work. I kept pressing and pressing, but they didn't work!" The trembling at her core seemed to expand suddenly until her whole body was shivering violently.

Rob put his arm around her, and she clung to him, trying to calm herself. "So it was a psychic attack," he said. "The goat was some kind of illusion—maybe an astral projection. At Durham I heard of psychics who could project a part of themselves in the shape of an animal. And the brakes had been tampered with—it must have been long-distance PK. The whole thing was a setup."

"And we could have been killed," Anna said thinly.

Gabriel's laugh was harsh. "Of course. They're playing for keeps."

Rob straightened his shoulders. "Well, the van's not worth salvaging—and besides, we'd better not let anybody find us here. They'll ask questions, want to call the police."

Kaitlyn could feel her heart skip a beat. She lifted her head to stare at Rob in dismay. "But—but, then, what do we *do?*"

"We go to my house," Anna said quietly. "My parents will help us."

Rob hesitated. "We agreed, no parents," he said. "We could end up putting them in danger—"

"But we don't have a *choice*," Anna said, just as quietly but with steel behind the softness. "We're stuck without a car or food, we don't have anywhere to sleep. . . . Listen to me, Rob. My parents can take care of themselves. Right now *we're* the ones in trouble."

"She's right," Lewis said soberly. "What else can we do? We can't afford a hotel and we can't sleep out here."

Rob nodded reluctantly. Kaitlyn allowed herself to feel some relief. Just the thought of having somewhere specific to go was comforting. But Anna's next words dispelled the comfort.

"It means we'll have to give up following the coast," Anna was saying. "We should just cut straight across to the Sound. We'll have to hitchhike, I guess."

"*Five of* us?" Gabriel said. "Who's going to pick up five teenagers?"

Secretly Kaitlyn agreed. Standing in the rain trying to get a ride—in a strange state—when there were five of you—and you had to be on the alert for the police . . . well, it wasn't her idea of fun. But what other choice did they have?

"We've got to try," Rob was saying. "At least, maybe somebody will take Anna and Kait with 'em—and then maybe the girls can find a phone and call Anna's folks."

Helping each other, they climbed through the wet ferns

and bracken, up the embankment, and to the road. Rob said
they had better walk a little distance away from the van to
lessen the chance that they'd be connected with it.

"We're lucky," he said. "You can't see the creek from the
road, and nobody was around to actually see the accident."

Kaitlyn tried to keep reminding herself she was lucky as
she stuck her thumb out, staring down the lonely road.

There weren't many cars. A long truck carrying huge logs
passed without stopping. So did a black Chevy pickup full of
orange and green fishing net.

Kaitlyn looked around as they waited. The rain had eased
to a drizzle, but the world had a sodden look that was rather
menacing. All the trees here, including the alders, were covered with thick mint-colored moss. It was a disturbing sight,
all those branches that weren't white or brown, but lumpy
unnatural green.

She felt a glow in the web just as Lewis asked, "What are
you doing, Rob?"

Rob was standing with his eyes shut, an expression of
concentration on his face. "Just moving energy around," he
said. "I could think better if this cut would start healing." He
opened his eyes, pulling the T-shirt bandage off. Kait saw with
relief that the cut had stopped bleeding. There was even a little
color in Rob's face.

"Okay," he said and smiled. "Now, how about the rest of
you? Anybody starting to hurt?"

Lewis shrugged; Anna shook her head. Gabriel kept looking down the road, ignoring the question.

Kaitlyn shifted, then said, "No, I'm fine." She wasn't; she was chilled and miserable and her entire left side had begun to ache. But she felt somehow that she didn't merit healing. She didn't *deserve* it.

"Kait—I can *feel* you're not," Rob was beginning, when Lewis said, "Another car!"

It was approaching slowly, an old Pontiac the color of pumpkin pie.

"It won't stop," Gabriel said sourly. "*Nobody's* going to stop for five teenagers."

The car passed them, and Kait got a glimpse of a young woman behind the rain-splattered window. Then brake lights flashed, and the car slowed to a stop.

"Come on!" Rob said.

As they reached the car, the driver's window opened. Kaitlyn heard the beat of Caribbean music, and then a voice. "You looking for a ride?"

It wasn't a young woman, Kaitlyn realized. It was a girl. A girl who didn't look any older than they were. She was slender and small-boned, with a pale and delicate face that contrasted sharply with her heavy shock of dark hair. Her eyes were gray-green.

"We sure are," Lewis said eagerly. Kaitlyn could feel his admiration in the web. "We're a little wet, though," he added apologetically. "Well, more than a little. A lot."

"Doesn't matter," the girl said carelessly. "The seats are vinyl—it's my granny's car. Get in."

Kaitlyn hesitated. There was something about this girl—she seemed fragile, but there was something almost furtive about her.

Rob? I'm not sure we should.

Rob glanced at Kait in surprise. *What's wrong?*

I don't know. She's just—does she seem okay to you?

She seems great to me, Lewis interrupted. *Jeez, what a babe. And I'm freezing out here.*

Kaitlyn still wasn't sure. *Anna?*

Anna had been walking around the back of the Pontiac, but had stopped at Kaitlyn's first message. Now she said gently, *You're probably still shaken up, Kait. I think she's fine—and besides, we can all fit in this car!*

"Yes, we can, can't we?" Gabriel said aloud, not seeming to mind the girl's inquisitive glance. Kaitlyn wondered how they must appear to the girl—all five of them standing frozen and silent—and then Gabriel suddenly coming out with this strange rhetorical question.

All right, let's do it, Kait said hastily. She was embarrassed, and she didn't want to argue anymore. But as Rob opened the door, she asked Gabriel, *What did you mean?*

Nothing. It's just an interesting coincidence that we fit, that's all.

Anna and Lewis got in the front with the girl. Kaitlyn slid

in the back seat after Rob, and Gabriel followed her. The white vinyl seats creaked under their weight.

"My name's Lydia," the girl said in that same careless voice. "Where are you going?"

They introduced themselves—or rather Lewis introduced them—and Anna said, "We're trying to get to Suquamish, near Poulsbo—but that's pretty far away. Where were you headed?"

Lydia shrugged. "I wasn't headed anywhere, really. I took the day off school to drive around."

"Oh, do you go to North Mason High? I have a cousin there."

Anna's question was perfectly innocent, but Lydia seemed affronted. "It's a private school," she said briefly. Then she said, "Are you getting enough heat back there? If I turn it too high, the windows steam up."

"It feels great," Rob said. He was holding Kaitlyn's hands in his own, rubbing them. And he was right, being in a warm dry car was wonderful. Kaitlyn's brain felt almost stupefied at the sudden luxury.

She was aware, though, that Lydia was watching them keenly, casting glances at Lewis and Anna beside her, then looking up into the rearview mirror to examine the three in the back. Although Lewis seemed to enjoy the scrutiny it made Kait uncomfortable, particularly when Lydia began frowning and chewing her lip in a speculative way.

"So what were you doing back there?" Lydia asked finally, very casually. "You're awfully wet."

"Oh. We were . . ." Lewis fumbled for words.

"We went for a hike," Gabriel said evenly. "We got caught in the rain."

"Looks more like you got caught in a flood."

"We found a creek," Gabriel said before Lewis could answer.

"So you guys are from around here?"

"From Suquamish," Anna said—and for her, at least, that was the truth.

"You take long hikes," Lydia said, looking in the rearview mirror again. Kait noticed that she had exactly three freckles on her small nose.

Somehow Lydia's skepticism had calmed Kait's own suspicions. It wasn't really furtiveness lurking in those gray-green eyes, she decided. It was more defensiveness, as if Lydia had been beaten up by life a great deal. Kaitlyn felt sympathetic.

They were driving inland, now, through stands of evergreen trees with tall bare trunks. To Kaitlyn, they looked like hundreds of soldiers standing at attention.

Lydia shook back her hair and tilted her chin up. "I hate going to private school," she said suddenly. "My parents make me."

Kaitlyn, relaxing in the warmth of the car, tried to think of something to say to that. But Lewis was already sympathizing. "That's too bad."

"It's so strict—and boring. Nothing exciting ever happens."

"I know. I went to private school once," Lewis said. Lydia changed the subject abruptly.

"Do you always take duffel bags when you go hiking?"

"Yes," Gabriel said. He seemed to be able to handle Lydia best. "We use them like backpacks," he said, seeming amused.

"Isn't that a little awkward?"

Gabriel didn't answer. Lewis just smiled engagingly.

There was another minute or so of fidgeting from Lydia, and then she burst out, "You're running away, aren't you? You don't really live around here at all. You're hitchhiking across the country or something—aren't you?"

Don't tell her anything, Gabriel thought to Lewis, just as Lydia said, "You don't have to tell me. I don't care. But I wish *I* could have an adventure sometime. I'm so tired of private riding clubs and country clubs and Key Clubs and the Assistance League." She was silent for a moment and then added, "I'll drive you to Suquamish if you'll tell me the way. I don't care how far it is."

Kaitlyn didn't know what to make of the girl. She was a strange, excitable creature—that was certain. And she felt left out, an outsider looking in on the five of them.

Kaitlyn remembered how that felt—being outside. Back in Ohio she had been outside everything. She'd been too different; her blue-ringed eyes had been too strange, her psychic drawings had been too spooky. No one at her old high school had wanted to consort with the local witch.

But she still wasn't sure about Lydia—and she didn't like the way Lydia pushed so hard to get in.

Don't tell her anything, she advised Lewis, echoing Gabriel's opinion. After a moment Lewis lifted his shoulders in acquiescence.

"We'd be grateful if you'd take us to Suquamish," Rob said gently, and then they all shut up and listened to the radio.

"Turn here," Anna said. "It's just down this street—there, that house with the Oldsmobile in front of it."

It was twilight, but Kaitlyn could see that the house was the same red-brown color as Anna's cedar basket. It must be made of cedar, she realized. The spruce and alder trees around it were becoming mere towering shapes as dark fell.

"We're here," Anna said softly.

A house, Kaitlyn thought. A real house with parents in it, adults who would help take care of them. For the moment it was all Kait wanted. She stretched her stiff, clammy legs and watched Gabriel reach for the door handle.

Lydia blurted, "I guess you weren't running away. I didn't know you really had somewhere to go. Sorry."

"It doesn't matter. Thanks for the ride," Rob said.

Lydia hunched her shoulders. "Sure," she said. It was the voice of someone who hasn't been invited to a party. Then she said in subdued tones, "Could I use your bathroom?"

"Oh—sure," Anna said. "Hang on, I'd better go inside first." *Mom isn't going to be expecting us,* she added silently.

Moving quickly and lightly, Anna ran up to the house. The others waited in the car, looking through steam-clouded windows. After a few minutes Anna came back, leading a short, motherly woman who looked bewildered but humorously resigned. Kait thought suddenly that she knew where Anna got her serenity.

"Come inside, all of you," the woman said. "I'm Mrs. Whiteraven, Anna's mother. Oh, my goodness, you're wet and half-frozen. Come in!"

They went in, and Lydia went with them.

Inside, Kaitlyn got a quick impression of a crowded, comfortable living room and two identical boys who looked about nine or ten. Then Anna's mother was hustling them into the back of the house, running hot baths and gathering clean clothes.

"You boys will just have to wear some of my husband's things," she said. "They'll be big, but they'll have to do."

Some time later Kaitlyn found herself warm and faintly damp from a bath, dressed in Anna's clothes and sitting in front of the fireplace.

"Your mother's nice," she whispered to Anna. "Isn't she a little surprised to have us turn up like this? Did she ask you any questions?"

Not yet. She's more interested in feeding us and getting us warm. But I know one thing—she hasn't heard anything from the Institute. She thought I was still at school.

They had to stop talking then because Anna's little brothers came in and started asking her about California. Anna managed to tell them about it without mentioning Mr. Zetes or the Institute.

Mrs. Whiteraven bustled back in. "Anna, your other friend was just waiting in the hall. I sent her to wash up. We'll have dinner in a few minutes, as soon as the boys are ready."

"But she isn't—" Anna began. She broke off as Lydia walked into the room, looking small and almost pathetic. It would be too rude to say "she isn't my friend" when Mrs. Whiteraven had just invited her to dinner.

After all, she did give us a ride, Anna said to Kaitlyn, who shrugged.

Rob, Gabriel, and Lewis appeared wearing billowing flannel shirts and jeans tightly belted to keep them on. Kaitlyn and Anna nobly refrained from giggling, but Lydia grinned. Lewis grinned back at her, unabashed. They sat down with Anna's mother and father at the table.

Dinner was hamburgers and smoked salmon, corn and broccoli and salad, with berry pie for dessert and Thomas Kemper's Old Fashioned Birch Soda to wash it down. Kaitlyn had never been so happy to see vegetables. All five of them from the Institute dug in with an enthusiasm that made Mrs.

Whiteraven's eyes widen, but she didn't ask any questions until they'd finished eating.

Then she wiped her hands on a dish towel, pushed her chair back, and said, "Now, suppose you kids explain what you're doing in Washington?"

CHAPTER 11

Kaitlyn looked from Anna's mother to Anna's father, a grave man with steady eyes who'd scarcely spoken during dinner. The kitchen was warm and quiet. Yellow light shone from the overhead lamp onto unfinished pine cupboards.

Then Kaitlyn looked at Rob. They were all looking at one another, all five who shared the web.

Should we? Anna asked.

Yes, Kaitlyn thought back, feeling agreement from the others. *But only your parents. Not . . .*

Anna waved a hand at her twin brothers. "You guys go play, okay? And . . ." She glanced at Lydia and faltered. Kaitlyn knew the problem; Anna was gentle by nature, and it was difficult to say "get out" to a guest who'd just eaten at the same table.

You're too soft-hearted, she thought, but Gabriel was already speaking.

"Maybe Lydia and I could take a walk outside," he said. "It's stopped raining now." Standing, he looked every inch the gallant gentleman—if you didn't count the mocking glint in his eyes. He extended his hand to Lydia courteously.

There wasn't much Lydia could do. She went rather pale, so that her three freckles stood out more prominently. Then she thanked Anna's parents and took Gabriel's hand. Lewis gave her a hurt look.

Be careful, Kaitlyn thought to Gabriel as he and Lydia walked out.

Of what? Psychic attacks—or her? he sent back, amused.

Anna's brothers went, too. And then there was no further excuse for delay. With one final look at her mind-mates, Anna took a deep breath and began telling her parents the whole story.

Almost the whole story. She left out some of the more grue-some bits and didn't mention the mind-link at all. But she told about Marisol, and the crystal that enhanced psychic power, and Mr. Zetes's plans for making his students into a psychic strike team. Rob went and got the files he'd taken from the hidden room.

"And we've been having these dreams," Anna said. "About a little peninsula with gray water all around it, and across from it is a cliff with trees and a white house. And we think that the people in the house might be sending us the dreams, trying to help us." She told about Kaitlyn's two encounters with the caramel-skinned man who came from the white house.

"He didn't seem to like the Institute," Kait put in. "And he showed me a picture of a garden with a huge crystal in it—like Mr. Z's crystal. We figure that maybe they know about these things."

Mrs. Whiteraven frowned. Her black eyes had been snapping and flashing throughout Anna's story, especially when Anna told about Mr. Z's plans. Mr. Whiteraven had merely gotten more and more grave-looking, one of his hands slowly clenching into a fist. Like Tony, they seemed to have no trouble accepting the reality of what Anna was saying.

Now Anna's mother spoke. "But—you're saying you set out for this white house without any idea where it is?"

"We have *some* idea," Anna said. "It's north. And we'll know it when we see it—the peninsula is lined with these strange rock piles. I keep thinking they're familiar somehow. They look like this." She got a pencil and began drawing on the back of one of the file folders. "No—Kait, you're the artist. Draw one."

Kaitlyn did her best, sketching one of the tall, irregular rock stacks. It came out looking a bit like a stone snowman with outspread arms.

"Oh, it's an *inuk shuk,*" Mrs. Whiteraven said.

Kaitlyn's head jerked up. "You *recognize* it?"

Anna's mother turned the paper, studying it. "Yes—I'm sure it's an *inuk shuk.* The Inuit used them for signals, you know, to show that a certain place was friendly or that visitors were welcome—"

"The *Inuit?*" Anna interrupted, choking. "You mean we have to go to Alaska?"

Her mother waved a hand, brow puckering. "I'm sure I've seen some of these much closer. . . . I know! It was somewhere on Vancouver Island. We took a trip there when you were about five or six. Yes, and I'm sure we saw them there."

Everyone began talking at once.

"Vancouver Island—that's Canada—" Rob said.

"Yes, but it's not far—there's a ferry," Anna said. "No *wonder* those things were familiar—"

"I've never been to Canada," said Lewis.

"But do you remember exactly *where* they were?" Kaitlyn was asking Mrs. Whiteraven.

"No, dear, I'm afraid not. It was a long time ago." Anna's mother chewed her lip gently, frowning at the picture. Then she sighed and shook her head.

"It doesn't matter," Rob said. His eyes were alight with excitement. "At least we know the general area. And somebody on the island has *got* to know where they are. We'll just keep asking."

Anna's mother put the paper down. "Now, just a minute," she said. She and her husband exchanged a glance.

Kaitlyn, looking from one of them to the other, had a sudden sinking feeling.

"Now," Mrs. Whiteraven said, turning away from her

husband. "You kids have been very brave and resourceful so far. But this idea about finding the white house—it's not practical. This isn't a problem for children."

"No," said Mr. Whiteraven. He'd been looking through the files Rob had brought. "It's a problem for the authorities. There's enough proof here to get your Mr. Zetes put away for a long time."

"But you don't understand how powerful he is," Anna said. "He's got friends everywhere. And Marisol's brother said that only magic could fight magic—"

"I hardly think Marisol's brother is an expert," her mother said tartly. "You should have gone to your parents in the first place. And that reminds me, you have to *call* your parents, now—all of you."

Kait hardened herself. "We can't tell them anything that would make them feel better. And if Mr. Zetes has some way of tapping the call—well, he'd know exactly where we are."

"If he doesn't already," Anna said softly.

"But . . ." Mrs. Whiteraven sighed and exchanged another look with her husband. "All right, *I'll* call them in the morning. I don't need to tell them exactly where you are until we get this thing straightened out."

"Straightened out how, ma'am?" Rob asked. His eyes had darkened.

"We'll talk to the elders, then to the police," Anna's mother said firmly. "That's the right thing to do."

Anna opened her mouth, then shut it again. *It's no good,* she told the others helplessly.

No. It isn't, Rob agreed.

Lewis said, *Jeeeez. I guess we should be relieved, but—*

Kaitlyn knew what he meant. Adults were in the picture now, taking charge, handling things. The authorities were going to be told. The five of them didn't have to worry anymore. She should have been happy.

So why did her chest feel so tight?

Two thoughts jostled in her brain. One was: After we got so far . . .

The other was: The adults don't know Mr. Z.

"Now we'll have to find places for you to sleep," Anna's mother was saying briskly. "You two boys can have the twins' room, and I'll put your friend Gabriel on the couch. Then Anna can share her room with you, Kait, and Lydia can go in the guest room—"

"*Lydia's* not sleeping here," Kaitlyn blurted, before thinking about how rude this sounded. "She's not one of us; she just gave us a ride."

Mrs. Whiteraven looked surprised. "Well, you can't expect her to drive all the way home now. It's too late, and she told me before dinner that she was tired. I've already invited her to stay overnight."

Kaitlyn started to groan, then realized that Rob and Anna and especially Lewis were looking at her reproachfully. In the web she could feel their bewilderment—they didn't understand what she had against Lydia.

Oh, well, what difference did it make anyway? Kait shrugged and bent her head.

Gabriel and Lydia came strolling through the door a few minutes later. Lydia didn't look particularly disappointed to have missed the kitchen conference. She kept glancing up at Gabriel through her lashes—a stratagem that seemed to amuse Gabriel and annoy Lewis. Kait and Anna left Rob to fill Gabriel in on what had happened while they helped make up the guest room bed.

So the quest is over? Gabriel asked. Kaitlyn could hear him perfectly even though he was in the kitchen and she was giving a final punch to Lydia's pillow.

We'll talk about it tomorrow, she told him grimly. She was tired.

And she was worried about Gabriel. Again. Still. She could tell that he was in pain—she could feel the tension shimmering under his surface. But somehow she didn't think he was going to let her help tonight.

He didn't. He wouldn't talk about it, either, not even when she managed to sneak a moment alone with him while the others were getting ready for bed.

"But what are you going to do?" She had dreadful visions of him sneaking into Anna's parents' room, too crazed to know what he was doing.

"Nothing," he said shortly, and then, with icy fury, "I'm a *guest* here."

So he'd caught her vision. And he had his own code of honor. But that didn't mean he could hold out all night. . . .

He was already walking away.

Kaitlyn climbed into Anna's double bed feeling uneasy and discouraged.

It was just dawn when she woke. She found herself staring at the luminous green numbers on Anna's clock radio, a knot twisting in her stomach. She could sense the others sleeping—even Gabriel. He was so restless that she could tell he hadn't been out anywhere.

Strangely, of all the things she had to worry about, the one bothering her was Lydia.

Forget Lydia, she told herself. But her mind kept spinning out the same questions. Who was Lydia, and why was she so eager to be with them? What was wrong with the girl? And why did Kait keep feeling she wasn't to be trusted?

There should be some way to tell, Kait thought. Some test or something. . . .

Kait sat up.

Then, quickly but as stealthily as possible, she slid out of bed and picked up her duffel bag. She took the bag into the bathroom and locked the door.

With the light on she fished through the bag until she found her art kit. The sealed Tupperware had survived the creek, and her pastels and erasers were safe. The sketchpad was damp, though.

Oh, well. Oil pastels didn't mind the damp. Kaitlyn picked up a black pastel stick, held it poised over the blank page, and shut her eyes.

She'd never done this before; trying to *make* a picture come when she didn't already feel the need to draw. Now she made use of some of Joyce's techniques, deliberately relaxing and shutting out the world.

Clear your mind. Now think of Lydia. Think of drawing Lydia. . . . Let the picture come. . . .

Black lines radiating downward. Kaitlyn saw the image and let her hand transfer it to the paper. Now some black grape mixed in. Blue for highlights—it was Lydia's hair. Then pale fleshtones for Lydia's face and celadon green for Lydia's eyes.

But she felt she needed the black again. Heavy strokes of black, lots of them, above and around Lydia's portrait, forming a silhouette that seemed to be cradling Lydia, encompassing her.

Kaitlyn's eyes opened all the way, and she stared at the drawing. That broad-shouldered silhouette with body lines that swept straight down like a man in a coat . . .

In one furious motion she was on her feet.

I'll kill her. Oh, my God, I'm going to *kill* her. . . .

She jerked open the bathroom door and headed for the guest room.

Lydia was a slender shape under the covers. Kait turned her over and grabbed her by the throat.

Lydia made a noise like Georgie Mouse. Her eyes showed white in the darkness.

"You nasty, spying, sneaking little *weasel*," Kait said and shook her a few times. She spoke softly, so as not to wake Anna's parents, and put most of her energy into the shaking.

Lydia made more noises. Kaitlyn thought she was trying to say, "What are you talking about?"

"I'll tell you what I'm talking about," she said, punctuating each word with a shake. Lydia was gripping her wrists with both hands, but was too weak to break Kait's hold. "You're working for Mr. Zetes, you little worm."

Squeaking feebly, Lydia tried to shake her head.

"Yes, you are! I *know* it. I'm psychic, remember?"

As Kaitlyn finished speaking, she sensed activity behind her. It was her mind-mates, crowding in the doorway. So much emotion, so close, had gotten through to all of them even in their sleep.

"Hey! What are you doing?" Lewis was saying in alarm, and Rob said, "Kait, what's happening? You woke everybody up. . . ."

Kaitlyn barely turned. "She's a spy!"

"What?" Charming in too-big pajamas, Rob came to stand beside the bed. When he saw Kaitlyn's grip on Lydia's throat, he reached instinctively. Lewis was right behind him.

"Don't, you guys. She's a spy—aren't you?" Kaitlyn tried to bang Lydia's head against the headboard, but didn't have enough leverage.

"Hey!"

"Kait, just calm down—"

"Admit it!" Kait told the struggling Lydia. "Admit it and I'll let you go!"

Just as Rob was putting his arms around Kait, trying to pull her away, Lydia nodded.

Kaitlyn let go. "I did a drawing that showed she's working for Mr. Zetes," she said to Rob. To Lydia, she added, "Tell them!"

Lydia was coughing and choking, trying to get enough air. Finally she managed to wheeze, "I'm a spy."

Rob dropped his arms, and Lewis looked almost comically dismayed. "What?"

A wave of ugly emotion came from Gabriel. Images of Lydia being chopped into little pieces and thrown in the ocean. Kaitlyn winced and for the first time realized that her hands were sore.

The others had gathered around the bed now. Anna was somber, and Lewis looked hurt and betrayed. Rob crossed his arms over his chest.

"All right," he said to Lydia. "Start talking."

Lydia sat up, small and ghostly in her white nightgown. She looked at each of the five rather threatening figures surrounding her bed.

"I am a spy," she said. "But I'm not working for Mr. Zetes."

"Oh, come off it," Kaitlyn said, and Gabriel said, "Of course you're not," in his silkiest, most sinister manner.

"I'm *not*. I don't work for him. . . . I'm his daughter."

Kaitlyn felt her jaw sag. Unbelievable—but, wait. Joyce *had* mentioned that Mr. Zetes had a daughter. . . .

She said the daughter was friends with Marisol, Rob agreed.

Kaitlyn remembered. She also remembered thinking that any daughter of Mr. Zetes's would have to be old, strangely old to be friends with Marisol.

"How old are you?" she said suspiciously to Lydia.

"Eighteen last month. Look, if you don't believe me, my driver's license is in my purse."

Gabriel picked a black Chanel purse off the floor and dumped its contents on the bed, ignoring Lydia's murmur of protest. He extracted a wallet.

"Lydia Zetes," he said, and showed the driver's license to the others.

"How did you *get* here?" Rob demanded.

Lydia blinked and swallowed. She was either on the verge of tears or an excellent actress, Kaitlyn thought. "I flew. On a plane."

"The astral plane?" Gabriel asked. He was very angry.

"On a *jet*," Lydia said. "My father sent me, and I got the car from a friend of his, a director of Boeing. My father called and told me where you'd be—"

"Which he knew because he set up a trap for us," Rob interrupted, seizing on this. "A trap with a goat. He knew if we didn't get killed in the accident, we'd be stranded—"

"Yes. And I was supposed to come along and help you—if any of you were still alive."

"You—little—" Words failed Kaitlyn. She grabbed for Lydia's throat again, but Gabriel was faster.

"Don't bother with it. *I'll* take care of her," he said. Kaitlyn sensed cold hunger.

Everyone in the web knew what he meant. The interesting thing was that *Lydia* seemed to know what he meant, too. She flinched, scooting back against the headboard.

"You don't understand! I'm not your enemy," she said in a voice laced with raw panic.

"Sure you're not," Lewis said.

"No, you're just his daughter," said Kaitlyn. Then she felt Anna's hand on her arm.

"Wait a minute," Anna said quietly. "At least let her say what she wants to." To Lydia, she said, softly but severely, "Go on."

Lydia gulped and addressed herself to Anna. "I know you won't believe me, but what I told you in the car was true. I *do* hate private school, and riding clubs, and country clubs. And I hate my father. All I ever wanted was to get away—"

"Yeah, yeah," Lewis said. Gabriel just laughed.

"It's *true*," Lydia said fiercely. "I hate what he does to people.

I didn't want to come after you, but it was my only chance."

Something about her voice made Lewis falter in his sneering. Kaitlyn could feel his indecision in the web.

"You weren't going to tell us, though, were you?" Kaitlyn said. "You'd never have told us who you were if I hadn't found out."

"I *was* going to," Lydia said. She squirmed. "I *wanted* to," she amended. "But I knew you wouldn't believe me."

"Oh, stop sniveling," Gabriel said.

Kaitlyn was looking at Rob. *I know I'm going to hate myself for asking this—but do you think it could be true?*

I . . . don't know. Rob grinned suddenly. *But maybe we can find out.*

He sat on the bed, taking Lydia by the shoulders, and looked into her face. She shrank back.

"Now listen to me," he said sternly. "You know that we're psychics, right? Well, Kaitlyn has the power to tell if you're lying or not." To Kait he said, *Go get your drawing stuff.*

Kaitlyn hid a smile and brought it from the bathroom. Rob went on, "All she has to do is make a drawing. And if that drawing says you're not telling the truth . . ." He shook his head darkly. "Now," he said, looking hard at Lydia again, "what's your story this time?"

Lydia looked at Kait, then at Rob. She lifted her chin. "It's the same. Everything I told you was true," she said steadily.

Kaitlyn made a few scribbles on the pad. Her gift didn't

work that way, of course, but she knew that the real test here was of Lydia's demeanor.

Well? she asked Rob.

Either she's telling the truth or she's the greatest actress in the world.

Like Joyce? Gabriel put in pointedly. *You know, I could probably tell if she's telling the truth. I could mind-link with her.*

Yeah, but what are the chances that she'd survive? Rob asked.

Gabriel shrugged. The hunger flickered again.

"Look, what was it you were supposed to do when you found us?" Kaitlyn asked Lydia.

"Keep you guys from going wherever you were going," she said promptly. "Convince you to go to the police or something instead—"

"He *wants* that? Your father?"

"Oh, yes. He knows he can fix the police. He's got lots of friends, and he can do things with the crystal. He's not afraid of police; he's afraid of *them*."

"Who?" Kaitlyn demanded.

"Them. The people of the crystal. He doesn't know where they are, but he's afraid you'll find them. They're the only ones who can stop him." She looked around. "*Now* do you believe me? Would I have told you that if I were your enemy?"

Kaitlyn could feel the wavering in the web, and the sudden resolution. Rob and Anna believed her. Lewis not only believed her but liked her again. Gabriel was cynical, but that was typical Gabriel. And Kait herself was convinced enough to have a new worry.

"If Mr. Z *wants* us to go to the police—" she began.

"Right," Rob said grimly.

"But we'll never convince my parents," Anna said.

"Right," Rob said again.

A feeling was stirring in Kaitlyn, part terror, part dismay, and part wild excitement.

Lewis gulped. "But that means—"

"Right," Rob said a third time. He grinned at Kait, his grin reflecting her bewildering mix of emotions. "The search," he announced to the room at large, "is back on."

Gabriel cursed.

Lydia was looking from one of them to another in bewilderment. "I don't understand."

"It means we're going to have to run away again," Rob said. "And if you really want to help us—"

"I do."

"—you can drive us to Vancouver Island. There's a ferry, right?" He glanced at Anna, who nodded.

"I'll do it," Lydia said simply. "When do we go?"

"Right *now*," Kaitlyn said. "We've got to get out of here before Anna's parents wake up."

"Okay, everybody," Rob said. "Grab your things and let's get moving."

CHAPTER 12

"The ferry leaves from Port Angeles at eight-twenty," Anna said as she and Kaitlyn hurriedly changed their clothes in her bedroom.

"It's started raining again," said Kaitlyn.

They all met a few minutes later in the front hallway. There were ominous stirring noises from the back of the house.

"Shouldn't you leave a note?" Lewis whispered.

Anna sighed. "They'll know," she said briefly.

"I'll leave them the files," Rob said. "Maybe they can do something with them."

Gabriel snorted.

Outside, the sky was cold and gray. The rain seemed to come at them horizontally as they drove to Port Angeles. If they kept the defroster on maximum, it cleared the windshield but scorched their skin; if they turned it down, the windshield immediately steamed over. If they opened the windows, it cleared everything but they froze.

At the ferry the water was navy blue with just a hint of green. They waited in a line of cars and finally drove onto a large boat. It cost twenty-five dollars, and Kaitlyn paid because Lydia only had credit cards.

On the passenger deck Kaitlyn watched the deep blue water slipping away on either side. We're on our way, she thought. To Canada. She had never been to a foreign country.

She was drinking a vending-machine Coke that Rob had brought her when Lewis rushed up, breathless.

"Trouble," he said. "I just talked to some kids in the bathroom. They said if you're under eighteen, you're supposed to have a letter of authorization to get into Canada."

"What?"

"A letter. From your parents or something, I guess. Telling who you are and how long you're going to be there."

"Oh, *terrific*." Kaitlyn looked at Rob, who shrugged.

"What can we do? We'll just hope they don't ask for one."

"I'm eighteen, anyway," Lydia said. "I'll drive and maybe the rest of you can fake it."

An hour later they cruised into Victoria Harbor. Kaitlyn's breath caught. The sun had come out, and the harbor was a picture begging to be painted. There were lots of little sailboats and lots of clean-looking pink and white buildings.

But she couldn't keep staring; they had to go downstairs

again and get in the car. They waited in another line at the customs checkpoint while the knot in Kaitlyn's stomach wound tighter and tighter.

"Where do you live?" a sunglassed customs officer asked Lydia.

Lydia's fingers barely tightened on the wheel. "In California," she said, smiling.

The customs officer didn't smile back. He asked to see Lydia's driver's license. He asked where they were going in Canada and how long they'd be staying. Lydia answered everything in a careless, sophisticated murmur. Then the officer bent a little at the waist to examine the inside of the car.

Look old, Kaitlyn told the others. They all sat up straight and tried to look mature and bored.

The customs officer didn't change expression. He glanced at each of them, then straightened.

"Any of you under eighteen?" he asked Lydia.

Kaitlyn's stomach gave a final sickening twist. Their driver's licenses would show the rest of them were *all* under eighteen. And then he'd ask for a letter. . . .

Lydia hesitated imperceptibly. Then she said "Oh, no." She said it lightly, with something like a toss of her head. Kaitlyn admired that. Although Lydia was slight, her manner was sophisticated and assured.

The customs officer hesitated. He was looking at Lewis— the one of them who looked youngest. Lydia glanced back at Lewis, too, and although her face was calm, her gaze was almost desperate. Pleading. Lewis's jaw set, and Kaitlyn felt a ripple in the web.

The customs officer had something hanging at his belt, a pager or walkie-talkie or something. Suddenly it began to shriek.

Not beep. *Wail.* It went off with a sound like an air-raid siren, a vibrating sound that put Kaitlyn's teeth on edge. People turned to look.

The customs officer was shaking the walkie-talkie, pressing buttons. The shrieking only went up in volume.

The officer looked from the device to the car as if hesitating. Then he grimaced, trying to muffle the electronic shrilling. With an impatient hand, he waved Lydia on.

"Go, go," Lewis whispered excitedly.

Lydia put the car in gear, and they glided off at a majestic five miles an hour. When they reached a main street, Kaitlyn let out her breath. They'd made it!

"Easier than I thought," Rob said.

In the back seat Lewis was chortling. "How about that? One for the home team!"

Kaitlyn turned on him. That ripple she'd felt in the web just before the shrieking began . . . "Lewis—did *you?*"

Lewis's grin widened, his eyes sparkling. "I figured if those creeps could sabotage us with long distance PK, I could handle a walkie-talkie. I just made a few little adjustments to give it some feedback."

Lydia glanced back at him again, and for the first time there was something like appreciation in her gray-green eyes. "Thanks," she said. "You saved my you-know-what." Lewis beamed.

Even Gabriel seemed grudgingly impressed. But he asked Lydia smoothly, "Who are those creeps, by the way? The ones who've been trying to kill us with psychic attacks."

"I don't know. Truly, I *don't*. I know my father has been doing something with the crystal—and he may have people helping him. But I don't know who."

"I wonder if they've stopped," Anna said suddenly. "I mean, there wasn't an attack last night. Maybe they've lost track of us."

"And maybe they're relying on somebody else to keep track," Gabriel said, with a meaningful look at Lydia. She gave something very much like a flounce without interfering with her driving.

"Where am I supposed to go now?" she asked.

There was a pause. Then Rob said, "We're not sure."

"You came here without knowing where you're *going?*"

"We don't know exactly. We're looking for—"

"Something," Gabriel said, interrupting Rob. Lewis frowned and Kaitlyn gave Gabriel an impatient look.

We decided to trust her. And she's going to find out anyway, as soon as we find it. . . .

"Then let her wait until we find it," Gabriel said aloud. "Why trust any further than we have to?"

Lydia's lips tightened, but she didn't say anything, and she didn't flounce again.

"I figure we have two choices," Rob said. "We can drive up and down the coast blindly, or we can *ask* people around here if they know where the—" He changed for an instant to silent speech: *the rock towers are.* "If Anna's mom recognized them, people on the island should know them."

"Can't *you* remember anything, Anna?" Lewis asked. "Your mom said you were on that trip, too."

"I was five," Anna said.

They decided to ask around. A man at a tourist shop sold them a map and directed them to the Royal British Columbia Museum. But although the museum people recognized Kaitlyn's sketch of an *inuk shuk,* they had no idea where any might be found on the island. Neither did anyone at the camera shop, or the bookstore, or the British imports store, or the native crafts shop. Neither did the librarians at the Victoria Library.

"Is it time to start driving around blindly?" Gabriel asked.

Lewis pulled out the map.

"We can drive either northeast or northwest," he said. "This island's sort of like a big oval and we're at the bottom. And before you ask, *nothing* on here looks like our Griffin's Pit. There're thousands of little peninsulas and things all over the coast, and no way to tell any of them apart."

"It's probably too small to be on the map, anyway," Rob said. "Flip a coin: Heads we go east, tails we go west."

Kaitlyn flipped a coin and it came up heads.

They drove northeast, following the coastline, stopping to check the ocean every few miles. They drove until it was dark, but they found nothing resembling the place in their dream.

"But the ocean is right," Anna said, standing on a rock and looking down into the blue-gray water. Gulls were crowded thickly around her—they took off when Kaitlyn or the others came near, but tolerated Anna as if she were a bird.

"It's *almost* right," Kaitlyn temporized. "Maybe we need to go farther north, or to try going west." It was frustrating to feel she was so close to the place, but not to be able to sense where it was.

"Well, we're not going to find anything tonight," Gabriel said. "The light's gone."

Kaitlyn heard the note of tension in his voice. Not just ordinary Gabriel-tension, but a fine edge that told her he was in trouble.

All day he'd been quieter than usual, withdrawn, as if he were wrapping himself around his private pain. His control was getting better, but his need was getting worse. It had been nearly thirty-six hours since Kaitlyn had caught him on the beach in Oregon.

And what on earth is he going to do tonight? Kaitlyn wondered.

"I beg your pardon?" Rob said, looking at her quickly.

She'd forgotten to screen her thoughts. Desperately hoping

he'd only caught the last bit, she said, "I was wondering what on earth we're going to do tonight. To sleep, I mean. We're almost broke—"

"And starving," Lewis put in.

"—and we certainly can't all sleep in this car."

"We'll have to find a cheap motel," Anna said. "We can afford one room, anyway, since it's off season. We'd better head back for Victoria."

In Victoria they found the Sitka Spruce Inn, which let them have a room with two twin beds for thirty-eight dollars and didn't ask any questions. The paint inside the room was peeling and the door to the bathroom didn't shut properly, but, as Anna pointed out, it did have beds.

At Rob's direction the girls got the beds. Lydia chose to share with Anna—clearly she hadn't forgotten the strangling. Kaitlyn curled up on the other, pulling the thin coverlet over her. The boys, sleeping on the carpet, had usurped the blankets.

She slept, but lightly. All that evening Gabriel had avoided her, refused to speak with her. Kait could tell by his cold determination that he was bent on solving his problem alone—and she didn't think that he was going to lie there and quietly endure it again tonight. By now she was closely enough attuned to him that she thought she'd wake up when he did.

It worked—mostly. Kaitlyn woke when the hotel door closed with a click. She could sense that Gabriel wasn't in the room.

Getting out of bed stealthily was almost routine now. The only shock came when Kaitlyn looked at the other bed and realized that there was only one figure in it.

Lydia was gone. Not in the bathroom, either. Just gone.

Kaitlyn crept out of the room feeling very grim.

She tracked Gabriel by his presence in the web, feeling him move away from her, following. She wondered if Lydia was with him.

Eventually she came out by the harbor.

Kaitlyn hadn't been afraid walking down the quaint, old-fashioned streets of Victoria. There were a few people out, and an atmosphere of sleepy safety blanketed the town. But here by the harbor it was very quiet, very lonely. The lights of boats and buildings reflected in the water, but it was still dark and the wharf was deserted.

She found Gabriel pacing in the shadows.

He looked something like a wild animal, a captured predator pacing out the confines of his cage. As Kaitlyn got closer, she could sense the intensity of his hunger.

"Where's Lydia?" she said.

He swung around to stare at her. "Can't you leave me alone?"

"*Are* you alone?"

There was no sound but the soft swish of water for a moment. Then Gabriel said with careful precision, "I have no idea where Lydia is. I came out by myself."

"Was she still in bed then?"

"I didn't look."

Kaitlyn sighed. All right, then, forget about Lydia, she told herself. There's nothing you can do. "Actually, I came out here to talk about *you*," she said to Gabriel.

Gabriel gave her a searing glance. All he said was "No."

"Gabriel—"

"It can't go on, Kaitlyn. Don't you see that? Why can't you just leave me to deal with things my way?"

"Because your way means people get hurt!"

He froze. Then he said distinctly, "So does yours."

Kaitlyn didn't understand—she wasn't sure she *wanted* to understand. Gabriel seemed . . . vulnerable . . . just now. She slapped down the strange, impossible thought that sprang to mind and said, "If you mean me, I can handle myself. If you mean Rob . . ."

The vulnerability disappeared instantly. Gabriel straightened and gave one of his most disturbing smiles.

"Let's say I meant Rob," he said. "What's he going to do when he finds out?"

"He'll understand. I wish you'd let me *tell* him. He might be able to help."

Gabriel's smile just grew more unpleasant. "You think so?"

"*I'm positive.* Rob likes to help people. And, believe it or not, I think he likes *you*. If you weren't so touchy—"

Gabriel waved a hand in sharp dismissal. "I don't want to talk about him."

"Fine. Let's talk about what you're going to do tonight. Going hunting? Going to find some girl walking alone and grab her?" Kaitlyn stepped closer as she spoke. Dim as it was, she could see the immediate wariness on Gabriel's face.

That's it, she thought. All I have to do is get near enough. His control is so close to breaking . . .

Gabriel didn't say anything, so she went on. "Whoever she is, she won't know what you're doing. She'll fight you, and that will hurt her. And she probably won't have enough energy, so you'll probably kill her. . . ."

Kaitlyn was very near now. She could see Gabriel's eyes, see the tortured struggle there. She could feel just the flash of his thought, quickly muffled. *Danger.* Quietly she said, "Is that what you want to happen?"

A muscle in his jaw jerked. "You know it isn't," he raged, equally quiet. "But there isn't any other choice—"

"Oh, Gabriel, don't be *stupid*," Kaitlyn said and put her arms around him.

He managed to resist for about one and a half seconds.

Then, with shaking hands, he pushed her hair off her neck. His lips were so near the place already. Kaitlyn bent her head to make it easy for him.

A feeling of something blowing open, breaking through . . .

and then something being released. Something like an electric current or a streak of lightning. Kaitlyn relaxed, giving willingly.

And felt her emotions rising to the surface, like blood rising to the surface of heated skin. Her caring for Gabriel, her longing to help him. She could sense his feelings, too.

It was only then that she realized, that she remembered, what the true danger in this was. Only then that she understood what Gabriel had meant by his warnings.

Because she could *feel* what he felt. And along with the gratitude, the sheer satisfaction and relief, were other emotions. Appreciation, joy, wonder, and—oh, dear God, *love*. . . .

Gabriel loved her.

She could see herself in his mind, an image so cloaked in glamour and ethereal grace that she could scarcely recognize it. A girl with red-gold hair like a meteor trail and smoky-blue eyes with strange rings in them. An exotic creature that burned like an eager flame. More witch than human.

How could she have been so *stupid?*

But it had never occurred to her that Gabriel, prickly, untouchable Gabriel, could fall in love with anyone. He'd changed too much since he'd loved Iris—and killed her. He'd become too hard, too bitter.

Only he hadn't.

There was no possibility of misunderstanding. Kaitlyn

could feel his emotions clearly—she was surrounded by them, immersed in them. After two days of deprivation Gabriel's control had splintered and his barriers dissolved completely. He realized what she was seeing, but he couldn't stop her, because he was too desperate in his feeding to fight.

Kait had the sense that they were staring at each other across a narrow chasm, both frozen in place, unable to hide from the other. She was seeing into Gabriel's naked soul. And that wasn't right, that wasn't fair, because she knew what he'd be seeing in her. Friendship and concern, that was all. She couldn't love Gabriel; she was already in love. . . .

But with Gabriel's emotions swirling around her, crashing around both of them like a storm-swelled wave, it was hard to remember that. It was hard to keep any rational thought in mind. Gabriel's love was pulling at her, dragging at her, demanding that she return it. That she give herself completely, open and give him everything. . . .

What are you doing to her?

Kaitlyn's heart stopped.

It was Rob's voice, and it shattered her world like a bolt of lightning. In one instant the sea-swept warmth of Gabriel's passion disappeared. The connection between them was cut off, and they sprang apart . . .

Like guilty lovers, Kaitlyn thought.

Rob was standing just below one of the wrought-iron

Victorian streetlights. He was fully dressed, but his hair was still rumpled into a lion's mane from sleep. He looked angry— and bewildered.

And despite his words, he hadn't grabbed Gabriel or tried to pull them apart. Which meant he knew. He must have sensed in the web that Kait wasn't being attacked.

There was a long moment when all three of them just stood. Like statues, Kaitlyn thought wildly. Pillars of salt. She knew that every second she delayed explaining made the thing look worse. But she still couldn't believe it was happening.

Gabriel seemed to be in shock, too. He stood as paralyzed as Kait, his gray eyes dilated.

At last Kait managed to speak through dry lips. "Rob, I was going to tell you—"

It was a terrible choice of words. Rob's face drained of color, and his golden eyes went so dark they were lightless.

"You don't need to," he said. "I saw." He swallowed and then said in an odd, husky voice, "I understand."

Then he turned quickly, almost running. Running away.

Rob, no! That's not what I meant! Rob, wait—

But Rob was almost at the concrete stairs leading to the harbor street. Hurrying to get out of range.

Kaitlyn cast one wild look after him. Then she looked at Gabriel, who was still standing motionless in the shadows. His face revealed nothing, but Kaitlyn could feel his pain.

Her heart was pounding madly. They both needed her,

and she could only help one of them. There was no more than a moment to choose.

With an agonized look at Gabriel, she whirled and ran after Rob.

She caught Rob beneath another streetlight, one with hanging baskets of flowers suspended from a crosspiece.

"Rob, please—you have to *listen* to me. You—"

She was almost hysterical, unable to finish her sentence. He turned, his eyes the wide hurt eyes of a child.

"It's all right," he said. With a jolt Kaitlyn realized something else. Those eyes were *blind*—he wasn't really seeing her. And he certainly wasn't listening.

"Rob, it's not what you think." The dreadful cliché rolled off her tongue before she could stop it. Then she said, with ferocious intensity, "It *isn't*. Aren't you even going to give me a chance to explain?"

That got through. Rob winced and recoiled just a bit, as if he'd rather run away again. But he said, "Of course you can explain."

She could see him bracing himself, waiting for an explanation of why she wanted to leave him. Frustration crested in her, overriding her fear. Words came out in a breathless rush.

"Gabriel and I weren't—we weren't doing anything wrong. I was giving him *energy,* Rob—like you do when you're healing. The crystal did something awful to him, and now he needs life energy every day. He's been in hell this last week. And if I don't help him, he'll hunt somebody down on the streets, and maybe kill them."

Rob blinked. He still looked like some tousled kid who'd been dealt a mortal blow, but now doubt was creeping into his expression. He repeated slowly, "The crystal?"

"I think that's what did it. He was never like this before. Now he needs the energy to stay alive. Rob, you *have* to believe me."

"But—why didn't you tell me?" Rob was shaking his head now, as if he had water in his ear. He looked dazed.

"I wanted to tell you, I did, but he wouldn't let me." And now I've betrayed his confidence, Kaitlyn thought. But there had been nothing else to do. She had to make Rob understand. "And no wonder he wouldn't, after the way you guys all talked about psychic vampires. He knew you'd be disgusted, and he couldn't stand that. So he kept it a secret."

Rob was wavering. Kait could see that he wanted to believe her, and that he was having trouble. Struggling for a leap of faith.

A voice behind Kaitlyn said, "It's all true."

CHAPTER 13

Kaitlyn whirled to see the most unlikely person imaginable. Lydia. Looking fragile and wistful, her blue-black hair a liquidy mass under the streetlight's soft illumination.

"You!" Kaitlyn said. "Where have you been? Why did you leave the room?"

Lydia hesitated, then shrugged. "I saw Gabriel leave. I wondered where he was going in the middle of the night, so I followed him to the wharf. And then I saw you come—"

"You spied on us!" It must have been Lydia she'd heard going out the door, Kaitlyn realized. Gabriel had already left.

"Yes," Lydia said, half miserably, half defiantly. "I spied on you. But it's a good thing I did!" She looked at Rob. "Kaitlyn kept saying she wanted to tell you. And she was only doing it because otherwise Gabriel would hurt people, maybe kill them. I don't understand exactly what it's all about, but I know she wasn't messing around with him."

Rob's whole body had relaxed—uncrumpling, Kaitlyn thought. And her own heartbeat was easing. Some of the nightmare feeling of unreality was fading away.

She looked at Rob and he looked at her. For a moment even communication in the web was unnecessary. Kait could see his love, and his longing.

Then, without quite knowing how she'd gotten there, she was in his arms.

"I'm sorry," Rob whispered. And then: *I'm so sorry, Kait. I thought . . . But I could understand why you might want to be with him. You're the only one he cares about. . . .*

It's my fault, Kaitlyn thought back, clinging to him as if she could make them into one body, fuse them together permanently. *I should have told you before, and I'm sorry. But—*

But we won't talk about it any more, Rob said, holding her more tightly. *We'll forget it ever happened.*

Yes. In that moment it seemed to Kaitlyn that she *could* forget. "But we have to make sure Gabriel's all right," she said aloud. "I left him by the wharf. . . ."

Slowly and reluctantly Rob let go of her. "We'll go now," he said. His face still bore the marks of recent emotion; there were shadows under his eyes and his mouth was not quite steady. But Kaitlyn could feel the quiet purpose in him. He wanted to help. "I'll explain to him that I didn't understand. All that talk about psychic vampires—I didn't know."

"I'll go, too," Lydia said. She had been watching them with open curiosity. For once, Kaitlyn didn't mind, and she gave Lydia a look of gratitude as they started walking. The girl might be nosy, she might be sneaky, and she might have a father who belonged in a horror movie—but she'd done Kaitlyn a good turn tonight. Kaitlyn wouldn't forget that.

Gabriel wasn't at the wharf.

"Hunting?" Rob said, looking at Kait with concern.

"I don't think so. He took enough from me—" Kaitlyn broke off as Rob's arm around her tightened. Rob was shaking his head.

"He can't do that anymore," he muttered. "It could hurt you. We'll have to figure something out. . . ." He shook his head again, preoccupied.

Kaitlyn said nothing. Her happiness was dimming a bit. She was all right with Rob again—but Gabriel was in bad trouble, worse even than Rob knew. She couldn't tell Rob what she'd seen in Gabriel's mind.

But she was dead certain Gabriel wasn't going to accept help from Rob—or from her, ever again.

The next morning Gabriel was back. Kaitlyn was surprised. She and Rob had returned to the hotel the night before to find

Anna and Lewis still sitting up. Rob had awakened them both when he found Kait, Gabriel, and Lydia missing.

At Rob's insistence Kait had explained as best she could about Gabriel's condition. Anna and Lewis had been shocked and sorry—and had promised to do anything they could to help.

But Gabriel didn't want help. The next morning he wouldn't talk to anyone and would barely glance at Kait. There was a strange, glittering look in his eyes, and all Kait could sense from him was determination.

He's hoping that the people in the white house can help him, she guessed. *And other than that, he doesn't care about anything*.

"We're in deep trouble financially," Anna was saying. "There's enough for gas and breakfast, maybe lunch, and then . . ."

"We'll just have to find the place today," Rob said, with typical Rob-ish optimism. But Kaitlyn knew what he left unspoken. They found the place today or they had to quit, resort to robbery, or use Lydia's credit cards and risk being traced.

"Let's go over what we're looking for," she said. What she really meant was that it was time to tell Lydia. *I think we can trust her,* she added, and Rob nodded. Lewis, of course, agreed wholeheartedly. Kaitlyn was getting a little worried about him—it was clear that he was more than infatuated with Lydia, but Lydia seemed to be the type to play the field.

Gabriel was the only one who might have objected, and he was sitting by the window, ignoring them all.

"A little peninsula thing with rocks on it," Lewis said promptly with a grin at Lydia.

"With *inuk shuk*," Anna said. "Lining both sides. And the shore behind it is rocky, and behind that is a bank with trees. Spruce and fir, I think. And maybe some scotch broom."

"And the ocean is cold and clean and the waves only come from the right," Kaitlyn put in.

"And it's called something like Griffin's Pit," Rob finished and smiled at her. There was still something of apology, of regret, about his slow smile this morning. Kait felt a twinge in her chest.

"Or Whiff and Spit or Wyvern's Bit," she said lightly, smiling back. Then she said, turning back toward Lydia, "And across from it is a cliff—although heaven knows how that can be, unless it's another little island. And on the cliff is a white house, and that's where we're going."

Lydia nodded. She wasn't stupid; she'd taken all of this in. Her eyes said "thank you" to Kait. "So where do we search today?"

"Flip a coin again," Lewis began, but Rob said, "Let Kaitlyn decide." When Kait looked at him, he added seriously, "Sometimes you have intuitions. And I trust . . . your instinct."

Kaitlyn's eyes stung. She understood; he trusted *her*.

"Let's go the other way today, west. The water didn't feel

quite right yesterday. Not . . . enclosed . . . enough." She herself wasn't sure what she meant by that, but everyone else nodded, accepting it.

They skipped breakfast and started driving northwest.

The weather was lovely for a change, and Kaitlyn found herself pathetically grateful for sunshine. Huge puffy white clouds drifted overhead. The coastal road quickly narrowed to one lane and trees crowded around them.

"It's the rain forest," Anna said. To Kaitlyn it was an almost frightening display of plant life. The road seemed to cut through a *solid* swath of vegetation. It was like a puzzle shaped like a wall on either side of the road—the pieces were different colors for different plants, but they interlocked solidly to fill all the space between the ground and the sky.

"We can't even *see* the ocean," Lewis said. "How're we supposed to tell if we're near the place?"

He was right. Kaitlyn groaned inwardly; maybe west had been a bad idea after all. Rob just said, "We'll have to go down side roads every so often and check. And we'll ask people again."

The problem was that there were few side roads and fewer people to ask. The road simply went on and on, winding through the forest, allowing them only occasional glimpses of the coast.

Kaitlyn tried not to feel discouraged, but as they drove farther and farther, her head began to buzz and the emptiness

in her middle to expand. She felt as if they'd been driving forever, through three states and a foreign country. And they were
never going to find the white house—in fact, the white house
probably didn't exist. . . .

"Hey," Lewis said. "Food."

It was another of the kiosks, like the ones that had sold
daffodils in Oregon. But this sign said BREAD DAYS: FRIDAY,
SATURDAY, SUNDAY.

"It's Sunday," Lewis said. "And I'm starving." They took
two loaves of multigrain bread—and paid for them, because
Rob insisted. Kaitlyn hadn't realized how hungry she was
until she took the first bite. The bread was dense and moist,
cool from the cold air outside. It had a nutty, nourishing
flavor, and Kait felt strength and optimism flowing back
through her.

"Let's stop *there*," she said as they passed a small building. A sign proclaimed it to be the SOOKE MUSEUM. She didn't
have much hope, first of all because the big museum in Victoria hadn't helped them, and second because this place looked
closed, but she was in the mood to try anything.

It *was* closed, but a woman finally answered Rob's persistent knocking. There were piles of books on the floor inside,
and a man with a pencil behind his ear, taking inventory.

"I'm sorry," the woman began, but Rob was already talking.

"We don't want to bother you, ma'am," he said, turning the
southern charm on full force. "We just have one question—

we're looking for a place that might be around here, and we thought you could maybe help us find it."

"What place?" the woman said with a harassed glance behind her, obviously impatient to get back to her work.

"Well, we don't exactly know the name. But it's like a little peninsula, and it's got these rock towers all up and down it."

Kaitlyn held up her drawing of the *inuk shuk*. Please, she was thinking. Oh, please . . .

The woman shook her head. Her look said she thought Kaitlyn and Rob were crazy. "No, I don't know where you'd find anything like that."

Kaitlyn's shoulders sagged. She and Rob glanced at each other in defeat. "Thank you," Rob said dully.

They both turned away and were actually leaving when the man inside the museum spoke up.

"Aren't there some of those things out at Whiffen Spit?"

Every cell in Kaitlyn's body turned into ice.

Whiffen Spit. Whiffen Spit, Whiffenspit, *Whiffenspit* . . . It was as if the whispering chorus of voices was once again in her mind.

Rob, fortunately, seemed able to move. He spun and got a foot in the door the woman was closing.

"What did you say?"

"Out at Whiffen Spit. I've got a map here somewhere. I don't know what the rocks are for, but they've been there as long as I can remember. . . ."

He went on talking, but Kait couldn't hear him over the roaring in her own ears. She wanted to scream, to run around crazily, to turn cartwheels. Anna and Lewis were clutching each other, laughing and gasping, trying to maintain their composure in front of the museum people. The whole web was vibrating with pure joy.

We found it! We found it! Kaitlyn told them. She had to tell someone.

Yeah, and it's Whiffenspit, Lewis said, running it together into one word as Kaitlyn had. *Not Griffin's Pit or Whippin' Bit—*

Rob was closest, Anna said. Whiff and Spit was actually pretty good.

Kaitlyn looked toward the car, where Lydia and Gabriel were standing as if declaring themselves both outsiders. Lydia was wide-eyed, watching with interest. Gabriel—

Gabriel, aren't you happy? Kaitlyn asked.

I'll be happy when I see it.

"Well, you're *going* to see it, ol' buddy," Rob said, turning and calling with a reckless disregard for the museum people. "I've got a map here!" He waved it triumphantly, his grin nearly splitting his face.

"Well, don't just stand around talking!" Kait said. "Let's go!"

They left the museum people staring after them.

"I can't believe it's real," Kaitlyn kept whispering as they drove.

"Look at this," Lewis was saying excitedly over her. "This map shows why there are only waves coming from the right. It's in the mouth of a little bay, and on the right side is the ocean. The other side is Sooke Basin, and there wouldn't be any waves there."

Rob turned on a narrow side road, nearly invisible between the trees. When he parked at the end, Kaitlyn was almost afraid to get out.

"Come on," Rob said, extending his hand. "We'll see it together."

Slowly, as if under a spell, Kaitlyn walked with him to the edge of the trees and looked down.

Then her throat swelled and she just stared.

It was the place. It looked exactly as it had in her dreams, a little spit of land pointing like a crooked finger into the water. It was lined with the same boulders, many with *inuk shuk* piled on top of them.

They walked down the rocky beach and onto Whiffen Spit.

Gravel crunched under Kaitlyn's feet. Gulls wheeled in the air, crying. It was all *so familiar. . . .*

"Don't," Rob whispered. "Oh, Kait." It was then that she realized she was crying.

"I'm just happy," she said. "Look." She pointed across the water. Far away, on a distant cliff covered with trees so green they were black, was a single white house.

"It's real," Rob said, and Kait knew he was feeling what she was. "It's really there."

Anna was kneeling by the edge of the spit, moving rocks. "Lewis, get that big one."

Lewis was showing Lydia around. "What are you doing?"

"Building an *inuk shuk*. I don't know why, but I think we should."

"Let's make it a good one," Rob said. He took hold of a large, flat rock, tried to lift it. "Kait—"

He didn't finish. Gabriel had taken hold of the other side.

The two of them looked at each other for a moment. Then Gabriel smiled, a thin smile touched with bitterness, but not with hatred.

Rob returned it with his own smile. Not as bright as usual, with something like apology behind it, and hope for the future.

Together, they lifted the stone and hauled it to Anna.

Everyone helped build the *inuk shuk*. It was a good big one, and sturdy. When they were done, Kait wiped wet dirt off her hands.

"Now it's time to find the white house," she said.

From the map they could see why there was land across the water. It was the other side of the mouth of Sooke Basin. They would have to drive back the way they'd come, and then all the way around the basin—or as far as the side roads would take them.

They drove for well over an hour, and then the road ran out.

"We'll have to walk from here," Rob said, looking into the dense mass of rain forest ahead.

"Let's just hope we don't get lost," Kait muttered.

It was cool and icy fresh in the forest. It smelled like Christmas trees and cedar and wetness. With every step Kaitlyn could hear her own feet squishing in the undergrowth and feel herself sinking—as if she were walking on cushions.

"It's sort of primeval, isn't it?" Lydia gasped, picking her way around a fallen log. "Makes you think of dinosaurs."

Kaitlyn knew what she meant. It was a place where people didn't belong, where the plant kingdom ruled. All around her things were growing on other things: ferns on trees, little seedlings on stumps, moss on everything.

"Did anybody ever see the movie *Babes in Toyland*?" Lewis asked in a muted voice. "Remember the Forest of No Return?"

They walked for several hours before they were certain they were lost.

"The problem is that we can't see the sun!" Rob said in exasperation. The sky had gone gray again, and between the clouds and the canopy of green above them, they had no way to get their bearings.

"The problem is that we shouldn't have just barged in here in the first place," Gabriel snapped back.

"How else are we supposed to get to the white house?"

"I don't know, but this is stupid."

Another argument, shaping up to be a classic. Kaitlyn turned away, to find Anna staring fixedly at something on a branch. A bird, Kaitlyn saw, blue with a high pointed crest.

"What is it?"

Anna answered without looking at her. "A Steller's jay."

"Oh. Is it rare?"

"No, but it's smart," Anna murmured. "Smart enough to recognize a clearing with a house. And it can get above the trees."

Understanding crashed in on Kaitlyn, and she had to suppress a whoop. She said in a choked voice, "You mean—"

"Yes. Hush." Anna went on staring at the bird. In the web, power thrummed around her, rose from her like waves of heat. The jay made a harsh noise like *shaaaack* and fluttered its wings.

Rob and Gabriel stopped arguing and turned to goggle.

"What's she *doing?*" Lydia hissed. Kait shushed her, but Anna answered.

"Seeing through its eyes," she murmured. "Giving it my vision—a white house." She continued to stare at the bird, her face rapt, her body swaying just slightly. Her fathomless owl's eyes were mystical, her long dark hair moved with her swaying.

She looks like a shaman, Kaitlyn thought. Some ancient priestess communing with nature, becoming part of it. Anna was the only one of them who really seemed to belong in the forest.

"It knows what to look for," Anna said at last. "Now—"

With a rapid-fire burst of noise like *shook, shook, shook,* the jay took off. It went straight up, into the canopy of branches— and disappeared.

"I know where it is," Anna said, her face still intent and trancelike. "Come on!"

They followed her, scrambling over mossy logs, splashing through shallow streams. It was rough going over steep ground, and Anna always seemed to be just on the verge of vanishing into the trees. They kept following until the light began to dim and Kaitlyn was ready to drop.

"We've got to take a rest," she gasped, stopping by a stream where huge fleshy yellow flowers grew.

"We can't stop now," Anna called back. "We're there."

Kaitlyn jumped up, feeling as if she could run a marathon. "Are you sure? Can you see it?"

"Come here," Anna said, standing with one hand on a moss-bedecked cedar. Kaitlyn looked over her shoulder.

"Oh . . ." she whispered.

The white house stood on a little knoll in a clearing. This close Kaitlyn could see it was not alone. There were several outbuildings around it, weathered and splintery. The house itself was bigger than Kaitlyn had thought.

"We made it," Rob whispered, behind her. Kaitlyn leaned against him, too full of emotion to speak, even in the web.

When they'd found Whiffen Spit, she'd felt like singing

and shouting. They had all been rowdy in celebration. But, here, shouting would have been wrong. This was a deeper happiness, mixed with something like reverence. For a long while they all just stood and looked at the house from their visions.

Then a harsh, drawn-out *shaaaak* broke into their reverie. The jay was fluttering on a branch, scolding them.

Anna laughed and looked at it, and it swooped away. "I told it thank you," she said. "And that it could leave. So now we'd better go forward, because we'll never find our way back."

Kaitlyn felt awkward and self-conscious as she walked out of the shelter of the trees, down toward the house. What if they don't want us here? she thought helplessly. What if it's all a mistake . . . ?

"Do you see any people?" Lewis whispered as they came abreast of the first outbuilding.

"No," Kaitlyn began, and then she did.

The building was a barn, and there was a woman inside. She was forking hay and dung, handling the big pitchfork very capably for someone as small and light as she was. When she saw Kaitlyn she stopped and looked without saying a word.

Kaitlyn stared at her, drymouthed. Then Rob spoke up.

"We're here," he said simply.

The woman was still looking at each of them. She was tiny and elegant, and Kait couldn't tell if she were Egyptian or Asian. Her eyes were tilted but blue, her skin was the color of coffee with cream. Her black hair was done in some complicated fashion, with silver ornaments.

Suddenly she smiled.

"Of course!" she said. "We've been expecting you. But I thought there were only five."

"We, uh, sort of picked up Lydia on the way," Rob said. "She's our friend, and we can vouch for her. But you do know us, ma'am?"

"Of course, of course!" She had an almost indefinable accent—not like the Canadians Kaitlyn had heard. "You're the children we've been calling to. And I'm Mereniang. Meren if that's too long. And you must come inside and meet the others."

Relief sifted through Kaitlyn. Everything was going to be all right. Their search was over.

"Yes, you must all come inside," Mereniang was saying, dusting off her hands. Then she looked at Gabriel. "Except him."

CHAPTER 14

"What?" Kaitlyn said, and Rob said, "What do you mean, except him?"

Mereniang turned. Her face was still pleasant, but Kait suddenly realized it was also remote. And her eyes . . .

Kaitlyn had seen eyes like that only once before, when the man with the caramel-colored skin had stopped her in the airport. When she'd looked into his eyes, she'd had the sense of centuries passing. Millennia. So many years that the very attempt to comprehend them sent her reeling.

There were ice ages in this woman's eyes, too.

Kaitlyn heard her own gasp. "Who *are* you?" she blurted before she could stop herself.

The enigmatic blue eyes dropped, veiled by heavy lashes. "I told you. Mereniang." Then the eyes lifted again, held steady. "One of the Fellowship," the woman said. "And we don't have many rules here, but this one can't be broken. No one may come into the house who has taken a human life."

She looked at Gabriel and added, "I'm sorry."

A wave of pure fury swept over Kait. She could feel herself flushing. But Rob spoke before she could, and he was as angry as she'd ever seen him.

"You can't do that!" he said. "Gabriel hasn't—what if it was self-defense?" he demanded incoherently.

"I'm sorry," Mereniang said again. "I can't change the rules. Aspect forbids it." She seemed regretful but composed, perfectly willing to stand here all evening and debate the issue. Relaxed but unbending, Kait thought dazedly. Absolutely unbending.

"Who's Aspect?" Lewis demanded.

"Not who. What. Aspect is our philosophy, and it doesn't make exceptions for accidental killing."

"But you can't just shut him out," Rob stormed. "You *can't.*"

"He'll be taken care of. There's a cabin beyond the gardens where he can stay. It's just that he can't enter the house."

The web was singing with outrage. Rob said flatly, "Then we can't enter it, either. We're not going without him!"

There was absolute conviction in his voice. And it rallied Kaitlyn out of her speechless daze. "He's right," she said. "We're not."

"He's one of us," Anna said.

"And it's a stupid rule!" Lewis added.

They were all standing shoulder to shoulder, united in their determination. All but Lydia, who stood aside looking uncertain—and Gabriel.

Gabriel had moved back, away from them. He was wearing the thin, faint smile he'd given Rob earlier.

"Go on," he said directly to Rob. "You have to."

"No, we don't." Rob was right in front of him now. Golden in the blue twilight, contrasting with Gabriel's pale face and dark hair. Sun and black hole, Kaitlyn thought. Eternal opposites. Only this time they were fighting *for* each other.

"Yes, you do," Gabriel said. "Go in there and find out what's going on. I'll wait. I don't care."

A lie Kait could feel clearly in the web. But no one mentioned it. Mereniang was still waiting with the patience of someone to whom minutes were nothing.

Slowly Rob let out his breath. "All right," he said at last. His voice was grim and the look he turned on Mereniang not friendly.

"Wait here," Mereniang told Gabriel. "Someone will come for you." She began walking toward the house.

Kaitlyn followed, but her legs felt heavy and she looked back twice. Gabriel looked almost small standing there by himself in the gathering darkness.

The white house was made of stone, and spacious inside, with a cathedral hush about it. The floor was stone, too. It might have been a temple.

But the furniture, what Kaitlyn could see of it, was simple. There were carved wooden benches and chairs that looked Colonial. She glimpsed a loom in one of the many recessed chambers.

"How old is this place?" she asked Mereniang.

"Old. And it's built on the remnants of an older house. But we'll talk about that later. Right now you're all tired and hungry—come in here and I'll bring you something to eat."

She ushered them into a room with an enormous fireplace and a long cedar table. Kaitlyn sat on a bench, feeling flustered, resentful, and *wrong*.

She went on feeling it as Mereniang returned, balancing a heavy wooden tray. A young girl was behind her, also carrying a tray.

"Tamsin," Mereniang introduced her. The girl was very pretty, with clusters of curly yellow hair and the profile of a Grecian maiden. Like Mereniang and the man at the airport, she seemed to have the characteristics of several different races, harmoniously blended.

But they're not what I expected, Kaitlyn told Rob wretchedly.

It wasn't that they weren't magical enough. They were almost *too* magical, despite their simple furniture and ordinary ways. There was something alien at the core of them, something disturbing about the way they stood and watched. Even the young girl, Tamsin, seemed older than the giant trees outside.

The food was good, though. Bread like the loaves they'd bought at the kiosk, fresh and nutty. Some soft, pale yellow cheese. A salad that seemed to be made of more wild plants than lettuce—flowers and what looked like weeds. But delicious. Some flat purply-brown things that looked like fruit roll-ups.

"They *are* fruit roll-ups," Anna said when Lewis asked. "They're made of salal berries and salmonberries."

There was no meat, not even fish.

"If you're finished, you can come meet the others," Mereniang said.

Kaitlyn bridled slightly. "What about Gabriel?"

"I've had someone take food to him."

"No, I mean, doesn't *he* get to meet the others? Or do you have a rule against that, too?"

Mereniang sighed. She clasped her small, square-fingered hands together. Then she put them on her hips.

"I'll do what I can," she said. "Tamsin, take them out to the rose garden. It's the only place warm enough. I'll be along."

The rose garden's warm? Lewis asked as they followed Tamsin outside.

Strangely enough, it was. There were roses blooming, too, all colors, crimson and golden-orange and blush pink. The light and warmth seemed to come from the fountain in the center of the walled garden.

No, not the fountain, Kaitlyn thought. The crystal in

the fountain. When she'd first seen it in a picture, she hadn't known what it was; she'd wondered if it was an ice sculpture or a column.

It wasn't like Mr. Z's crystal. That monstrosity had been covered with obscene growths, smaller crystals that sprouted like parasites from the main body. This crystal was clean and pure, all straight lines and perfect facets.

And it was glowing gently. Pulsing with a soft, milky light that warmed the air around it.

"Energy," Rob said, holding a hand up to feel it. "It's got a bioenergetic field."

Kaitlyn felt a ripple in the web and was turning even as Gabriel said, "Beats a campfire."

"You're here!" Rob said. They all gathered around him happily. Even Lydia was smiling.

At the same moment Mereniang came through the other entrance in the wall with a group of people.

"This is Timon," she said. The man who stepped forward actually looked old. He was tall but frail and white-haired. His lined face was gentle, the skin almost transparent.

Is he the leader? Kaitlyn asked silently.

"I am a poet and historian," Timon said. "But as the oldest member of the colony, I am sometimes forced to make decisions." He gave a gently ironic smile.

Kaitlyn stared at him, her heartbeat quickening. Had he *heard* that?

"And this is LeShan."

"We've already met," Gabriel said and showed his teeth.

It was the caramel-skinned man from the airport. His hair was a pale shimmery brown, like silver birch. His eyes were slanting and very dark, and they flashed at Gabriel dangerously.

"I remember," he said. "The last time I saw you, you had a knife at my throat."

"And you were on top of Kaitlyn," Gabriel said, causing some consternation among the rest of the Fellowship.

"I was trying to warn you!" LeShan snapped, moving forward.

Mereniang was frowning. "LeShan," she said. LeShan went on glaring. "LeShan, Aspect!"

LeShan subsided, stepping back.

If Aspect was a nonviolent philosophy, Kait had the feeling that LeShan had a little trouble with it. She remembered that he'd had a temper.

"Now," Timon said. "Sit down if you'd like. We'll try to answer your questions."

Kaitlyn sat on one of the cool stone benches that lined the wall. She had so many questions she didn't know which to ask first. In the silence she could hear the singing of frogs and the gentle trickle of water in the fountain. The air was heady with the scent of roses. The pale, milky light of the crystal gave a gentle radiance to Timon's thin hair and Mereniang's lovely face.

No one else was speaking. Lewis nudged her. *Go on.*

"Who are you people?" Kait asked finally.

Timon smiled. "The last survivors of an ancient race. The people of the crystal."

"That's what I heard," Lydia said. "I've heard people use that name, but I don't know what it *means.*"

"Our civilization used crystals for generating and focusing energy. Not just any crystals—they had to be perfectly pure and faceted in a certain way. We called them great crystals or firestones. They were used as power stations; we extracted energy from them the way you extract the energy of heat from coal."

"Is that possible?" Rob said.

"For us it was. But we were a nation of psychics; our society was based on psychic power." Timon nodded toward the crystal in the fountain. "*That* is the last perfect crystal, and we use it to generate the energy to sustain this place. Without it, we would be helpless. You see, the crystals do more than just supply technical power. They sustain *us.* In the old country they could rejuvenate us; here they merely stop the ravages of time."

Is that why so many of them have young faces and old eyes? Kaitlyn wondered. But Lewis was speaking up.

"There's nothing like that in history books," he said. "Nothing about a country that used crystals for power."

"I'm afraid it was before what you consider history," Timon

said. "I promise you, the civilization did exist. Plato spoke of it, although he was only repeating stories *he'd* heard. A land where the fairest and noblest race of people lived. Their country was formed of alternating rings of land and water, and their city was surrounded by three walls. They dug up a metal called *orichalcum,* which was as precious as gold and shone with a red light, and they used it to decorate the inner wall."

Kaitlyn was gasping. For as Timon spoke, she *saw* what he described. Images were flooding into her mind, as they had when Joyce had pressed a tiny shard of crystal to her third eye. She saw a city with three circular walls, one of brass, one of tin, and one which glowed red-gold. The city itself was barbaric in its splendor—buildings were coated with silver, their pinnacles with gold.

"They had everything," Timon said in his gentle voice. "Plants of every type; herb, root, and leaf. Hot springs and mineral baths. Excellent soil for growing things. Aqueducts, gardens, temples, docks, libraries, places of learning."

Kaitlyn saw it all. Groves of beautiful trees intermingled with the beautiful buildings. And people living among them without racial strife, in harmony.

"But what *happened?*" she said. "Where did it all go?"

LeShan answered. "They lost respect for the earth. They took and took, without giving anything back."

"They destroyed the environment?" Anna asked.

"It wasn't quite as simple as that," Timon said softly. "In

the final days there was a rift between the people who used their powers for good and those who had chosen the service of evil. You see, the crystals could just as easily work evil as good, they could be turned to torture and destruction. A number of people joined the Dark Lodge and began to use them this way."

"And meanwhile the 'good' psychic masters were demanding too much of their own crystals," LeShan put in. "They were greedy. When the energy broadcast from the crystals was tuned too high, it caused an artificial imbalance. It caused earthquakes first, then floods."

"And so the land was destroyed," Timon said sadly. "Most of the people died with it. But a few clairvoyants escaped—they'd been able to predict what was going to happen. Some of them went to Egypt, some to Peru. And some"—he lifted his head and looked at Kait's group—"to Northern America."

Kaitlyn narrowed her eyes. There had been no pictures in her head to accompany Timon's last words. "This—destruction," she said. "It wouldn't have involved a continent sinking or anything, would it? Like a lost continent?"

Timon just smiled. "Ours is certainly a lost race," he said, then went on without answering the question. "This little enclave is all that remains of our people. We came here a long time ago, with the hope of living simply, in peace. We don't bother the outside world, and most of the time it doesn't bother us."

Kaitlyn wanted to pursue her question, but Rob was asking another one. "But, you know, Mr. Zetes—the man we ran
away from—he has a crystal, too."

Members of the Fellowship were nodding grimly. "We're
the only pure survivors," Mereniang said. "But others escaped
and intermarried with the natives of their new lands. Your Mr.
Zetes is a descendent of one of those people. He must have
inherited that crystal—or possibly unearthed it after it had
been hidden for centuries."

"It *looks* different from yours," Rob said. "It's all covered
with things like spikes."

"It's evil," Mereniang said simply, her ageless blue eyes
clear and sad.

"Well, it did something to Gabriel," Rob said. In the web
Kaitlyn could feel Gabriel tense in anticipation. Although he
was keeping himself under tight control, she could tell he was
both hopeful and resentful. And that he was beginning to suf-
fer as he did every night—he needed energy, soon.

"Mr. Z hooked Gabriel up to it," Rob was going on. "Like
you said, for torture. But afterward—well, it had permanent
effects."

Mereniang looked at Gabriel, then moved to look at him
more closely. She put a hand on his forehead, over his third
eye. Gabriel flinched but didn't step back.

"Now, just let me . . ." Mereniang's sentence trailed off. Her
eyes were focused on something invisible, her whole attitude one

of listening. Kaitlyn had seen Rob look like that when he was healing.

"I see." Mereniang's face had become very serious. She took her hand away. "The crystal stepped up your metabolism. You burn your own energy now so quickly that you need an outside supply."

The words were dispassionate, but Kait was certain she could detect something less impartial in those ageless blue eyes. A certain fastidious distaste.

Oh, God, no, Kait thought. If Gabriel senses that . . .

"There's one thing that might help," Mereniang said. "Put your hands on the crystal."

Gabriel looked at her sharply. Then, slowly, he turned to the crystal in the center of the garden. His face seemed particularly pale in the cool white light as he approached it. After a brief hesitation, he touched one hand to a milky, pulsating facet.

"Both hands," Mereniang said.

Gabriel put his other hand on the crystal. As soon as it touched, his body jerked as if an electrical current had been sent through it. In the web Kaitlyn felt a flare of power.

She was on her feet in alarm. So was Rob, so were the others. But what she felt in the web now was energy flowing, flowing *into* Gabriel. It was cold, and it elicited none of the wild gratitude and joy she'd felt in Gabriel when he took energy from her—but it was feeding him nevertheless. Sustaining him.

She sat down again. Gabriel took his hands away. He stood with his head down for a moment, and Kaitlyn could see that he was breathing quickly. Then he turned.

"Am I cured?" he asked, looking straight at Mereniang.

"Oh—no." For the first time the dark woman looked uncomfortable. She couldn't seem to hold Gabriel's eyes. "I'm afraid there *is* no cure, except possibly the destruction of the crystal that made you this way. But any crystal which produces energy can help you—"

Rob interrupted, too overwrought to be polite. "Just a minute. You mean destroying Mr. Zetes's crystal will cure him?"

"Possibly."

"Well, then, what are we waiting for? Let's destroy it!"

Mereniang looked helplessly at Timon. All the members of the Fellowship were looking at one another in the same way.

"It isn't that easy," Timon told Rob gently. "To destroy that crystal, we would first have to destroy *this* crystal. The only way to shatter it would be to unite it with a shard from a crystal that is still pure. Still perfect."

"And this is the last perfect crystal," Mereniang reminded them.

"So—you can't help us," Rob said after a moment.

"Not in that, I'm afraid," Mereniang said quietly. Timon sighed.

Kait was looking at Gabriel. His shoulders had sagged abruptly, as if taking on a heavy weight. His head was slightly

459

bent. In the web all she could feel were the walls he was doggedly building brick by brick. She could only guess what he must be feeling.

She knew what her other mind-mates were feeling, though—alarm. The Fellowship couldn't cure Gabriel's psychic vampirism. Well, then, what about their other problem?

"There's something else we wanted to ask you about," Lewis said nervously. "See, when we were trying to figure out what Mr. Z was up to—well, it's a long story, but we ended up with this telepathic link. All of us, you know. And we can't get rid of it."

"Telepathy is one of the gifts of the old race," Timon said. His old eyes rested on Kait briefly, and he smiled. "The ability to communicate mind to mind is a wonderful thing."

"But we can't *stop*," Lewis said. "Gabriel got us linked, and now we can't get unlinked."

Timon looked at Gabriel. So did Mereniang and several of the others, as if to say, "You again?" Kaitlyn had the distinct impression that they thought he was a troublemaker. She sensed a flash of anger from Gabriel, quickly stifled.

"Yes, well, I'm afraid there's not much we can do about that, either," Mereniang said. "We can study it, of course, but a five-way link is a stable pattern. Usually it can only be broken by—"

"The death of one of the members," Kaitlyn and Anna said in chorus. They looked at each other in despair.

"Or distance," Timon said. "If you were to put physical distance between the members—that wouldn't break the link, of course, but you wouldn't feel it as much."

Rob was rumpling his already tousled hair. "But, look, the really important thing is Mr. Zetes. We understand if you can't fix Gabriel or break the link—but you *are* going to help us against Mr. Z, aren't you?"

There was one of those dreadful pauses which spoke louder than words.

"We are a peaceful race," Timon said at last, almost apologetically.

"But he's *afraid* of you. He thinks you're the only threat to him." Rob glanced for confirmation at Lydia, who nodded.

"We don't have the power of destruction," Mereniang said. LeShan was grinding one fist into his palm—Kaitlyn sensed that he, at least, wished they did.

Rob was still protesting. "You mean there's nothing you can do to stop him? Do you realize what he's *up* to?"

"We are not warriors," Timon said. "Only the youngest of us can even leave this place and travel in the outside world. The rest are too feeble—too old." He sighed again and rubbed his lined forehead.

"But can't you do something psychically?" Kaitlyn asked. "Mr. Z's been attacking us long distance."

"It would give away our location," LeShan said grimly, and Timon nodded.

"Your Mr. Zetes *does* have the power of destruction. If he discovers this place, he will attack us. We are only safe as long as it remains a secret."

Gabriel lifted his head and spoke for the first time in a long while. "You're awfully trusting of *us,* then."

Timon smiled faintly. "When you first came here, Mereniang looked into your hearts. None of you has come to betray us."

Kaitlyn had been listening with growing frustration. Suddenly she couldn't keep quiet any longer. She found herself standing, words bursting out of her throat.

"You can't help Gabriel and you can't help break the link and you won't help us fight Mr. Zetes—so what did you *bring* us here for?"

There was age-old sadness in Mereniang's eyes. Endless regret, tempered with the serenity of resignation.

"To give you a refuge," the dark woman said. "We want you to stay here. Forever."

CHAPTER 15

"**B**ut what about Gabriel?" Kaitlyn said. It was the first thing she could think of.

"He can stay, too."

"Without going in the *house?*"

Before Mereniang could answer, Rob spoke. "Look, *nobody's* deciding to stay right now. This is something we've got to think over—"

"It's the only place you'll be safe," Mereniang said. "We've had a lot of visitors over the years, but we've asked very few to stay with us. We do it when they have no choice—no other safety."

"Are there any here now?" Kait asked, looking at the Fellowship behind Mereniang.

"The last died a long time ago. But he lived longer than he would have in the outside world—and so will you. You are part of our race, and the crystal will help sustain you."

Lewis was twisting his baseball cap. "What do you mean, 'part of your race'?"

Timon spread his hands. "All psychics are descendants of the old race. Somewhere among your ancestors was one of the people of the crystal. The old blood has awakened in you." He looked at each of them earnestly. "My children, you *belong* here."

Kait didn't know what to say. She'd never felt so confused and disoriented in her life. The Fellowship was nothing that she had expected, and the discovery left her numb, in shock. Meanwhile, the web was a jumble of conflicting emotions that made it impossible for her to tell what any particular one of the others was thinking.

It was Rob who saved them, speaking steadily. "We're proud that you think we're good enough to join you, sir," he said to Timon. He'd regained his natural courtesy. "And we'd like to thank you. But this is something we're going to have to talk over a bit. You understand that." It was a statement, but Rob scanned the faces of the Fellowship questioningly.

Mereniang looked vaguely annoyed, but Timon said, "Of course. Of course. You're all tired, and you'll find it easier to think tomorrow. There's no hurry."

Kaitlyn still felt like arguing with somebody—but Timon was right. She was swaying on her feet. Tomorrow they'd all be fresh, and less emotional.

"We'll talk to them again about Mr. Zetes then," Rob

whispered to her under cover of the meeting breaking up.

Kaitlyn nodded and glanced around for Gabriel. He was talking to Lydia, but he stopped when he saw her looking.

"Are you going to be all right?" she asked him.

His eyes were opaque—as if they'd filmed over with gray spiderweb. "Sure," he said. "They've got a little cot for me in the toolshed."

"Oh, Gabriel . . . Maybe we should all stay there with you. Do you want me to ask Meren—"

"No," Gabriel said vehemently. Then he added more smoothly, "Don't worry about me. I'll be fine. Get your sleep."

Walls, walls, walls. Kaitlyn sighed.

Then, oddly, he said: "Good night, Kait."

Kaitlyn blinked. Had he ever said good night to her before? "I—good night, Gabriel."

Then Mereniang gathered them up and took them into the house, leaving Gabriel with a couple of the men.

It was as they were entering the house that Kaitlyn remembered a question she'd forgotten to ask. "Meren, do you know about the *inuk shuk* on Whiffen Spit?"

"Timon knows the most about them."

"Well, I was just wondering why they were there. And if they meant anything."

Timon was smiling reminiscently. "Ancient peoples started the tradition. They came down as traders from the north and left some of their stone language here. They called this a place of good magic, and they built their friendship signs on the spit that points to it."

Timon was still smiling, lost in thought. "That was a very long time ago," he said. "We've watched the world change all around us—but we have remained unchanged."

There was a note of pride in his voice, and a tinge of arrogance in Mereniang's face.

Kait looked at Timon. "Don't you think change is sometimes good?"

Timon came out of his reverie, looking startled. But no one answered her.

Kaitlyn's bedroom was very plain, with a bed built into the wall, a chair, and a washbasin under a mirror. It was the first time she'd slept alone—without the others—in a week. She didn't like it, but she was so tired she fell asleep quickly anyway.

Alone in the tool shed, Gabriel was awake.

So Mereniang had "looked into their hearts," had she? He smiled wryly. What the Fellowship didn't seem to realize was that hearts could change. *He* had changed since he'd come here.

It was a change that had started last night. Last night on the wharf when he'd discovered his feelings for Kaitlyn—and Kaitlyn had made her choice.

It wasn't her fault. Strangely enough, it wasn't Kessler's, either. They belonged together, both honest, both good.

But that didn't mean Gabriel had to stick around and watch it.

And now, tonight, his last hope had disappeared. The people of the crystal couldn't free him. They didn't even *want* to. And he'd seen the disgust and condemnation in their eyes.

Live here? In their outbuildings? Face that condemnation every day? And watch Kessler and Kait romancing each other?

Gabriel's lips drew back from his teeth in a fierce smile. He didn't think so.

I should be grateful to the Fellowship, he thought. They've shown me what I really am, simply in contrast to what *they* are. Back in the old days I'd have joined the Dark Lodge and hunted these gutless wimps out of existence.

It was a fairly simple equation. He didn't belong with the good guys, the white hats. Therefore, he must belong with the other side.

Not a new revelation, but a rediscovery. Kait had almost made him forget what he really was. She'd almost convinced him that he could live on the light side, that he wasn't a killer by nature. Well, tomorrow she'd see how wrong she'd been.

Gabriel stepped back a little to look at the body on the toolshed floor.

The man's name had been Theo. The Fellowship had sent him to spend the night out here—whether as companion or guard Gabriel didn't know. Now he was in a coma. Not quite dead, but getting there.

Gabriel had mind-linked with him to take knowledge from his brain. Including the knowledge of a secret trail through the otherwise impassable forest.

The extra energy had been nice, too.

Now the only thing Gabriel was waiting for was Lydia. He'd whispered a few words to her in the rose garden, asking her to come tonight and meet him. He was fairly certain she'd show up.

And then Gabriel would ask her if she really wanted to spend the next seventy years with a commune of doddering old hippies. Or if life might not be better back in sunny California, where Gabriel had the feeling that Mr. Zetes was setting up a little Dark Lodge of his own.

Lydia was weak. He thought he could persuade her. And if he couldn't—well, she could join Theo on the floor. Lewis would be unhappy, but what did Lewis matter?

For just an instant an image flashed through his mind of what would happen if he *could* persuade her. What would happen here, to the Fellowship, once he gave Mr. Zetes the information needed to home in on the white house. It wouldn't be a pretty picture. And Kait would be in the middle of it. . . .

Gabriel shook the thought off and bared his teeth again.

He had to at least have the courage of his convictions. If he was going to be evil, he'd *be* evil, all the way. From now on there were no half measures.

And besides, Kessler would be here. He'd just have to take care of Kaitlyn himself.

A footstep sounded outside the shed. Gabriel turned to meet Lydia, smiling.

Someone was shouting.

Kaitlyn could hear it even in her sleep, as she slowly drifted toward consciousness. By the time she was fully awake, it was more than one person, and the web was singing with alarm.

She ran out, pulling on her clothes. Broadcasting *What's happening?* to anyone that could hear.

I don't know, Rob sent back. *Everyone's upset. Something's happened.* . . .

People were running in the hallways of the white house. Kaitlyn spotted Tamsin and swooped on her. "What's going *on?*"

"Your friends," Tamsin said. She had olive-dark eyes, contrasting strangely with her golden hair. "The boy outside and the small girl . . ."

"Gabriel and Lydia? *What?*"

"They're gone," Mereniang said, appearing from a recessed room. "And the man we had guarding Gabriel is nearly dead."

Kaitlyn's heart plummeted. Endlessly, it seemed. She couldn't move or breathe.

It couldn't be true. It *couldn't.* Gabriel wouldn't have done a thing like that. . . .

But then she remembered how he'd looked last night. His gray eyes so opaque, his walls so high. As if he'd lost all hope.

And she certainly couldn't sense him anywhere in the web. She could feel only Rob and Lewis and Anna, who were coming to join her now in the hallway.

Rob put an arm around her to support her. Kaitlyn needed it; she thought her knees might give out.

Lewis was looking wretched and unbelieving. "Lydia went, too?" he asked pathetically. Mereniang just nodded.

"But they can't have gone far," Kait whispered, finding her voice. "They can't get through the forest."

"The guard knew a path. Gabriel entered his mind. He knows what the guard knew." Mereniang spoke with very little emotion.

"It must have been Lydia," Rob exploded. "Gabriel wouldn't have done it on his own. Lydia must have talked him into it, somehow." Kaitlyn could feel his pain and Lewis's fighting each other, building exponentially, magnifying her own distress.

Mereniang shook her head once, decisively. "If anything, it was the other way around. I realized last night that Gabriel was dangerous; that was why I sent Theo to watch him. But I underestimated *how* dangerous he was."

Kaitlyn felt a wave of sickness. "I still can't believe it. It couldn't have been his fault—"

"And I still don't think it was Lydia's fault," Lewis began.

"It doesn't matter whose fault it is," Mereniang said sharply, interrupting both of them. "And there's no time to argue. We have to prepare for an attack."

Lewis looked confused and horrified. "You're going to attack—?"

"No! We're going to *be* attacked. As soon as those two communicate with your Mr. Zetes. They must have run away to join him."

This time the wave of sickness almost drowned Kaitlyn. She heard Anna whisper, "Oh, no . . ."

And she tried to convince herself that Gabriel wouldn't tell Mr. Zetes, that he'd just run away. But the violent beating of her own heart contradicted her.

"Mereniang! We need you in the garden!" The voice came from a doorway.

Mereniang turned. "I'm coming!" She looked back at Kaitlyn's group. "Stay inside. The worst of it will be out there." And then she was running.

Kaitlyn held on to Rob, her only anchor in a spinning world. *Do you think he'll do it?*

Rob's arms tightened around her. *I don't know.*

Rob, is it our fault?

The hardest question, the one she knew would haunt her dreams if she lived through today. She could feel Lewis's hurt despair. Before Rob could answer, the attack began.

A cold wind blew down the corridor. Not just cold air; a gale. It whipped Kaitlyn's hair against her cheeks and tore loose strands from Anna's braid. It cut through their clothing like a newly sharpened knife.

And with it came a rattling. The wooden bench against the wall began to tremble, at first with a fine vibration, then more and more violently. Kaitlyn could hear the banging of doors swinging on their hinges, and the crash of things falling off shelves and walls.

It was so sudden that for a moment all she could do was stand and cling to Rob. Her temperature seemed to have dropped by degrees. A violent shivering racked her body.

"Stay together," Rob shouted, reaching out for Anna and Lewis. They grabbed hold, all four of them clutching each other. It was like trying to stand in a blizzard.

There was a wild ringing in Kaitlyn's ears—like the sound she'd heard once in the van. The sound of a crystal glass being stroked, only this went on and on, and it was pitched at a frequency that hurt. That pierced like needles, making it almost impossible to think.

And the *smell*. The odor of rotting flesh, of raw sewage. The wind forced it into her nostrils.

"What are they trying to do? Stink us all out?" Lewis shouted.

"Meren said it would be worse outside!" Anna shouted back. It was no good using telepathy, the entire web was vibrating with that piercing note.

"And they said she was needed in the *garden!*" Rob shouted. "The garden—where the crystal is. Come on!"

"Come on *where?*" Lewis yelled.

"To the rose garden! Maybe we can do something to help!"

They stumbled and staggered getting out of the house. Outside, the wind was worse, and the sky was black with clouds. It didn't seem to be morning at all, but an eerie and unnatural twilight.

"Come on!" Rob kept shouting, and somehow they made it to the garden.

The smell was coming from here, and so was the ringing sound. The roses were tattered, their petals torn off by the wind. A few petals still whirled in the air.

"Oh, God—the crystal!" Anna shouted.

Most of the Fellowship seemed to be gathered around it, and many of them, including Timon and Mereniang, had their hands on it. The crystal itself was pulsating wildly, but not with the gentle milky light Kait had seen before. Every color of the rainbow seemed to be fighting and flashing in its depths. It was dazzling, almost impossible to look at.

But that wasn't what Anna had meant. It was something much worse. Superimposed on the rose garden crystal was another, a phantom crystal without any color. A monstrosity with growths sprouting from every facet.

The crystal from Mr. Z's basement, Kait thought dazedly. Or, rather, its astral image. And around that corrupted crystal were the astral images of the attackers, visible like ghosts among the bodies of the Fellowship.

The gray people, the ones she'd seen in the van. She just hadn't seen the crystal then. They were leaning around it, touching it with their hands and foreheads. Using its power—

—to do what? Kaitlyn thought suddenly. "What are they trying to do?" she shouted to Rob.

"They're trying to destroy our crystal," one of the Fellowship answered. A sturdy woman who was in the outer circle around the fountain. "They've set up a vibration to shatter it. They won't be able to do it, though, not while all our power is protecting it."

"Can we help?" Rob yelled.

The woman just shook her head, looking back at the crystal. But Rob and Kaitlyn both moved past her, struck by a common impulse to get as close as possible to what was happening. They squeezed through the crowd and ended up behind Timon and Mereniang.

Timon's frail body was shaking so hard that Kaitlyn felt a stab of fear. She was shaking herself—not with cold, now, but with the vibrations of the crystal. The ground, the fountain, everything was trembling, as if resonating to a single, terrible note.

"So much—evil. So much—"

It was a gasp, and Kaitlyn could barely hear it. But she saw Timon's lips moving and she caught the words. His lined face was white, his eyes wide and clouded.

"I didn't know," he gasped. "I didn't realize—and to do such things to *children* . . ."

Kaitlyn didn't understand. She looked at Mereniang and saw that the dark woman's face was also twisted with horror. Those blue eyes narrowed and streamed with tears.

Then Kait looked at the gray people.

They were more defined than she'd ever seen them before. It was almost as if they were actually materializing here, as if they might appear physically at any moment. She could see their bodies, their hands—and their faces.

One of them was familiar. Kaitlyn had seen that face before—or at least a picture of it. On a folder labeled SABRINA JESSICA GALLO.

But Mr. Zetes had told her they'd all gone insane. Every one of his first students, everyone in the pilot study.

Maybe he didn't mind them being insane. Maybe it was easier to control them that way. . . .

Kaitlyn could feel tears on her own cheeks. Timon was right. Mr. Zetes was absolutely evil.

And he seemed to be winning. The crystal in the fountain was vibrating ever more frenetically. The kaleidoscope of colors disappearing into the misty gray of the other crystal. She could actually see the corrupted crystal more clearly now.

"Timon, let go!" Mereniang was calling. "You're too old for this! The crystal should be sustaining you, not the other way around."

But Timon didn't seem to hear her. "So evil," he said again and again. "I didn't realize how evil. . . ."

"Rob, we've got to do something!" Kaitlyn shouted.

But it was Timon who answered, in a telepathic voice that cut through the ringing in the web. A voice so strong that Kaitlyn whirled to stare at him.

Yes! We must do something. We must let go of the crystal!

Mereniang was staring, too, her eyes and mouth open. "Timon, if we release it—"

Do it! the telepathic voice roared back. *Everyone, do it now!*

And with that, Timon stepped away, taking his hands off the crystal.

Kaitlyn's head was spinning. She watched as the other members of the Fellowship looked at each other wildly, in obvious distress. Then, suddenly, she saw another figure step back.

It was LeShan, his lynx eyes flashing, holding his empty hands in the air.

Another one of the Fellowship stepped away, and another. Finally only Mereniang was holding on.

Let go! Timon shouted.

The crystal was trembling visibly. The piercing note rang higher and higher in Kaitlyn's ears.

"Let go," Timon whispered, as if his strength had suddenly given out. "Someone—make her . . . She'll be destroyed. . . ."

Rob surged forward. He grabbed Mereniang around the waist and pulled. Her palms came away from the crystal, and they both fell to the ground.

The terrible ringing became a terrible crashing. The sound

of a million goblets falling to the floor. A sound that deafened Kaitlyn, echoing in every nerve.

The great crystal was shattering.

It was almost like an explosion, although the only thing flying outward was light. A burst of radiance that left Kaitlyn blind as well as deaf. Imprinted on her eyelids she had a picture of thousands of shards hanging in air.

She fell to her knees, arms wrapped around her head protectively.

When she opened her eyes, the world had changed. The wind was gone. So was the smell.

So were the crystals—both of them. The gray crystal had simply vanished, along with the gray people. The other one, the last perfect crystal in the world, was lying in splinters in the water of the fountain.

Dizzy and unbelieving, Kaitlyn looked around.

Timon was lying on the grass, one hand curled on his chest. His eyes were shut, his face waxen.

Rob was picking himself up from under Mereniang, who was crying.

"Why?" the dark woman demanded. It was what Kait wanted to know herself. "Why, why?"

Timon's eyelids fluttered.

"Take a shard and give it to the children," he whispered.

CHAPTER 16

Mereniang looked both bewildered and horrified. She didn't move. But LeShan took two quick steps and thrust a hand into the fountain.

"Here," he said, holding out one of the shards toward Rob.

Rob didn't glance up. He was kneeling by Timon, one hand on the old man's upper chest.

"Hang on," he said. Then he glanced up at Mereniang. "He's so weak! It's as if his life-force has disappeared. . . ."

"The crystal was sustaining him," Mereniang said. Her blue eyes, though still fixed on Timon, were dull. She had withdrawn into herself, arms wrapped around her body. "When it shattered, his life ended."

"He's not dead yet!" Rob said fiercely. He shut his eyes,

placing his free hand on Timon's forehead. Kaitlyn could sense the healing energy flowing from him.

"No," Timon whispered. "It's no use, and I need you to listen to me."

"Don't talk," Rob ordered, but Kait went to kneel by the old man. She needed to understand what was happening.

"Why did you do it?" she asked.

Timon's eyes opened. There was a strange serenity in their depths. He even managed something like a smile.

"You were right," he said faintly. "Change is good—or at least necessary. Take the shard."

LeShan was still holding out the crystal. Kaitlyn looked from him to Timon. Then she reached out her hand.

The shard was almost as thick as her wrist and a foot long. It was cold and heavy and the facets were very sharp. One sliced into her thumb when she tested the edge.

"Take it back with you, and do what needs to be done," Timon whispered. His voice was almost inaudible now. Rob was sweating, his hands trembling, but Timon seemed to be fading away.

"Some things are so evil they must be fought. . . ."

A shiver went through Timon's frame, and a strange sound came from his lungs. Death rattle, Kaitlyn thought, too numb to move. It was almost like hearing a soul leave a body.

Timon's eyes were wide, staring at the sky. But now they were unseeing.

Kaitlyn's throat felt tight and swollen. Her eyes filled, tears spilling over. All around her the members of the Fellowship were milling about, like a flock of birds thrown into confusion. They didn't seem to know what to do now that Timon was dead and the crystal shattered.

And Rob's chest was heaving. His hair was dark with sweat, his eyes dark with grief. A healer who had lost the battle.

Kaitlyn scooted over to him, glad to have some problem she could understand. She put her arms around him. She felt a ripple in the newly free web and saw Lewis and Anna come to kneel beside her.

They put their arms around both Kait and Rob. All of them holding on as they had in the blizzard. Clinging to one another because they were all they had.

"All right, you lot!" LeShan was shouting. "Timon's gone, but we're still alive. We're going to have to think for ourselves. And we don't have time to stand around!"

"We're going to have to leave, of course," LeShan said. He seemed to have taken charge while Mereniang was grieving. Kaitlyn was glad; LeShan might be aggressive and quick-tempered, but she found him much easier to understand than the rest of the Fellowship.

They were all standing in the central hallway of the white house. Around them the Fellowship was busying itself, packing and carrying, moving and loading. "You think Mr. Zetes will attack again," Rob said. It wasn't a question.

"Yes, that was just the beginning. He's removed our defenses—and that was probably all he *could* do at one go. Next time it'll be for the kill." A tall woman looked in from another hallway. "LeShan, are the children coming with us? I'm trying to arrange transportation."

LeShan looked at Kait and the others.

"Well?" he said.

No one spoke at first. Then Rob said, "Let me get this clear. Timon's idea was that we should go back down to Mr. Zetes, and use the shard of your crystal to destroy *his* crystal."

"It's the only way to do it," LeShan said. "But that doesn't mean you have to."

"Timon *died* so we could have a shard," Anna said. Her normally gentle face was severe.

"And I *still* don't understand," Kait burst out. "Why did everyone listen to him? You were dead-set against fighting before—what made you all change your minds?"

LeShan's lip curled. "I don't think they all *did* change their minds. They're just used to obeying Timon. He might not have considered himself the leader, but everyone let him do the thinking."

"And he changed his mind because of the attack?" Lewis said uncertainly.

"Because of Sabrina," Kaitlyn said. Everyone looked at her. "Didn't you *see?*" she asked.

Lewis blinked. "Who's Sabrina?"

"Sabrina Jessica Gallo. She was one of the gray people. I didn't realize it before because I couldn't see her face."

"Are you sure?" Rob asked.

"Positive. I saw her clearly this time. And I guess that means the other gray people are the other old students. They all looked young to me."

"That was what Timon sensed," LeShan said. His lips were still curled slightly, as if he had an unpleasant taste in his mouth. "We all sensed it, everyone who was touching the crystal. The attackers were *children*—none of them over twenty. And their minds were twisted . . . I can't explain it."

"They were insane," Kaitlyn told him rather calmly. "That's what Mr. Zetes said, that the crystal had driven them crazy. And that's why I never thought of him using them to attack us. I had the idea they were in institutions somewhere."

"Maybe Mr. Z got them out," Lewis said hollowly.

LeShan grimaced. "In any case, we could feel their agony— and their evil. None of us realized evil like that still existed in the world. I think *we* had the idea that it died when our country died."

"And you're not going to tell us what that country was, are you?" Kaitlyn asked. She'd been meaning to get the question in since yesterday.

LeShan seemed not to hear her. "If you four go back down to fight this man, it will be dangerous," he said. "I won't pretend otherwise. And you can't rely on any help from us. I've got to make sure all these people get settled somewhere—and by the time I'm free, it may be all over with you."

"Thanks," Rob said dryly.

"If I can help after that, I will. But it's your decision."

"We'd be safe if we went with you?" Kaitlyn asked. She felt almost wistful.

"Reasonably safe. Nobody can promise perfect safety."

Kaitlyn sighed. She looked at Rob, and at Lewis and Anna. They were all looking at one another, too.

Do we really have a choice? Rob asked.

The longer we wait, the stronger Mr. Z will get, Anna said. Her thought smoldered with conviction.

We might as well finish what we started, Lewis put in, sounding resigned. He'd bounced back remarkably quickly from his upset. With his natural resilience and optimism, he was even now hoping for the best in Lydia—Kait could tell.

Kaitlyn had a different reason for wanting to go back. Yes, she wanted to stop Mr. Zetes, but there was something more important.

Gabriel, she told the others.

There was an immediate swell of emotion. Some of it was anger, bewilderment, feelings of betrayal. But there was sympathy, too, and determination—and love.

You're right, Rob thought. *If he really is going to join Mr. Zetes—*

I'm afraid he is, Kaitlyn broke in. *I should have thought of it last night. Meren said that any crystal that produces energy could feed him. And Mr. Z's crystal certainly produces energy.*

You think that's why he left? Anna asked.

I don't know. I doubt that's all of it. But I think he'd rather get energy from a crystal than from people. And the more contact he has with that crystal—

"The worse he'll get," Rob said aloud. "The more like Sabrina and those other poor jerks."

"We've got to stop *that*," Lewis said, startled.

Rob looked at him, and then smiled. It was just the ghost of his normal grin, but it warmed Kaitlyn immeasurably.

"You're right," he said. "We've got to stop it."

"My parents may be able to help," Anna said. "I'm sure they've been trying."

LeShan said, "I'll arrange your transportation."

That was all he said, but his lynx eyes flashed at Kaitlyn. She had the impression that he was desperately proud of them.

"Wait, there's one more thing," she said anxiously. "I wanted to ask you before, but I never got the chance. There's this girl back in California. Mr. Zetes put her into a coma somehow—with drugs, we think. I told her brother that we'd ask you for help, but . . ."

Her voice trailed off. She could feel Rob's concern regarding Marisol, and his chagrin over forgetting—but LeShan's face was impassive.

Of course they won't be able to help, she thought. *They're not doctors. I was stupid for even asking...*

She didn't want to imagine Marisol's brother's face when she told him.

LeShan was nonchalant. "The perfect crystals had the virtue of curing most diseases," he said. "Even a shard ought to do something to help your friend."

Kaitlyn's breath came out in a rush. She hadn't even realized she was holding it, but suddenly her heart was lighter.

LeShan was walking away, but he glanced back over his shoulder and grinned.

"So it's just us again," Lewis said. They were waiting for LeShan to bring them a guide through the forest. Kaitlyn was carrying her duffel bag, which held her clothes—all dirty by now—and her art kit. She had the crystal shard in her other hand.

"We're the only ones we have to rely on," Kaitlyn agreed.

Anna said, "That's all anybody ever has, really."

"Yeah, but all that driving, all that searching," Lewis said. "All for nothing."

Rob looked at him quickly. "It *wasn't* for nothing. We're stronger now. We know more. And we finally have a weapon."

"Right," Anna said. "We set out to find this place and we did. We wanted to find a way to stop Mr. Z and we have."

"Sure. It's all over but the screaming," Lewis said, but he smiled.

Kaitlyn looked back at the white house, now looted and empty. She was wondering if she *could* have stayed if things had been different. If Gabriel hadn't betrayed them, if the Fellowship were staying, could she have made her home here? Would it have been a place where she could have belonged?

"If we can destroy the crystal, we can cure Gabriel, too," Rob was saying.

Kaitlyn looked at him fondly. No, she thought. I don't belong with the Fellowship. I belong with Rob—and Lewis, and Anna, and Gabriel, too. Wherever they are, I'm home.

"Right," she said to Rob. "So let's go do it. The search is on again."

She looked down at the shard. As a ray of sun broke through the clouds, it flashed like diamond.

THE PASSION

For Pat McDonald, editor extraordinaire,
whose keen insight helped shape my visions, and whose boundless
patience allowed me to perfect them

CHAPTER 1

A dog barked, shattering the midnight silence. Gabriel glanced up briefly, his psychic senses alert. Then he went back to breaking into the house.

In a moment, the lock on the door gave way to his lock-pick. The door swung open.

Gabriel smiled.

There were four people awake in the house. One of them Kaitlyn. Beautiful Kaitlyn with the red-gold hair. A pity he might have to destroy her—but he was her enemy from now on. He couldn't afford weakness.

He was working for Mr. Zetes now. And Mr. Zetes needed something—a shard from the last perfect crystal in the world. Kaitlyn had it . . . Gabriel was going to take it.

As simple as that.

If anyone tried to stop him, he was going to have to hurt them. Even Kaitlyn.

For just an instant there was a tightening in his chest. Then his face hardened and he moved stealthily into the dark house.

"Give up, Kaitlyn."

Kaitlyn looked into Gabriel's dark gray eyes.

"How did you get *in* here?" she said.

Gabriel smiled silkily. "Breaking and entering is one of my new talents."

"This is Marisol's house," Rob said from behind him. "You can't just—"

"But I *have* just. Don't expect help; I've put everybody outside to sleep. I'm here, and I think you know why."

They all stared at him: Kaitlyn and Rob and Lewis and Anna. They were refugees, runaways from the Zetes Institute for Psychic Research, and Marisol's family had taken them in. Marisol herself was absent; once a research assistant at the Institute, she'd found out too much and ended up in a coma. But her family had been kind—and now Kaitlyn had brought more trouble on them.

It was past midnight. The four of them had been sitting up in the room Marisol's brother had assigned the girls, talking and trying to figure out what to do next. And then the door had opened to reveal Gabriel.

Kaitlyn, who was standing directly in front of the handsome mahogany desk by Marisol's bed, made her face utterly blank. She tried to make her mind blank, too.

Anna and Lewis, who were sitting on the bed, were looking just as blank, and Rob's mind was just one wash of golden light. Nothing for Gabriel to grab onto.

It didn't matter. He looked past Kaitlyn, at the desk, and his smile was dazzling and dangerous.

"Give up," he said again. "I want it, and I'm going to get it."

"We don't know what you're talking about," Rob said flatly, taking a step toward him.

Gabriel answered without turning to look at Rob. He was still smiling but his eyes were dark. "A shard of the last perfect crystal," he said. "Do you want to play hot and cold—or should I just take it?" He looked at the desk again.

"*If* we did have it, we wouldn't be giving it to you," Rob said. "We'd use it to destroy your boss—he is your boss now, isn't he?"

Gabriel's smile froze. His eyes narrowed slightly, and Kaitlyn could see darkness filling them. But his voice was calm and easygoing. "Sure, he's my boss. And you'd better stay away from him or you're going to get hurt."

Kaitlyn could feel a stinging behind her eyes. She didn't believe this was happening, she *didn't*. Gabriel was standing here like a stranger, warning them away from Mr. Zetes. From *Mr. Zetes,* the man who'd tried to make them into psychic weapons to sell to the highest bidder, who'd tried to kill them when they rebelled. Who'd hounded them all the way up to Canada when they ran away from him, and who was clearly still after them now that they'd returned to fight him. They'd hoped Marisol's house would be a safe place to hide from him—but they'd been wrong.

"How *can* you, Gabriel?" Anna said in her low, clear voice, and Kaitlyn knew she was feeling the same thing. Anna Eva Whiteraven's face—usually serene between its dark braids of hair—was now clouded. "How can you join him? After everything he's done—"

"—and everything he's going to do," Lewis put in. Lewis Chao was normally as cheerful as Anna was serene, but now his almond-shaped eyes were bleak.

"He's bad, Gabriel; he's bad, and you know it," Rob said, closing in from behind. Rob Kessler wasn't built for menace either, but just now with his tousled blond hair and blazing golden eyes he looked like an avenging angel.

"And he'll turn on *you* in the end," Kaitlyn said, adding her voice to the chorus against Gabriel. In her mind she added herself to the group: Kaitlyn Fairchild, not as gentle as Anna and Lewis or as good as Rob, a girl with fiery hair and a temper. And eyes that people called witchy, smoky blue with darker blue rings in them. Right now, Kait fixed these eyes mercilessly on Gabriel, staring him down.

Gabriel Wolfe threw back his head and laughed.

As always, it almost took Kaitlyn's breath away. Gabriel was so handsome it was frightening. His pale skin made his dark hair look even darker, like the silky pelt of some animal—

like his namesake. A wolf, a predator in his bones, who enjoyed stalking and toying with his prey.

Of course he's bad, Gabriel said. Kaitlyn heard the words in her head, rather than with her ears, and the tone was amused and mocking. *I'm bad, too—or hadn't you noticed?*

Tiny needles of pain jabbed into Kaitlyn's temples.

She managed not to gasp, but she could sense Anna's alarm, and Lewis's and Rob's.

Gabriel had gotten stronger.

Kaitlyn could feel it through the psychic web that connected the five of them, the web that Gabriel had created. The web that would link them until one of the five died. They were all psychics: Rob was a healer and Kaitlyn saw the future, Lewis was psychokinetic and Anna controlled animals—but Gabriel was a telepath. He fused minds. He'd fused *their* minds, the five of them, by accident, and now they were like the arms of a starfish: separate but part of one being.

Gabriel's power had always been strongest, but now it rocked Kaitlyn with its force. His mental voice had been amused, yes—but it had also been like a white-hot poker burning the words directly into her brain.

By contrast, Lewis's thought sounded weak and distant. *I'm scared.*

Kaitlyn glanced at him quickly and saw that he hadn't meant it to be heard. That was the problem with telepathy, with the web that connected them, held them close. It held them *too* close, sometimes, throwing their private thoughts into the public forum. Leaving them totally exposed, naked to one another. Unable to hide anything.

Realization flashed through her, and she looked back at Gabriel.

"That's it, isn't it?" she said. "Why you left. It was too much for you, being so close. It was too intimate—"

"No."

"Gabriel, we all feel the same way," Anna said, picking up on Kaitlyn's theme. "We'd all like some privacy. But we're your friends—"

Gabriel's smile was savage. "I don't need friends."

"Well, you've got them, boy," Rob said softly. He moved in another step and his hand closed on Gabriel's shoulder. With a gesture that made it look easy, he turned Gabriel around.

Kaitlyn could feel Gabriel's startled outrage in the web. Rob ignored it, speaking quietly and seriously, looking Gabriel straight in the face. His anger was gone, and so was the usual defensiveness that flared between him and Gabriel, the male rivalry, the jostling for position. Rob was struggling with his pride, his internal honesty conquering it. Forcing himself to be vulnerable with Gabriel.

"We're more than friends," he said. "We're part of each other, all of us. You made us that way. You linked us together to save our lives—and now you're telling us you've defected to the bad guys? That you're our enemy?" He shook his head. "I don't believe it."

"That's because you're an idealistic idiot," Gabriel hissed, his voice as soft as Rob's, but feral and menacing. He didn't try to move out of Rob's grip. "Believe it, country boy—because if you mess with me, you're going to be sorry."

Rob shook his head. He had a look in his eyes that Kaitlyn knew well, and his jaw was at his most stubborn. "You can't fool me, Gabriel. You act like a dumb tough guy but you're not, you're smart. One of the smartest people I've ever met. You could make something of yourself—"

"I *am*—" Gabriel began, but Rob went on, gentle and relentless.

"You act like you don't care about people, but that's not true either. You saved us all from the crystal when Joyce and Mr. Z were trying to kill us with it. You saved us again when they trapped us at the Institute. You helped Kaitlyn save us from that psychic attack in the van."

And then Rob did something that astonished Kaitlyn. He actually *shook* Gabriel. Once again, startled outrage washed through the web, but before Gabriel could say anything Rob was speaking again, fierce and insistent.

"I don't know what you're trying to prove, but it's no good. *It's no good.* You care about us; you can't change that. Why don't you just give in and admit it, Gabriel? Why don't you stop this nonsense right now?"

Kaitlyn's breath was caught in her throat. She didn't *dare* breathe, didn't dare move. Rob was walking on a tightrope above razors and knives. He was insane—but it was working.

Gabriel's body had relaxed slightly, some of the predator-tension draining out of it. And though Kaitlyn couldn't see his eyes, she guessed that they were lightening, a warm gray instead of cold. His presence in the web was warming, too; Kaitlyn no longer got images of stalactites and glaciers. Under the burning heat of Rob's golden eyes, Gabriel's icebergs were cracking up.

"We all care about you," Rob said, never letting up the intensity. "And your place is right here. Come back to us and help us get rid of Mr. Z, okay? Okay, Gabriel?"

And then he made his mistake.

He'd been speaking vehemently, throwing his words into Gabriel's face, and Gabriel had been listening as if he couldn't help it. Almost as if he were hypnotized. But now Rob switched to nonverbal communication to punch his message directly into Gabriel's mind. Kaitlyn knew why he did it—telepathy was forceful and intimate. Too intimate. Her cry of warning was lost as Gabriel snapped.

Come back, Rob was saying. *Come back, Gabriel—okay?*

Kaitlyn felt fury building in Gabriel like a tsunami. *Rob*, she thought. *Rob, don't—*

Leave me ALONE!

The mental shout was like a physical blow. Literally. It

threw Rob backward, body spasming in total reflex as the signals from his own brain scrambled. He fell with every muscle contracted, his face twisted, his fingers clawed. Kaitlyn felt a spasm of sheer terror on his behalf. She wanted to run to him, but she couldn't. Gabriel was between them and her legs wouldn't move. Anna and Lewis stood frozen as well.

I don't need any of you, Gabriel said, still with enough force to numb Kaitlyn's mind. *You're wrong about me. I'm no part of you. You can't even imagine what I am, what I've become.*

"I can," Kaitlyn gasped. She was thinking of what Mr. Zetes's crystal had done to him, what it had made him. A psychic vampire, who needed to drain life energy from others to live himself. She could feel the ghost of teeth in her spine, just at the base of the neck. As if a single sharp tooth were piercing the skin there.

The memory brought a certain fear, but no revulsion. And anxious as she was to get to Rob and help him, she wanted to help Gabriel, too.

"It's not your fault, Gabriel," she whispered. "You think you're evil because of what you can do with your mind, because of what the crystal made you do. But it's not your fault. You didn't ask for it. And you're not evil."

"That's where you're wrong." Gabriel had turned to face her, and she saw that he was calmer. But the ice was back in his eyes, the cold, lucid madness that was more terrifying than any rage. When he smiled, goose-flesh broke out on Kait's arms.

"I've known what I am for a long time," he said conversationally. "The crystal didn't change me, it just enhanced my abilities. And it made me accept myself." His smile widened, and Kaitlyn had a primal instinct to run. "If you've got the darkness in your nature, you might as well enjoy it. Might as well go where you belong."

"To Mr. Zetes," Anna whispered, her lovely, high-cheekboned face drawn with disgust.

Gabriel shrugged. "He has a vision. He thinks psychics like me have a place in the world—on top. I'm superior to the rest of the lousy race, I'm smarter, stronger, *better*. I deserve to *rule*. And I'm not going to let any of you stop me."

Kaitlyn shook her head, struggling with words. "Gabriel— I don't believe that. You're *not*—"

"I *am*. And if you try to keep me from getting that shard, I'm going to prove it to you."

He was looking at the desk again. Kaitlyn drew herself up a little. Rob was still lying helpless on the floor, Lewis and Anna seemed frozen. There was nobody but her to stop him.

"You can't have it," she said.

"Get out of the way."

"I said, you can't have it." To her amazement, her voice was fairly steady.

He moved closer to her, his gray eyes filling her field of vision, filling the world. *Don't make me do it, Kaitlyn. I'm not your friend anymore. I'm your hunter. Go home and stay away from Mr. Z and you won't get hurt.*

Kaitlyn looked into his handsome pale face. *If you want the shard, you'll have to take it by force.*

"Whatever you say," Gabriel murmured. His eyes were the color of a spiderweb. Kaitlyn felt the touch of his mind like a searing caress and then the world exploded in pain.

CHAPTER 2

"Kaitlyn!"

Dimly Kait heard Rob's shout, felt him struggling to get to his feet. Then, when he couldn't, beginning to crawl. She could barely sense him for the overwhelming pain in her head.

Anna and Lewis were closer and she could hear them shouting, too.

"Let go of her!"

"What are you doing to her?"

Gabriel brushed them away and kept on doing it. The pain increased—like fire. Kaitlyn had only one memory that would compare to it: being connected to the crystal. The big crystal, the impure one, the one Mr. Zetes used for enhancing psychic powers—and for torture.

Waves of red-streaked agony that peaked very quickly and died away just as another wave was coming. Kaitlyn's own muscle tension held her rigid, standing motionless under it. Kept her from getting away, kept her from screaming. It wasn't heroism. She didn't have the air.

Stop it, damn you! Stop it!

Rob had gotten to her, somehow. His hands were on her, and golden healing energy flooded up to combat the red-streaked anguish. His powers were protecting her.

"Leave her alone," Rob said hoarsely, and pulled Kaitlyn away from Gabriel, toward the bed.

Gabriel regarded the cleared path in front of him thoughtfully. "That was all I wanted," he murmured.

He opened the middle drawer of the mahogany desk and took out the crystal shard.

Kaitlyn was gasping for breath. Rob put her down on the bed, one arm still around her protectively. Kait could sense his trembling anger, and the shocked fury of Lewis and Anna—and she was surprised to find that she herself felt very little resentment toward Gabriel. There had been a look in his eyes just before he blasted her—as if he'd had to turn himself off to do it. To squelch his own emotions.

Now he turned to face them, and the shard flashed in the bright light of Marisol's halogen lamp. It was the size and shape of a small unicorn's horn, a foot long, multifaceted. It glittered not like crystal, but like diamond.

"It's not yours," Anna said in a low voice. She and Lewis had flanked Rob and Kaitlyn, the four of them presenting a united front to Gabriel. "The Fellowship gave it to Kait."

"The Fellowship," Gabriel sneered. "Those gutless do-gooders. If I'd lived in the old days, I'd have joined a Dark Lodge and hunted them out of existence."

Not gutless, Kaitlyn thought. Gabriel's words brought the faces of the Fellowship to her mind: Timon, frail but wise; Mereniang, cool and discerning; LeShan, lynx-eyed and impatient. They were the last survivors of an ancient race, the race that had used the crystals. They didn't interfere with the affairs of humanity—but they'd made an exception for Kaitlyn's group. They'd given up their own power to give Kaitlyn a weapon against Mr. Zetes.

"And now Mr. Z is forming a Dark Lodge of his own," she said, looking at Gabriel steadily.

"You could call it that. A psychic strike team. And *I'm* going to lead it," Gabriel said negligently, stroking the crystal. That was dangerous, as Kait could have told him. One of the facets cut his finger and he frowned at the drop of blood absently. He seemed to feel no danger from the others; he didn't even bother to look at them.

"This would have been useless to you anyway," he said. "You were planning to take it to the crystal, right? Put them together and set up a resonance that would shatter both."

Kaitlyn didn't know *what* the scientific theory was. LeShan had told them that this shard would destroy Mr. Z's crystal, that was all. She watched a drop of Gabriel's blood fall onto the hardwood floor.

"But to do that, you'd have to get to the crystal," Gabriel continued. "And you can't. The old man has it under a combination lock—and PK won't help with that, will it, Lewis? Eight random numbers to guess?"

He sounded almost jolly—and he was right, Kaitlyn knew. Lewis could move objects with his mind using psychokinesis, but that wouldn't help him figure out a combination.

Lewis had flushed slightly, but he didn't answer Gabriel's question. Instead he said, "Is Lydia still in this with you?"

"Your little sweetheart?" Gabriel grinned nastily. "Better give up on her, too. She's back under her father's thumb. She never liked you, anyway."

Pity, Kaitlyn thought. Lydia Zetes was a spy and a traitor, sent by her father to snoop on them as they traveled to Canada to find the Fellowship—but Kaitlyn felt vaguely sorry for her. Being under Mr. Z's thumb was a fate she wouldn't wish on anybody.

"It's like I told Kaitlyn," Gabriel said calmly. "You might as well all go home. You can't get at the crystal. The police wouldn't believe you—the old man has them taken care of. He's taking care of the ones Anna's parents contacted, too, by the way. And the Fellowship can't even help themselves. So there's really no point in you staying. Why don't you go home before I have to hurt you again?"

Rob had been silent so far—too angry with Gabriel to find words. Now he found them, standing up to face Gabriel directly once again. Kaitlyn didn't need the web to sense his rage—it was written in every line of his body, in the burning of his golden eyes.

"You're a traitor," he told Gabriel simply. "And if you won't join us, we'll fight you. With everything we've got."

His voice was quiet, but it shook. Not just rage, Kaitlyn thought suddenly. Rob was *hurt*—he felt personally betrayed. He hadn't believed Gabriel would hurt Kait—and Gabriel had proved him wrong. It had become a battle between them, Rob and Gabriel, the two in the group who had always fought most fiercely together, felt the most antagonism for each other, taken the positions farthest apart.

And who knew how to push each other's buttons. Rob was going on, his voice not quiet now but rushed and reckless.

"You know what I think? I think Kait was wrong—it's not the web you can't stand. It's not the intimacy. It's the *freedom*. Having to make your own choices, be responsible for yourself. That's what you can't take. You'd rather be a slave to the crystal than deal with freedom."

Gabriel lowered the shard, his eyes darkening. Kaitlyn grabbed for Rob's arm, but he seemed oblivious to her.

"I'm right, aren't I?" Rob said, with a short, strange laugh, as if delighted to have hurt Gabriel. It was so vicious and contemptuous it didn't sound like Rob. "Mr. Z tells you what to do—and you *like* that. It's what you're used to, after all those years locked up in CHAD. Hell, you probably *miss* being in jail—"

Gabriel went white and hit him.

Not mentally—Kaitlyn had the impression that he was too angry for that. He hit with his fist, catching Rob square in the mouth. Rob's head jerked back and he went down.

With the fluid, easy movements of a predator, Gabriel reached for him again. Kaitlyn found herself on her feet and between them.

"No!" She fumbled for Gabriel, meaning to restrain him or at least hinder him—and somehow found herself grabbing the crystal. It was cold and hard. She held onto it and Gabriel, still trying to get to Rob, let go.

Lewis and Anna were around Gabriel now, seizing any part of him they could reach and clinging. Kaitlyn managed to detach herself from the group and back away, clutching the crystal to her chest. Gabriel didn't seem to care; his eyes were fixed on Rob.

Who was scrambling up, wiping blood from his mouth with the back of his hand. He looked savagely triumphant at having gotten Gabriel to lose control. Kaitlyn realized he wasn't thinking anymore, just feeling. He was lost in his hurt and betrayal and anger, lashing out in a way she'd never seen before.

God, we've changed, she thought, sick with dismay. We've all changed from being in such close contact with one another. Rob used to be so pure and now he's furious . . . just like a regular human being, her mind added, unasked.

And he's *wrong*—and I've got to stop this. Before the two of them actually kill each other.

"Come on," Rob was saying. "D'you have the guts to go one on one with me? No hocus-pocus, just our fists. You man enough for that, boy?"

Gabriel pulled off his jacket, despite the efforts of Anna and Lewis to keep him still. Strapped to his forearm was a knife in some kind of spring-loaded mechanism.

Oh, *great,* Kaitlyn thought. She held on to the crystal shard more tightly. She knew she should get it to safety—but where *was* safety? Gabriel could follow anywhere she went; could take the knowledge of where it was hidden out of her mind. And besides, she couldn't leave and let Gabriel and Rob fight.

She decided to gamble.

"Here's the crystal, Gabriel," she said. "I've got it—and the only way you're going to get it is the way you did before." *But I'm hoping you won't,* she added mentally. *You said yourself that it's not going to do us any good. We can't get to Mr. Z's crystal—so what difference does it make? Why not just go back and tell him you couldn't find it?*

She was trying to give him a way out. If he didn't *really* want to hurt them . . .

Gabriel hesitated. His mouth was tight; his eyes hard. But she could see uncertainty in his face. He stood very still a moment, then, abruptly, he started toward her.

Kaitlyn's mind blanked out in fear and surprise. Behind her, the door opened.

"Hey, are you guys still up—?" The sleepy voice broke off.

It was Tony, Marisol's brother, wearing cutoff shorts as pajama bottoms. He was rubbing his eyes and frowning. Clearly whatever Gabriel had done to keep the Diaz family asleep had worn off.

"Who's that?" Tony demanded, staring at Gabriel. Then he blinked and the frown disappeared.

"Hey, it's you. I remember you from last time. Come back to get the *brujo,* huh?"

He seemed happier to see Gabriel than he had been to see the rest of them, Kait thought. Maybe because Gabriel was somebody he could relate to—another tough guy. Or maybe because he thought that of all of them, Gabriel was most likely to be able to get Mr. Zetes. Tony hated Mr. Z with a passion; called him "El Diablo" or "El Gato"—both names for the devil, and longed for him to be sent *abajo*—down below to hell—where he belonged.

The five who shared the web were all frozen by the presence of a stranger, like figures in a tableau. Tony went on talking cheerfully; he didn't seem to feel the tension in the room or see the blood on Rob's chin.

"I see you got the *cuchillo*—the magic knife for Marisol. I couldn't believe it when they told me. A real old-fashioned charm, right? After all those doctors said she'd never wake up— we'll show 'em!" He grinned, his usually sullen features almost glowing. He did everything but slap Gabriel on the back.

Kaitlyn looked at Gabriel sharply, saw what she'd suspected—

that he hadn't known the shard could cure Marisol. Maybe she should have told him, but she hadn't liked the idea of giving Mr. Z any further information. He'd find a way of using it against them somehow.

For now, though, it had given Gabriel pause. He seemed thrown off balance by Tony's gratitude and good humor. Embarrassed.

"Well, Gabriel certainly helped us to get the shard," Kait said—and that was true enough. If Gabriel hadn't defected, the Fellowship's crystal wouldn't have been reduced to shards in the first place. "And he would want Marisol to get well."

Rob was quietly wiping his bloody mouth again. He'd backed off when Tony came in, and Kaitlyn could feel through the web that he was calming down. Gabriel looked at him, then at Kaitlyn, and finally at Tony.

"We'll have a big party when all this is over," Tony said. "A real blowout. I've got some friends in a garage band. As soon as Marisol is better." He ran a hand through his curly mahogany hair.

Kaitlyn pressed the crystal to her chest and looked at Gabriel.

He held her gaze a minute with eyes as dark and unfathomable as storm clouds. For the first time that night she consciously noticed the scar on his forehead—a crescent-shaped mark left by his encounter with Mr. Z's crystal. Right now it seemed to stand out against the pale skin.

Then, looking suddenly tired, Gabriel shrugged. His eyelids drooped, hooding those depthless eyes.

"I've got to go," he said.

"You can stay," Tony offered immediately. "There's plenty of room."

"No, I can't. But I'll be back." He said the last to Kaitlyn and Rob, with heavy emphasis. Kait couldn't mistake his meaning. "I'll be back—soon."

He picked up his jacket and walked out the door. Kaitlyn felt her breath come out in a rush. She found she was holding the crystal so hard it hurt.

Tony yawned. "So, are you guys coming to bed? I put sleeping bags on the floor."

"Just give us a minute," Rob said. "We have to talk something over."

Tony left. Rob shut the door after him, then turned to face the others.

He isn't as calm as I thought, Kaitlyn realized. Rob's jaw was set, his skin pale under its tan.

"Now," Rob said. "What to do."

Kaitlyn shifted. "He did go away," she pointed out. "Without the crystal."

Rob angled a sharp glance at her. "Are you defending him?"

"No. But—"

"Good. Because it doesn't matter if he went away. He'll be back. You heard him."

L.J. SMITH

Anna opened her mouth, then shut it and sighed. She put a hand to her forehead. Her usual serenity was in tatters, but she seemed to be regaining it, gathering it around her like a cloak. "Rob's right, Kaitlyn," she said slowly. "Gabriel did say that—and he *meant* it."

Kaitlyn lowered her arms and looked at the crystal. It was heavy and cold, and on one facet was a pinkish smear. Gabriel's blood. "But what can we *do?*" she said.

"That's what I want to know." Lewis's round, open face was tense. "What can we do against him? He knows where we are—"

"We'll have to get out," Rob said. "That's obvious. And another thing that's obvious—Gabriel's our enemy now. I meant it when I said we'd fight him. We've got to do whatever's necessary from now on."

Kaitlyn felt very cold.

Lewis was sober. "Geez," he breathed. Then he said, "I guess if we have to stop him, we will."

"Not just that. If we have to hunt him, we will, too. We may have to destroy Mr. Zetes—and that may include Gabriel. If it does, it does. We'll do whatever it takes," Rob said. "We don't have any choice."

Lewis looked even less happy, but he nodded slowly, scratching his nose. Frightened, Kaitlyn turned to Anna.

Anna's lovely face was set. "I agree," she said quietly. "Although I hope he'll come to his senses and it won't be

512

necessary—for now he's our enemy. We have to treat him that way." Her dark eyes were sad but stern. Kaitlyn understood—Anna's nature was peaceful, but she had the pragmatism of Nature itself. Sometimes hard choices had to be made, sometimes even sacrifices.

They were all in agreement, all united against Gabriel. And they were looking at Kaitlyn.

That was when Kaitlyn realized what she had to do.

It came to her in a dazzling burst of inspiration, almost like one of her pictures. A crazy plan, completely insane—but she had to do *something*. She couldn't let Rob destroy Gabriel—not only for Gabriel's sake, but for Rob's. If he succeeded, he would be changed forever.

The first item in her plan was not to let anyone know she was planning it.

So she composed her face and did her best to veil her thoughts. It wasn't easy to hide things from mind-mates, but she'd gotten a lot of practice in the past week or so. Looking as resigned and grim as possible, she said, "I agree, too."

She was worried that they might be suspicious—but she was with three of the most unsuspicious people in the world. Rob nodded, looking genuinely grim and resigned himself, Anna shook her head sadly, and Lewis sighed.

"We'll hope for the best," Rob said. "Meanwhile, I guess we should get some sleep. We'll have to get up early and get moving."

Which means I don't have much time, Kaitlyn thought, and then she tried to smoke-veil that, too. "It's a good idea," she said, going over to the desk and putting the crystal shard back in.

Lewis said good night and left, chewing one thumbnail and looking wistful. About Gabriel? Kaitlyn wondered. Or Lydia? Anna departed for the bathroom and Kait and Rob were left alone.

"I'm sorry about all this," Rob said. "And especially sorry he hurt you. That was—unspeakable." His eyes were dark, dark gold.

"It doesn't matter." Kaitlyn was still cold—and drawn to Rob's warmth like a moth to a flame. Especially now, when there might be no tomorrow . . . but he couldn't know that. She reached for him and he took her in his arms.

Their first kiss was a little desperate, on both sides. Then Rob calmed down, and his tranquility spread to Kait. Oh, nice. Warm tingles, warm golden haze.

It was harder now to cloak her thoughts from him. But she had to, he couldn't suspect that they were going to be separated for the first time since they'd met. Kaitlyn clung to him and concentrated on thinking about how much she loved him. How she wanted to engrave him on her memory . . .

"Kait, are you all right?" he whispered. He held her face between his hands, searching her eyes.

"Yes. I just—want to be close." She couldn't get close enough.

You've changed me, she thought. Not just showing me that boys aren't all pond scum. You've made me different, made me look at the broader picture. Given me vision.

Oh, Rob, I love you.

"I love you, Kait," he whispered back.

And *that* meant it was time to stop. She was losing her control; he was reading her thoughts. Reluctantly Kaitlyn pulled back.

"You said it yourself. We're going to need our sleep," she told him.

He hesitated, grimacing. Then nodded, yielding. "See you tomorrow."

"Sleep well, Rob."

You're so good, Rob, she thought as the door closed behind him. And so protective of me. You wouldn't let me do it. . . .

There was a map of Oakland on the desk; they'd bought it to find their way back to Marisol's house. She put it in her duffel bag with the rest of her worldly possessions—a change of clothes bought with the Fellowship's money and her art kit—and pulled a pair of underwear over it. Maybe there was a way to leave the bag in the bathroom . . . yes, and she could wear a nightgown over her clothing. . . .

"Need something?" Anna's voice said from behind her. Guilt stricken, Kaitlyn froze in place.

CHAPTER 3

Blank your mind! Kaitlyn told herself.

She'd been caught red-handed, thinking about things that would *make* Anna suspicious—if Anna had been listening. And everything tonight depended on Anna not suspecting.

"Just trying to figure out what to wear tomorrow," Kait said lightly, giving the bag a final rummage-through. "Not that I have much choice; I'm beginning to feel like Thoreau."

"With his one old suit?" Anna laughed, and Kaitlyn felt the knot in her stomach ease. "Well, I'm sure Marisol would lend you something if she knew what an emergency it was. Why don't you look in the closet?" Anna was going to the closet herself as she spoke. "Whew! This girl liked clothes. I bet we can both find something to fit."

I love you, Kaitlyn thought, as Anna pulled out a long slim

cotton-knit dress and said, "This looks like you, Kait." I love you and Lewis almost as much as I do Rob. You're all so *decent*—and that's why he's going to beat you if you're not careful.

She forced her mind away from that and looked around the room. Marisol's room was like Marisol herself—an unpredictable mixture. Neat with messy, old with new. Like the big mahogany desk, with its silky-ruddy finish scratched and stained, as if it had been given by a loving grandmother to a careless teenager who used it for mixing perfume and storing a CD player. Or the leather miniskirt peeping out of a hamper just below the picture of the Virgin Mary.

A pair of expensive sunglasses were lying half under the bed's dust ruffle. Kait picked them up and absently twisted one gold earpiece back into shape.

"How about this?" Anna was saying, and Kait whistled. It was a very sexy, very feminine dress: spandex bodice fitting to just below the hips then flaring to a sheer chiffon skirt. Tiny gold clasps held the cap sleeves. A *radical* dress, black, that would make the wearer look slim as a statue.

"For you?" Kait said.

"No, you, dummy. It would make the boys swallow their tongues." Anna started to put the dress back. "Come to think of it, you don't need any more boy trouble. You've got two panting after you already."

"This kind of dress might get a girl *out* of trouble," Kait said hastily, taking the hanger. Spandex and chiffon wouldn't wrinkle, and she would need all the weapons she could gather if her plan went through. An outfit like this might make Gabriel sit up and take notice, and seducing Gabriel was item number one on her date book.

She folded the dress small and put it in her duffel bag. Anna chuckled, shaking her head.

Is this really me doing this? Kait wondered. Kaitlyn Brady Fairchild, who used to think Levi's jeans were high fashion? But if she was going to be Mata Hari, she might as well do it thoroughly.

What she said was, "Anna? Do you think about boys?"

"Hmm?" Anna was peering into the closet.

"I mean, you seem so *wise* about them. You always seem to know what they'll do. But you don't seem to go after them."

Anna laughed. "Well, we've been pretty busy lately with other things."

Kaitlyn looked at her curiously. "Have you ever had one you really liked?"

There was the barest instant of hesitation before Anna answered. She was looking at another dress, fingering some sequins that were coming off. Then smiled and shrugged. "Yeah, I guess I found somebody worth caring for once."

"What happened?"

"Well—not much."

Kaitlyn, still watching curiously, realized with surprise that Anna's thoughts were veiled. It was like seeing lights behind a paper wall—she could sense color but not shape. Is that what my veiling looks like? she wondered, and barely had the wits to ask, "Why not?"

"Oh—it would never have worked out. He was together with somebody already. My best friend."

"Really?" Thoughts of veiling had led to thoughts of *what* she was veiling, and Kaitlyn was by now utterly distracted. She hardly knew what she was saying, much less what Anna was. "You should have gone for it. I'll bet you could have *taken* him. With your looks . . ."

Anna grinned ruefully and shook her head. "I would never do that. It would be wrong." She put the sequinned dress back in the closet. "Now, bed," she said firmly.

"Um." Kaitlyn was still distracted. Thinking: I'm casual, I'm calm, I'm confident. She hurried to the bathroom and came back with her clothes still on under the billowing flannel nightgown she'd gotten at Anna's house.

She'd acquired it on the trip *up* to Canada, because they hadn't stopped by Anna's home in Puget Sound on the way back down. They'd accepted money and a 1956 Chevy Bel Air from the Fellowship and taken Route 101 all the way down the coast, driving all day for three days, avoiding Anna's parents. Avoiding *any* parents—they hadn't contacted Lewis's in San Francisco or Rob's in North Carolina or Kaitlyn's father in Ohio. They'd agreed on this early as a necessity; parents would only get worried and angry and would never, never agree to their kids doing what had to be done.

But from what Gabriel had said, Anna's parents had gone to the police anyway. They'd had proof of what Mr. Z was up to—files Rob had stolen from the Institute, detailing Mr. Z's experiments with his first group of students . . . but obviously even proof wasn't enough. Mr. Z had the police sewn up.

No one from the outside could take him down.

Kaitlyn sighed and pulled the covers more tightly over herself. She was focused on Anna, lying beside her in Marisol's bed; listening to Anna's breathing, monitoring Anna's presence in the web.

When she was certain Anna was asleep, she quietly slipped out from under the covers.

I'm going out to see Rob, she projected, not loud enough to wake the other girl, but loud enough, she hoped, to wiggle into Anna's subconscious. That way, if Anna noticed her missing in the next few hours, she might assume Kaitlyn was in the living room and not worry.

Kait tiptoed to the bathroom, where she'd managed to leave her duffel bag. She stripped off the flannel nightgown and crammed it on top of the black dress and Marisol's designer sunglasses. Then she crept down the hallway and noiselessly let herself out the back door.

There was no moon, but the stars were frosty-pale in the night sky. Oakland was too big a city for them to make much of a show, and for a moment Kaitlyn felt a pang of homesickness.

Out by Piqua Road in Thoroughfare, the sky would be pitch-black, huge, and serene.

No time to think about that. Keep moving and find a phone booth, girl.

Back in Thoroughfare, she would have been terrified of walking around a strange city at night—not to mention daunted by the task of trying to get to *another* strange city, at least thirty or forty miles away. But she was a different Kaitlyn than she'd been back in Thoroughfare. She'd dealt with things then *that* Kaitlyn had never dreamed of, she'd traveled all the way to Canada without any adult to help, and she'd learned to rely on her own resources. Now she had no choice. She couldn't wait until morning—she'd never get away from the others in the daytime. She didn't have money for a cab. Still, there must be a way to get across the bay to San Carlos; she just had to find it.

With an almost frightening coolheadedness, she set out to find the way.

This wasn't a bad area of town, and she found a phone booth with an undamaged phone book. She looked up Public Transportation in the local area pages—thank heaven, it said that most of the buses ran twenty-four hours a day. She could even see the basic route she'd have to take: up to San Francisco to get across the water, then south down to San Carlos.

But now, how to *find* a bus that was running at this hour? Well, first thing was to find the bus line. Wincing a little, she tore the AC Transit map out of the phone book—a rotten thing to do, but this was an emergency. Using that and the map of Oakland she navigated her way to MacArthur Street, where the map showed the "N" bus running all night.

Once there, she heaved a sigh of relief. A twenty-four-hour gas station at the corner of MacArthur and Seventy-third. The attendant told her that the bus ran hourly, and the next one would come at 3:07. He seemed nice, a college age boy with shiny black skin and a flattop, and Kaitlyn hung around his booth until she saw the bus approaching.

The bus driver was nice, too, and let her sit behind him. He was a fat man with an endless supply of ham sandwiches wrapped in greasy paper, which he took from a bag under his seat. He offered Kait one; she accepted politely but didn't eat it, just looked out the window at the dark buildings and yellowish streetlights.

This was *really* an adventure. Going to Canada, she'd been with the others. But now she was alone and out of mind-shot—she could scream mentally and none of them would hear. As they approached the Bay Bridge, its swooping girders lit up like Christmas, Kaitlyn felt a thrill of joy in life. She clutched her duffel bag with both hands, sitting up very straight on her seat.

When they got to the terminal where she'd have to change buses, the driver scratched under his chins. "What you want now is the San Mateo line, okay? You go across the street and wait for the Seven B—it'll be along in about an hour. They keep the terminal closed because of homeless people, so you got to wait outside." He closed the bus door, shouting, "Good luck, sweetie."

Kaitlyn gulped and crossed the street.

I'm not afraid of homeless people, she told herself. I *was* a homeless person; I slept in a vacant lot, and in a van on the beach, and . . .

But when a man with a plaid jacket over his head came toward her pushing a shopping cart, she felt her heart begin to pound.

He was coming closer and closer. She couldn't see what was in the cart; it was covered with newspapers. She couldn't see his *face* either, she only thought it was a man because of the husky build.

He kept coming, slowly. Why slowly? So he could check her out? Kaitlyn's heart was going faster and faster, and her joy in life had disappeared. She'd been stupid, stupid to go wandering around at night by herself. If she'd only stayed in her nice safe bed . . .

The figure under the plaid jacket was almost on her now. And there was no place to run. She was on a deserted street in a dangerous city and she couldn't even see a phone booth. The only thing she could think of to do was sit up straight and pretend she didn't even see him. Act as if she weren't afraid.

He was right in front of her now. For an instant a streetlight shone into the hood of his jacket, and Kaitlyn saw his face.

An old man, with grizzled hair and gentle features. He looked a little baffled and his lips moved as he walked—as he *shuffled*. That was why he was going so slowly, because he was old.

Or, Kaitlyn thought suddenly, maybe because he's weak or hungry. It would make *me* hungry to push a shopping cart around at four o'clock in the morning.

It was one of those moments when impulse overrode thought. Kaitlyn pulled the ham sandwich out of her duffel bag.

"Want a sandwich?" she said, which was exactly what the bus driver had said to her. "It's Virginia ham."

The old man took the sandwich. His eyes wandered over Kaitlyn for a moment and he gave a smile of astonishing sweetness. Then he shuffled on.

Kaitlyn felt very happy.

She was cold and tired, though, by the time the bus came. It wasn't a nice bus like the "N." It had a lot of graffiti on the outside and split vinyl seats on the inside. There was chewing gum on the floor and it smelled like a bathroom.

But Kaitlyn was too sleepy to care, too sleepy to ask to sit behind the driver. She didn't pay much attention to the tall man in the torn overcoat until he got off the bus with her.

Then she realized he was following her. It was nine or ten

blocks walk to the Institute, and by the third block she was sure. What hadn't happened in the depths of Oakland or the wilds of San Francisco was happening here.

Or . . . he might be okay. Like the man with the shopping cart. But the man of the cart hadn't been following her.

What to do? Knock on somebody's door? This was a residential neighborhood, but all the houses were dark. Run? Kaitlyn was a good runner; she could probably outdistance the man if he wasn't in good shape.

But she couldn't seem to make herself do *anything*. Her legs just kept walking mechanically down Exmoor Street, while shivers ran up her spine at the thought of him behind her. It was as if she were caught in some dream, where the monsters couldn't get her as long as she didn't show she was afraid.

When she turned a corner she glanced back at him. Foxy red hair—she could see that under a streetlight. His clothes were ragged but he looked strong, athletic. Like somebody who could easily overtake a seventeen-year-old girl running.

That was what she saw with her eyes. With her other sense—the one that sometimes showed her the future—she got no picture but a distinct impression. *Bad.* This man was *bad*, dangerous, full of evil thoughts. He wanted to do something bad to *her*.

Everything seemed to go clear and cold. Time stretched and all Kait's instincts were turned to survival. Her brain was whirring furiously, but no matter which way she turned the situation looked the same. Very bad. No inspiration came about to save herself.

And underneath her thoughts ran a sickening litany: I should have known I couldn't get away with this. Wandering around at night on my own . . . I should have *known*.

Think of something, girl. *Think*. If you can't run, you'd better find shelter, fast.

All the houses around her looked asleep, locked-up. She had a horrible certainty that no one would let her in . . . but she had to do *something*. Kait felt a sort of wrenching in her guts—and then she had turned and was heading for the nearest house, taking the single porch step in a jump and landing on the welcome mat. Something inside her cringed from banging on the door, even in this extremity, but she clamped down on the cringe and *did* it. Hollow bangs echoed—not loud enough, to Kait's ears. She saw a doorbell, pushed on it frantically. She kept pounding, using the side of her fist because it hurt less than using her knuckles.

Inside, she could hear only silence. No reaction to her noisy intrusion. No footsteps running to the door.

Oh, God, *answer!* Come here and answer your door, you idiots!

Kaitlyn looked behind her and her heart nearly jumped out of her body.

Because the foxy man was *there;* he was standing on the walkway of the house. Looking at her.

And he was veryveryvery bad. His mind was full of things that Kaitlyn couldn't sense directly, but that when put together sounded like one long scream. He'd done things to other girls—he wanted to do them to her.

No sound from the house. No help. And she was cornered prey here on the porch. Kait made her decision in an instant. She was off the porch and running, running for the Institute, before the man could move a step.

She heard her own pounding footsteps in the street—and pounding feet behind her. Her breath began to sob.

And it was dark and she was *confused*. She didn't know which way the Institute was anymore. Somewhere around here she turned left—but *where?* It was a street that sounded like a flower or plant—but she couldn't read street signs anyway.

That street looked familiar. Kait swerved toward it, trying to get a glimpse of the sign. Ivy Street—was that right? There was no time to debate. She veered down the street, trying to push her legs into going faster . . . and realized almost instantly that it was a mistake.

A cul-de-sac. When she reached the end, she'd be caught.

She glanced behind her. He was there, running, overcoat flapping like the wings of a bird of prey. He was ungainly but very fast.

She wasn't even going to make it to the end of the cul-de-sac. If she ran to a house, he'd grab her as she stood on the porch. If she slowed, he'd tackle her from behind. If she tried to double back, he'd cut her off.

The only thing she could think of to do was stand and fight.

Once again, the feeling of clear coldness swept over her. Right, then. She pulled up short, staggering a little, and whirled. She was standing in the widest part of the cul-de-sac, surrounded by parked cars.

He saw her and stumbled, slowing down, hesitating. Then, at a shambling half-run, he started toward her again. Kaitlyn stood her ground.

She was glad she hadn't dropped her duffel bag. Maybe she could use it as a weapon. Or maybe there was something *in* it to use. . . .

No, everything was too soft. Except the pencils, but they were in her art kit. She'd never get them out in time.

Then I'll use my fingers to stab his eyes out, she thought savagely. And my knees and my feet and fists. Adrenaline was singing in her veins; she was almost *glad* of the chance to fight. The things she sensed inside him made her want to rip him to pieces. He'd killed, he was a killer.

"Come on, you creep," she said, and realized she was saying it out loud.

He came. He was grinning, a crazy-happy grin. His eyes were crazy, too. Kaitlyn tensed her muscles and then he was on her.

CHAPTER 4

Gabriel was blocking the world out, but the scream came through.

He was pacing in front of the Institute, loitering. He'd been out all night, and didn't particularly want to go in. Not that anyone inside now would bother him—but he still had an impulse to avoid the place. He'd screwed up; he hadn't gotten the crystal shard. And tonight he'd have to explain to *him*.

Zetes. Gabriel felt a muscle in his jaw twitch. He understood now why Marisol had been so afraid of the old man. He had a sort of malevolent power about him, a power that was best observed in day-to-day living. He seemed to drain the will out of everyone around him. Not suddenly, the way Gabriel drained life energy, but slowly. People around him began to feel nervous and exhausted—and dazed. Like birds looking into the eyes of a snake.

A quiet form of terrorization.

Gabriel didn't intend to be terrorized. But now that he'd chosen his path, he needed Zetes. The old man had the structure, the organization, the contacts. Gabriel planned to use all those things on his journey to the top.

He was debating going in when the scream sliced through his consciousness. It wasn't a vocal sound, purely mental. It was composed of hate and anger as well as fear. And it was Kaitlyn.

Close. North and west of him, he thought. He was moving before he thought anything else.

And he probably couldn't have explained why if anyone had asked him.

He moved with the smooth long steps of a hunting wolf. The scream came again—the sound of someone fighting for her life. Gabriel moved faster, homing in on it.

Ivy Street. It was coming from down there—and now he could see it, in the streetlights at the end of the cul-de-sac. He couldn't hear anything except mentally; Kaitlyn never did scream out loud when she was in trouble.

Gabriel reached the grappling figures at a dead run. A red-haired man was on top of Kaitlyn, and she was biting, kicking, and clawing. The man was considerably damaged but sure to win in the end. He was heavier and stronger, he could outlast her.

Déjà vu, Gabriel thought. Once in back of the Institute he'd found another man attacking Kaitlyn—a man who'd turned out to be from the Fellowship. This one, Gabriel thought, eyeing the unwashed hair and unsavory appearance of Kaitlyn's attacker, was unlikely to be anything but a bum.

He could just leave things as they were. The old man would be happy to hear Kaitlyn was dead, and it would mean one less person keeping the shard from them. But . . .

All these thoughts flashed through Gabriel's mind in seconds. Before he'd even consciously come to a conclusion, he was reaching for the man.

He tangled a hand in the back of the dirty overcoat and pulled, yanking the man up. Kaitlyn rolled out from under, and he could hear the surprise in her mind. *Gabriel!*

So she hadn't seen him. Well, she'd been busy trying to stay alive. The man in the overcoat was reacting now, pulling away. He saw Gabriel and threw a punch.

Gabriel ducked around it. He jerked his arm and the knife in his sleeve *snicked* out. His hand closed around it, feeling the welcome weight, the smoothness of the handle.

The man's eyes got big.

Just like Wolverine, Gabriel thought, cutting the knife in front of him in a practice move. The red-haired man's eyes followed it. He was scared; Gabriel could already taste the flavor of his fear.

But don't worry about the knife, he thought, knowing the man couldn't hear him. That's just a distraction, to keep you watching . . . while I do *this*. . . .

Gabriel's other hand rose almost gracefully, gracefully and stealthily, and touched the man on the back of the spine. Just above the soiled collar of the overcoat, just at the nape of the neck.

His fingers made contact with skin, found the transfer point. He could find it easier with his mouth, but he wasn't going any nearer this filthy derelict than he had to. There was a feeling of breakage, as if something was tearing loose. The red-haired man stiffened violently, his muscles jerking. Then Gabriel felt it—the rush of energy, like blue-white light streaking up from the transfer point, fountaining into the air. Into Gabriel's fingers, filling channels and rushing through them, warming his entire body.

Ahhhhh.

It was something like a cold drink on a hot day—a cold drink in a tall glass, with ice cubes clinking against the inside and drops of water condensing on the outside. And it was something like getting your second wind when running—a sudden feeling of strength and peace and vigor. And it was something like standing on the bow of a catamaran with the wind in your face. It wasn't *much* like any of those things, but they were as close as Gabriel could get to the feelings of refreshment and vitality and excitement.

Drinking pure life, that was what it was. And even from a filthy derelict, it tasted pretty good. This guy had been more alive, in his creepy, slimy way, than most. Gabriel let go of him, then pushed the knife back into its casing.

The red-haired man gave a shudder and collapsed, falling as if he'd been deboned. On the ground, he twitched once and was still. He smelled bad.

Kaitlyn, breathing hard, was getting to her feet.

"Is he dead?" she asked.

"No, he's got a gasp or two left. But he's not at all well."

"You enjoyed that." Her eyebrows were arched in scorn and her smoky blue eyes flashed. Wispy red curls clung to her forehead; the rest of her hair was loose in a glorious flame-colored waterfall. She looked flushed and windblown and very beautiful.

Gabriel looked away angrily. He *wouldn't* think about her, he wouldn't see how beautiful she was, how fair her skin was or the way her breathing moved her chest. She belonged to someone else, and she meant *nothing* to him.

He said, looking at the huddled figure on the ground, "You were doing a pretty good job on him yourself."

Kaitlyn shivered, then controlled it. Her voice was softer when she answered. "I could see he was full of nasty things. His mind was . . ." She shivered again.

"You could see into his mind?" Gabriel asked sharply.

"Not exactly. I could *sense* it somehow—sort of like a feeling or a smell. I couldn't tell exactly what he was thinking." She looked up at Gabriel, hesitated, then took a deep breath. "I'm sorry. I didn't say thank you. But I *am* glad you showed up. If you hadn't . . ." Her voice trailed off again.

He ignored this last. "Maybe being in the web has made you slightly telepathic for other people—or maybe that guy was slightly telepathic." He touched the overcoat with the toe of his running shoe. Then he looked at Kait. "Where are the others?"

Kaitlyn drew herself up, looked back calmly. "What others?"

"You know what others." Gabriel stretched out his senses, listening for the slightest hint of their presence. Nothing. He narrowed his eyes at Kaitlyn. "They've got to be around somewhere. You wouldn't come out here alone."

"Wouldn't I? I *am* alone. I came on the bus; it was easy. Aren't you going to ask why?"

Behind her, the sky was green and palest pink, shading to ultramarine in the west. The last stars were going out, the first light was touching her hair with red-gold. She stood slim and proud as some medieval witch princess against the dawn. Gabriel had to work to keep his face expressionless, to keep his presence in the web icy. "All right," he said. "What are you doing here?"

"What do you mean, she's *gone?*" Rob demanded.

"She's gone," Anna repeated miserably. "I woke up and looked and there she wasn't. She isn't *here*."

Lewis rolled over in his sleeping bag, squinting and scratching. "Did you check in the, uh . . ."

"Of course I've checked in the bathroom. I've looked *everywhere,* and she's just not anywhere. Her bag is gone, too, Rob."

"What?" It came out a yell. Anna clapped a hand over his mouth, and Rob stared at her over it.

If her bag's gone, she's gone, he said telepathically after a moment.

That's what I've been telling you, Anna replied. Her beautiful dark eyes were wide but calm. Anna always could keep her head in a crisis—and Rob was close to losing his. Ever since last night his emotions had been in a turmoil.

With an effort he collected himself. *No, I mean that she's gone for a while—and probably of her own free will. Somebody kidnapping her wouldn't have taken the bag.*

"But—why would she leave?" Lewis asked, sitting up. "I mean, she *wouldn't* leave, but if she did leave—well, why?"

Rob looked past the dark, heavy shapes of the living room furniture to the window. It was just dawn.

"I think . . . she's maybe gone to the Institute."

The other two stared at him.

"No," Anna said.

Rob lifted his shoulders, lip caught between his lower teeth. He was still looking out the window. "I think yes."

"But *why?*" Lewis said. Rob barely heard him. He was looking at the sky, translucently blue, like glass. Kait was out there somewhere. . . .

"Rob!" Lewis was shaking him. *"Why* would she have gone to the Institute?" he demanded.

"I don't know," Rob said, coming back to earth. "But she might have an idea she can influence Gabriel—or maybe she wants to try something on Mr. Zetes."

Anna and Lewis audibly let air out of their lungs. "I thought—I mean I thought you were saying . . ."

Rob blinked at him, bewildered.

"He thought you were saying that Kait defected like Gabriel," Anna said crisply. *"I* knew she didn't, but I thought maybe *you* thought she did."

"Of course she wouldn't do that," Rob said, shocked. It was hard for him to understand other people sometimes— they seemed so quick to think the worst about each other, even their friends. He knew better, Kaitlyn wasn't capable of anything evil.

"But she must have gone in the middle of the night," Lewis was saying. "You think she took the car?"

"The car's out front. I looked before I woke you up," Anna said. "I don't know *how* she could make it."

"She'd find a way," Rob said briefly. Kaitlyn was silk and fire—over a steel-hard core of determination. "No, she'll get there, if that's where she's going. The question is, what do we do about it?"

"What *can* we do?" Lewis said.

There were sounds of stirring in the back of the house.

Marisol's parents. Rob glanced that way, then back out the window.

"We'll have to get to her somehow. Find her and get her out of there."

"Get her out," Anna said quietly. It wasn't a question, it was a confirmation.

"We *have* to," Rob said. "I don't know what she has in mind, but it's not going to work. Not in that house of lunatics. They're dangerous. They'll kill her."

"I came to see you," Kaitlyn said, and moved closer to him.

She could tell he wasn't buying it.

"It's *true*. Look at me, feel my thoughts. I came here to see you, Gabriel."

She was taking a chance. But she *had* come to see him, that much was true, and after he'd just saved her life she was genuinely glad to see him. He could sense that much safely. And she was betting he wouldn't search below the surface, because that would mean getting close, letting *her* sense *him*. She had the strong feeling he didn't want that.

He was looking at her hard, his gray eyes narrowed against the light. Beautiful north light, slanting around them, making the modest houses look enchanted, making even Gabriel look golden and warm. She could only guess how it made her look.

Gabriel dropped his eyes. His psychic senses had brushed

her mind as lightly as a moth's wing. "So you came to see me," he said.

"I've missed you," Kaitlyn said, and that was also true. She'd missed his razor wit and the mocking humor that glinted behind his eyes and his strength in the web. "I want to join you."

It was such a whopping huge lie that she expected to *feel* the alarms going off in his head. But he'd withdrawn his mental probing and veiled himself. He wouldn't even look at her properly.

"Don't be stupid," Gabriel said, in a voice suddenly gone weak.

Kaitlyn saw her advantage and pounced. "I *did*. I decided last night. I don't like Mr. Z, but I think some of the things he says are true. We have infinite possibilities—we just need room. Freedom. And we *are* superior to other people."

Gabriel seemed to have gathered himself. "You don't go in for that stuff."

"Why shouldn't I? I'm tired of running. I want to be with you, and I want power. What's wrong with that?"

His mouth had gone hard. "Nothing's wrong—only you don't believe it."

"Test me." Kaitlyn's heart was pounding with the risk. "Gabriel, I didn't know what we had together until you left. I care about you." This was it, the time to see whether she was true Hollywood material. She stepped even closer to Gabriel, almost touching him. "Believe me."

If he wanted, he could reach into her mind and rip the truth out. Her thin shields wouldn't hold against him.

But he didn't try to probe her brain. He kissed her instead.

Kaitlyn surrendered to the kiss deliberately—she knew she had to, and she felt a flash of triumph. Small-town girl makes good. A star is born!

Then the triumph was swept away by something much stronger and deeper. Something fierce and joyous—and *pure*. They were clinging together, he was holding her as hard as she was holding him.

Electricity seemed to arc between them. Everywhere they touched Kaitlyn could feel the sparks. His hand tangled in her hair, and she was frighteningly moved by the tiny tugs, the little pain it caused as his fingers worked. His lips brushed against hers again and again.

An ache was starting inside Kaitlyn. They were together, *together*, so close, and she wanted to be closer. A trembling thrill raced through her—and then a flash of light. His fingers were on the nape of her neck.

A flash of light—it was beginning. The sparks becoming a blue-white torrent. In a moment the transfer point would open, and her energy would flood into him.

The ultimate sharing—but she *couldn't*. Their minds would be open to each other. She would have no shields—he would see everything.

Kaitlyn tried to pull away . . . but it didn't work. He was

holding her and she couldn't seem to let go of him. She didn't have the will—and in a moment he would *see*—

A garage door roared to life.

Kaitlyn jumped and was saved. Gabriel lifted his head, looking at a house near them. Kaitlyn took the moment to step away.

The world was coming to life around them. It wasn't dawn but daylight. The door to another house was opening; a cat was running up a walkway. No one had noticed the tall boy standing in the street kissing a girl, or the crumpled figure at their feet.

"But they'll see us in a minute," Kaitlyn whispered. "Let's go."

They walked quickly. At the intersection, Kaitlyn looked at him. "Which way to the Institute?"

"You really want to go there?" He looked doubtful, but not contemptuous as before. She'd convinced him.

"I want to be with you."

Gabriel was confused. Confused and vulnerable—there was something fragile in his eyes. "But—I hurt you."

"You didn't want to." Kaitlyn was sure of that suddenly. She'd thought so before, but now she was *sure.*

"I don't know," he said shortly. "I don't know anything anymore."

"*I* know. Forget about it." She could tell he was still bewildered, but she figured that was probably good. The more off balance, the less he'd be likely to analyze her. She was still dizzy and bewildered herself from that kiss.

Oh, God, what am I getting myself into?

She decided to think about it later.

"Is Joyce still running things?" Joyce Piper was the woman who'd recruited them both last winter—who'd made the Institute seem like a legitimate place. Even now Kaitlyn had a hard time believing she was as bad as Mr. Z.

"If you can call it running things. She's supposed to be in charge, but—well, you'll see."

Kaitlyn felt a surge of victory, suppressed it. He wasn't arguing anymore. He was assuming she'd come, and that they'd let her in.

I'm going to do it, she thought. She suddenly realized that it was wonderful good luck that she was arriving with Gabriel. He was going to help her immeasurably.

As they neared the Institute she thought, stand tall, walk tall. She held her head up. The first time she'd come here she'd been overwhelmed by anxiety. Worry about her new roommates—would they like her, would they accept her? Now she had much more serious things to worry about, but she had a purpose. She knew she looked cool and confident, almost regal.

She reached into her duffel bag and pulled out Marisol's sunglasses. Put them on, flicked back her hair.

Now I'm ready.

Gabriel glanced at her. "Those new?"

"Well, I don't figure Marisol needs them anymore." She saw him raise his eyebrows at her new hardheartedness.

The Institute was *purple.* Well, of course she remembered that, but it was still a shock to see how truly purple it was. A wild thrill of homesickness ran through her.

"Come on," Gabriel said, and led her to the door. It was locked. He rattled in exasperation.

"I forgot the key—"

"What about your new talent for breaking and entering?"

But the door opened. Joyce was standing there, her short blond hair slick and wet. She was wearing a pink sweater and leggings.

As always, an aura of energy surrounded her, as if she might suddenly spring into action at any moment. Her aquamarine eyes were sparkling with life.

"Gabriel, where have—" She broke off, her eyes widening. She'd seen Kaitlyn.

For a moment they just stood and looked at each other. Under her cool exterior, Kaitlyn's heart was pounding. She *had* to convince Joyce, she had to. But she could feel the waves of suspicion radiating from the blond woman.

Once, Joyce had fooled her, had fooled all of them. Now it was Kaitlyn's turn. Kait felt just like one of those Federal agents infiltrating the Mafia.

And you know what they do to *them,* she thought.

"Joyce—" she began, making her voice gentle and persuasive.

Joyce didn't even glance at her. "Gabriel," she said in a grating whisper, "get her the hell out of here."

CHAPTER 5

Kaitlyn stared at Joyce in dismay. There was a buzzing in her ears, and she couldn't speak.

Gabriel saved her. "Wait until you hear what she has to say."

Joyce glanced from one of them to the other. Finally she said, "Did you get the crystal shard?"

"I couldn't find it," Gabriel answered without any discernible pause. "They have it hidden someplace else. But what difference does it make?"

"What *dif*—" Joyce clamped her lips together and threw a glance behind her, as if worried she'd be overheard. "The difference is that *he's* going to be here tonight, wanting it."

"Look, are you going to let us in or not?"

Joyce let out a stifled breath, turned her gem-hard eyes on Kaitlyn again. She gazed for a long moment, then she abruptly reached out and snatched the sunglasses from Kaitlyn's face.

Kait was startled but wouldn't show it; she returned the aqua-marine gaze steadily.

"All right," Joyce said at last. "Come in. But this had better be good."

"It's good if you want another clairvoyant," Gabriel said once they were in the living room. "You know Frost isn't very good."

Joyce sat down, one trim pink leg crossed over the other. "You've got to be kidding," she said shortly.

"I want to join you," Kaitlyn said. The buzzing was gone from her ears; she could speak in cool, nonchalant tones.

"I'm sure!" Joyce said. *Her* tone was sarcastic.

"Would I bring her here if it wasn't true?" Gabriel asked. He flashed one of his brilliant, unsettling smiles. Before Joyce could reply he added, "I've looked into her mind. She's sincere. So why don't we just cut the bull? I'm hungry."

"*Why* would she want to join us?" Joyce demanded. She looked shaken by Gabriel's conviction.

Kaitlyn went through her speech about believing Mr. Z's theories about psychics and supreme power. She was getting good at it by now. And, she was finding, it was fairly easy to sell it to people who wanted power themselves. It was a motivation they could understand.

At the end of the oration Joyce bit her lip. "I don't know. What about the others? Your friends."

"What about them?" Kaitlyn said coldly.

"You were involved with Rob Kessler. Don't deny it."

Kaitlyn could feel Gabriel waiting for the answer, too. "We broke up," she said. She wished, suddenly, that she had thought more about this part of the story. "I was interested in Gabriel and that made him furious. Besides," she added with happy inspiration, "he likes Anna."

She had no idea what made her say it, but it had an unexpected effect on both Joyce and Gabriel. Joyce's eyebrows went up, but some of the tightness went out of her mouth. Gabriel hissed in a sharp breath—like someone about to say, I knew it all the time.

Kaitlyn was startled. She hadn't *meant* that. Rob had never given any sign—and neither had Anna—or at least she didn't *think* so. . . .

And she couldn't think about it now. She had to stay firmly in the moment. She fixed her eyes on Joyce, who was looking torn.

"Look," Kait said. "This is straight up. I wouldn't come here if I wasn't serious—I wouldn't put my *dad* in that much danger." She held Joyce's gaze. "Because you guys can do things to him, right? I wouldn't risk that." In fact, it wasn't something she had realized until a little while ago. Mr. Z's psychics could attack over any distance, and if they found out the truth about Kait, he'd be an obvious target. Now it was too late to turn back—the only way to protect her dad was to make her act good.

"Hmm. But you went all the way to Canada to *fight* us."

"Sure. I went to the Fellowship and found it was a crock. They can't even help themselves, much less anyone else. And—it's not that I don't care about Rob and the others anymore, but I can't stick with them when they're going to lose. I want to be on the winning side."

"You and Lydia," Joyce said, grimly amused. It was another hit; Kait could tell. "Well, if nothing else I suppose we can use you as a hostage," Joyce murmured.

"In that case, can we get some breakfast?" Gabriel asked, not waiting to see what Kaitlyn's reaction would be.

"Right," Joyce said briefly, handing Kaitlyn the sunglasses. "Nobody else is up yet. Get it yourselves."

A little different from the cheerful-homemaker attitude you had before, Kaitlyn thought, not bothering to shield it from Gabriel. He grinned.

The kitchen was different. Dirty, for one thing; there were dishes in the sink and Coke cans spilling out of the wastebasket. A cardboard box full of sloppily shut take-out containers was on the counter.

Chinese food, Kaitlyn saw. *Joyce never let us have take-out Chinese. And those boxes of Frosted Flakes and Captain Crunch in the pantry—what had happened to Joyce's health food kick? An act?*

"I told you she wasn't exactly running things anymore," Gabriel said under his breath, slanting a quirky glance at her.

Oh. Kaitlyn shrugged and poured herself a bowl of Captain Crunch.

When they were finished eating, Joyce said, "Right, go upstairs and get yourself cleaned up. You can go in Lydia's room for now—then we'll see about further arrangements when *he* comes tonight."

Kaitlyn was surprised. "Lydia's living here?"

"I told you," Gabriel said. "Under her father's thumb."

As she and Gabriel reached the landing, Kait said, "Which room do you have now?"

"The same as before." He indicated the best room in the house, the big one that had cable hookup and a balcony. Then he gave her an evil glance. "Want to share it with me? You can use the Jacuzzi. And the king-size bed."

"I think Joyce would put her foot down about *that*," Kaitlyn said.

She didn't know which room was Lydia's, but she knocked lightly on the door of the room she used to share with Anna. Then she looked in.

Lydia, small in an oversize T-shirt, was just getting out of bed. She saw Kaitlyn and squeaked. Her eyes darted around the room, looking for an exit, then she took a sideways step toward the bathroom door.

Kaitlyn chuckled. In a way, it was a relief to see someone more scared than she was. "What's the hurry?" she said, feeling lazy and dangerous. Like Gabriel.

Lydia seemed to be paralyzed. She wriggled a little, like a worm on a hook, then she blurted, "He made me do it. I didn't want to leave you in Canada."

"Oh, Lydia, you're such a liar. You did it for the same reason I did. You wanted to be on the winning side."

Lydia's cat-tilted green eyes opened even wider. She was a pretty little thing, with a pale and delicate face and a heavy shock of black hair. Or she would have been pretty if she hadn't always looked so guilty and slinking, Kait thought.

"The same reason you did?" Lydia breathed. "You mean—Father brought you here—?"

"I came on my own, to join you guys," Kaitlyn said firmly. "Joyce said I could share this room." She swung her duffel bag over the twin bed that wasn't rumpled, and dropped it with a thump.

She'd expected Lydia to look awed or understanding. Instead, Lydia looked as if she thought Kait was crazy.

"You *came on your own* . . ." Then she stopped and shook her head. "Well, you're right about one thing," she said. "My father is going to win. He always wins." She looked away, lip curling.

Kaitlyn eyed her thoughtfully. "Lydia, how come you're at the Institute? You're not psychic—are you?"

Lydia shrugged vaguely. "My father wanted me here. So Joyce could watch me, I think."

And you didn't really answer the question, Kaitlyn thought.

Gabriel had said that if Kait had picked up the red-haired man's thoughts, either she or the red-haired man must be slightly telepathic. But Kaitlyn had been able to tell how Joyce felt about her, and now she was getting strong feelings from Lydia. It wasn't that she could tell exactly what they were thinking; more that she could get a sense of their general mood.

So I'm a telepath? It was a weird and unsettling thought. Telepathy in the web didn't count; Gabriel had hooked them together. But to sense other people's feelings was something new.

Like just now she could tell that Lydia had a lot on her mind—which meant she might be induced to talk.

"So what's it like around here?" Kaitlyn asked casually.

Lydia's lip curled farther, but she just shrugged again and said, "Have you met the others?"

"No. Well, I mean, I've seen their astral forms before, on the way to Canada."

"You'll probably like those better than their real forms."

"Well, why don't you introduce me?" Kait suggested. She wasn't really as interested in the dark psychics as in the routine around here—something that might give her an idea where Mr. Z kept the crystal. But any information would be helpful, and she figured it was better to be aggressive in meeting Mr. Z's new students. She didn't want them to think she was afraid of them.

"You *want* to see them?" Lydia was afraid of them.

"Yeah, come on, show me the psychic psychos." Kaitlyn kept her tone light and was rewarded with a faint, admiring grin. "Let's tour the zoo."

In the hallway, they nearly ran into Joyce. She glanced at them and then knocked briskly at the door of what had once been the common room for Kait's group. Without waiting for an answer, she threw the door open.

"Everybody up! Renny, you have to get to school; Mac, we start testing in ten minutes. If you want any breakfast, you'd better move it."

She moved on, to yell at another door. "Bri! School! Frost! Testing!"

Kaitlyn, with a clear view of the first room, had to keep herself from gasping.

Oh, my God, I don't believe it.

The room was now a bedroom—sort of. Like a bedroom from a flophouse, Kaitlyn thought. No, *worse.* Like a bedroom from one of those abandoned buildings you see on the news. Across one wall the words "NO FEAR" were spray-painted. *Spray-painted.* Most of the curtains were down and one of the windows in the alcove was broken. There was a large hole in the plaster of one wall and another in the door.

And the room was filthy: It wasn't just the motorcycle helmet and the traffic cones on the floor, or the stray bits of clothing draped over every piece of furniture, or the cups overflowing with cigarette butts. There were cookie crumbs and ashes and potato chips mashed into the carpet, and mud on almost everything. Kaitlyn marveled at how they'd managed to get it so dirty in such a short time.

A boy wearing only boxer shorts was standing up. He was big and lanky, with hair so short it was almost nonexistent, and dark, evil, knowing eyes. A skinhead? Kaitlyn wondered. He looked like the kind of guy you would hire as an assassin, and his mind felt like the red-haired man's.

"Jackal Mac," Lydia whispered. "His real name's John MacCorkendale."

Jackal eyes, Kaitlyn thought. That's it.

The other boy was younger, Kaitlyn's age. He had skin the color of creamed coffee and a little, lean, quick body. His face was narrow, his features clean and sharp. The glasses perched on his nose did nothing to make him look less tough. A smart kid gone bad, Kait thought. The brains of the operation? She couldn't get a clear feeling about his mood.

"That's Paul Renfrew, Renny," Lydia whispered—and ducked. Jackal Mac had thrown a size twelve combat boot at her.

Kaitlyn ducked, too. Then she stood frozen as the huge guy rushed toward them, all arms and legs.

"What are you doing here? What do you want?" he snarled, right in Kaitlyn's face.

Oh, Lord, she thought. His *tongue* is pierced. It was, with what looked like a metal bolt.

Renny had come, too, light as a sparrow, his eyes merry and malicious. He circled Kaitlyn, picked up a strand of her hair by the ends.

"Ouch! That burns!" he said. "But the curves are okay." He smoothed a hand over Kait's behind. "I like her better in the flesh."

Kaitlyn reacted without thinking. She whirled around and her hand made sharp contact with Renny's cheek. It knocked his glasses askew.

"You don't ever do that," she said through her teeth. It brought back every moment of loathing she'd ever felt for a boy. Boys, with their big meaty hands and their big sloppy grins . . . she pulled her arm back in preparation for another slap.

Jackal Mac caught her wrist from behind. "Hey, she fights! I like that."

Kaitlyn jerked her hand out of his grasp. "You haven't seen anything yet," she told them, and gave her best wolfish grin. It wasn't acting. This was genuine, from the heart.

They both laughed, although Renny was rubbing his cheek.

Kaitlyn turned on her heel. "Come on, Lydia. Let's meet the others."

Lydia had been crouching by the stairway. Now she straightened up slightly and hurried toward the second door Joyce had shouted at. It was the room Rob and Lewis had shared in the old days.

The door was ajar; Lydia pushed it open. Kaitlyn braced herself for more destruction.

She wasn't disappointed. Once again the curtains were down, although here they'd been replaced by black sheets. There was a black candle burning on the dresser, dripping wax, and an upside-down pentagram scrawled on the mirror in lipstick. *Glamour* magazines lay open on the floor, and there was the inevitable scattering of clothing and garbage.

There was a girl on each of the twin beds.

"Laurie Frost," Lydia said. She didn't seem quite so afraid of the girls. "Frost, this is Kaitlyn—"

"I know her," the girl said sharply, sitting up. She had blond hair even lighter than Joyce's, and much messier. Her face was beautiful, although the permanently flared nostrils gave it a look of perpetual disdain. She was wearing a red lace teddy and as she raised a hand to flick hair out of her eyes Kaitlyn saw that she had long silvery nails. They were pierced with tiny rings like earrings.

"She's one of *them*. The ones who ran away," Frost said in a menacing hiss.

"Hey, yeah," the other girl said.

There was no need for Lydia to introduce her. Kaitlyn recognized her from a picture on a file folder in Mr. Z's office. Except that the picture had been of a pretty, wholesome girl with dark hair and a vivid face. Now she was still pretty—in a bizarre way. There were streaks of cerulean blue in her hair, and black smudges of makeup surrounding her eyes. Her face was hard, her jaw belligerent.

Sabrina Jessica Gallo, Kaitlyn thought. We meet at last.

"I know you, too," Kaitlyn said. She kept her voice cool and returned Bri's stare boldly. "And I'm not running away now. I came back."

Bri and Frost looked at each other, then back at Kait. They burst into nasty laughter, Bri barking, Frost tittering.

"Right back into the mousetrap," Frost said, flicking her long, silvery nails. "It's Kaitlyn, right? What do they call you, Kaitlyn? Kaitykins? Kitty? Kit Cat?"

Bri took it up. "Kit Kat? Pretty Kitty? Pretty Pretty?"

They dissolved into laughter again.

"We'll have to make the Kitty Kat welcome," Frost said. Her wide, pale blue eyes were spiteful but slightly unfocused. Kaitlyn wondered if she were hung over from something—or maybe that was just the way these people *were*. The Fellowship had sensed insanity in them, and what Kaitlyn sensed now was that each of them was a little bit *off*. Aggressive, malicious—but not very focused. As if there were an inner fogginess in each of them. They weren't even properly suspicious; they weren't asking the right questions.

And Kait wasn't sure what to do with them while they were pointing and giggling at her like kindergartners.

"Sabrina and Frost, I said *now!*" Joyce's voice came from the corridor, cracking like a whip. The girls kept giggling. Joyce pushed past Kaitlyn like a blond meteor and began yelling at them, picking clothes up off the floor.

Kaitlyn shook her head, putting on an expression of genteel astonishment for Joyce's benefit. Then she turned to Lydia.

"I think I've seen enough," she said, and made an exit.

A few minutes later Joyce came into Lydia's room. Her sleek hair was ruffled and she was flushed, but her aquamarine eyes were still hard.

"You can stay in this room today," she said to Kaitlyn. "I don't want you going downstairs while I'm doing testing."

"That's fine with me. I didn't get any sleep last night."

"Good luck napping," Joyce said grimly.

But in a surprisingly short time, the upper floor was still. Lydia, Renny, and Bri had departed for school; Jackal Mac and Frost were presumably being tested. Gabriel's door was locked.

Kaitlyn lay down on her old familiar bed—and realized how tired she really was. She felt wrung out, drained not only of energy, but of emotion. She'd meant to lie awake and make a plan, but she fell asleep almost instantly.

She woke a long time later. Warm, diffuse afternoon light filled the room. Silence filled her ears.

She got up and grabbed for the headboard as a wave of giddiness swept her. Breathing slowly, she held her head down until she felt steadier.

Then she crept in stocking feet to the door.

Still silence. She went to the stairway and turned her head, ear pointed downstairs. No sound. She descended quietly.

If Joyce saw her, she'd say she was hungry, and when was dinnertime anyway?

But Joyce didn't appear. The lower floor seemed deserted. Kaitlyn was alone in the house.

Okay, don't panic. This is terrific, the perfect opportunity. What do you want to look at first?

If I were a big ugly crystal, where would I be?

One obvious place was the secret room in the basement. But Kaitlyn couldn't get in that; Lewis had always used PK to find the hidden spring in the panel. Another place was in Mr. Z's house in San Francisco, where he'd kept it before. But Kaitlyn couldn't do anything about that today. Sometime she'd have to find a way to get to San Francisco.

For now . . . well, Joyce hadn't wanted her to see the testing. So Kait would start with the labs.

The front lab was as she remembered it, weird machines, a folding screen with seashells appliquéd on it, chairs and couches, bookcases, a stereo. There was no graffiti. Kaitlyn looked briefly into each of the study carrels that lined the walls, but she knew already that the crystal could never fit into something so small. She found only more equipment.

I wonder what their powers are? she thought, envisioning each of the students she'd met. I forgot to ask Lydia. Gabriel said something about Frost being clairvoyant, but the others— I'll bet they do something *bizarre.*

She turned to the back lab . . . and found it locked.

Aha!

It had never been locked before. Kaitlyn found it extremely suspicious that it should be locked now.

But her jubilation changed to despair a minute later as she realized a basic truth. If it was locked, she *couldn't get in.*

But wait, wait. Joyce had always kept a house key on top of the bulletin board in the kitchen, for anybody to grab when they were leaving the house. Sometimes people had the same locks on the inside doors of a house as the outside. If that key were still there . . . and if it fit . . .

In a moment she was in the quiet, darkening kitchen, fingers searching anxiously on the top of the bulletin board's frame. She found some dust, a dead fly . . . and a key.

Eureka! Praying all the way, Kaitlyn hurried back to the lab. She held key to lock, almost dropping it in her nervousness.

It's *got* to work, it's *got* to work. . . .

The key slipped in. It fit! She waggled it. It turned!

The doorknob turned, too. Kait pushed and the door was open. She stepped in and shut the door behind her.

The back lab was dim—it had been a garage and had only a small window. Kaitlyn blinked, trying to make out shapes. She didn't dare turn on a light.

There were bookcases here, too, and more equipment. And a steel room like a bank vault.

A Faraday cage.

Kaitlyn remembered Joyce telling her about it. It was for complete isolation in testing. Soundproof, electronically shielded. They had put Gabriel in there.

Kait remembered herself begging Joyce to promise *she'd* never have to go in.

Her mouth was dry. She tried to swallow, but her throat seemed to stick together. She walked toward the gray bulk of the steel vault, one hand lifted as if she were blind.

Cool metal met her fingers.

If I were a crystal, I'd be somewhere like this. Shielded, enclosed. With enough room for everybody to get in and crowd around me.

Kaitlyn's fingers slid over the metal. Her former tranquility in the face of danger was gone, and her heart wasn't just pounding, it was *thundering*. If the crystal was really in there, she had to see it. But she didn't really want to see it—and to be alone with that obscene thing . . . in the dark. . . .

Kaitlyn's skin was crawling and her knees felt unsteady. But her fingers kept searching. She found something like a handle.

You can do it. You can do it.

She pulled.

At first, she thought the sound she heard was the vault door clicking. Then she realized it was somebody opening the lab door behind her.

CHAPTER 6

What does a spy do when she's caught?

Kait's stomach plummeted. She recognized the voice, even before she whirled around to see the figure silhouetted in the door.

Light shone behind him. Broad shoulders, then body lines that swept straight down. A man wearing a greatcoat.

"Are you finding anything to interest you?" Mr. Zetes asked, his gold-headed cane swinging in his hand.

Oh, God. The buzzing was back in Kaitlyn's ears and she couldn't answer. Couldn't move, either, although her heart was shaking her body.

"Would you like to see what's inside there?"

Say something, idiot. Say anything, *anything*.

Her dry lips moved. "I—no. I—I was just—"

Mr. Zetes stepped forward, snapped on the overhead light. "Go on, take a closer look," he said.

But Kaitlyn couldn't look away from his face. The first time she'd seen this man, she'd thought him courtly and aristocratic. His white hair, aquiline nose, and piercing dark eyes made him look like some English earl. And if an occasional grim smile flashed across his face, she was sure that he had a heart of gold underneath.

She'd found out differently.

Now, his eyes held her with an almost hypnotic power. Boring into her mind, gnawing. He looked more telepathic than Gabriel. His measured, imperious voice seemed to resound in her blood.

"Of course you want to see it," he said, and Kaitlyn's throat closed on her protests. He advanced on her slowly and steadily. "Look at it, Kaitlyn. It's a very sturdy Faraday cage. Look."

Against her will, Kaitlyn's head turned.

"It's natural that you would be interested in it—and in what's inside. Have you seen that yet?"

Kaitlyn shook her head. Now that she wasn't looking into those eyes, she found she could speak—a little. "Mr. Zetes—I wasn't—"

"Joyce told me that you had come back to join us." Mr. Z's voice was rhythmic . . . almost soothing. "I was very pleased. You have great talents, you know, Kaitlyn. And a keen, inquiring mind."

As he spoke he unlocked the vault with a key, grasped the handle. Kaitlyn was speechless again with fear. Please, she was thinking. Please, I don't want to see, just let me go.

"And now your curiosity can be satisfied. Go in, Kaitlyn."

He pulled the steel door open. There was a single lamp inside, the battery-driven kind that clamps on walls. It gave enough light for Kaitlyn to see the object below.

Not the crystal. A sort of tank, made of dark metal.

Bewildered, forgetting herself, Kaitlyn took a step forward. The tank was almost like a Dumpster trash can, except that instead of being rectangular it had one side which slanted steeply. A door was set in that steeply slanting side. It looked like the door to a hurricane cellar, leading down.

There were all sorts of pipes, cables, and hoses attached to the tank. One machine beside it looked like the electroencephalograph Joyce had used to measure Kaitlyn's brain waves. There were other machines Kaitlyn didn't recognize.

The tank itself felt like a giant economy-size coffin.

"What . . . is it?" Kaitlyn whispered. Dread was clogging her chest like ice. The thing gave off an aura of pure evil.

"Just a piece of testing equipment, my dear," Mr. Zetes said. "It's called an isolation tank. The ultimate Ganzfeld cocoon. Put a subject inside, and she is surrounded by perfect darkness and perfect silence. No light or sound can penetrate. It's filled with water, so she can't feel the effects of gravity or her own body. There is no sensory stimulation of any kind. Under those conditions, a person—"

Would go insane, Kaitlyn thought. She recoiled from the tank violently, turning away. Just the idea of it, to be abandoned in utter darkness and silence, was making her physically sick.

Mr. Z's hand caught her, holding her lightly but firmly. "Would be undistracted by outside influences, free to extend her psychic powers to the fullest. Just as you did when Joyce blindfolded you, my dear. Do you remember that?"

He had turned to look at her, holding her terrified gaze with his. She hadn't missed his use of personal pronouns. Put a subject inside and *she* can't feel *her* own body.

"As I said earlier, you have very great talents, Kaitlyn. Which I would like to see developed to their fullest."

He was pulling her toward the tank.

And she couldn't resist. That measured voice, that precise grip . . . she had no will of her own.

"Have you heard of the Greek concept of *arete,* my dear?" He had put aside his cane and was opening the hurricane-cellar door. "Self-actualization, becoming all you can be." He was pushing her toward the open door. "What do you think you can be, Kaitlyn?"

A black hole gaped in front of her. Kaitlyn was going into it.

"Mr. Zetes!"

The voice was thin and distant in Kaitlyn's ears. All she could see was the hole.

"Mr. Zetes, I didn't realize you were here. What are you doing?"

The pressure on Kait's neck eased and she could move of

her own volition again. She turned and saw Joyce in the doorway. Gabriel and Lydia were behind her.

Then Kaitlyn simply stood, blinking and trying to breathe. Mr. Z was going over to Joyce, talking to her in an undertone. Kaitlyn saw Joyce look up at her in surprise, then shake her head.

"I'm sorry, but there's no help for it," Mr. Z said, with mild regret, as if saying "I'm sorry, but we'll have to cut expenses."

He's talking about my imminent demise, Kaitlyn realized, and suddenly she was talking, gabbling.

"Joyce, I'm sorry. I know I shouldn't have gone inside here, but I wanted to see what changes you'd made, and there was nobody around to ask, and—I'm *sorry.* I didn't mean anything by it."

Joyce looked at her, hesitated, then nodded. She beckoned Mr. Z into the front lab and began talking to him. Kaitlyn followed slowly, warily.

She couldn't hear everything, but what she heard stopped her breath. Joyce was defending her, championing her to Mr. Z.

"The Institute can use her," Joyce said, her tanned face earnest—and strained with what looked like repressed desperation. "She's well-balanced, conscientious, reliable. Unlike the rest of—" She broke off. "She'll be an asset."

And Gabriel was agreeing.

"I can vouch for her," he said. Kaitlyn felt a surge of gratitude—and admiration for his level, dispassionate gray eyes. "I've probed her mind and she's sincere."

Even Lydia was chiming in—after everyone else, of course.

"She *wants* to be here—and I want her for my roommate. Please let her stay."

Listening to it, Kaitlyn was almost convinced herself. They all sounded so *sure*.

And somehow it worked—or seemed to work. Mr. Z stopped shaking his head regretfully and looked thoughtful. At last he shifted his jaw, drew a deep breath, and nodded.

"All right, I'm willing to give her a chance," he said. "I'd like to see a little more penitence in her—some signs of remorse—but I trust your judgment, Joyce. And we could certainly use another remote-viewer." He turned to give Kaitlyn a benevolent smile. "You and Lydia go along to dinner. I want a word with Gabriel."

It's over, Kaitlyn realized. They're not going to kill me; they're going to feed me. Her heart was only beginning to return to its normal rate. She tried to hide the trembling in her legs as she followed Lydia.

But it slowed her down, and before she could get out of the front lab she heard Mr. Z speak to Joyce again.

"Give her a chance, but watch her. And have Laurie Frost watch her, too. She's intuitive; she'll pick up on anything subversive. And if she finds something . . . you know what to do."

A sigh from Joyce. "Emmanuel . . . you know what I think about your 'final solution'—"

"We'll send her out on a job soon. That ought to prove something."

"Kait, are you coming?" Lydia called from the kitchen.

Kait went through the door, but dawdled on the other side. Mr. Z was speaking again.

"Gabriel, I'm afraid you've been careless."

Gabriel's voice was restrained but defiant. "About the shard? You haven't heard—"

"Not about that," Mr. Zetes said in his unhurried way. "Joyce explained that to me. But there was a man found half-dead on Ivy Street. He had all the signs of someone drained of life energy. The police have been making inquiries."

"Oh."

"*Very* careless of you to do that in our own neighborhood— and the man might talk." Mr. Z's voice dropped to an icy whisper. "Next time, *finish the job*."

Kaitlyn was shivering when Gabriel came through the door. She was barely able to give him a smile of gratitude.

Thanks.

He shrugged. *No problem.*

Dinner started off quietly. Joyce served bacon cheeseburgers, fare that never would have been allowed in the old days. The psychics eyed Kaitlyn from around the long table, but didn't say much. Kait had the feeling they were biding their time.

"So where was everybody this afternoon?" she asked Lydia, trying for normalcy.

"I was in Marin. Riding lessons," Lydia said in subdued tones—she never seemed to talk loudly around the other students.

"I was asleep," Gabriel said lazily.

No one else answered, including Joyce, who returned to the kitchen. Kaitlyn dropped the subject and ate fries. It was interesting, though—the ones who'd been out were also the ones who would have been involved in testing. Could they have been in San Francisco? In Mr. Z's house—with the crystal?

She made a mental note to follow up on the question.

What Joyce said next might have been coincidence.

"So you've seen the isolation tank."

Kaitlyn almost inhaled a fry. "Yes. Have—has anybody really been in that thing?"

"Sure, it's cool," Bri said. She shut her eyes and leaned her head back. "Cosmic, man! Groooovy." Her expression of ecstasy was marred by the fact that her open mouth was full of half-chewed hamburger.

"Shut your face, you slut!" Frost snapped, flicking a pickle chip at her.

"Who's a slut, you bimbo?" Bri returned cordially, chewing. "Jimbo bimbo. Mumbo jumbo."

They both laughed: Frost shrilly, Bri gruffly.

Jackal Mac glared. "Quit with the freakin' noise," he said brutally. "You make me sick with that freakin' noise." He had been eating with fervent single-mindedness, the way Kaitlyn imagined a coyote might eat.

"I like to see girls have a good time," Renny said. He was eating with finicky precision, gesturing with a french fry. "Don't you, Mac?"

"You making fun of me? You making fun of *me*, man?"

Kaitlyn blinked. It was a non sequitur; she didn't follow Mac's logic. But it didn't take logic to read the sudden fury in his slitted eyes.

He stood up, towering over the table, leaning across to stare at Renny. "I said, you makin' fun of *me?*" he bellowed.

Renny let him have it with a hamburger in the face.

Kaitlyn gaped. The hamburger had been dripping with ketchup and Thousand Island dressing. Renny had thoughtfully removed the bun, so Jackal Mac got the full benefit of the condiments.

Bri shrieked with laughter. "What a pitch, what a pitch! Pitch, snitch!"

"Think that's *funny?*" Jackal Mac seized her by the hair and slammed her face into her plate. He began to grind it around and around. The giggles turned to screams.

Kaitlyn was now gasping. Frost plunged her long nails into a bowl of coleslaw and came out with a juicy handful. She threw it at Mac, but it scattered over the table, hitting Renny, too.

Renny seized a bottle of Clearly Canadian water—the fizzy kind.

"Time to go." Gabriel caught Kaitlyn by the arm above the elbow and neatly lifted her from the chair out of the way of a burst of carbonated water. Lydia was already scuttling out of the room.

"But he's going to kill her!" Kaitlyn gasped. Mac was still grinding Bri's face into the plate.

"So?" Gabriel piloted her toward the kitchen.

"No, I mean, *really*. I think that plate cracked; he's going to *kill* her."

"I said, 'so?'"

There was the sound of shattering glass and Kaitlyn looked back. Jackal Mac had stopped grinding Bri's face; Renny was now slashing at him with a broken Clearly Canadian bottle.

"Oh, my *God*—"

"Come on."

In the kitchen, Joyce was washing dishes.

"Joyce, they're—"

"It happens every night," Joyce said shortly. "Leave it alone."

"Every night?"

Gabriel stretched, looking bored. Then he smiled. "Let's go up to my balcony," he said to Kaitlyn. "I need some air."

"No, I—I want to help Joyce with the dishes." There was no point in trying to deceive him about such a minor thing, so she added, *I want to talk to her a minute. I didn't have time earlier.*

"Suit yourself." Gabriel's voice was unexpectedly cold; his expression was stony. "I'll be busy later." He left.

Kaitlyn didn't understand why he was angry, but there was nothing to do about it. She was a spy, she had information to gather. Picking up a dish, she said abruptly, "Joyce, why do you put up with it?"

"With Gabriel? I don't know, why do you?"

"With *them*." Kaitlyn jerked her chin toward the dining room, where yells and crashes could still be heard.

Joyce gritted her teeth and scrubbed viciously at a greasy pan with a soap pad. "Because I have to."

"No really. Everything's so crazy now—and it seems like it's against everything you believe in." Kaitlyn was getting incoherent—maybe the scare before dinner was still affecting her. She had the feeling that she should shut up, but instead she blundered on. "I mean, you seem like the kind of person who really *believes* in things, and I just don't understand—"

"You want to know why? I'll show you!" With a soapy hand, Joyce seized something that had been on the counter, underneath the Chinese take-out containers.

It was a magazine, the *Journal of Parapsychology*.

"My name is going to be in this! The lead article. And not just this." Joyce's face was contorted, it reminded Kaitlyn of the way she'd looked when she'd held Gabriel's bleeding forehead against the crystal, trying to kill him. Overcome by maniacal passion.

"Not just this, but in *Nature, Science, The American Journal of Psychology, The New England Journal of Medicine*," Joyce raved. "Multidisciplinary journals, the most prestigious journals in the world. My name and my work."

Dear God, she's a mad scientist, Kaitlyn thought. She was almost spellbound by the ranting woman.

"And that's just the beginning. Awards. Grants. A full professorship at the school of *my* choice. And, incidentally, a little trinket called the Nobel Prize."

Kait thought at first that she was joking. But there was no humor in those glazed aquamarine eyes. Joyce looked as insane as any of the psycho psychics.

Could he have hit her with the crystal, too? Kaitlyn wondered dazedly. Or could it be some sort of cumulative effect from being around it, like secondhand smoke?

But she knew that no matter what the crystal had done to warp and magnify the desire, it was Joyce's desire in the first place. Kaitlyn had finally discovered what made Joyce run; she had just seen into the woman's soul.

"That's why I put up with it, and why I'm going to put up with anything. So that the cause of science can be advanced. And so I can get *what I'm due.*"

As suddenly as she had grabbed it, Joyce dropped the magazine she'd been shaking in front of Kaitlyn's eyes. She turned back to the sink.

"Now, why don't you take a walk," she said in a voice suddenly gone dull. "I can wash the dishes by myself."

Numb, Kaitlyn walked out of the kitchen. She avoided the dining room, went through the front lab and up the stairs.

Gabriel's door was locked. Well, she should have expected

that, really. She'd managed to offend two of the three people who'd championed her tonight. Might as well try for a perfect score, she thought philosophically, and headed for the room she was to share with Lydia.

But Lydia proved to be impossible to offend or talk to at all. She was in bed with the covers pulled over her head. Whether she was sulking or simply scared, Kaitlyn didn't know. She wouldn't come out.

So *moody*, Kaitlyn thought.

It was a very long, very dull evening. Kait listened to the other psychics stagger up to their various rooms, then a TV blared from one room, a stereo from the other. It spoiled Kaitlyn's concentration for the one thing that might have relaxed her: drawing.

And this room depressed her. All her possessions had disappeared from it—thrown away when the new students came in. Anna's raven mask was lying in a corner. Like a piece of garbage. Kait didn't dare hang it up where it belonged.

Finally, she decided to take a bath and follow Lydia's example. She had a long soak, curled up in bed—and then there was nothing to do but think.

Scenes from the day kept floating through her mind. The face of the red-haired man . . . Gabriel's face in the dawn light. Mr. Z's silhouette.

I've got to make plans, she thought. Mysteries to investigate. Ways to find the crystal. But her mind couldn't focus on one thing, it kept skipping.

Joyce defended me . . . I fooled the fooler. And what convinced her was that Rob and I had broken up . . . because Rob liked Anna.

What an idea. How odd. And Gabriel fell for it, too.

She must be sleepy. Her mind skipped again, her thoughts becoming less and less cohesive. I hope Gabriel isn't really angry with me. I need him. Oh, God, all the things I said to him . . .

Was that wrong? To let him think I'm in love with him? But it wasn't completely a lie. I do care about him. . . .

As much as I do about Rob?

It was a heretical thought, and one which jerked her fully awake. She realized she had been half-dreaming.

But the thought wouldn't go away.

In Canada she had discovered that Gabriel loved her. Loved her in a vulnerable, childlike way she could never have believed if she hadn't *seen* it, felt it in his mind. He had been completely open to her, so warm, so joyous . . .

. . . the way he was this morning, her mind whispered.

But in Canada she hadn't loved him. Or at least she hadn't been in love.

You couldn't be in love with two people at the same time. You *couldn't* . . .

Could you?

Suddenly Kaitlyn felt icy cold. Her hands were cold, her face was cold. As if someone had opened a window somewhere inside her and let a glacial wind blow in.

If I loved Gabriel . . . if I loved both of them . . .

How could I choose?

How could I choose?

The words were ringing so loudly in her head that she didn't notice the very real noise in her room. Not until a shadow loomed on the wall beside her.

Terror swept her. For an instant she thought it was Mr. Z—and then she saw Gabriel beside her bed.

Oh, Lord, did he hear my thought? She groped for shields, found she didn't have any. She was burned out.

But Gabriel was smiling, looking at her from under heavy eyelids. He would never have smiled like that if he had heard. "Ready to try out the balcony now?" he asked.

Kaitlyn looked at him, slowly regaining her composure. He was looking particularly gorgeous, and dangerous as darkness. She felt a magnetic pull drawing her to him.

But she was exhausted. Unshielded. And she had just discovered a crisis within herself that threatened to bring the world crashing down.

I can't go with him. It would be insane.

The magnetic pull only got stronger. She wanted to be held. She wanted him to hold her.

"Come on," Gabriel whispered, and took her hand. He caressed the palm with his thumb. "Kiss me, Kait."

CHAPTER 7

Kaitlyn was shaking her head at him. What on earth
could the girl mean?

Gabriel could tell she wanted to come. He'd read
the line in some old book somewhere, probably during one of
his stints in solitary. "She trembled at his touch." Reading it,
he'd sneered—but now he was seeing the real thing. When he
reached down to take her hand, Kaitlyn trembled.

So what was the problem?

I'm tired, she projected in a whisper.

Oh, come on. Sitting on a balcony is relaxing.

He could tell she was going through some struggle. Mad
because of the way he'd acted after dinner? Or . . .

Did it have something to do with what he'd seen this
afternoon?

His mood darkened. *Is there something wrong?* he asked
silkily.

"No, of course not," she said very quickly. On the other bed a lump under the comforter stirred. Gabriel eyed it with distaste.

Kaitlyn was getting up. Gabriel's lip twitched at the sight of her nightgown—it was flannel and tentlike, covering her from throat to ankle. Quite a bit different from Frost, who had pirouetted in front of him dressed in what looked like a transparent red handkerchief the first night he'd met her. She'd made it clear, too, that she didn't mind if he took the handkerchief off.

Kaitlyn, by contrast, was holding the neck of her nightgown closed as she briskly walked to his room.

She paused there to look at the walls. "You do the graffiti?"

He snorted. *Mac. He was living here.*

"And what did he think when you asked him to get out?"

Gabriel said nothing, waited until she turned around. Then he gave her one of his most disturbing smiles. *I didn't ask.*

"Oh." She didn't pursue it. She stepped through the open sliding glass door onto the balcony. "It's a nice night," she murmured.

It was—a soft moonless night, with stars showing between branches of the olive trees. The air was warm, but Kaitlyn had her arms wrapped around herself.

Gabriel went still.

Maybe it was the simplest explanation after all. Maybe he'd been wrong about her trembling—or wrong about the reason. Not desire . . . but fear.

"Kaitlyn." Instinctively, he used words instead of thoughts, giving her the distance she seemed to need. "Kait, you don't have to . . . I mean, you *know* that, don't you?"

She turned quickly, as if startled. But then she didn't seem to know what to say. He could search her thoughts—he could sense them even now, like silver fish darting and gliding in clear water—but he *wouldn't*. He would wait for her to tell him.

She was staring at him, breathing lightly. "Oh, Gabriel. I do know. And I can't explain—I'm just . . . oh, it's been a hard day."

Then she put her hands over her face. She started to cry, with her hair falling around her, and little quick intakes of breath.

Gabriel stood transfixed.

Kaitlyn the indomitable—crying. She did it so seldom that he was too amazed at first to react. When he could move, he could think of only one thing to do.

He took her in his arms, and Kaitlyn clung to him. Clung tightly—and after a moment lifted a tear-stained face to him.

The kisses were soft and slow and very passionate. It was strange to do this without touching her mind, but he wasn't going to be the first to initiate contact. He'd wait for her. Meanwhile, it was a sort of pleasurable agony to restrain himself.

And it was good just to hold her and touch the softness of her skin. He wanted to hold her hard, not to hurt her but to keep her safe, to show her that he was strong enough to protect her. Her beauty was like fire and strange music, and he loved her.

And he *could* love her, because she didn't belong to anyone else, and she loved him back. She'd given it all up for him.

For an instant he felt a flicker of guilt at that, but it was swept aside by a fierce desire to hold her closer. To *be* closer. He couldn't keep himself in check any longer. He reached for her mind, a tendril of thought extending to caress her senses.

Kaitlyn recoiled. Not just pulling away from his mind, but pulling out of his arms. He could feel her trying to fling up shields against him.

Leaving him stricken, utterly bewildered, and bereft. Cold because she'd taken all the warmth in the universe away with her.

Suspicion knifed through him, unavoidable this time.

What is it you don't want me to see?

"Nothing!" She was frightened—no, panicked. His suspicion swelled until it was larger than both of them, until it blocked out everything else. He threw words at her like stones.

"You're lying! Don't you think I can tell?" He stared at her, controlling his breath, forcing his voice into velvety-iron tones. "It wouldn't have something to do with Kessler coming around here this afternoon, would it?"

"Rob—here?"

"Yeah. I felt his mind and tracked him down to the red-wood trees out back. You're telling me you didn't know?"

Her eyes were still wide with surprise—but he saw, and felt, the flash of guilt. And his suspicions were confirmed.

"What are you really doing here, Kaitlyn?"

"I told you. I—"

"Stop lying to me!" Again he had to stop to control himself. When he spoke again his voice was like ice because he was made of ice. "You didn't break it off with him, did you? And you're not here to join us. You're a spy."

"That's not true. You won't even give me a chance—"

"I told them all that I'd seen into your mind—but I never really did. You made sure of that. You did a wonderful job of tricking me."

Her eyes were large and fierce with pain. "I didn't trick you," she said in a ragged voice. "And if you think I'm a spy, then why don't you go tell Joyce? Why don't you tell them all?"

He was calm, now, because a block of ice can't feel. "No, I won't do that. I'll let you do it to yourself. And you will, sooner or later—probably sooner, because the old man isn't stupid and Frost will pick things up. You'll betray yourself."

There was a blue flame of defiance in her eyes now. "I'm telling you, I am not a spy," she said.

"Oh, right. You're perfectly sincere. I believe you completely." Quick as a striking snake, he bent over her, thrusting his face close to hers. "That's fine, as long as you remember one thing. Keep out of my way. If you mess with *my* plans, angel—no mercy."

Then he left, stalking out of the room to be alone with his dark bitterness.

Kaitlyn cried herself to sleep.

"Bri—school! Frost—testing!"

The shouting voice in the hall woke Kaitlyn. She felt languid and stupid, with a stuffed-up nose and a bad headache.

The door banged open. "Lydia—school! Kaitlyn, you're going to school, too. I arranged it yesterday, and I'm coming in with you today."

Thanks for telling me, Kaitlyn thought, but she got up—painfully, because every muscle seemed to be aching. She stumbled to the bathroom and began to go through the routine of dressing like a programmed robot. Shower, first.

The warm water felt good on her upturned face, but her mind kept leaping back to what had happened with Gabriel last night. At first everything had been so wonderful—and then . . . it had hurt her to see his eyes like holes in his face and his mouth tight to keep it from working.

You ought to be glad it all turned awful, a voice inside her whispered. Because if it had stayed good—well, what would you do? What would you do about Rob?

She didn't *know* what she would have done. Her entire middle was a tight ball of anguish and she was so confused.

It didn't matter. Gabriel hated her now, anyway. And that

was *good*, because she was going to be true to Rob. It was good—except for the minor fact that Gabriel might denounce her to Mr. Z and get her killed.

Tears mingled with the shower spray on her face. Kaitlyn turned her head aside to take a deep, shuddering breath, and that was why she didn't see the shower curtain being pulled open.

The first thing she knew was a rough hand closing around her wet arm.

"What do you think you're doing? Get out of there!" Bri shouted, adding a string of expletives. Kaitlyn had to step over the side of the tub or fall over it—she was being dragged out. Naked and stunned, she shook her hair back and stared at the other girl.

"You think you can use all the hot water again? Like you did last night?" That was the gist of what Bri was yelling, although actually every other word was a curse. Kaitlyn stood dripping on the tile floor, dumbfounded.

"You think you're better than us, don't you?" Bri shouted. "You're Little Miss Responsible, teacher's pet. You can use all the water you want to. You've never had it hard."

The sentences were disjointed, and again Kaitlyn had that sense of something being *off*, as if Bri couldn't actually get a fix on what was making her angry. But her anger and resentment were clear enough.

"Everybody's darling," she mocked, cocking her head back and forth, with a finger to her chin—a bizarre Shirley Temple impersonation. "Looks so *sweet—*"

Something snapped. Kaitlyn's temper had always been combustible, and now it ignited like rocket accelerant touched with a match. Naked as she was, she seized Bri and slammed her against a wall. Then she pulled her away and slammed her back again. Bri's mouth fell open and her eyes showed white. She fought, but fury gave Kaitlyn inhuman strength.

"You think I've always had things easy?" she yelled into Bri's face. "You don't know how it was back in Ohio. I was from the wrong side of the tracks anyway, but to top it off, *I was a witch.* You think I don't know what it's like to have people cross themselves when you look at them? When I was five the bus driver wouldn't take me to school—she said my mom ought to get me blessed. And then my mom died—"

Tears were sliding down Kaitlyn's cheeks, and she was losing her anger. She slammed Bri again and got it back.

"Kids at school would run up and touch me for a dare. And adults would get so nervous when I talked to them—Mr. Rukelhaus used to get a *twitch* in his eye. I grew up feeling like something that ought to be put in the zoo. Don't tell me I don't know what it's like. *Don't tell me!*"

She was winding down, her breath slowly calming. So was Bri's.

"You dye your hair blue and do stuff to look weird—but you're doing it yourself, and you can change it. I can't change my eyes. And I can't change what I am."

Suddenly embarrassed, Kaitlyn let go of Bri's arms and looked around for a towel.

"You're okay," Bri said in a voice Kaitlyn hadn't heard her use before. Not a sneering tough-girl voice. Kait looked around, startled.

"Yeah, you're okay. I thought you were a goody-goody wimp, but you're not. And I think your eyes are cool."

She looked more sane than she had since Kait had met her.

"I—well, thanks. Thank you." Kait didn't know whether to apologize or not; she settled for saying, "You can use the shower now."

Bri gave a friendly nod.

It's strange, Kait thought as Joyce drove her to school. Bri, Lydia, and Renny had gone in Lydia's car. It's strange, but for a while there she sounded just like Marisol. What was it Marisol said that first night? *You kids think you're so smart—so superior to everyone else.*

But we *didn't* think that; it was just Marisol's paranoia—a very particular kind of paranoia. Kaitlyn shot a look at Joyce under her eyelashes. And Joyce has that kind, too—thinking she isn't getting what she's due.

They *all* think the world is out to get them—that they're special and superior but everybody is persecuting them. Can the crystal do that?

If it can, it's no wonder they're out to get the world first.

Joyce checked her in to school, and Kaitlyn found herself going to the same classes she had when she'd come to the Institute. The teachers put her absence down as a vacation, which was mildly amusing. It was surrealistic, like being in a dream, to sit in British literature again, with all these kids whose lives were quiet and boring and completely safe. Who hadn't had *anything* happen to them in the last few weeks; who hadn't changed at all. Kaitlyn felt out of step with the whole world.

Watch it, kid. Don't *you* get paranoid.

At lunch several people asked her to sit with them. Not just one group, but two, called to her in the cafeteria. It was the sort of thing Kaitlyn had always dreamed about, but now it seemed trivial. She was looking for Lydia—she wanted to talk to that girl.

Lydia wasn't in evidence. Bri and Renny were off in a corner, bullying people and probably extorting lunch money. Kaitlyn wondered how their teachers dealt with them.

I'll look around by the tennis courts, she thought. Maybe Lydia's eating her lunch out there.

She was crossing in front of the PE building when she saw three people crowded in the doorway of the boy's locker room. They were looking out from behind the little wall that kept people from seeing in the open doors, and they seemed ready to duck back at any moment. The weird thing was that one of them was a girl. A girl with long dark braids . . .

And the tallest boy had hair that shone in the sun like old gold. Kaitlyn's heart leaped into her mouth and choked her. She ran.

"Rob—you shouldn't be here," she gasped as she got behind the wall. And then she was hugging him hard, overcome by how dear and familiar and honest, and loyal and safe he was. His emotions wide open—not icy and shielded. She could *feel* how much he cared for her, how glad he was that she was alive and unhurt.

"I'm fine," she said, pulling back. "Really. And I'm sorry for running away without telling you—and I don't know why you're not mad."

Lewis and Anna were crowding around her, smiling, patting her as if to make sure she was real. They were *all* so dear and good and forgiving. . . .

"We were *worried* about you," Anna said.

"We camped out yesterday near the Institute hoping you'd come out," Lewis said. "But you never did."

"No—and *you* can't do that ever again," Kait said shakily. "Gabriel saw you. I don't think anybody else did, thank God, but he's bad enough."

"We won't have to do it again," Rob said, smiling. "Because we've got you now. We'll take you with us—even though we don't exactly have a place to go yet. Tony's working on that."

Kait thought he had never looked so handsome. His eyes were amber-gold, clear and full of light like the summer sky.

His face was full of trust and happiness. She could feel the radiant energy of his love.

"Rob . . . I can't." The change in his expression made her feel as if she'd hit an innocent child in the face.

"You can." Then, as she kept shaking her head: *"Why not?"*

"For one thing, if I disappear, they'll think I've betrayed them and they'll do something to my father. I *know* they will; I feel it in Joyce. And for another thing—Rob, it's *working.* I've got them snowed. They believe I've come back to join them and I've already had a chance to look around the house." She didn't dare tell him what had come of that; she had the feeling that if Rob knew, she'd be slung over his shoulders caveman style, being carried out of San Carlos.

"But what are you looking for? Kait, *why* did you come back here?" Anna said.

"Couldn't you figure that out? I'm looking for the crystal."

Rob nodded. "I thought it was something like that. But you don't need to live there, Kait. We'll break in sometime; we'll find a way."

"No, you won't. Rob, there are *five* psychics there, besides Lydia and Joyce, and they're all crazy-paranoid. Literally. We need somebody on the inside, who can move around the house freely, and who can figure out what's going on. Because I don't just want to find the crystal, I want to find the way to destroy it. I need to know everybody's schedule, figure out a time when we can get to it with the shard. We can't just go running in some afternoon waving it over our heads. They'll slaughter us."

"We'll fight back," Rob said grimly, his jaw at its most stubborn.

"They'll still slaughter us. They're *loonies*. You haven't seen what they've done to the house—" Kaitlyn caught herself. Too much description of the danger—she was about to get slung over Rob's shoulder. She changed tracks fast. "But they trust me. This morning one of the girls said I was okay. And Joyce wants me around because the rest of them are so far into the twilight zone. So I think everything will work out—if you'll just please let me get on with it."

Rob took a long, deep breath. "Kaitlyn, I can't. It's just too dangerous. I'd rather walk in and fight it out with Gabriel myself—"

"I *know* you would." And that's just what you're *not* going to do, Kait thought. "But it's not just Gabriel—you haven't seen the others. There's a guy called Jackal Mac who's about eight feet tall and has a shaved head and muscles like a gorilla. And I don't even *know* what his psychic power is, but I know that they're all hopped up on the crystal. It makes them stronger, and it makes them crazier."

"Then I don't want you with them."

"I *have* to be. Someone has to be. Don't you see that?" Kaitlyn felt her eyes filling—they seemed to do that a lot these days—and then she decided to do something dishonorable. To use those tears. She let them come, and she asked Rob, "Don't you trust me?"

She could see how it hurt him. His own eyes had a suspicious shine, but he answered steadily, "You know I do."

"Then why won't you let me do this? Don't you think I'm capable enough?"

It was completely unfair, as well as being unkind. And it worked. Rob had to admit that he thought she was very capable. The only one of them who could pull such a thing off. He even had to admit, finally, that it was a thing that probably needed to be done.

"Then why won't you *let* me?"

Rob gave in.

"But we'll come back and check on you next Monday."

"It's too dangerous, even at school—"

"Don't push it, Kait," Rob said. "Either you let us check on you regularly or you don't stay at all. We'll be here on Monday at lunch. If you don't show up, we're coming in after you."

Kaitlyn sighed, knowing Rob wasn't going to budge. "Okay. And I'll call when I find the crystal and I know a time we can get to it. Oh, Lewis—I should have thought of this before. How do you make the secret panel slide back?"

Lewis's almond-shaped eyes widened in dismay. "Huh? Kait—I don't know!"

"Yes, you do. Something inside you knows, because you do it."

"But I can't say it in words—and besides, you don't have PK."

"Neither does Joyce or Mr. Z, and the panel was made for them. And if you can't say it in words, just think it to me. Just think *about* it and let me listen."

Lewis was reluctant and doubtful, but he screwed up his face and began to think. "I just sort of feel around with my fingers—I mean with my mind—behind the wood. Like this. And I feel something metallic here. And then when I get to about here . . ."

"It opens! So the springs or whatever have to be in those places. You're a good visual thinker, I can see just what parts of the panel you mean." Kait made a note of the images, freezing them in her memory as she hugged him. "Thanks, Lewis."

And I'll mention you to Lydia, she added soundlessly, because a picture of Lydia was running underneath all Lewis's other thoughts.

She felt his shy embarrassment, like a mental blush. *Thanks, Kait.*

Then she hugged Rob again. *I'm glad you came.*

Be careful, he sent back to her, and she wished she could just go on hugging him, standing here and feeling safe. He was so good and she cared about him so much.

When she hugged Anna she projected a private message. *Take care of him for me—please?*

Anna nodded, biting her lip to keep the tears back.

Kait left without looking behind her.

The rest of the school day was uneventful, but Kait felt exhausted. She was fumbling in her locker after the last bell rang, when Bri came running interference through the crowd.

"Hurry up," she said in her boyish voice. "Come on; Joyce is waiting for you. She sent me to get you."

"What's the rush?" Kait asked nervously. Bri's dark eyes were snapping; her cheeks were flushed with excitement.

"Black Lightning strikes! Mr. Zetes has a job for us."

CHAPTER 8

Kait hurried toward Joyce's car with a knot in her stomach. She didn't know what kind of jobs Mr. Z had the kids do, but she knew she wasn't going to like it.

As it turned out, though, Joyce wasn't rushing them to the job. She was taking four of them shopping.

Gabriel, Renny, Frost, and Kaitlyn. They dropped Bri at the Institute where she stood on the sidewalk screaming with rage.

"It's not her fault, but she just doesn't look the part," Joyce said rather calmly as she headed for the freeway. "I told her not to put that blue in her hair."

Kaitlyn, squashed between Frost and Renny in the tiny backseat, felt as if she had lost her only friend. Not that she would rely on Bri, actually, or trust her as far as she could throw her. But the other three were openly hostile; Gabriel wasn't speaking to her, Renny kept whispering obscene suggestions in her ear, and Frost gave her a spiteful pinch whenever she thought Joyce wouldn't notice.

"What part doesn't she look?" Kait asked faintly.

"You'll see." Joyce drove them to a mall and pulled up in front of Macy's. There she ensconced Gabriel and Renny in the men's department and hustled Kait and Frost to the women's. She pushed Kait past Liz Claiborne and into Anne Klein.

"Now we're going to find you each a suit. Tweed, I think. Brown, anyway. Very conservative, only a little slit in the skirt."

Kaitlyn didn't know whether to laugh or groan. She'd never had a suit before, so this should have been exciting—but tweed?

It wasn't so bad when she got it on. Joyce pulled her hair back and Kait eyed herself in the mirror thoughtfully. She looked very trim and serious, like the librarian in a movie who starts out with her hair in a bun and horn-rim glasses and then blossoms by the end of the picture.

Frost's transformation was even more amazing. Her normal attire was a style Kait had privately dubbed "slunge"— a cross between sleaze and grunge. But in a double-breasted brown wool suit, she looked like another librarian—from the neck down.

"When we get home, you'll lose the lipstick—all of it— and half the mascara," Joyce told her. "And you'll put that rat's nest into a French twist. Also lose the gum."

The boys were equally transmogrified by three-piece Mani suits and leather shoes. Joyce paid for everything and hustled them out of the store.

"When do you tell us what we're doing?" Gabriel asked in the car.

"You'll hear the details at home. But basically it's a burglary."

Kaitlyn's stomach knotted again.

"So what now?" Anna asked. They were sitting in a Taco Bell in Daly City. Tony had promised to find them a place to stay with one of his friends—an apartment in San Francisco. But he hadn't found the place yet, and Rob was worried about staying any longer at Tony's house. So they spent as much time as possible outdoors, where they might be hard to find.

For the first time since Kaitlyn had disappeared Rob had an appetite.

But he would never in a hundred years have imagined he'd have left her at the Institute. The little witch—he still wasn't quite sure how she'd persuaded him. Of *course,* she was capable, but even a capable person could easily get killed there.

She'd asked him to trust her, that was it. All right, then, by God, he'd trust her. It was hard to let her go—he didn't think anyone realized how hard. He would very much have preferred to go himself. But . . .

I believe in you, Kaitlyn Fairchild, he thought. Just please God keep yourself safe.

He was so deep in his own thoughts that Anna had to poke him and ask silently, *I said, what now, Rob?*

"Huh? Oh, sorry." He stopped sucking on his Coke, considered. "Well, we've been too busy watching Kait to take care of Marisol. I guess we'd better do that now. Tony said his parents wouldn't be at the hospital till tonight, so it's a good time."

"Should we get Tony to go with us?" Lewis asked.

Rob thought. "No, I guess not. If it doesn't work, it'll be pretty hard on him to watch. We'll find some way to make them let us in." Tony had warned them that Marisol wasn't allowed visitors, except family.

They drove to St. Luke's Hospital in San Francisco, and Rob took the crystal shard out of the glove compartment. It was a crazy place to keep it, but they had to take it with them wherever they went. He slipped it into the sleeve of his sweater—it was just about as long as his forearm—and they strolled into the hospital.

On the third floor Rob beckoned a nurse—"Ma'am? Could I ask you a question?"—and sweet-talked her while Lewis and Anna snuck in Marisol's room. Then when all the nurse's phones began to ring at once, he snuck in himself. The ringing was provided by Lewis's PK, a neat trick, in Rob's opinion.

Inside the room, he felt Anna's shock. She was trying bravely to conceal it, but it showed through. He squeezed her shoulder and she smiled at him gratefully, then she stopped smiling and moved away so abruptly that he was startled.

Upset, probably. Marisol looked bad. Rob remembered her as a vivid, handsome girl, all tumbled red-brown hair and full pouting lips. But now . . .

She was painfully thin. There were all sorts of tubes and wires and monitors attached to her. Her right arm was on top of the blanket, with the wrist cocked at an impossible angle, turned in against the forearm. And she *moved*—her head twisted constantly, writhing on her neck, her brown eyes partway open but unseeing. Her breathing was frightening to hear: She seemed to be sucking air in through clenched teeth as she grimaced.

I thought people in comas were quiet, Lewis thought shakily.

Rob knew better. He'd been in a coma himself, after meeting a mountain at fifty miles an hour. He'd been hang gliding at Raven's Roost off the Blue Ridge Parkway, and he'd hit wind shear and stalled out. He'd broken both arms, both legs, his jaw, enough ribs to puncture a lung . . . and his neck. A hangman's fracture—so called because it's the same place your neck breaks when they hang you. Nobody expected him to live, but a long while later he'd woken to find himself in a Stryker frame and his granddaddy crying.

He'd spent months in bed and during those months he'd discovered his powers. Maybe they'd been there all along, and he'd just never sat still long enough to notice them, or maybe they were a gift because God was sorry about smashing a li'l ol' farm boy into that mountain. Either way, it had changed his life, made him see what a dumb sucker he'd always been, how selfish and shortsighted. Before, he'd aspired to being a guard for the Blue Devils at Duke. After, he aspired to help some.

Now, he felt shame flood up to drown him. How could he have left Marisol like this a day longer than she needed to be? He shouldn't have waited, not even to watch out for Kait. There was no excuse for it—he was still a dumb sucker and a selfish jerk. Fat lot of help he'd given Marisol.

This time Anna squeezed *his* shoulder. *None of us realized,* she said. *And we don't even know if we can help her, now. But let's try.*

He nodded, strengthened by her gentle practicality. Then, with one glance up at a picture of the Madonna and Child above the bed, he pulled the crystal out of his sleeve. It was cold and heavy in his hand. He wasn't sure where to apply it— LeShan hadn't said anything about that. After some thought he gently touched it to her forehead, the site of the third eye. A powerful energy center.

And nothing happened.

Rob waited, and waited some more. The tip of the shard rested between lank strands of red-brown hair. Marisol's head kept twisting. There was no change in her energy level.

"It's not working," Lewis whispered.

Fear pricked at Rob like tiny hornet stings. Was it his fault? Had he left it too long?

Then he thought, maybe the crystal needs a little help.

He took a deep breath, shut his eyes, and concentrated.

He never could explain exactly how he did his healing—how he knew what to do. But somehow he could feel what was wrong with a person. He could see different kinds of energy running through them like bright-colored rivers—and sometimes not flowing, but dark and stagnant, stuck. Marisol was almost all stuck. There was some sort of blockage between brain and body, and nothing was flowing either way.

How to fix that? Well, maybe start with the third eye, send energy through the crystal until it pushed hard enough against the plugs to blow them free.

Gold energy, flooding down the crystal. The crystal swirled it in a spiral and amplified it, heightening it with every turn. So that was how this thing worked!

More energy. More. Keep it flowing. He could see it flowing into Marisol, now, or at least trying to. Her third eye was stopped up as if somebody had wedged a cork in there. The energy built up behind it, roiling and gold and getting hotter by the minute. Rob felt sweat break out on his forehead. It dripped into his eyes and burned.

Ignore it. Send more energy. More, more.

Rob was breathing hard, a little frightened by what was happening. The energy was a crackling, spinning mass now, so hot and dense that he could barely hold onto the crystal. It was like trying to control a high-pressure fire hose. And trying to send more energy in was like trying to pump air into a critically overinflated bicycle tire. Something had to give.

Something did. Like a cork blowing out of a bottle, the blockage flew out of Marisol's third eye. The force of the energy behind it chased it down her body and out the soles of her feet almost faster than Rob's eye could follow.

Gold everywhere. Marisol's entire body was encased in gold as the energy raced around, rushing through veins and capillaries, circulating at a wildly accelerated speed. An internal whirlpool bath. God, it was going to kill the girl. Nobody was meant to have that much energy.

Rob jerked the crystal away from her forehead.

Marisol's body had been straining, her back arching as the energy shot through her. Now she fell back and lay completely still for the first time since they'd walked in. Her eyes were shut. Rob realized suddenly that one of her monitors was blaring like an alarm going off.

Then, as he watched, her right hand began to move. The fingers unclenched, the wrist relaxed. It looked like a normal hand again.

"Oh, God," Lewis whispered. "Oh, look at that."

Rob couldn't speak. The alarm went on blaring. And Marisol's eyes opened.

Not halfway. All the way. Rob could see the intelligence in them. He reached out to touch her cheek, and she blinked and looked scared.

"It's okay," he told her, loud over the alarm. "You're going to be all right, you understand?"

She nodded uncertainly.

Running footsteps sounded outside the door. A sturdy nurse burst in, got almost to the bed before she skidded and saw Rob.

"What do you think you're doing in here? Did you touch anything?" she demanded, hands on hips—and then she took a good look at Marisol.

"Ma'am, I think she's feeling a little better," Rob said, and smiled because he couldn't help it.

The nurse was looking from Marisol to the monitors. She broke into a huge grin, switched the monitor off, and took Marisol's pulse.

"How're you feeling, darlin'?" she asked with tears shining in her eyes. "You just hang on one minute so I can get Doctor Hirata. Your mama's going to be so happy." Then she rushed out of the room without yelling at Rob.

"I think we'd better go before Doctor Hirata gets here," Lewis whispered. "He might ask some awkward questions."

"You're right." Rob grinned at Marisol, touched her cheek again. "I'll tell your brother you're awake, okay? And he'll be over here as fast as he can drive. And your parents, too . . ."

"Rob," Lewis whispered urgently.

They made it to the back stairs without being caught. On the second landing they stopped and whacked each other in glee.

"We did it!" Rob whispered, his voice echoing in the empty stairwell. "We did it!"

"*You* did it," Anna said. Her dark eyes were glowing and wise. It wasn't true, it had been the crystal, but her praise made Rob feel warm to the tips of his fingers.

He hugged Lewis and felt happy. Then he hugged Anna and felt a surge of something different from what he felt for Lewis. Stronger . . . warmer.

It confused him. He'd only felt something like it once before—when he'd found Kaitlyn alive down in Mr. Z's basement. It was almost like pain in its intensity, but it wasn't pain.

Then he pulled back, shocked and mortified. How could he let himself feel like that about anyone but Kaitlyn? How could he let himself feel even a little like that?

And he knew Anna could tell, and that she was upset, because she wouldn't meet his eyes and she was holding herself shielded. She was disgusted with him, and no wonder.

Well, one thing was for certain. It would never happen again, never.

They walked down the rest of the stairs with only Lewis talking.

"All right, this is the place," Gabriel said. It was an imposing stone building on a one-way street in the financial district of San Francisco. Through the metal-framed glass doors Kait could see a guard at a little booth.

"Joyce said the guard won't give us any trouble. We sign in with the names she told us. The law firm is Digby, Hamilton, and Miles, the floor is sixteen."

He didn't look at Kaitlyn as he spoke and he didn't glance at her as they went inside. She didn't seem to exist for him anymore. But Joyce had told them to go in pairs, and Kait was supposed to walk by Gabriel. She tried to do it without showing any more expression than he did.

The guard was wearing a red coat and talking on a cell phone. He barely looked at them as Gabriel flipped through papers on a clipboard. Gabriel signed, and then it was Kait's turn. She wrote *Eileen Cullen, Digby, Hamilton, and Miles, 16,* and *11:17,* on the appropriate lines. The 11:17 was the "Time In."

Frost and Renny signed in and they crossed the tile mosaic floor to a bank of brass elevators. A man in jeans was polishing the brass, and Kaitlyn stared at her neat brown Amalfi shoes while they waited—it seemed a long time—for the elevator.

Once inside, Gabriel pushed a large black button for floor sixteen. The button stuck. The elevator started, slowly, and with a wheeze.

Renny was snickering and Frost let out a torrent of gasping giggles.

"Do you know what I signed for my name?" Renny asked, banging the elevator door. "I signed Jimi Hendrix. And I put for the company, Dewey, Cheatum, and Howe. Get it? Dewey, Cheatum, and Howe for a law firm!"

"And I put Ima Pseudonym," Frost said, tittering.

Kaitlyn's heart gave a violent thud and began racing. She stared at them, appalled. They *looked* normal now: Frost's hair was pulled back elegantly and she was wearing only one earring in each ear and Renny could have been a junior accountant. But underneath they were still the same raving loonies.

"Are you guys *nuts?*" she hissed. "If that guard takes a look at that sheet—oh, God, or if the next person who signs in just *glances* up—we are *dead. Dead.* How could you do such a thing?"

Renny just waved a hand at her, weak with laughter. Frost sneered.

Kait turned to Gabriel to share her horror. It was a reflex— she should have known better. However horrified he might have been a minute ago, he now shrugged and flashed a quick, mocking smile.

"Good one," he said to Renny.

"I knew *you* had a sense of humor," Frost purred, running a silvery fingernail up Gabriel's gray wool sleeve. She ran it all the way to his crisp white collar, then toyed with the dark hair behind his ear.

Kaitlyn gave her a blistering glare through narrowed eyes. Then she stared at the elevator buttons, fuming silently. She didn't like this job. She *still* hadn't been told what they were doing—what can you burglarize in a law firm? She didn't even know what psychic powers Frost and Renny had. And now she had to worry about what other insane things they might decide to do.

The elevator doors opened.

"What a dump," Renny said, and snickered. Gabriel cast an appreciative look around. The walls were paneled in some beautiful reddish gold wood and the floor was dark green marble. Through glass doors Kait could see what looked like a conference room.

Gabriel glanced at the map Joyce had given him. "Now we go right."

They passed rest room doors—even those looked opulent—and entered a hallway with dark green carpeting. They stopped when they came to a set of doors blocking their way. The doors were very big and heavy; they looked like metal, but when Kaitlyn touched one it was wood. And locked.

"This is it," Gabriel said. "Okay, Renny."

But Renny was gone. Frost, standing a little way back, said, "He had to go to the little boys' room." She was struggling to keep a straight face.

Kaitlyn clenched her fists. She'd seen the graffiti at the Institute; she could just bet what he was doing in there. "Now what?" she snarled at Gabriel. "Look, are you going in there to get him, or am I?"

Gabriel ignored her, but she could see the tightness of his jaw. He started toward the bathroom, but at that moment Renny came out, his face the picture of innocence.

"I would have thought," Gabriel said without looking at Kait, "that you'd be happy if we screwed this up. After all, you're not really one of us . . . are you?"

Kaitlyn felt chilled. "I am, even if you don't believe it," she said, working to put sincerity in her voice. "And maybe I don't like stealing things, but I don't want to get caught and sent to jail, either." As Renny approached, walking cockily, she added in an undertone, "I don't even know why we *brought* him."

"Then watch and see," Gabriel said tersely. "Renny, this is it. From here on you need a security pass."

The device on the wall looked vaguely familiar. It was like the machines at the gas station that you slide a credit card through to charge gas automatically.

"Yeah, magnetic," Renny muttered. He pushed his glasses back with an index finger on the nosepiece and ran a hand over the security pass reader. "Anybody looking?" he said.

"No, but do it fast," Gabriel replied.

Renny stroked the device again and again. His face was wrinkled up, monkeylike. Kaitlyn chewed her lip and watched the central area from which they'd just come. Anybody stepping out of an elevator would see them.

"There you are, baby," Renny whispered suddenly. And the right hand door swung open.

So now Kaitlyn knew. Renny had PK, psychokinesis; he could move objects by power of mind alone. Including the little mechanisms inside security pass readers, apparently.

Just like Lewis, Kaitlyn thought. I wonder if there's something about short guys.

The door closed behind them when they went through.

Gabriel led them quickly down the hallway. On the left other hallways branched away; on the right were secretaries' carrels with computers on the desks. Behind the carrels were office doors, with names on brass nameplates beside them. Kaitlyn saw one nameplate that said WAR ROOM.

Maybe law is more exciting than I thought.

They came to another set of the big doors and Renny dealt with them in the same way. They walked down another hallway.

The farther they got into private territory, the more frightened Kait was. If anyone caught them here, they would have some explaining to do. Joyce hadn't given them any advice about that—Kaitlyn had the sick feeling that Gabriel might be expected to use his power.

"What are we *looking* for, anyway?" Kait whispered to Gabriel between her teeth. "I mean, have they got the Mona Lisa here or something?"

"Keep your stupid mouth shut. Anyone walking up one of those hallways could hear us."

Kaitlyn was stunned into silence. Gabriel had never spoken to her like that before. And he hadn't said a word about Renny and Frost doing really dangerous things.

She blinked and set her teeth, determined not to speak again, no matter what.

"This is it," Gabriel said at last. The nameplate on the door said E. Marshall Winston. "Locked," Gabriel said. "Renny, open it. Everybody else keep your eyes out. If anybody sees us here, we've had it."

CHAPTER 9

Kaitlyn stared down the hall until she saw red after-images. She was sweating onto her white silk blouse. Then she heard a snap and the door opened.

"Frost, keep watching out. Renny, come with me."

Kaitlyn felt sure Gabriel wanted her to keep watching, too, but couldn't bring himself to name her. She followed Renny into the dark office. Gabriel was pulling the shades, cutting out the night.

"She said Mr. Z thought it would probably be in the file cabinet—I guess that's this." He went over to a wooden credenza with file drawers built in. "Locked."

Renny took care of that, while Gabriel shone a penlight on the drawers. Kaitlyn's heart was thumping, quick and hard. She was watching a crime being committed—a serious, major crime. And if they got caught, she was as guilty as any of the others.

Renny stepped back and Gabriel pulled the top file drawer out. Then he cursed softly, closed it, and pulled out the lower one.

It was crammed with hanging files in green folders, each one neatly labeled. Kaitlyn watched the penlight illuminate labels: Taggart and Altshuld—Reorganization. Star Systematics—Merger. Slater Inc.—Liquidation. TCW—Refinancing.

"Yes!" Gabriel whispered. He pulled out the thick hanging file that said TCW.

Inside were a lot of manila folders. Gabriel began going through them deftly. It all seemed to be paper, mostly white paper covered with courier type, a few booklets with paper as thin as Bible pages.

In a strange way, Kaitlyn felt relieved. It didn't seem so wrong to steal paper, even if it was important paper. It wasn't like taking money or jewels.

Gabriel's breath hissed out.

He was peering into a manila envelope. He pulled out the papers inside it, scattering them on the credenza's flat top, and shone the light on them.

Kaitlyn squinted, trying to make out what they were. They looked like certificates or something, heavy blue-gray paper, with a fancy border around the edges.

Then her eyes focused on tiny words Gabriel was tracing with his finger. Pay to Bearer . . .

Oh, my *God*.

Kaitlyn stood paralyzed, the print swimming before her eyes. She kept staring at the number on the bond, sure it couldn't be right, but it kept saying the same thing.

U.S. $1,000,000.

One million dollars.

And there were lots of the things. A pile of them.

Gabriel was flipping through, counting under his breath. "Twenty," he said at last. "That's right." He gathered the bonds up in his hands and caressed them. He was wearing the same expression Kaitlyn had seen when they toured Mr. Z's mansion. Like Scrooge counting his gold pieces.

Kaitlyn forgot her vow not to speak. "We're stealing twenty million dollars?" she whispered.

"A drop in the bucket," Gabriel said, and caressed the bonds again. Then he straightened up and began to briskly put the other folders back into the drawer. "We don't want a custodian or somebody to see anything's wrong tonight. Not until we get out of the building."

When the drawer was shut, he put the manila envelope inside his jacket. "Let's go."

Nobody was in the hall and they passed the first set of doors safely. From this side, the doors just pushed open. Kaitlyn didn't know whether to be nauseated or relieved. They were committing a felony. Gabriel was walking around with twenty *million* stolen dollars against his chest. And the horrible thing was that they were getting away with it.

Of course, on the brighter side, they were getting away with it. Kaitlyn wasn't going to jail.

That was when the two men stepped out of an office in front of them.

Kaitlyn's heart jumped into her mouth and then *burst*. Her feet were rooted to the floor and her hands and arms were numb. Her chest was squeezed so tightly that there was no room for her lungs to breathe.

Still, at first she thought the men wouldn't look her way. They did. Then she thought they wouldn't keep looking, wouldn't stare—because surely she was frightened *enough,* she'd been punished enough already. She wanted nothing to do with a life of crime.

But the men kept looking, and then the men were walking toward Kaitlyn's group. And then their mouths were moving. That was all Kaitlyn could take in at first, that the mouths were moving. She couldn't hear what they were saying, everybody seemed to be underwater or in a dream.

But a minute later her mind ran it all back for her, sharp and clear. "What are you doing here? You're not interns."

And there was suspicion in the voices, or at least a sense of wrongness. And Kaitlyn knew that if somebody didn't come up with something quick, that suspicion was going to harden and gel and they'd be trapped like flies in amber.

Think, girl. Think, *think.*

But for once, absolutely nothing came to her. Her quick

brain was useless. All she could think of was the lump under Gabriel's black-flecked gray jacket, which was starting to look as big as an elephant inside a boa constrictor.

That was when Frost stepped in.

She moved forward in a slithery, silky way totally at odds with her brown suit. Kaitlyn saw her smile at the two men and take their hands.

God, not *now,* Kaitlyn thought. Flirting won't stop them. But this passed in a flash, because Frost was talking, and not in a sexy way, but bright and cheerful.

"You must be—Jim and Chris," she said, hanging on to their hands like somebody at a tea party. "My uncle told me about you. You're in the corporate group, right?"

The two men looked at her, then at each other.

"We're just looking around. I'm thinking of coming here in a few years, and these are my friends. My uncle said it would be all right, and he gave me his security pass."

"Your uncle?" one of the men said, not as sharp as before, but bewildered.

"Mr. Morshower. He's a senior partner—but you know him, because he knows you. Why don't you call him at home and check it out? He'll tell you everything's okay."

"Oh, Sam," one of the young men said weakly. Funny that Kaitlyn had suddenly realized they were young. "I mean, Mr. Morshower." He threw a look at the other young man and said, "We won't bother him."

"No, no. I insist," Frost said. "Please call him." She actually picked up a phone from one of the secretaries' desks.

"That's all right," said the second young man. He looked unhappy. For the first time Kaitlyn was able to look at them as people. One had brown hair and one had black hair, but they were both wearing white shirts and striped ties knotted all the way up, even at this hour, and they both looked pale and somewhat harassed.

"Are you sure?" Frost asked, sounding disappointed. She put the phone back. The young men gave wry, watery smiles.

"Can you find your way out?" they asked, and Frost said of course, they could. Kaitlyn hardly dared to say anything, but she managed to smile at them as she walked past, and back down the hall, and toward the elevators.

Her chest was squeezed again, but this time the pressure was from inside. She was so bursting with laughter that she could hardly contain it until they were in the elevator.

Then they were all laughing, howling, shrieking, almost falling down. Renny did fall down, drumming his heels on the elevator floor. They were insane. Kaitlyn very nearly kissed Frost.

"But how did you know?" she said. "Did Joyce tell you?"

"No, no." Frost tossed her ash blond head impatiently. "I got it from them. I could've done it just from a piece of their clothing or one of those stupid fat silver pens they had in their pockets."

"Those were Montblanc pens. And they weren't silver, they

L. J. SMITH

were platinum," Gabriel said quietly, and then they all had to be quiet because they'd reached the lobby. Frost swerved toward the red-coated guard to sign out, but Gabriel pushed her past him and into the street. The guard looked after them, came to the door.

"Step on it," Kait said to Gabriel as they scrambled into Joyce's car.

"It's called psychometry," Frost said to Kait after another period of hilarity. Gabriel was driving wildly through the streets of San Francisco.

Kaitlyn had heard of psychometry. You could tell a person's whole history by handling a personal object. "But why did you pick Mr. Morshower?"

"Because I could tell they were afraid of him. They were supposed to have something—a merger agreement?—sent to his client by the FedEx deadline today and they haven't done it."

Frost reeled the words off glibly, but Kaitlyn could tell she wasn't really interested anymore. And the resourcefulness and sanity that seemed to have taken her over during the crisis was fading. The inner fogginess was coming back. It was as if intelligence were a tool this girl used, and then threw away when it wasn't needed anymore.

That put a damper on Kaitlyn's excitement. The feeling of having brilliantly outwitted a cruel world was dying away. For a while it had made her breathless, but now . . .

We really are crooks, she thought with a mental sigh.

And she was afraid of Frost's powers. Anybody who could find out that much about you with a touch was dangerous. Frost had already touched Kait when they were in the backseat of Joyce's car. Had she found anything out?

Must not have, Kaitlyn concluded, or Joyce wouldn't have sent me. Maybe it helps that I've developed shields in the web. But I'll have to be careful—one false step and . . .

"Just try not to get a ticket," she said to Gabriel, who was rounding a corner wildly.

He didn't answer. Great. He wasn't speaking to her again.

"Did I pass?" Kait asked Joyce.

Joyce looked at her, going through all the signs of being startled.

"What do you mean?"

"It was a test, wasn't it? So, did I pass or fail? I didn't do much."

They were sitting up in Joyce's room, drinking herbal tea in the wee hours of the morning. Renny and Frost had gone upstairs to drink something stronger, and Gabriel had gone with them, never glancing at Kait.

"Yes, it was a test," Joyce said at last. "The money will come in handy, but mostly I had to make sure that you were really one of us. Now you're a full member of the team—and if you ever think of crossing us, remember that you've participated in a felony. The police take a dim view of that."

She took a sip of tea and mused briefly. "You and Gabriel passed," she added. "As for Frost and Renny . . ."

"They did most of the work."

"But from what you've said, they also did a lot of stupid things." For a moment Kait thought Joyce was going to go on, to confide in her. But then Joyce stood up and said shortly, "We'll stick to other kinds of jobs from now on. Long distance, maybe. Mac is good at that."

"Is he?" Kait asked innocently. "What's his power? I don't know what he or Bri do."

She held her breath, sure Joyce wouldn't tell her. But Joyce shrugged and said, "His specialty is astral projection, actually."

Let your mind do the walking, Kait thought. It was Lewis's phrase. So Mac was responsible for the astral projections and psychic attacks against them on the way to Canada. "But we saw at least four figures," she blurted before she thought. "And one of them was Bri—I *recognized* her."

Joyce was setting the clock radio by the bedside and answered impatiently and almost absently. "Mac used to guide them, help them get away and then help them get back into their bodies. But anybody can do astral projection if they have the power of the crys—" She broke off so quickly her little white teeth actually snapped shut. Then she said, "Bed, Kaitlyn. It's way past time."

I knew they used the crystal to project themselves, Kait

thought. I saw it beside their astral forms. But she didn't tell Joyce. She said, "Okay, but are you going to tell me what Bri does?"

"No. I'm going to go to bed."

And that was all Kaitlyn could get out of her.

Upstairs, Kaitlyn could hear the voices in Gabriel's room. Gabriel and Frost and Renny? Gabriel and Frost? There was no way to find out.

"Too bad I can't do astral projection," she muttered.

Lydia was asleep, of course, so there was no chance to talk to her. And no way to try out the secret panel downstairs—it was directly across from Joyce's room.

Nothing to do, then, but go to sleep . . . but it took her a long time to relax, and when she did, she had nightmares.

The next morning she saw Frost coming out of Gabriel's room.

Gabriel came out a moment later, while Kaitlyn was still standing motionless by the stairs. He was shrugging into his T-shirt. He looked particularly handsome in a just-roused, early morning way. His hair was very wavy, as if someone had run fingers through it to release the curl, his eyes were hooded and lazy and there was a faint smile of satisfaction on his lips.

Kaitlyn discovered that she wanted to kill him. The image that came to her mind was of hitting him with a rolling pin, but not in an amusing, comic-book sort of way. In a way that would make splinters of bone fly and splatter the walls with blood.

His expression changed very slightly when he saw her standing there. His eyes narrowed and his mouth soured. But he held her gaze stonily and walked by her without speaking.

"Today you'll do some testing," Joyce said to Kaitlyn after breakfast.

But before starting with Kait, Joyce settled the other psychics in. Testing had changed since the old days, Kaitlyn thought. Then, Joyce's experiments had been scientific, the kind of thing you could report in a journal article. Now, everything seemed oriented toward crime.

Jackal Mac, wearing swim trunks full of holes, was led toward the back lab with the isolation tank, and Kait heard Joyce saying, "Just take a look inside that safe in the city, see if the papers are there. Then try the long-distance job, check out that furnace."

Astral projection for felons, Kait thought. Is that how they knew the twenty million was in that filing cabinet? But how did they know to look in a filing cabinet in the first place?

Renny was practicing his PK, but not on a random event generator as Lewis had done. He had a collection of locks in front of him, as well as diagrams that looked like the insides of locks. Without touching anything, he was making the locks open and close.

Aha, Kait thought. Well, that makes sense. He needs to

know what part of the lock to push with his mind to open it. PK doesn't give you magical knowledge about locks, just the power to poke around inside them.

It explained Gabriel's comment about Lewis not being able to open the combination lock on the crystal—wherever the crystal *was*. Kaitlyn would bet her last dime that Mr. Z had some sort of fiendishly complicated locking device, something that Lewis couldn't get a diagram for. Which meant the only way to open the lock would be to somehow figure out the eight numbers in the combination.

Whoa, girl. Take it easy. You've got to *find* that crystal first.

As soon as she'd thought it, Kaitlyn shifted nervously. Gabriel and Frost were sitting across the room by the stereo. But *he* was studying a pile of CDs and *she* couldn't tell anything unless she touched a person. Besides, she seemed to be studying Gabriel. She was looking more sleazy than grungy today, in an orange top cut so low that you could ski down the bare skin in front. Her hair had returned to its usual uncombed state and her lips were vivid tangerine.

"What are you doing?" Kait asked Bri, as a diversion.

Bri glanced up. "Can't you tell?"

She was holding a plumb bob on its line above a map. The plumb bob and line looked just like what Kaitlyn's father had used to determine if a surface was vertical, just a small weight hanging freely from a cord. The map was upside down to Kaitlyn and she could only make out "—Charlotte Islands."

"I'm dowsing," Bri said. She gave a boyish grin at Kait's surprise.

"I thought you used a forked stick for dowsing."

"No, stupid. That's for dowsing for water or gold or something. This kind is to find things that are far away, and you can do it for *anything*."

"Oh." As Kaitlyn watched, the plumb bob began to swing in circles over a section of the map.

"See? All you got to do is think of what you're looking for. Sasha used to do the other kind of dowsing, only he didn't use a stick. He used coat hangers shaped like *ls*."

"Sasha?"

"Oh, yeah. You never met him." Bri snorted laughter. "He was blond and pretty cute, critty pute. Cute."

"Was he one of Mr. Z's first students?" Kaitlyn asked quickly. "Part of the pilot study, like you?" Bri seemed to be on the verge of one of those bizarre attacks which always ended in her repeating nonsense words until it drove everyone crazy.

"Yeah, him and Parté King. Not his real name. Parté King was a bike messenger in the city, a real skinny guy. Both terrific psychics."

"But what happened to them? Are they dead?"

"Huh? They—" Suddenly Bri's face turned cold, as if someone had turned off a light switch inside her. She looked up at Kait and her face was hard. "Yeah, they're dead," she said. "Sasha and Parté King. You wanna make something of it?"

Joyce was coming out of the back lab. Kaitlyn moved away from Bri's carrel feeling depressed.

The dark psychics were nicer to her now, sure, but it was like a geyser pool bubbling between eruptions. Ready to go off in her face at any minute.

The doorbell rang.

"That's the volunteers—would you get them, Gabriel?" Joyce said bustling around with her clipboard. "Frost, I'm going to have you do some psychometry with them; Kait, I'm going to start you with some remote viewing."

She sat Kaitlyn in a carrel with a photograph in front of her. It was an eight-by-ten glossy of a wall safe.

"I want you to concentrate on the picture and draw anything that comes into your mind," she said. "Try to imagine what might be *in* the safe, okay?"

"Okay," Kaitlyn said, concealing a surge of rebellion. This was *not* legitimate research, and she was losing her taste for larceny.

"I'm going to put this on your forehead," Joyce added, producing a piece of masking tape.

This time the surge was one of alarm, and Kait couldn't hide it. "An electrode over my third eye?" she asked as lightly as she could.

"You know what it is. Since you haven't been exposed to the big crystal, we'll use this to enhance your powers."

"Well, why don't you expose me to the big crystal, then?" Kait asked recklessly. "Those little chips give me a headache, and—"

"Sorry, that's up to Mr. Zetes, and he doesn't want you anywhere near it. Now, hold still." Joyce's tone said she'd had enough. Her eyes had gone as hard as gems and she barely pushed aside Kaitlyn's bangs before slapping the tape on Kait's forehead.

Kait felt the piece of crystal cold against her skin. It was bigger than the piece Joyce had used in the old days, maybe because now Joyce wasn't trying to conceal it. This one felt the size of a quarter.

Knowing where it came from, she could scarcely keep herself from tearing the tape off. But then she saw Gabriel in the doorway, looking sardonic and amused.

You don't have anything against the crystal, do you? After all, you're one of us. . . .

Kaitlyn shot back, *I'm not one of* them. *But I guess you are.*

Right, angel. I'm one of them—and don't you forget it.

Kaitlyn left the tape alone.

But she didn't want to help Joyce with the safe. She stared at the photograph, then shut her eyes and just scribbled, taking the time to think.

She understood now how the dark psychics had attacked them on the road to Canada. First Bri probably dowsed to figure out where they were. Then Jackal Mac guided their astral forms to the right location. After that, they could assault their victims with weird apparitions or with Renny's long-distance PK. Simple. You could terrorize people without ever going near them.

And now Joyce was expecting her to join in the long-distance crime wave, to help them visualize some safe to break into.

Wait a minute.

If she could see into a safe, why not a room? Why not try to visualize the secret room below the stairway?

Without opening her eyes, Kait groped for a new piece of paper. She'd never tried to visualize a specific place before, but the remote viewing process was old hat by now. Stretch out and let your thoughts drift. Block out any external noises. Let the darkness take you down. . . .

And now, think of the secret room. Think of walking up to the door, visualize that hallway lit by fluorescent greenish light. Walk up to the door . . . and let the darkness take you. . . .

Her hand began to cramp and itch.

Then it was dancing and skidding over the paper, moving of its own accord while Kaitlyn floated in darkness. Sketching fluidly, easily. Kaitlyn held her breath and tried not to be anxious, tried not to think or feel anything.

Okay, slowing down—is it done yet? Can I look?

She couldn't resist the temptation. One eye opened, then both were open and wide. Chills swept over her, as she stared, not at the piece of paper her hand was still working on, but at the first one, the one that was supposed to be only scribbles.

Oh, God, what *is* it? What have I done?

CHAPTER 10

I t wasn't her usual style. It was cartoonish, but *gruesome* cartoonish, like the new breed of comic books. At first Kait thought it might be a picture of her beating Gabriel to death with a rolling pin.

But those long tear-shaped things flying out at the edges were flames. Flames, fire. It was a fireball or an explosion, circular, with smoke billowing every which way, and the shock waves moving outward like ripples on a pond.

And in the center was a stick figure of a person. Like Itchy the cat after Scratchy hits him with a flamethrower. Arms waving, legs splayed in a grotesque dance.

Ha, ha.

Except that since Kait's drawings always came true, somebody was going to get burned. Somebody involved with that safe, maybe? Kait tried to recapture what she'd been thinking about while scribbling. Too much. Psychic attacks, Canada,

Bri dowsing, Jackal Mac on the astral plane, Renny's PK. And the safe, of course, even though she'd tried not to think about it.

This picture could involve any of those things. Kait had a very bad feeling about it, made worse by a nagging, growing headache.

What about the other picture? The one that was supposed to be visualizing the secret room? Kait looked at it and wanted to slam her fist on the table.

Garbage! Trash! Not literally, but the drawing was useless. It wasn't the inside of a room at all, and it certainly didn't show a crystal. It was a line drawing of a sailing ship on a pretty, wavy ocean. Sitting on the deck, right below the sails, was a Christmas tree. A nice little Christmas tree with garland and a star on top.

Kaitlyn's eyes were stinging with pain and fury. The first picture left her helpless. The second was useless.

And that makes *me* completely hopeless.

Suddenly she couldn't hold her feelings in. She crumpled them up with a savage motion and threw them as hard as she could at Frost. One hit Frost on the cheek, the other hit Frost's volunteer.

"Kaitlyn!" Joyce shouted. Frost leaped up, one hand to her cheek. Then she made a rush for Kait, her nails clawed.

"Frost!" Joyce shouted.

Kaitlyn put a foot out to block Frost. In elementary school

she'd been a pretty good fighter, and right now it felt good to fend Frost off. And if Frost whacked her, she was going to whack right back. She felt calm and queenly standing there ready to kick Frost in the chest.

"Come on, snowflake," she said. "Come get me!"

"I will, you!" Frost shrieked, charging again.

"Gabriel, help me! Renny, you stay in that seat!" Joyce shouted.

Joyce and Gabriel dragged Frost back and sat her down hard in a chair. Kait was tempted to go after her, but didn't.

"Now," Joyce said in a voice to cut through steel, "what is going on?"

"I got mad," Kaitlyn said, not at all sorry. "Everything I draw is *trash*."

"Smash," Bri said quietly. Kait had an urge to snicker.

Joyce was staring at Kait, lips compressed, brow furrowed. Abruptly, she pulled the tape off Kait's forehead.

"How do you feel?" she said.

"Bad. I have a headache."

"Right," Joyce muttered. "All right, you go upstairs and lie down. But first you pick up those papers and put them in the trash can where they belong."

Stiff-backed, Kait stalked over to the crumpled wads, picked them up. Then, as Joyce turned back to her clipboard, she faked throwing them at Frost again. Frost went red, and Kait hurried out of the room.

Upstairs, she shut the door of her bedroom and wondered what had come over her.

Was she crazy? No, of course—it was the crystal. Joyce had used a big piece of the crystal and it had made Kaitlyn act like the psycho psychics.

And I must be pretty crazy to start with, because it didn't take much, Kaitlyn thought. Maybe Bri and the others were a lot saner than me to begin with. I wish I could have seen them before . . .

She let out her breath, trying to make sense of her feelings. She'd really been furious there, furious and completely indifferent to any consequences her actions might have. She would happily have scratched Frost's eyes out.

Well, maybe that wasn't so crazy. After all . . .

Kaitlyn sat on the bed heavily. She kept trying to tell herself she didn't care about Gabriel—but if she didn't care, why did she hate Frost so much today?

And Gabriel certainly didn't jump up to defend me, she thought. He probably enjoyed watching us fight.

Kait rubbed her throbbing forehead, wishing she could go outside and lie under a tree. She needed air. Idly, she toyed with the balls of paper in her other hand.

Then she looked up as the door opened.

"Can I come in? My riding lesson was canceled this morning," Lydia said. She sounded depressed.

"It's your room," Kaitlyn said.

She kept rolling the paper balls around, squashing them against each other. She'd taken them so Frost wouldn't pick them out of the trash can and laugh at them—but was that the only reason? Now she wondered if it hadn't also been some survival instinct kicking in.

None of her drawings was really worthless. Maybe she'd better keep them.

"What's the matter?" Lydia asked.

Kait frowned. Lydia was picking *now* to talk? "I've got a headache," she said shortly, and dropped the paper balls in a drawer.

Then she remembered her promise to Lewis. She glanced at Lydia out of the side of her eye.

The smaller girl looked very neat in a brown riding habit. Her heavy dark hair was pulled away from her small pale face, and her green eyes showed up more than ever. Neat and rich—and miserable.

"Have you got a boyfriend?" Kait asked abruptly.

"Huh? No." She hesitated, then added, "I'm not after Gabriel, if that's what you mean."

"It isn't." Kait didn't want to talk about Gabriel. "I was thinking about Lewis—did you ever notice him?"

Lydia looked startled—almost frightened. "Lewis! You mean Lewis Chao?"

"No, I mean Lewis and Clark. Of course Lewis Chao. What do you think of him?"

"Well . . . he was nice to me. Even when the rest of you weren't."

"Well, he thinks you're nice, too. And I told him—" Kaitlyn caught herself. Oh, Lord, this headache was making her stupid. She'd almost said that she'd told Lewis *yesterday* she'd bring him up. Frantically, she tried to think of another way to end the sentence.

"I told him that you'd think you were too good for him. That you'd just laugh at him. That was a long time ago," Kaitlyn finished at random.

Lydia's eyes seemed to turn a darker green. "I wouldn't laugh. I like nice guys," she said. "I don't think *you're* very nice. You're turning out just like them," she added, and left the room, slamming the door.

Kaitlyn leaned back against the headboard, convinced she just wasn't cut out to be a spy.

And she still didn't feel quite herself. One thing was certain, she couldn't let Joyce put her in contact with the crystal again. It made her lose control, and when she lost control anything could happen.

And another thing was certain, too. She couldn't use her power to visualize the hidden room downstairs, and Joyce wasn't going to let her anywhere near it. So the only solution was for her to go down there herself.

But *when?*

Still rubbing her forehead, Kaitlyn toed her sneakers off and lay down.

At first she shut her eyes just to ease the headache. But soon her thoughts began to unwind and her muscles relaxed. This time there were no nightmares.

When she woke she had that feeling of desertion again. The house seemed too quiet, the warm air too still.

At least her headache was gone. Moving slowly, she got off the bed and tiptoed to the door.

Silence.

Oh, they *wouldn't* leave me alone again. Not unless it's a trap. If it's a trap, I'm not going anywhere.

But she had a *right* to go downstairs. She lived here; she was a full member of the team. She could be going down to get a diet soda or an apple.

Down the stairs, then.

And she had a right to look around downstairs. She could be looking for the others; she could be lonely. She kept the right words on her lips.

"Joyce, I just wanted to ask you—"

But Joyce wasn't in her room.

"Are you guys still testing—?"

But the front lab was empty. So was the back lab.

And the kitchen, and the dining room, and the living room. Kaitlyn pushed aside the living room curtains to look outside the house. Nobody playing hacki sack or Frisbee tag. Only juniper hedges and acacia trees. She couldn't even see Joyce's car.

Okay, so maybe it's a trap. But it's too good an opportunity to miss.

Heart beating in her throat, Kaitlyn crept toward the paneled hallway under the staircase.

The middle panel, she thought, with one guilty glance behind her at the French doors leading to Joyce's room. She ran her fingers over the smooth dark wood, reaching up to find the crack that was the top of the door.

Okay, she was in front of it. Now to find the place Lewis had showed her. She shut her eyes and concentrated on the images she'd gotten from Lewis. They weren't exactly visual, more like just a feeling of how she should move her hands. He'd found something around this level—and then he'd pushed with his mind. She would push with her fingers.

And then he'd moved over *this* way, and down, and pushed again. Kaitlyn pushed again, pressing hard.

Something clicked.

Kaitlyn's eyes flew open. I did it! I actually did it!

Excitement bubbled up from her toes, fizzling out to fill every part of her body. She was *impressed* with herself.

The middle panel had disappeared, sliding to the left. Stairs led downward, illuminated only by faint reddish lights at foot-level.

The bubbles seemed to be making a fizzing in her ears now, but Kaitlyn tried to listen over it. Still, silence.

Okay. Going down.

With each step into the red dimness, she felt a little of the effervescence leaving her. This wasn't a nice place. If she'd been a few years younger, it would have made her think of trolls.

At the bottom she groped for the light switch she knew should be there—and then snatched her fingers back. Too much light wasn't good. If there was somebody in the room at the end of the hall, they might notice.

But if she didn't turn on the light, she'd have to walk the whole way in darkness. Just the thought made her knees unsteady.

There was no help for it. Tensing her muscles, she put a hand on the wall to guide her and began walking forward. In a moment she had to put the other hand out to feel for obstacles. She was blind.

Each step was hard, and she had to clench her teeth tighter and tighter to make herself keep going. The red staircase behind her began to feel more and more tempting.

Oh, God, what if somebody came and saw the panel open and closed it *and locked her in here?*

The thought was so terrible that she almost turned around and ran. Instead, she used the energy to force herself forward. And *one* more step, and *one* more step—

Her outstretched fingers encountered a door.

Her need for light was so great that she reached automatically for the knob, without listening to see what might be on the other side. But instead of a knob, her fingers found something like a calculator built into the door.

What was it? She could feel little square bumps in a regular pattern. It really did feel like a calculator.

Oh, you idiot. You *idiot.* You must still be stupid from the testing this morning. It's a combination lock. Not one of those padlock kinds; one of the fancy ones, where you punch numbers on a keypad.

And if this was the combination lock, then behind that door . . .

It was *in* there. That grotesque thing with the obscene crystalline growths all over it. It was squatting in there just a few feet away.

Kaitlyn was swamped by a feeling of evil.

And then—she heard noises.

From behind the door.

They were in there with it.

Oh, God, I'm so stupid, I'm so stupid. Of course, they're in there. This is where they go in the afternoons, they go to the crystal, and they're all sitting in there around it *right now.*

Don't panic, don't panic, she told herself, but it was too late. She *was* panicking. She hadn't even asked Lewis how to shut the secret panel. She was incompetent and stupid and they were right inside there and she didn't have time to get away.

Another noise sounded—very close to the door.

Suddenly Kaitlyn was moving, without thinking, without

caring where she was going. With great stocking-footed leaps she was sailing down the hallway toward the red stairs. She reached the first step and began to scramble up, banging her knee, ignoring it, scrambling on. Using her hands. She got to the top of the stairs and the white light of the hallway blazed into her eyes. That light was the only thing that stopped her, kept her from running through the living room and out of the house—or up to her bedroom to hide under the bed. She was almost like an animal in her blind instinct to get under cover.

"Kaitlyn, what on *earth*—?"

The voice was high and light, surprised. Kaitlyn turned terrified eyes on Lydia.

"What happened? Did they do something to you?" Lydia was looking past her down the stairs.

A tiny bit of Kaitlyn's mind returned. There was a chance, just a chance for help—for salvation. Lydia knew about the panel; Lydia seemed worried about Kaitlyn.

"Oh, Lydia," she said, and her voice came out a croak. "I—I . . ."

She'd meant to lie, to say that she'd been down with the others and she'd gotten scared. But somehow what came out was, "Oh, Lydia, I know I shouldn't have gone down there. But Joyce never lets me do anything. I just wanted to see—and now Joyce is going to be *furious*. I don't know how to get the panel shut."

Lydia was looking at her with level green eyes.

"I just want to do the things they do," Kaitlyn said, then blurted, "I'm sorry if I was mean to you before."

There was a pause. Kaitlyn's heart was beating so hard she was dizzy. Lydia was staring down at the staircase, lower lip caught between her teeth.

Finally she looked up. "So you want to do the things they do. You're one of them. Okay." She leaned forward and touched the left wall quickly, in three different places.

The panel slid shut, concealing the gaping hole.

Kaitlyn stood, not knowing what to do. Lydia stared at the floor.

"Be careful, Kaitlyn," Lydia said, and then she hurried away before Kaitlyn could recover.

Kaitlyn stood under the spray of hot water, trying to get warm. Her legs were still wobbly and she was developing a magnificent bruise on one knee.

Lydia knew.

There was no doubt in Kaitlyn's mind. The one in the house who wasn't psychic was the one who'd found her out. Kaitlyn's lies hadn't fooled her for a minute.

So why had she helped Kaitlyn?

Oh, it didn't matter. Just please let her not tell Joyce. Kaitlyn flexed her cold hands under the flood of water.

But there was no way to ensure that. The only way to keep safe was to leave. And Kaitlyn couldn't do that. No matter how frightened she was, she couldn't leave when she'd come so far. If she could just stick it out until Monday—and if she could get Rob to give her the shard—

—and if she could figure out the combination.

She had to, to get into that room alone.

Drying herself as she went, Kaitlyn headed for her art kit.

Last time she hadn't been concentrating on the right thing. She'd been trying to see inside the room—and heaven only knew why she'd gotten the garbage she had. Maybe Joyce kept a Christmas tree in with the crystal. Maybe there was a ship in a bottle in there. Anyway, now she knew what to think about.

Numbers. She needed numbers for that combination lock. And with her own art materials, with her beloved pastels and her faithful sketchbook, she was going to get those numbers.

Door shut tight, ceiling light off. Kaitlyn threw a T-shirt over the lamp on the nightstand to dim it. Okay, that was the proper ambiance. Hair swathed in a towel, feet tucked under her, she put pastel to paper.

She had never worked so hard at blanking her mind. She *threw* herself down the chute into the waiting darkness. The itch and cramp took over her fingers and she felt them moving, reaching out to snatch new pastel sticks, swirling colors across the page.

A few minutes later she looked at what she'd done.

I can't believe it. I can't *believe* it!

It was another ship with a Christmas tree.

This time in color. The ship's sails were dove white, the planks were tinted sienna brown, the pretty curly waves were three shades of blue. And standing proudly on the deck was a celadon green Christmas tree with poppy red garland and a yellow ocher star.

Kaitlyn wadded the paper up in a fury and threw it at the mirror.

She wanted to break things. She wanted to throw something heavier—

The door burst open.

Instantly, Kaitlyn's fury disappeared and terror rushed in to fill the vacuum. Lydia had told them. They had all run up here to get her. She could hear thudding footsteps in the hall behind the figure in her doorway.

"Hey, Kait, how come it's so dark in here?" Bri shouted. Without waiting for an answer, she added, "Come on! Get dressed!"

For what, execution? Kait wondered. She heard her own voice saying almost quietly, "Why?"

"Because we're celebrating! We're all going out to the club! Come on, get dressed, put your best duds on. Plenty of *guys*," Bri added slyly. "You got something to wear? I could lend you something."

"Uh—that's okay, I've got something," Kaitlyn said hastily. She could just imagine what sort of "duds" Bri might have to lend. But Bri's urgency was contagious, and Kaitlyn felt herself being propelled toward the closet. "I've got a black dress—but why are we celebrating?"

"We did a job this afternoon," Bri said, shaking her clasped hands over her head like a boxer. "An astral job, a real big job. We killed LeShan."

"I met her on the stairs. She said she had to see you," Tony's friend said. Rob, Lewis, and Anna were sitting in the tiny one-room apartment. Rob peered behind Tony's friend at the person who had to see them.

"I've been tracking you from house to house," the girl said. She had clusters of curly yellow hair and the profile of a Grecian maiden. Despite the yellow hair, her complexion was olive and her eyes almond-shaped like Lewis's. She was very pretty.

And familiar. "I know you," Rob said. "You were—you were with the Fellowship."

"Tamsin," Anna said, before the girl could.

The girl—Tamsin—nodded at her. She looked as if she were trying to smile, but it didn't work. The smile turned into a trembling of her lips, then her head went down and she started to cry.

From the doorway, Tony's friend said, "I'll catch you guys later," and left hurriedly.

"What is it?" Rob was trying to lead the girl to a chair. His initial excitement at seeing her had deflated like a pricked balloon. He'd thought the Fellowship had sent someone to help.

"I came to help," the girl choked out, as if she could hear his thought—and probably she could. The Fellowship were all psychics. "LeShan sent me."

"Then what's the matter?" Anna asked quietly, putting a gentle hand on Tamsin's quivering shoulder.

"Nothing was the matter—until a little while ago. Then I felt it. I felt him die. LeShan is dead."

Rob's skin tingled with shock. He had to swallow hard. "Are you sure?"

"I *felt* it. We thought we'd be safe from them on our new island. But they must have found him. I felt him die."

She's really upset, Lewis said silently.

She was, Rob thought. Not just upset but helpless—the way the people of the Fellowship tended to be when they didn't have a leader. He didn't send the thought to Lewis because he had the feeling Tamsin could hear.

"And now I don't know what to do," Tamsin said, almost wailing it. "LeShan was going to tell me when I got here. I came all this way and I can't help you at all."

Rob looked at Anna, as if he might find something comforting to say in her face. Anna was so wise. But Anna's gaze, dark and liquid with tears, held his only a moment, then quickly dropped.

Angry with himself, Rob put an arm around Tamsin. He said, "Maybe Meren—"

"Mereniang is dead, too," Tamsin whispered. "She died on the way to the island. There's no help anywhere, no hope!"

CHAPTER 11

Kaitlyn sat on Lydia's bed with the black dress on her lap. She had been reaching for it, glad that she'd brought it and that it had hung out with no wrinkles, when Bri had told her.

Now she just sat. She didn't need to ask Bri any questions. She knew the whole truth.

Queen Charlotte Islands. That's what the map had said. In Canada. That must have been where the Fellowship had gone when they'd left Vancouver Island. Bri had dowsed for them with that map.

And Jackal Mac had checked the furnace out. Some furnace where the Fellowship were living. Kaitlyn knew because she had a picture of it—a picture of a fireball, of a furnace exploding. And a man in the middle of it.

All of them had gathered around the crystal this evening and sent out their astral forms. They'd left their bodies and gone to the Queen Charlotte Islands and then Renny had used his PK.

Oh, LeShan. Kaitlyn twisted the chiffon of the black dress between brutal fingers. I liked you. I really liked you. You were arrogant and angry and impatient and I really, really liked you. You were *alive*.

Caramel-colored skin. Slanting lynx eyes. Softly curling hair that seemed to have an inner luminescence, pale and shimmering brown. And a spirit that burned like midnight fire.

Dead.

And now Kaitlyn had to go and celebrate. No way to get out of it. They would know if she tried to make some excuse. If she was going to be one of them, she had to hate the Fellowship as they did.

Feeling very brittle, very light, and unstable, Kait went over to the mirror. She pulled off the towel and her clothes and put on the black dress. She began to mechanically run her fingers through her wet hair, when she suddenly realized something.

I look like a witch.

In the dim light, with her long hair falling about her shoulders, drying just enough to be a halo of red, with the black dress and her bare feet and the pallor of her face . . .

I do. I look extremely witchy. Like somebody who might go walking down the street like this, barefoot, hair wild in the breeze, singing strange songs, and all the people peeping out at me from behind their curtains.

The fitted spandex bodice *did* make her look slim as a statue, and the sheer chiffon skirt swirled from hip to midcalf. But it wasn't vanity that held her there looking. It was a new sense of her own competence, of determination.

Anybody who looks this witchy *must* be able to call down a curse. And that's what I'm going to do. Somehow, I'll make them all pay, LeShan. I'll avenge your death. I promise.

I promise.

People were calling outside. Lydia was opening the door apologetically.

"I just heard," she said. She looked as hangdog and slinking as Kaitlyn had ever seen her, but also bitterly satisfied, as if she'd been proved right. "I told you my father would win. He always does. You were smart to come in on this side, Kait."

"Could I borrow a pair of nylons?" Kaitlyn asked.

Mr. Z was in the living room when they all came downstairs. Kaitlyn supposed he'd been in the hidden room with them, directing the work. He gave Kaitlyn a courtly nod as she walked toward him in a pair of shoes borrowed from Frost.

He looked amiable, but Kaitlyn could *feel* his savage joy. He knew she was hurting and he liked that.

"Have a good time, Kaitlyn," he said.

Kaitlyn lifted her head, refusing to give him the satisfaction.

Gabriel was there, too, handsome in dark clothes. Kaitlyn turned appraising eyes on him. He didn't look disturbed over LeShan's death—but then he had no reason to like the Fellowship.

Their philosophy said they couldn't open their doors to anyone who'd taken a human life . . . no matter what the circumstances. Because Gabriel had killed by accident and in self-defense, they refused to let him in. So now Gabriel wasn't upset.

Everyone else was delirious with happiness.

Mr. Z saw them off, and they took two cars. Kait rode in Lydia's car with Bri and Renny. Joyce took Gabriel, Frost, and Jackal Mac. Kait spent the drive plotting how to make them all pay—Gabriel, too.

The club was called Dark Carnival. Kaitlyn stopped musing on revenge to stare. It was like nothing she'd ever seen before.

There was a line of people waiting to get in the door. People wearing *everything*. Unimaginable outfits. They looked bizarre and more than a little scary.

Traffic stopped the car for a while near the door and Kaitlyn was able to watch what was going on. A doorkeeper with a lip-ring and a Liverpool accent was saying who could get in immediately, who should wait, and who should just go home. Those who got in: a guy with purple glittery lipstick and silver aluminum curlicues for hair. A girl in an evening gown of black spiderweb. A chic Italian-looking girl in a white unitard and black velvet shorts—very short.

"He keeps out people who aren't cool enough," Bri said in Kaitlyn's ear, leaning heavily on her back. "You have to be either famous or completely beautiful or—"

Or dressed like a cross between a Busby Berkeley show and something from a science fiction movie, Kaitlyn thought.

"So how are we going to get in?" she asked quietly.

She was watching the losers—the people who couldn't get in. The normal people who weren't exciting or weird enough, waiting outside behind cords, sometimes crying.

"We've got invitations," Lydia said in a dead voice. "My father has connections."

She was right. The doorkeeper let them right in.

Inside there were strobe lights, super black lights, and colored lights, all flashing in an atmosphere so full of smoke Kaitlyn could hardly see anything but the flashing rainbow.

The music was loud, a throbbing beat that people had to shout over. On the dance floor a girl with long shiny hair was kicking high over her head.

"Isn't it great?" Bri yelled.

Kaitlyn didn't know what it was. Loud. Weird. Exciting, if you were in the mood to celebrate, but surreal if you weren't.

I'm going to avenge you, LeShan. I promise.

She glimpsed Joyce walking toward the dance floor. Jackal Mac, the lights reflecting on his head, was giving an order to a scantily clad cocktail waitress.

Where was Gabriel?

Bri had disappeared. Kait was surrounded by people with wings, people dressed in cellophane, people with spikes for fingernails. Everywhere she looked were falls of Day-Glo hair.

Enormous false eyelashes. Slanted eyebrows, silver-glittering eyebrows. No eyebrows. Pierced bodies.

If she hadn't been so cold with anger over LeShan, Kaitlyn might have been scared. But just now nothing could touch her. A man in a leopard-skin unitard and a mask beckoned her to dance and she followed him to the floor. She didn't really know much about dancing, except what she'd done at home, watching the TV and dreaming.

It was too loud to talk, and she didn't really care what the leopard-man thought of her—so it was the perfect opportunity to muse on revenge again.

And that was how she solved the mystery of the combination lock.

It wasn't like in books, where the faithful sidekick makes some offhand remark and then the famous detective sees all. There was no particular reason why it came to her. But every minute or so her mind would go back to her problem.

I need to get to that crystal. Which means I need to get the combination.

And once when her mind went back to it, she thought, "But maybe I already have the combination. One drawing was a real prophecy. What about the other?"

And then the other thought was simply *there,* fullblown, a question asking itself in her mind: How can a Christmas tree and a ship be eight numbers?

Well, *Christmas* had a number, of course. A date. December

the twenty-fifth, 12/25. Or 25/12 if you were thinking the twenty-fifth of December.

The dark room rocked under Kaitlyn's feet. The leopard-skin man was walking away, but she didn't care. She backed up to a railing, her eyes on the flashing lights.

She was trembling with excitement, her mind racing to follow this new idea to the end, like a spark running down a line of powder.

The ship. The ship is another number. And what number? It could be the number of masts or the number of crew or the number of voyages it made. Or a date, a date when the ship sailed—but what kind of ship is it?

A window opened in her stomach and she felt hollow with dismay. She didn't know anything about ships. How long would it take to research, to speculate?

No, stop. Don't panic. The picture was drawn by your unconscious, so it can't be much smarter than you are. It couldn't take a date and make it into a ship if you didn't *know* the date and ship already.

But I'm so stupid, Kaitlyn argued back. Rotten in history. I only know the simplest dates—like "In fourteen hundred ninety-two . . ."

Columbus sailed the ocean blue.

That sparkly, curly blue ocean. Three colors of blue. Drawn with an excess of care.

She'd found the answer.

Kaitlyn knew it, she felt certain. But a nagging murmur of dissent was starting in her brain. Mr. Z wouldn't make the combination that simple. He wouldn't begin it—or end it—with 1492. Anyone *glancing* at it would remember. Someone breaking in might try it at random.

That was when Kaitlyn had her second brainstorm. Supposing the combination didn't begin or end with 1492—not all together. The Christmas tree had been in the middle of the ship, so supposing the combination was 14/12/25/92. Or 14/25/12/92.

Good heavens, or even 1/12/25/492. Or . . .

Kaitlyn cut her busy brain off. I'll think of all the possibilities later. But I'll try the easy ones first. And I'll—

A guy with a bald head was darting a black-stained tongue at her. Kaitlyn recoiled, then realized it was Jackal Mac.

"What's the matter? Scared of me?"

Kaitlyn stared into the jackal eyes. "No," she said flatly.

"Then come dance."

No, Kaitlyn thought. But she was a spy and her most important job was to not get caught until she got the shard to the crystal. Nothing else was important.

"Okay," she said, and they danced.

She didn't like the way he moved in on her. Not like slow dancing, he wasn't trying to hold her, but he kept moving toward her, forcing her to back up. Otherwise his swinging arms and gyrating hips would have made contact.

She saw Frost and Gabriel together on the floor. Frost fit right in here; she was wearing a silver baby doll dress and silver ankle boots. She kept brushing against Gabriel's body as she danced.

Well, at least she wasn't as exposed as that woman wearing a negligee. Or that man painted orange who seemed to be wearing almost *nothing*.

"Hey, baby! Pay attention!"

Jackal Mac was closing in again. Kaitlyn stepped back and collided with a woman in space-age neon sunglasses.

"Sorry," she muttered, inaudibly over the music. She edged away, heading for a deserted space below the bandstand. "Look, Mac, I'm kind of tired—"

"Sit down and rest."

He was backing her farther into the space, below and slightly behind the stage. Kaitlyn tripped over a cord or cable. She couldn't keep walking backward like this.

"I think I just want something to drink. Would you like something?"

It was strange that her voice was so calm. Because suddenly she was very scared.

They were in an isolated little nook here, where the music was loudest. No one from the dance floor could really see them. Certainly no one could hear them. It was smoky and dark and humid and it felt like a trap.

"Yeah, I'm kinda thirsty," Jackal Mac said, but he was

blocking the way out. His eyes gleamed in the dimness. He had one hand up, resting on the stage, and suddenly Kaitlyn got a whiff of his sweat.

Danger.

It was like red warning lights flashing in her head, like the sound of sirens. She could *feel* his mind, cluttered and trashed and nasty as his bedroom. Nasty as the red-haired man had been.

"I'm thirsty, you know, but not for a drink. Gabriel told me how you used to take care of him."

Not like the red-haired man after all. Jackal Mac had a different aberration. He didn't want to hurt her body, he wanted to suck her brain out.

You bastard, Kaitlyn thought with white-hot fury, but she didn't mean Jackal Mac. Her hatred was for Gabriel.

He'd told this—animal—about what Kait had done for him. The most private moments she'd ever had with anyone. Kaitlyn felt as if she'd been violated already, ripped open for everyone to see.

"What else did Gabriel tell you?" she said in a voice that was hard and distant and unafraid.

Jackal Mac was surprised. His head bobbed, apelike, then his black-stained tongue came out to lick his lips.

"He said you were always chasing him. I guess you like it, huh?" Sliding his arm down to shoulder level, he moved closer. "So you gonna make this easy, or what?"

Kaitlyn held her ground. "You're not a telepath. I don't know what you think—"

"Who says you need to be a telepath?" Mac laughed. "This is about energy, pretty girl. We all need energy. Everybody who's a friend of the crystal."

The crystal. Of course. Mr. Z's way of keeping them all in line. It had made them all psychic vampires like Gabriel. And it satisfied them all, provided them with energy . . . unless you were like Jackal Mac and wanted something extra.

He wants me to be afraid, Kait thought. He enjoys that, and he'll like draining my energy best if I'm fighting and screaming. That little extra kick.

I hate you, Gabriel. I *hate* you.

But it didn't prevent her from saying what needed to be said.

"And you think Gabriel's going to like it if you mess around with me?" she asked. "He didn't like you messing with his room."

Mac's eyes took on an almost injured expression.

"I wouldn't touch Gabriel's woman," he said. "But that's Frost now. He was the one who said I should check you out."

His teeth shone white in the darkness.

For an instant, Kaitlyn felt only numb. Gabriel had thrown her to Jackal Mac like a bone. How could she *live* with that?

And then survival instinct took over and she realized that she wouldn't have to live with it if she didn't do something fast.

Jackal Mac was reaching for her with his blunt, restless hands. She knew the routine. There were several transfer points, but third eye to third eye or lips to spine were best. She would bet that Mac wanted her spine.

So *relax*. Relax and let him get behind you. No, pretend you're going to cooperate.

A part of her mind was yammering at her, insisting that there was a way to yell for help. A vocal scream would be lost in the throbbing music, but she could scream mentally. Gabriel had come the last time; he might come if he thought Mac was killing her.

But I *won't* scream, she thought, cold washing over her like an icy waterfall. I won't scream even if he does kill me. I wouldn't take Gabriel's help if I knew it would save my life.

Gabriel had set this human beast on her. Let Gabriel live with the consequences. Besides, he might hear her screams and just smile.

"Come on," Kaitlyn said to Mac, aware she hardly sounded seductive. "I don't mind. Just let me get my hair out of the way."

His hands with their ugly, chewed-up nails hovered in the air. She stepped toward him, but to one side, grasping her hair with one hand, pulling it off her neck, watching his eyes follow her movements greedily.

"Okay and just let me do—*this*." While his eyes were on her bare shoulders, she slammed a heel into his shin. He made a thick, startled sound of surprise and pain, more like a pig than a jackal. He lunged toward her—

—but she had kicked the loose cord between his feet. He stumbled, tangled in it. Kaitlyn didn't wait to see if he recovered his balance or not. She was running.

She reached the dance floor, plunged into the crowd. Fell into someone's arms. A poetic-looking young man wearing a shirt with a large collar and flowing white sleeves.

"Hey—"

Kaitlyn reeled away. Where was Joyce? Nobody else could keep Mac from following her out here, from dragging her back. . . .

There. Joyce and Lydia. Kaitlyn wove unsteadily toward them through the crowd.

"Joyce—"

She didn't get any farther. A roar was beginning behind her. Jackal Mac was parting the crowd like Moses parting the Red Sea. But unlike Moses, he was doing it with fists and elbows, and the Red Sea was getting mad.

"You don't need to explain," Joyce said tightly to Kaitlyn.

As Kaitlyn watched, Mac ran into a short woman with lacquered hair. He shoved her aside. A large man wearing chains lunged forward to grab him.

"Here comes Renny," Lydia said.

Renny appeared with a bottle. Kait couldn't tell if he was attacking Mac or defending him, but suddenly glasses were flying, people were throwing punches. Jackal Mac picked up a chair and lifted it over his head.

Screams split through the music. Hefty men in suits were running in from all directions.

"You girls get out of here," Joyce said. Kaitlyn could feel that she was angry and exasperated almost to tears. Here she was, out to celebrate in her pink St. John dress with the rhinestones, and Mac was ruining everything. If Kaitlyn hadn't known why Joyce was celebrating, she might have felt sorry for her.

As it was, she took Lydia's arm and propelled her toward the Exit sign. Lydia waited until they were in the car to speak.

"What happened?"

Kait shook her head, then leaned her temple against the cool window. Everything inside her was sick and sore. Not from Mac's attack. From knowing Gabriel had egged him on. And from the hole in the universe where LeShan had been.

It's a filthy world, she thought slowly. But I'm going to do my part to clean it up. And then I'll never have to look at Gabriel again. I'll go as far away from here as I can go.

It was very late when she heard Joyce bring the others home that night. There was a lot of thudding on the stairs, a lot of banging and laughing and cursing.

"They scare me," Lydia said softly from the other bed. "The way they are. What they can do."

They scared Kaitlyn, too. She wanted to say something

comforting about how things were going to change, but she didn't dare. Lydia wasn't evil, but she was weak—and besides, no one was to be trusted. *No one.*

"Think about something else," Kaitlyn said. "Did you ever find a cow alarm clock around here?"

"No. A what?"

"An alarm clock shaped like a cow. It was Lewis's. It used to go off every morning, this sound like a cowbell and then a voice shouting 'Wake up! Don't sleep your life away!' And then it would moo."

Lydia giggled faintly. "I wish I'd seen that. It sounds—like Lewis."

"Actually, it sounded like a cow." Kaitlyn could hear Lydia snorting softly in the darkness for a while, then silence. She pulled the covers over her head and went to sleep.

The next day she was confronted with a problem. Everyone else was exhausted and lethargic, so Joyce had canceled all testing. She had the day to herself—but she couldn't figure out how to get in touch with Rob.

Call the Diaz house? Not from inside the Institute. Much too risky. And she had no excuse for walking off alone to find a pay phone. She didn't want to do anything that might look suspicious.

But she *needed* to talk to Rob, to tell him to bring the shard on Monday. She didn't want to waste any more time.

She was sitting at the desk in her room, tapping a pencil

and wondering if she dared ask to borrow Lydia's car, when a noise at the window made her turn around.

A kitten. A big kitten, almost a cat. It was pawing at the screen.

Kaitlyn almost smiled despite her mood. You funny baby, how did you get all the way up here? she wondered, and went to open the screen. The kitten butted its head against her and rasped her knuckle with a tongue like a furled pink leaf until Kait rubbed the black velveteen fur between its ears.

What a funny collar. Way too thick. That must hurt you. . . .

It was a piece of paper, wrapped around and around the blue nylon stretch collar and secured with masking tape.

A note.

Suddenly Kaitlyn's heart was beating hard. She looked down into the backyard below the window. Nobody in sight. Then she glanced over her shoulder, toward the closed door of the bedroom.

Eyes on the door, she pulled at the tape with her fingernails, tearing the note free.

CHAPTER 12

THE MAN AT THE AIRPORT AND THE LADY WITH THE
PITCHFORK ARE DEAD. THE WATER'S TOO HOT. MEET
ME AT THE OLD RENDEZVOUS SOON AND THE DISH WILL
RUN AWAY WITH THE SPOON. PICK YOUR TIME, JUST LET
ME KNOW. SEND A MESSAGE IN A BOTTLE.

The note was neither addressed nor signed—Rob had thought it less risky that way, Kaitlyn supposed. But she understood what it said.

Mereniang was dead, too. LeShan was the man who'd accosted her at the airport, and the first time they'd seen Meren she'd been pitching cow dung. Rob thought Kaitlyn was in too much danger now, and he wanted her to come to the gym, where he'd whisk her away from the Institute permanently. She was supposed to pick a time when she could get away and send a note back.

Kaitlyn sat for a moment, rolling the pencil between her fingers. Then she straightened her shoulders, tore a sheet out of her sketchbook and began to write in a heavy, determined hand.

The hotter the water, the better witches Like it. No date today. Same time, same pLace tomorrow. Bring the magic knife. I've done my homework and know my numbers.

She hoped Rob would remember Tony saying "I see you got the magic knife for Marisol." And she hoped he would understand that she *couldn't* leave now; she knew where the crystal was kept and she knew the combination to get to it.

The kitten was nudging her, rolling, asking for pets. Kaitlyn stroked it, then wrapped the note around its collar and taped it securely. She opened the screen and held her breath.

Out went the kitten, without a backward glance. Anna must have implanted the suggestions very well.

Now, Kaitlyn thought, leaning back. Nothing to do but ⸱ for tomorrow at noon. And hope Rob keeps his date.

⸱ it alone," Rob said.

⸱ It's the only possible way."

It was noon on Monday. They were hiding in the gym itself, which seemed safer than the entrance.

Kaitlyn looked at Lewis and Anna for help, but they were both looking pretty helpless. As if they couldn't figure things out. Rob was the one who'd made up his mind.

"I can't let you take it back to the Institute by yourself. I'm going with you—I'll sneak in whenever you do."

He just wasn't thinking it through. "But what if we get caught sneaking into the house?"

"What if *you* get caught with the crystal? That would be just as bad as being seen with me."

"No, it *wouldn't,*" Kaitlyn said, straining to keep her voice patient. "I can hide the crystal—or at least there's a chance that I could hide it quick if I heard somebody coming. But I can't hide *you.* What am I going to do, stick you under a sofa pillow?"

Rob was trying to be patient, too—she could see and feel it. And he was losing the battle. "It's . . . just . . . too . . . dangerous," he said with slow emphasis. "Do you really think I'm going to sit around, safe in somebody's apartment, while you take all the risk? What does that make me?"

"Smart. Rob, I'm hoping I can get to the crystal today, but that may not be possible. Joyce could have the lab door open; somebody could be sitting in the living room where they can see the secret panel. I may have to wait around for days and watch for my chance. *You* can't sit that long in the house with me—or even outside," she added, cutting him off. "Gabriel would feel you there, just like he did before. And then it would be all over, he's really our enemy now."

She had thought this through, and she didn't intend to budge. And she could see Rob knew it. His expression suddenly changed; his jaw set, his mouth straightened into a grim line. A golden blaze sparked in his eyes. He looked, Kaitlyn thought, like a good guy pushed too far.

Without a word, he reached for her, grabbed her around the waist. Kaitlyn felt herself lifted, her feet leaving the wooden gym floor.

"I'm sorry, but I've had enough," he said. "You're coming back to the car."

A few days ago, Kaitlyn might have thought this funny. But now . . .

Put me down!

The volume of it shocked Rob into loosening his grip. The sheer fury in her eyes kept his mouth shut as Kaitlyn pulled away from him.

Anna and Lewis were shocked, too—and frightened. Kaitlyn knew they could feel the anger pouring off her like invisible waves. She stood like a queen, feeling tall and terrible and when she spoke each word came out like a white-hot chip of steel.

"I am *not* an object, something to be picked up or carried away or passed around. *Gabriel* thought that's what I was. He was wrong. You're both wrong," she said to Rob.

His hair was tousled, making her suddenly think of a

little boy. His eyes were dark amber and wide. There was utter silence in the gym.

"*I* am the only one who can decide what will happen to me," Kaitlyn went on very quietly. "No one else. *Me.* And I've already made my decision. I'm going back to that place and I'm going to try to stop them any way I can. Whether you give me the shard or not is *your* decision, but I'm going back anyway."

She had never spoken to him like this before, and she could see that he was confounded. Stricken. Kaitlyn tried to make her voice gentler, but she could hear the steel underneath it.

"Rob, don't you see, this thing is bigger than just us. You're the one who taught me that things can be bigger than people. You made me *want* to make a difference. And now I have a chance to do it. Timon died and LeShan died and Mereniang died, and if somebody doesn't stop the Institute more people are going to die. I *have* to try and stop that."

Rob was nodding slowly. He swallowed and said, "I understand. But if something happened to you—"

"If something terrible happens to me, then at least I know that *I* chose it. I went because I decided to go. But *you* don't have anything to do with it. . . . Do you understand?"

Anna was crying. Lewis was almost crying.

And Rob—seemed shocked into submission. He looked at Anna as if that were somehow his final appeal.

Anna blinked away tears. Her face was compassionate, sad—and still. Too deep a stillness to be simply resignation.

"Kait's right," she said. "She'll go if she says she'll go. You can't say for her. Nobody can ever say for somebody else."

Then Rob looked back at Kait, slowly, and she knew that he was seeing her as an equal for the first time. An equal not just in brains or psychic power or resourcefulness, but in every way, with exactly as much right to risk her life as he had to risk his.

Equal and *separate*. It was as if at that moment they split apart, became two independent creatures. If Rob had ever had a fault in their relationship, it was thinking he had to protect her. And Kaitlyn had encouraged it in a way, by thinking that she needed to be protected. Now, all at once, they were both realizing it wasn't true.

And once Kait knew that, she realized that in the last few minutes she had grown in his eyes. Rob respected her more, even loved her more than ever before . . . in a different way.

But he was still having a hard time grasping that he was *really* going to have to stand here and watch her walk away and take the risk herself. So he gave it one last try, not with force, but with entreaty.

"You know, I've been wondering if we should maybe wait just a little to use the shard, anyway. It did cure Marisol, you know. You didn't see that, Kait, but it was wonderful. And there are a lot of other people in that hospital. I was kind of hoping . . ." He shrugged, his face wistful.

Kaitlyn was moved. But before she could speak, Anna did.

Anna's face was even more compassionate than before, more sad—and more certain.

"No, Rob," she said quietly. "That's the one thing we *can't* do. It doesn't belong to us; it's just on loan. Timon gave it to us for destroying the crystal. We *can't* just go around using that much power that isn't really ours. Something bad would come of it."

Then she put a gentle hand on Rob's shoulder. "You've got power of your own that you can use to help people—and that should be enough. You'll have your chance, Rob."

Rob stared at her for a long moment, then nodded. He looked from her to Kaitlyn, and through the web, Kaitlyn got just a glimpse of his thought. He was awed and a little confused at being caught between these two farsighted women. She could feel him wondering how they'd gotten so wise while he'd stayed dumb.

And thinking there was nothing for him to do but agree.

"So it's settled," Kaitlyn said quietly. "I'll take the shard and go back to the Institute, and you'll go back to Tony's friend's apartment."

"We left Tamsin there," Anna said. "We'll tell her what you're doing. She'll be rooting for you, Kait, and so will Marisol."

Kaitlyn was glad to talk about something ordinary, because she had the feeling that any minute she might start crying. "Marisol's really that much better?"

"She's still in the hospital because her muscles are weak and she has to learn to use them again. But Tony says it'll only be a few days before she's walking. Oh, Kait, I wish you could have seen his face when he came to see us! And his mom and dad—they called and just thanked us over and over. We couldn't get them off the phone."

"And Tony said he was going to light a candle for you," Lewis put in. "You know, in church. Because Rob told him you were in danger."

Kaitlyn's throat was swollen and her eyes kept filling with warmth. She gulped. "I'd better take it and get going."

Rob knelt and opened the duffel bag he'd brought. He took out the crystal shard, opened Kaitlyn's backpack, and put it in. Kaitlyn knew that he was doing it himself as a sort of symbolic offering, an admission that she was right. She also knew that he had to fight to make every move.

He stood up, very pale, and held the backpack out to her.

"Call us when it's over," he said. "Or if you think you can't do it before tomorrow. And, Kait?"

"Yes?"

"If you don't call us by tomorrow, I'm coming in. That's not negotiable, Kaitlyn; that's *my* choice. If I don't hear from you, I'm assuming that something's gone wrong, and all bets are off."

What could Kaitlyn say?

Good luck, Lewis said silently as she hugged him. *I'll be thinking about you.*

Be careful, Anna said. *Be as clever as Raven and get yourself out safe.* She added a few words in Suquamish, and Kaitlyn didn't need a translation. It was a blessing.

Last of all, she hugged Rob. His eyes were still sore from the hard lesson he'd just learned. He held on to her very tightly. *Please come back to me. I'll be waiting.*

How many times had women said that to their men who were going off to war?

The swelling in Kaitlyn's throat was getting bigger by the minute. *I love you all,* she told them. Then she turned around and walked toward the back door of the gym, feeling their eyes on her. She knew they stood in perfect silence as she went out onto the blacktop, and then onto the baseball field, watching and watching until she was out of sight.

Kaitlyn was heading straight back for the Institute. It was only about a mile. She'd told Rob that she might have to wait for days to get to the crystal, but she knew that her best chance was right now. Bri, Renny, and Lydia were at school—and Gabriel was supposed to be. That left Frost and Jackal Mac in the house with Joyce.

I should be able to get in without them noticing, she thought. *And then maybe they'll all go into the back lab or something, and I can get to the panel.*

The walk was actually pleasant. Kaitlyn found herself noticing the sky, which was a beautiful blue with just the right amount of wispy clouds. The sun was warm on her shoulders, and the hedges by the sidewalk were dotted with starlike yellow flowers. It's spring, she thought.

Strange how you enjoyed the world more when you thought there was a chance you might be leaving it soon.

Even the Institute looked exotic and beautiful, like a giant grape monument.

Now came the hard part. She had to sneak in so as not to get caught, but do it without *looking* sneaky. So that if she *were* caught, she could say she'd come home from school sick.

After some thought, she let herself in the kitchen door. The kitchen was right by the front lab, but no one in the lab could see her until she passed the lab doorway.

Music was coming from the lab. Good, that should cover any sounds. Squaring her shoulders, Kait walked boldly by the lab doorway, forcing herself to glance inside casually, forcing herself not to tiptoe.

That one glance showed her Frost sorting through a tray full of watches and keys, while Joyce sat beside her with a notebook. Frost was facing the back lab—great. Joyce was facing Frost, but bent over her notebook. Pretty good.

Jackal Mac was nowhere in sight. Kait prayed he was in the back lab, in the tank.

Still forcing herself *not* to be stealthy, not to creep, she walked through the dining room and out and around the staircase. She looked around the corner and saw the little hallway that led to the other door of the lab.

Okay, how to make this look casual? I've got to wait here . . . maybe I'm tying my shoe.

Without taking her eyes off the figures in the lab, she knelt and undid her shoelace. Then she stayed that way, with the laces in her hands, watching Joyce.

I can't go into the hall until she turns around or goes into the back lab. It takes a few seconds to get the panel to slide back, she could just glance up and see me from where she is now.

Time dragged by. The backpack began to feel heavy, dragging at Kaitlyn's shoulders.

Come on, Joyce. Move. Go get a book from the case or something. Go change the CD. Do anything, just *move.*

Joyce stayed put. After what seemed like an hour, Kaitlyn decided that she was going to have to risk stepping out anyway— and then she saw Joyce was getting up.

Kait's vision seemed to go double. Joyce's face was a tan blur. Then Joyce's back was a pink blur. Joyce was going into the back lab.

Oh, thank you! Thank you!

The instant the last bit of pink disappeared, Kaitlyn stepped into the hall. No time to be stealthy, no point in looking casual. All that mattered was to be *quick.*

Her fingers stabbed out at the wood paneling, once and then again. The click seemed agonizingly loud. She threw a glance at Frost—Frost still had her back turned.

The panel had recessed. Kaitlyn stepped into the gaping hole.

Down the stairs. Quick. Quick.

She'd never learned the secret of closing the panel from inside. Well, it didn't matter much. As long as she got to the crystal. She didn't care if they discovered her after that.

As she reached the bottom stair she shrugged off her backpack and pulled out a flashlight. She'd taken it from the kitchen drawer that morning.

Quick. Move quick. The little circle of light showed her the way.

Aha. There it is.

The combination lock shone softly on the wall by the door, looking like something from a science fiction set. A door to the starship *Enterprise.*

Although her heart was beating in all sorts of funny places—her throat, her ears, her fingertips—Kaitlyn felt calm. She'd rehearsed this all in her mind last night.

Put the backpack down. Flashlight in your teeth. Take out the paper with the possible combinations on it. Make every move count.

Paper in one hand, she began to punch in numbers with the other.

Each little rubber pad gave under her fingertips, and the number she'd punched appeared on an LED display at the top.

1 . . . 4 . . . 1 . . . 2 . . . 2 . . . 5 . . . 9 . . . 2. Enter.

Nothing. The LED display blanked out.

Okay. *Next!*

1 . . . 4 . . . 2 . . . 5 . . . 1 . . . 2 . . . 9 . . . 2.

Again, nothing. Tiny threads of panic began to unwind in Kaitlyn's gut. Okay, so she still had six combinations to go, but she'd used the best two. What if Mr. Z had changed the numbers? She should have drawn again last night to make sure. Oh, God, she hadn't even *thought* of that. . . .

Wait a minute. I didn't press Enter.

She pressed it. Immediately she heard a sort of pleasant hum, an accepting sound that reminded her of an ATM machine getting to work.

With a soft click, the door opened away from her.

I did it! It worked! Oh, thank you, Columbus—I'll love you forever!

Her heart was beating all over now, her entire skin tingling with the pulses. Excitement and fear swam inside her, and she had to take a deep breath to keep her head.

Okay, quick, now, *quick.* A light might be seen upstairs, so get the shard out first.

She fumbled getting it out of the backpack. The flashlight kept sliding out from under her chin. The paper with the combinations had fallen on the floor. She ignored it.

Okay. *Got it.*

With both hands, she held the crystal shard.

It had never felt so good to her. Cold and heavy and sharp, it was like a weapon in her hand, strengthening her. It seemed to be telling her, *Don't worry about anything from here on in.*

All you have to do is get me to the crystal. I'll take care of things from there.

Yes, Kaitlyn thought. Now.

In the end, it had almost been too easy. Why had Rob been so worried about her?

Standing tall, holding the crystal like a spear, she pushed the door open and stepped into the office. It was dark and she'd lost the flashlight. She reached for the wall, fingers groping across it. She found a light switch and got ready to throw it, planning to charge toward the great crystal as soon as she could see. A battle yell, some legacy of distant Irish ancestors, gathered in her throat.

Now . . .

She threw the switch—and froze.

The charge never happened. The crystal was there, all right, huge and deformed and grotesque as she remembered. But it wasn't alone. There were two—other things—in front of it.

Kaitlyn's eyes opened wide as she saw them. She felt her lips stretching open, not for a battle yell, but for a scream. A scream of perfect terror.

CHAPTER 13

At first all Kaitlyn was able to take in was her feeling of disgust and horror. It was something like the disgust she'd felt at home when her dad would turn over a shovelful of earth in the garden—and reveal something soft and squirmy or hard and chitinous hiding underneath.

A little like that, but magnified hundreds and thousands of times.

She guessed these two things were human. Or had started out that way. But they looked so deformed and felt so *wrong*, they gave her the sick feeling she'd gotten when she first saw a potato bug, that huge, unnatural, semicrustacean-looking insect. Or when she'd seen her first picture by Hieronymus Bosch, the artist who did scenes from hell, with people who had lobsters' claws or windows in their bodies.

The other thing she knew immediately was that they

were guard dogs. Mr. Z's new guard dogs, put here to protect the crystal.

Sasha and Parté King.

She knew them from Bri's descriptions—although it took a lot of imagination. Sasha had skin that was chalky white, unnaturally white, like something that had never seen the sun. Almost translucent, with lines of blue veins showing through. His eyes were like the red eyes of albino mice, or the blind eyes of cave fish.

He did have blond hair, as Bri had said. Hair that was not just unkempt but *full of things*. Bits of garbage and paper like the rubbish that covered the floor.

He looked like a slug: white, flaccid, immobile.

Then there was Parté King—whatever that weird name might mean. Bri had said he was skinny. Now he was skeletally thin, wasted away like someone about to die. Skin stretched across his bones—almost as if he had an exoskeleton, like a bug. His brown hair was falling out in clumps, exposing naked skull.

He looked like some kind of cricket, as if he would rattle if you shook him.

And they were both alive, even though they looked like nothing that could survive long. Kaitlyn realized with a qualm of pure horror that they *lived* down here, alone and insane, chained to the floor. Biting at people's ankles, grinning face-splitting grins.

She thought she was going to vomit.

"Muh-muh-muh," Sasha said, beaming. His teeth were wet; wetness spilled onto his chin. He made a wormlike movement toward her.

I should run, Kaitlyn thought dispassionately. Her thought seemed to die somewhere before it got to her legs. She stood still and watched the swollen white grub thing inching across the floor toward her. It was like a human being in the process of mutating into something. A pupa.

They weren't going to let her get to the crystal. She could feel the power of their minds like a curtain across the room. So strong it almost knocked her over, invading all her senses. The touch of their minds made her think of rotting things, bugs, pus.

Parté King was making a clicking noise in his throat. Pushing himself into a sitting position. They both wore canvas jackets which held their arms behind their backs with many straps.

Straitjackets.

Below that they wore garbage bags. Kaitlyn couldn't make sense of that until she realized: diapers.

Run, you stupid girl. Please run now.

Parté King fell over backward, his stick legs waving slowly in the air.

"Ch-ch-ch-ch-ch." He was still grinning.

So this is what happens to Mr. Z's old students. It could happen to you, too. A little too much time near the crystal and . . .

Hey, but they're still terrific psychics!

Please, *run*.

At last she seemed to tune in to her brain's terrified whimpering pleas. She turned around to run. She saw the open door of the office, took a wavering step toward it.

And ran into a sort of invisible wall, a thickening of the air. Cold air. Or maybe there was nothing wrong with the air, and it was just her muscles.

She couldn't move a step closer to the door. They had her, they were draining her volition, her will to run. She couldn't get away, and maybe she'd known that all the time.

Sasha laughed bubbles, like a baby.

"You poor things," Kaitlyn whispered. Pitying them didn't change an ounce of her loathing for them. She knew somehow that they were beyond any kind of healing. Hurt worse than Marisol in her coma.

Even if they would let her approach them with the crystal shard, even if she were a healer like Rob, it wouldn't help. Kaitlyn *knew*.

Her knees were giving out. She let it happen, sitting on the floor and watching the creatures who shared it with her crawl closer. There was nothing to do.

Nothing except wait for Mr. Zetes to come.

"I thought you'd bring that to me," Mr. Zetes said. "Thank you, my dear."

He held his hand out for the shard. Kaitlyn looked at the

long fingers with their square, perfectly manicured nails. She tried to stab him.

It was stupid. There were the human pupae behind her, dragging her every gesture into slow motion, and there were the psycho psychics behind Mr. Z. They'd all come to see the fun. Besides, Mr. Z himself was strong.

He took the shard from her, hurting her wrist. Deliberately, she thought.

"In a way, it's too bad you decided to come out of the closet now," Mr. Z said. "I wish you'd kept the pretense up for just a few more days. My next job for you was silencing the Diaz family."

His handsome old face was absolutely diabolical.

"I like your old students," Kaitlyn choked out. "The ones with very good minds. What a waste."

"Muh-muh-*muhhhh*," Sasha drooled behind her. "Muhhh."

Mr. Z glanced at him almost fondly. "They're still useful," he said. "The crystal has made them more powerful than ever, in a way, it's allowed them to achieve their true potential. I'm afraid you can't join them, though." He turned slightly, speaking over his shoulder.

"John, please put this in Joyce's room. Laurie and Sabrina, take Kaitlyn upstairs and get her ready. Paul, watch them."

Who are all those people? Kaitlyn thought whimsically. Jackal Mac took the shard and disappeared, presumably heading for Mr. Z's car. Frost and Bri stepped forward and each took her by an arm, leading her out of the office. Renny followed.

Joyce and Lydia were standing in the hallway by the hidden panel. Frost and Bri marched Kaitlyn by them.

As they reached the second floor, Kait spoke. "What's going to happen to me?"

"Never mind." Frost gave her a push and Kaitlyn stumbled into the room Frost and Bri shared. Frost's face was sparkling with malicious triumph. She looked almost beautiful, like a Christmas tree angel with hair made of spun glass. She had on bubble-gum pink lipstick, so glossy it reflected light.

"Bri? You going to tell me?"

Bri looked angry instead of triumphant. "You sneak. You dirty spy." Her deep boyish voice was rough with anger and revulsion. "You get what you deserve."

Renny stood just outside Bri's door, arms folded, his clean-cut narrow features severe. He looked like an executioner.

Frost was groping through a pile of clothes on the floor. "Here. Put this on."

It was a bathing suit, one piece, black-and-white striped.

Kaitlyn thought of saying "Why?"—but there wasn't any point. She said, "I'm not going to undress in front of *him*."

"Mr. Z told me to watch," Renny said. Not lecherously. Flatly.

"You got better things to worry about," Bri said, her voice harsh.

Kaitlyn decided not to argue. Bri was right; what difference did it make at this point? She turned her back to the door and stripped, ignoring Renny like a piece of furniture. She tried to hold her head high, make every movement regal and indifferent. Even so, by the time she had pulled the bathing suit on her face was burning, her eyes full of tears.

Frost tittered and snapped the elastic on Kaitlyn's back. But Bri said nothing and kept her head down. Even Renny seemed to avoid Kaitlyn's gaze as she turned around again.

"I'm ready."

They marched her downstairs.

Not back to the crystal room. Into the front lab. The door to the back lab was open.

And then Kaitlyn knew.

I will not scream, she told herself. I won't whimper and I won't scream. They'll just enjoy it more. They'd love me to start screaming.

But she was afraid she *would* scream. Or that she might even beg.

"Is everything ready?" Mr. Z asked Joyce. Joyce was standing in the doorway to the back lab. She nodded.

Jackal Mac was staring at Kaitlyn as if he wanted to drink her face through his eyes. His evil jackal eyes. His mouth was partly open, making her think of a panting dog.

Loving this. Loving it.

"You're going to end up like the ones downstairs," Kaitlyn told him. Jackal Mac grinned like a fox.

Mr. Zetes made a gesture, a formal gesture that reminded Kaitlyn of the first time she'd heard him speak. When he'd welcomed her and Rob and the others to the Institute, telling them how special they all were. It seemed like years ago.

"Now," Mr. Z said, addressing the whole group, "I think you all know the situation. We've discovered a spy. I'm afraid I suspected this from the beginning, but I decided to give her a chance." He looked at Joyce, who looked back with a blank face. "However, there's no longer any doubt about why she came to us. So I think the best solution is my original one."

He looked at each of the others in the room and spoke with genteel emphasis. "I want you all to witness this, because I want you to understand what happens when you break faith with me. Does anyone have any questions?"

The lab was silent. Dust motes hung in the slanting afternoon light. No one had a question.

"All right. John and Paul, take her in. Joyce will handle the equipment."

Fight, Kaitlyn thought. That was different than screaming. As Mac and Renny reached for her, she ducked sideways and tried to run, throwing a mule kick as she went.

But they were ready for her. Mac wasn't going to be faked out again. He simply tackled her as if she'd been a two-hundred-pound quarterback, knocking her to the floor. Kaitlyn saw stars and had a horrible sense of not enough air. She'd had the breath knocked out of her.

There was a confused time, and then she realized she was sitting up, being whacked on the back. She whooped in air. Then, before she could really get her bearings, she was being hauled to her feet.

Fighting was no good. She was helpless.

Then she heard a voice, thin, high, and frightened. To her astonishment, she realized it was Lydia.

"Please don't do it. Please don't—Father."

Lydia was standing in front of Mr. Z. Her pale hands were clenched together at waist level, not as if she were praying, but as if she were trying to hold her guts in.

"She can't fight you anymore, and you know it. You could just send her away. She'd never tell anyone about us; she'd just go away and be quiet and live. Wouldn't you, Kaitlyn?" Lydia turned huge green eyes on Kait. Her lips were white, but there was a fierceness in those eyes that Kaitlyn admired.

Good for you, Lydia, she thought. You finally stood up to him. You spoke out, even when nobody else would.

But someone else was speaking.

"Lydia has a point, Emmanuel," Joyce said in a low, carefully controlled voice. "I really don't know if we have to go this far. I'm not entirely comfortable with this."

Kaitlyn stared at her. Joyce's hair was sleek as seal fur, her tanned face was smooth. Yet Kaitlyn caught a sense of inner agitation almost as great as Lydia's.

Thank you, Joyce. I knew it couldn't all be an act. There's something good in you, deep down.

Kaitlyn glanced at the others.

Bri was shifting from foot to foot, scratching her blue-streaked head. Her face was flushed; she looked as if there were something she wanted to say. Renny was scowling, seeming angry but uncertain.

Only Jackal Mac and Frost still looked eager and enthusiastic. Frost's eyes were shining with an almost romantic fervor, and Jackal Mac was licking his lips with his pierced tongue.

"Anyone else?" Mr. Z asked in a voice of terrible quiet. Then he turned on Joyce. "It's lucky for you that I know you aren't serious. You've managed to overcome your discomfort in much more squeamish situations than this. And you will now, of course—because you wouldn't want to join her in that tank. Or visit the room downstairs overnight."

A sort of shudder passed over Joyce's face. Her aquamarine eyes seemed to unfocus.

"And the same goes for the rest of you," Mr. Zetes said. "Including *you*." He was looking at Lydia. He hadn't raised a fist; he hadn't even raised his voice. But Lydia flinched, and everyone else went still. His very presence cowed them all.

"Every one of you would go to jail for years if the police found out what you've been doing these last weeks," Mr. Zetes said, his face composed and Satanic. "But the police will never have to deal with you. Because *I* will, if you cross me. Your old classmates downstairs will help. There is nowhere you can go to get away from us, nowhere you can hide that we can't find you. The power of the crystal can reach out across the globe and swat you like a fly."

Silence and stillness. The psychics watched the floor. Not even Frost was smirking now.

"Now," Mr. Z said in a grating whisper, "does anyone still have any objections?"

Some people shook their heads. Lydia, her shoulders hunched miserably, was one of them. Others just stayed still and quiet, as if hoping Mr. Z wouldn't look at them.

"Gabriel?" Mr. Zetes said.

Kaitlyn looked up in surprise. She hadn't realized Gabriel had arrived; she'd barely noticed his absence before.

He was frowning, looking like somebody who's arrived at a party to find it had started an hour earlier without him. "What's going on?" he said. He repeated it to Kaitlyn silently, his narrowed eyes on the black-and-white bathing suit. *What's going on? What did you do?*

"A disciplinary matter," Mr. Zetes said. "I hope there won't be any more like it in the future."

Kaitlyn didn't wait for him to finish, but spoke to Gabriel over his words. *None of your business. I despise you.* She threw the full weight of her contempt at him like someone throwing beer cans and rocks and bricks. And then, because Rob had taught her how to hurt him, she added, *Jailbird. You'd better do everything he says or he'll send for the police.*

She hadn't realized how much she hated him before this moment. All the loathing that she somehow hadn't felt toward Renny or even Jackal Mac and Frost, she felt for him. All the anger and betrayal. If she'd been closer, she would have tried to spit on him.

Gabriel's face hardened. She felt him pull away, felt the ice of his shields. He didn't say another word.

"All right," Mr. Z said. "You boys take her in; then we'll all go into the city for dinner. I think this calls for another celebration."

There was no point in fighting any longer. Mac and Renny dragged Kaitlyn into the back lab. She stood motionless in their grip while Joyce forced a mouthpiece into her mouth. It was connected to an air hose like a scuba diver's.

Now Joyce was pulling gloves over her hands and forcing her into a canvas jacket like the ones the creatures downstairs were wearing. Kaitlyn's arms were crossed, useless. Weights were being attached to a belt around her waist, and to her ankles.

She heard a voice behind her: Mr. Zetes. "Goodbye, my dear. Pleasant dreams."

And then Joyce was sticking something in her ears. Some kind of earplugs. Suddenly Kaitlyn was deaf.

They were pushing her forward.

The isolation tank still looked like a Dumpster. A lopsided

Dumpster with a hurricane door. The door was open and they were forcing her inside.

She couldn't help it; she was going into this *thing*. This thing that they were going to close on her, that they were going to bury her in alive.

As the dark metal walls rose around her and the water came up to meet her, Kaitlyn's nerve broke. She did scream. Or at least, she tried. But the thing in her mouth muffled it like a gag and the earplugs dulled the rest of the sound. There was only silence as water enveloped her. And darkness.

She twisted, trying to get on her back, to see the door. To see the light for one last instant . . .

But all she saw was a rapidly diminishing rectangle of white. Then the metal door clanged shut. It was the last sound she was to hear.

Right from the beginning, it was very bad.

Remembering Bri's words ("Sure, it's cool. Cosmic, man!"), she had hoped that the tank might be pleasant at first. Or at least bearable. But it wasn't. It was a death trap, and from the first instant Kaitlyn felt a screaming inside her that wouldn't stop.

Maybe the difference was that she knew she was in here for good. They weren't going to let her out in an hour or a few hours or a day. They were going to keep her in here for as long as it took, until she was a *thing*, a drooling, vacant-eyed lump of flesh with no mind.

Her first thought was to try and beat the system. She would make her own noise; she would make herself feel. But even the loudest humming was dim and soon her throat grew sore. After a while she wasn't sure whether she was humming or not.

It was very difficult to kick with the weights on her legs, and when she did manage, she found the tank was lined with something like rubber inside. Between the drag of weights and water and the give of the rubber padding, she couldn't feel much of anything.

She couldn't pinch with her fingers, either, the gloves prevented that and dulled all sensation. Her arms were immobilized. She couldn't even chew her lips—the mouthpiece prevented it.

More, all these exertions tired her out. After trying everything she could think of, she was exhausted, unable to do anything but float inertly. The weights were gauged to keep her floating right in the middle of the water, away from the top and bottom of the tank, and the water temperature was gauged so that she had no sensation of hot or cold.

It was then that she began to realize the true horror of her situation.

It was dark. She couldn't *see*. She couldn't see *anything*.

And she couldn't hear. The silence was so deep, so profound, that she began to wonder if she really remembered what sound was.

In the endless dark silence, her body began to dissolve.

Once, when she'd just turned thirteen, she'd had a nightmare of a disembodied arm in her bed. She had half-woken one night to find that she'd been lying with her arms pressed together under her body, and that one of them had gone to sleep. She could feel it with her other hand: a cool, unnaturally limp arm. In her not-awake state, it seemed as if someone had put a severed dead arm in her bed. Her own arm was foreign to her.

After that, all her nightmares were of the cool blue arm snuggling up to her chin and then dragging her under the bed.

Now Kaitlyn felt as if *all* her limbs had gone to sleep. At first it seemed that her body had gone dead, and then she realized she didn't *have* a body anymore. At least, there was no way to prove she did.

If there were arms and legs in the tank, they weren't hers. They were dead, unholy, other peoples' limbs, floating around her, ready to kill her.

After a while, even the sense that there were other peoples' limbs around her faded. There was *nothing* around her.

She had no sense of being trapped inside the little Dumpster tank. She had no sense of being anywhere. She was alone in pure space, and around her was nowhere, nothingness, absence, emptiness.

The world had disappeared because she couldn't sense it. She'd never realized it before, but the world *was* her senses. She had never known anything but her internal map of it, made up from what she saw and heard. And now there was no sight, no sound, no map, no world. She couldn't keep hold of the conviction that there *was* a world outside—or that there was an outside.

Did the word *outside* have meaning? Could something be outside the universe?

Maybe there had never really been anything except her.

Could she really remember what the color "yellow" was? Or the feeling of "silk"?

No. It had all been a joke or a dream. Neither of those things existed. These ideas of "touch" or "taste" or "hearing"— she'd made them up to get away from the emptiness.

She had always been alone in the emptiness. Just her, just K—

Who was she? For an instant there, she'd almost had a name, but now it was gone. She was nameless.

She didn't exist either.

There was no person thinking this. No "I" to make words about it.

There was no . . . no . . . no . . .

A silent scream ripped outward. Then:

Kaitlyn!

CHAPTER 14

Gabriel was frightened.

Frost sat beside him during dinner—Mr. Z's orders, he was certain. She touched him every other minute, stroking his wrist, patting his shoulder. Again, he felt certain, on Mr. Z's orders.

They wanted to know if he would try and reach Kaitlyn with his mind.

But the restaurant in San Francisco was too far from the Institute. Kaitlyn was long out of range, as Joyce must have told Mr. Z. Gabriel didn't even try to stretch out his mind; instead he worked on convincing everyone that he didn't want to. That he hated Kaitlyn as much as Jackal Mac did.

He must have done a good job, because Lydia was looking at him with burning green hatred in her eyes—when her father's head was turned, of course.

She wasn't the only one who looked unhappy. Bri had

eaten almost none of her dinner. Renny kept swallowing as if he felt sick. And Joyce was holding herself rigid and expressionless, her aquamarine eyes fixed on the candle in the center of the table.

The club they went to next was also far away from San Carlos—but not quite as far. Frost left his side to dance with Mac. As soon as she was gone, Gabriel slipped the piece of crystal he had palmed out of his pocket.

It should increase his range—but enough? He wasn't sure. The only time he'd managed a telepathic link over such a long distance was when he'd been in agonizing pain.

He had to try.

With Mr. Z smoking a cigar and smiling benevolently at the dancers on the floor, Gabriel clutched the tiny chip of crystal and sent out his mind.

But the frightening thing was that even when he felt he'd stretched out far enough, he couldn't feel Kaitlyn. Her place in the web was filled with nothingness. Not even a wall, only blankness. Nobody nowhere.

Desperate, he kept calling her name.

There was a vision in her mind.

Whose mind? It didn't matter. Maybe there wasn't a mind at all, but only the vision.

A rose, full and blooming, with lush petals. The petals were a warm color that she had forgotten. At first it was a nice image, all those petals on one stem, separate but connected. It reminded her of something. But then the vision went bad. The petals turned black, the color of the emptiness. The rose began to drip blood. It was hurt, mortally wounded. The petals began to fall . . . and on each there was a face, and the face was *screaming*. . . .

Kaitlyn! Kaitlyn, can you hear me?

Petals falling, dripping. Like tears.

Kaitlyn! Oh God, please answer me. Please, Kaitlyn. Kaitlyn!

There was desperation in the voice. Whose voice? And who was it talking to?

I couldn't contact you before. He had Frost sitting by me, touching me. She would have known. But now I have them convinced I don't want to talk to you—oh, please, Kaitlyn; answer. It's Gabriel.

Suddenly there was another vision. A hand dripping blood. Onto a floor. Gabriel's hand, cut by the crystal shard, dripping onto Marisol's floor.

And she had seen it, she, Kaitlyn. She was Kaitlyn.

She had a self again.

Gabriel?

His voice came back, at a volume that hurt her. *Yes. Kaitlyn, talk to me.*

Gabriel, is it really you? I thought . . . you'd be mad. After I said . . .

She wasn't sure what she'd said. Or even what "saying" was.

Kaitlyn, don't be—don't even think about that. Are you all right?

It was a stupid question. Kaitlyn had no way to answer it in words, so she sent along the thin, quivering strand of the web that connected them a vision of what the emptiness was like. Nothingness, void, absence . . .

Stop. Please stop now. Oh God, Kait, what can I do?

Kaitlyn could feel the black well trying to suck her back into it; all she had to hold on to was the slender connection with Gabriel, like a tiny shaft of light in a dungeon. It was keeping her sane at the moment, but it wasn't enough. She needed more, she needed . . .

You need to see and hear, Gabriel said.

I don't even remember what those things are like, Kaitlyn told him. She could feel hysteria bubbling in her, stealing her rationality.

Gabriel said simply, *I'll show you.*

And then he began to give her things, with his mind. Things *he* had seen and heard, things from his memory. He gave her everything.

"Remember what the sun's like? It's hot and yellow and so bright you can't look at it. Like this. See?" In her sense-starved condition his voice seemed like a real voice not like telepathy. He was giving her the sound of talking. And sending her a picture. As soon as Kaitlyn saw it she remembered. The sun.

That's good, she said. *It feels good.*

"That's what it looks like in summer. I grew up in New York, and sometimes in the summer my mom would take me to this place by the ocean—remember the ocean?"

Blue-green coolness. Hot sand between the toes, gritty sand in the bathing trunks. Water foaming and hissing, children shrieking. The smell and taste of salt.

Kaitlyn drank it all in greedily, hungry for every nuance of sight or sound. *More, please. More.*

"We'd go up to the boardwalk, just her and me. She'd always buy me a hot dog and an ice cream. She didn't have much money, because the old man drank it all, but sometimes she'd make him give her a dollar to fix something he really liked for dinner. Then she'd get me the ice cream—remember ice cream?"

Creamy, blobby coldness. Stickiness on her chin. Rich, dark taste of chocolate.

I remember. Thank you, Gabriel.

He gave her more. All his best memories, everything he could think of that was good. Every golden afternoon, every skateboard ride, every moment with his mother when he was seven years old and sick with the fever that gave him his power.

Everything he was, he gave to her.

Kaitlyn devoured the sensations, filling herself with the reality of the world outside. She was drenched in sunshine and cool wind and the smell of burning leaves and the taste of

Halloween candy. And music; she hadn't realized how Gabriel loved music. At fourteen, he'd wanted to play in a garage band. He was jamming with the drummer one night, trying to get more in sync—and then the drummer was lying on the floor, clutching his head. Pierced by Gabriel's mind. When Gabriel tried to help him up, he ran screaming.

A week later, Gabriel was on his way to the psychic research center in Durham, where his principal and his mother and the social worker hoped someone could teach him control. His father's last word to him had been: "Freak."

"Never mind about that," Gabriel said. He was giving her only good things, nothing depressing. She could feel that he didn't want her to see his father's stubbly face with the bleary red eyes. Or feel the burning hot shock of his father's belt.

It's all right, Kaitlyn said. *I mean, I won't look at anything you don't want me to, but you don't have to worry about me . . . and I won't ever tell anyone, and I'm so sorry. Oh, Gabriel, I'm so sorry. And . . .*

She wanted to tell him that she understood him now, in a way she'd never understood anyone before. Because she was *with* him. It wasn't even like being in the web; it was much closer than that, much deeper. He'd torn down all the barriers and put his soul into her hands.

I love you, she told him.

"I love you, Kaitlyn. From the very beginning."

She got a sense then, of how he saw her. Bits and pieces from his memories of her. Her eyes, smoky blue, with the strange dark rings in them, framed by heavy black lashes. Her skin tasting like peaches. Her hair crackling when she brushed it, flame-colored, silky but full of electricity.

She could sense, too, scraps of what he'd thought about her over the weeks. Lines from their lives together. *That kind of girl might be too interesting, might tempt you to get involved . . . A girl who challenged him, who could be his equal . . . Her mind was a place of blue pools and blazing meteors . . . She stood slim and proud as some medieval witch princess against the dawn.*

"And then I thought you'd betrayed me," he said. "But you really came to protect me, didn't you?"

With that, Kaitlyn realized that he'd seen as deeply into her mind as she'd seen into his. She had thought he was the one giving, while she had only received . . . but of course, he'd had to join with her completely in order to share his life with her.

He knew everything, now.

And then he came on something that sent shock waves through Kaitlyn.

"Jackal Mac said—*what?*"

Kaitlyn could feel the memory he was looking at. *He said you told him to check me out.*

Gabriel's cold anger filled the universe.

"I never said that. I never talked to him about you at all."

I know, Gabriel. She did know, she was certain.

"But Lydia knew how you gave me energy on the trip to Canada. She must have told him—"

Gabriel, forget about it. His fury was hurting her, filling her with images of death, of Jackal Mac spitting up bone splinters. *Please think me something nice.*

So he did. All that night, he thought her beautiful music and hillsides of wild mustard flowers and the smell of fresh pencil shavings and the taste of banana marshmallow candies. And the touch of his hands, the way he would do it if she ever got back in the world again.

Rob stared at the edges of the afghan that served Tony's friend for a window curtain. He didn't move, because he didn't want to disturb the others; Anna and Lewis and Tamsin on the floor. Even the black kitten Tony had given Anna was lying curled and still. But Rob couldn't sleep.

Light was showing around the blanket edges. Morning. And Kaitlyn hadn't called last night.

He had a very bad feeling.

There was no good reason for it. Kaitlyn had told them she might have to wait and watch for her chance. That was probably what she was doing.

But Rob was empty and sick with fear.

Rob?

He turned to see Anna looking up at him. There was no sign of drowsiness in her face or her dark eyes.

I couldn't sleep, either. She put a hand on his arm and he put his hand over it. Just the feel of her warmth gave him some comfort.

You want to go and look for her now, don't you?

Rob turned from the window again. Her steady gaze, her calm face, and her gentle presence in the web all strengthened him.

"Yes," he whispered.

Then we'll go. I think we should, too. Let's wake up Lewis and Tamsin.

Kaitlyn knew it was morning because Gabriel said so.

"I think they're going to take you out soon. Mr. Zetes drove up a little while ago, and now Joyce is knocking on all the doors upstairs."

Another circus, huh? Kaitlyn asked. She didn't know how she felt about the outside world anymore, but the thought of everyone staring at her was definitely appalling.

"I'll be with you," Gabriel said.

As the night had gone on, she'd gotten more and more of an odd sense from him. A feeling that ran beneath the thoughts they were sharing, that he was keeping away from her. Although it was tightly controlled, she recognized it as pain.

Gabriel, are you all right? I feel—are you hurt, somehow?

"I have a sort of headache. It's no problem. Do you feel it now?"

Once again, she had the sense that he was concealing something. But concealing it better.

"Okay, Joyce is telling us to come downstairs." After a moment, he said, "We're in the lab."

Yeah, time for the unveiling. Kaitlyn laughed silently, nervously. *I wonder what they're going to think. I suppose I should act crazy.*

"I think it's your best chance. Kait—I don't know how I can save you right now. The others don't like what the old man is doing—I think Joyce asked him to take you out this soon—but they're afraid of him. And I can only fight one of them at a time."

Kaitlyn knew. Gabriel's destructive power operated most strongly when he could touch his victim, and it took time. He couldn't hold off Jackal Mac and Renny while killing Mr. Z, for instance.

And you're weak, she told him. *From helping me, I know. I'm sorry. But we'll manage somehow—maybe they'll just put me back in the tank.*

Then she realized something that made the blood start beating in her ears. *Gabriel, wait, wait! Rob is coming. I forgot.* She'd forgotten about the outside world. *All you need to do is wait until he gets here, then he can help.*

"It depends on what Mr. Z is going to do to you, whether we can wait. He's giving a speech now. On and on."

I don't want to hear it. Gabriel, you do know that Rob didn't mean the things he said at Marisol's house. He was mad at you. Hurt. And he felt betrayed. But that's because he really cares about you. You know that, don't you?

Even now, Gabriel refused to say it. But Kaitlyn had seen inside him too deeply to be fooled. Her question was rhetorical. Gabriel *did* know. His feelings for Rob were all mixed up with guilt and jealousy and resentment of Rob's effortless ability to do good and be good, and to go through life being loved. But Kaitlyn thought that Rob would be pleased with the feeling Gabriel had under that. He admired Rob. Respected him. Would have liked to be somebody Rob could like.

But he does like you, Kaitlyn said again, and then she realized they were opening the door of the tank.

The clang was a different sort of sound than Gabriel's mental voice, and she thought that if she had really been in silence all yesterday afternoon and night—maybe fifteen hours at a guess—she wouldn't have recognized what sound was anymore, and screamed in fear. She was spared having to fake that because they couldn't hear her.

Hands pulled at her, the touch as shriekingly dissonant as the door clang. Everything was so *harsh.* Her skin was so sensitized that even the gentlest pressure would have hurt, and these hands weren't gentle.

Then light struck her eyes. It both hurt and dazzled, confusing her. She couldn't really see anything, only the whiteness, with occasional shapes blocking it. Squinting helped a little, but tears still ran down her face.

It didn't matter; she was soaking wet everywhere. She could feel the harsh hands taking off the strait-jacket and weights, removing the mouthpiece. Then, just as she began to really see, she was turned around to face Mr. Zetes.

She was white and wrinkled. Her mouth hurt, she had cramps in her arms and shoulders, and her legs wouldn't support her. She was dripping all over the floor.

"She can't stand up," Joyce said crisply. "Bri, get a chair."

They put her in the chair. Mr. Z looked at her.

Now, what? Kaitlyn asked Gabriel. *I don't think I can scream. Should I just sort of look vacant?*

Try it, he commanded. Now that she could hear real voices, his telepathic voice seemed different. She knew it wasn't sound.

"Can you understand me, Kaitlyn?" Mr. Zetes was asking. "Do you know where you are?"

His expression was avid and eager. Like a connoisseur just about to take the first sip of wine, stopping to inhale the bouquet. If he thought she was crazy enough, he'd say, "Ahhh."

Kaitlyn tried to look mad. She gazed at him, doing her version of the human pupa stare. She wondered if she should try to say, "Muh-muh-muh"—but she was afraid she would do it wrong. Instead, she tried to smile the way Sasha had.

She saw in an instant that it wasn't any good. Mr. Z was an

expert on insane people—he collected them. His piercing eyes widened and then narrowed as he looked at her. Kaitlyn would have sworn she could see a red spark somewhere in their depths.

Then his white brows drew together over his aquiline nose and his mouth made a bitter, scornful line. He planted his gold-headed cane on the ground and stood tall, like some patriarch from the Bible. Except that he looked instead like *El Diablo, El Gato,* Satan.

"It's failed," he said. He looked at Joyce. "Why?"

"I don't know. I have no idea." Even Kaitlyn could hear the relief in the shaky voice. Joyce's hand on Kaitlyn's back pressed gently, out of Mr. Z's sight.

"This girl tried to destroy us. Not once. Time and again." Mr. Z's voice was shaking, too—with repressed anger.

Joyce straightened. "I had nothing to do with it, Emmanuel. I don't know how she came through like this. But now that she has—"

Mr. Z's face had been undergoing a struggle—one instant molded by satanic fury, the next smoothing as it was suppressed. Almost like Claymation, Kaitlyn thought. But now he had himself under control. His lips curved in a smile of grim delight.

"Now that she has, we'll just have to try the other solution," he told Joyce. "The crystal will take care of her."

Kaitlyn felt a falling in her stomach. She looked at Gabriel, who was standing with Renny and Jackal Mac and Lydia, all in a row behind Mr. Z. And at that instant she heard:

Kaitlyn? Kaitlyn, this is Rob. Am I in range yet?

Rob! Oh, thank God, Rob, you're early, thank God.

She felt the flash of Gabriel's response as well. Desperate relief.

Rob, where are you? Kaitlyn demanded.

At the end of the block. We were worried you might be in trouble.

We are! Rob, you'd better hurry.

At the same time Gabriel was saying, *If you can make a distraction, I can try to get Kait out.*

Then Kaitlyn snapped to the real world. Frost had darted forward and grabbed her hand, wrapping her silver-nailed fingers around it.

"Mr. Zetes, I know how she did it!" Frost shrieked, her voice thin and sharp with spite. "She's talking to them! She was talking to them just now, and she's scared they'll get caught because they're coming right here!"

Kaitlyn jerked her hand away as if she'd touched a live coal. Red fury exploded inside her and she kept pulling her hand back to get distance, and then she slapped Frost's cheek as hard as she could.

But Gabriel kept his head. She could hear him yelling a warning to Rob. *Stay where you are! They just found out about you! Don't come near the house!*

"Quickly," Mr. Z said, and his smile was more delighted than ever. He rolled the words in his mouth as if enjoying them.

"John, Laurie, Paul—help Kaitlyn downstairs, please. Everyone else follow. Hurry now. This should be very interesting."

Kaitlyn tried to fight Mac and Frost and Renny, but her limbs were too weak. She was more of a hindrance by just being limp.

Gabriel didn't fight, either—probably too many of them, Kaitlyn thought. But she didn't understand why he seemed to be hanging back, the last one down the stairs to the hidden room. She tried to get a look at him as they carried her down, but she couldn't see.

"I want to kill him myself!" Gabriel shouted from the floor above. Kaitlyn felt the pang of a new terror. What if the crystal had driven Gabriel crazy like the others? And it was just showing up now?

Gabriel—

He wouldn't answer her. Because Frost was touching her? She didn't know.

"Come down!" Mr. Zetes shouted as he punched in the combination to the office.

Kaitlyn didn't want to go in there. Did not. She struggled with fresh strength as they carried her through the door.

Then the smell and the psychic feel of the human pupae struck her and she went limp.

They carried her past the crystal to the only piece of furniture in the room, a chair. Everyone else was crowding in. Mr. Z was herding them, gesturing them to pack themselves more tightly. Like somebody trying to fit more people into an elevator. Gabriel was the last. He stepped back to join the others who were lining the walls.

Then Mr. Zetes backed up. He stood, leaning both hands on his cane, looking at the doorway with anticipation.

"They won't come," Kaitlyn told him. Her voice was earnest; she just wished it was steady. "I warned them and they're too smart to come when they know you're waiting."

Mr. Zetes smiled. "Do you hear that, my dear? The kitchen door breaking."

Rob? Are you in the house? Rob, listen to me—don't do it. Stay away! Stay away!

But the imperious tone that had worked with him in the gym did nothing now.

This is my choice, Kaitlyn, Rob said. And Kaitlyn heard footsteps on the stairs.

CHAPTER 15

"Rob, go back!" Kaitlyn screamed aloud.

Rob came in. He was flushed and windblown, his hair a golden lion's mane, his eyes full of all the light of the sky. He had run down the stairs, but he took the step into the room calmly, face alert and purposeful, assessing his chances. Looking for Kaitlyn and the way to get her out.

"Leave," Kaitlyn whispered.

Anna and Lewis were right behind Rob. Stepping over the threshold and into the trap. Behind them was a girl Kaitlyn recognized vaguely . . . yellow curls and tilted eyes . . . of course, it was Tamsin.

"A visitor from the Fellowship!" Mr. Zetes said. "We are greatly honored." He actually bowed over his cane.

He didn't move to shut the door. He didn't have to. Once they were all in, he nudged Parté King with his foot, not quite a kick.

Kaitlyn felt power swelling out to hold the new arrivals in the room. As if a fence had been stretched across the open doorway. Rob stared at the lolling creatures on the floor, his face going pale under his tan, the light in his eyes fading with shock.

And even as he stared, he was caught, his movements dragged into slow motion. So were the others. Like flies in flypaper, Kaitlyn thought. Gnats in a web.

"What did you do to them?" Rob whispered, looking slowly from Sasha to Mr. Zetes.

"The unfortunate pilot study," Mr. Zetes said blandly. "Don't look so alarmed. You'll find it isn't so bad after a while."

"Muhhh," said Sasha.

Rob tried to move toward Mr. Zetes—Kaitlyn saw the determination in his face, saw his muscles cord as he strained. But Sasha and Parté King were watching him. Their power surged up to hold Rob tighter. Kaitlyn could *feel* it happening as well as see it. Rob stopped fighting and stood panting.

"You should have stayed away, Rob," Joyce said, in a voice that seemed on the edge of tears. "I wish you had; I really do."

Rob didn't glance at her. He looked at Kaitlyn.

I'm sorry, Kait. I blew it.

Kaitlyn felt wetness spill from her eyes. *I'm the one who's sorry. It's my fault we're all here.* She looked at Tamsin, wondering if there was any hope. The people of the Fellowship were born to a psychic race, they had all sorts of ancient knowledge. Was there some weapon . . . ?

But Tamsin's face undeceived her. Tamsin was gazing mutely at the two creatures on the floor, her lips parted with pity and helpless sorrow. She didn't even seem to recognize the possibility of fighting.

Aspect, Kaitlyn thought. The philosophy of the Fellowship. Nonviolence, passive resistance.

It wasn't going to get Tamsin very far here.

"I didn't realize that this morning would be so productive," Mr. Zetes said happily. He was doing everything but rubbing his hands, gloating. "These last two days have been splendid—just splendid. And now we'll finish up."

He took a step toward Rob, unaffected by the dragging power of the human pupae.

"I'm going to leave you down here to get acquainted with my former students," he said. "I think in a short time you'll all be on the same level of communication—especially if I tie you in actual contact with the crystal. Contact is quite painful, especially in large doses in the beginning. But of course you know that already."

"We can't just disappear," Anna said. "Our parents will come looking. My parents know about you already. They'll find out what you've done and then they'll kill you."

"In other words, I won't get away with it," Mr. Zetes translated, still bland. "Go on, say it, my dear, I don't mind the cliché.

But the fact is that I *will* get away with it. Literally, you see. I have many different residences across the country; even abroad. And the crystal isn't as much of an encumbrance as you might think. I've already brought it to the United States from a very far place." He looked at Tamsin as if this were a shared joke.

She didn't respond. He shrugged very slightly and went on. "So, you see, I can take my crystal and my students wherever I go—and that's all I need. I'll leave you here, of course. In your parents' care."

He gave his terrible smile.

Kaitlyn was proud of her mind-mates. They stood in the doorway, snarled with invisible thread, but none of them broke down or showed any fear. Anna's head was high on her slim neck, her dark eyes proud and self-contained. Lewis stood squarely, fists clenched, his round face stern and unreadable. Rob looked like a young and angry angel.

I love you, Kaitlyn told them. *I love you and I'm so proud of you.*

A voice broke into her admiration.

"I won't go with you! I'll stay here with them," Lydia said passionately.

Mr. Zetes frowned just a little. "Don't be ridiculous."

"I won't go! I hate what you're doing. I hate *you!*" Lydia's elbows were at her sides, fists held shaking near her shoulders. "I don't care if you win this time; I don't care what happens to me; I don't care, I don't *care*—"

"Be quiet!" Mr. Zetes said brutally. Lydia was quiet. But she shook her head, dark hair flying from side to side.

"You'll do as you're told," Mr. Zetes said. "Or you *will* be left here, and I don't think you'll like that." He looked at Joyce, his pleasure in the morning obviously spoiled. "All right," he said abruptly. "Let's finish, so we can get to breakfast. Take those chains off the boys and bring them over here."

Kaitlyn's eyes went to the chains on Parté King and Sasha. They had one on each ankle. Which meant one for her, Rob, Anna, and Lewis each. Tamsin probably wouldn't try to fight.

Then Kaitlyn looked up, because something was wrong. Joyce wasn't moving to obey Mr. Zetes. She was shaking her head.

"I'm not asking you to do it, I'm telling you. Joyce!"

Joyce shook her head again, slowly and decisively, her aquamarine eyes on Mr. Z's face.

"Good for you, Joyce," Kaitlyn said. To Mr. Zetes, she said, "Can't you see? They're all turning against you. It's going to keep happening, too. You can't win."

Mr. Zetes had gone purple.

"Disobedience! Disobedience and insubordination!" he shouted. "Is there anyone here who still understands loyalty?" The piercing eyes flashed around the room. Bri and Renny looked away from him: Bri glowering, Renny with his shoulders angrily hunched. They were both shaking their heads slowly.

Mr. Z's gaze settled on Jackal Mac. "John! Take the key from Joyce and remove those chains immediately!"

Jackal Mac obeyed. He started to feel all over Joyce's pockets for the key, but she slapped his hand away and pulled it out, slowly, staring at Mr. Zetes all the while.

Shambling to the center of the room, Mac unlocked the chains from Sasha.

"Give them to me," Mr. Zetes said impatiently. "Then remove the others."

When Mac did, Mr. Z looked at Rob. Kaitlyn could see that he was fighting to regain his smiling malevolence. But he couldn't do it. He was an angry old man taking revenge.

"Go ahead and struggle," he told Rob. "You won't be able to move. And when I have you chained, these boys on the floor will move you step by step until you touch the crystal. The great crystal, the last of the ancient firestones. Go ahead, take a look at it."

He gestured at the obscene thing towering in the middle of the floor, the crystal that shone with its own milky impure light. The machine of death waiting for them all.

"The moment you touch it, your mind will start to burn," Mr. Zetes went on with some of his old fervor. "In a matter of hours it will burn *out*. Like a gutted house. Your powers will remain, but *you* will not." Kneeling, he brought the chain to Rob's ankle. "And now . . ."

"I don't think so," Gabriel said.

While Mr. Zetes had been talking to Rob, while the human pupae were busy keeping Rob tightly controlled for the chaining, while Jackal Mac was unlocking the other chains, Gabriel had been inching forward. Kaitlyn had seen it, but hadn't known what he could do. He was empty-handed. The pupae would stop any kind of a fight.

But as Gabriel spoke, she heard a swishing *snick.* The sound she'd heard in Marisol's room and on Ivy Street, when his spring-loaded knife snapped out of his sleeve.

Only this time it wasn't a knife.

He was holding the crystal shard by its thick end, holding it underhanded, like a sword ready to thrust up. Its tip was only a foot or so from the giant crystal in the center of the room.

Now Kaitlyn understood why he had been the last one downstairs. He'd been in Joyce's room, getting the shard.

"Don't close that chain," Gabriel said. "Or I'll put it on the crystal."

Kaitlyn heard a metallic click and knew that Mr. Z had done it anyway. He straightened up to look at Gabriel. He was alarmed but not panicked, Kaitlyn thought.

"Now, Gabriel," he said, and moved a little toward him.

Just a little. Gabriel stiffened. The tip of the shard quivered. Kaitlyn could see it reaching for one of the outgrowths of the crystal, like a stalactite and a stalagmite trying to kiss.

"Stay there!"

Mr. Z stopped.

"Now," Gabriel said. "Everyone who doesn't want to die, step back."

At the same time, Mr. Z was kicking the human pupae. "Stop him! Push him back against the wall."

Parté King, the cricketlike one, rolled over on his side to look at Gabriel. Sasha turned his swollen white head. They were both smiling their face-splitting grins.

Kaitlyn felt the power surge up again, sweeping around Gabriel like sticky running tree sap around a fly, turning to amber to hold him. She saw Gabriel start to lunge forward, then freeze in place, the tip of the shard only inches from a jagged outgrowth.

Her throat swelled, and then she was shouting. "Come on! Everybody! If we all move at once—maybe they can't hold us."

She stood, heard Mr. Z yell, and felt the drag of air. She fought it, shouting, "Get to the shard! Somebody get to the shard!"

Then it seemed everyone was either trying to move, or trying to stop someone from moving. Bri was trying to move. Her glower had turned to a look of grim resolve, and Kaitlyn realized she'd finally decided which side she was on. Frost was stopping her, blocking her like a basketball guard. Renny was trying to move. Jackal Mac had abandoned the chains and was grappling with him in slow motion.

Rob and Anna and Lewis were all struggling to get to Gabriel, mostly with their feet stuck to the floor, but occasionally managing a step. Even Tamsin was trying. Mr. Z was turning round and round among them, raising his cane, shouting. He couldn't deal with them all at once.

Then Kaitlyn saw that Lydia was free and moving—slowly but steadily—toward Gabriel and the shard.

"Joyce!" Mr. Zetes shouted. "Stop her! She's right beside you! Stop her!"

But Joyce shook her head. "It's time it was over, Emmanuel," she said. In an instant, she and Lydia were caught in the sticky air, too. Lydia still struggled on desperately.

"Hold them!" Mr. Zetes shouted, and began beating Sasha and Parté King with his cane. "Hold them all! Hold them all!"

Kaitlyn heard the savage swishing sound of the cane, and the dull thud of the blows. She saw Gabriel's face tighten, saw it go grim with purpose. The shard quivered, moved an inch toward the crystal.

"Gabriel," Mr. Zetes said. "Think of all your ambitions. You wanted to go to the top. Have everything good. Money, power, position—all the things in life you deserve."

Gabriel was panting, sweat trickling down his temples.

"Recognition of your superiority—you'll never have any of it without me," Mr. Z went on frantically. "What about all that, Gabriel? Everything you always wanted?"

Gabriel lifted his head just enough to look Mr. Z in the eye. "The hell with it."

Then he gritted his teeth and the shard moved again.

Mr. Zetes lost control.

He began to scream, shrill and piercing, and to beat Sasha again. "Stop him! Stop him! Stop him!"

Sasha's voice rose, too, for the first time since Kaitlyn had seen him. "Muh-muh! *Muhhhh! Muhhhh! Moooooootheeerrrr!*"

Kaitlyn screamed herself then. She was crying wildly, fighting the air.

Then suddenly the drag disappeared. The air was air again. Everything that happened next happened in an instant, so that Kaitlyn's mind took it in like a still photograph, receiving the impressions before she could really process them.

She was moving freely. Sasha had turned to look at Mr. Zetes. She could see Sasha's face, not white anymore, but red with the fury of a squalling infant. And then Mr. Zetes was flying toward the crystal, *flying,* as if a giant hand had thrown him. He smashed into it, into its heavy solidity and sword-sharp outcrops at the same instant that Gabriel thrust the shard forward like a rapier.

It all happened at once. Although Kaitlyn's body was free there was no time to *do* anything, only time for one thought, sent out to her mind-mates as she saw the shard stab toward the crystal. With Gabriel still holding it—

Protect Gabriel! Put your thoughts—around him—

The words weren't very clear, but her intent was. She felt everyone in the web, Rob, Lewis, and Anna, joining with her to help shield Gabriel's mind from the destruction.

Mr. Z's high, keening wail came at the same instant, just as the shard made contact with one translucent facet of the crystal.

And then—

There were all sorts of sounds woven together in the great crashing that came next. There was the sound of an axe crashing through glass, and the sound of a sonic boom that rattled the windows. There was the rushing sound of a freight train passing by very close. There was a metallic sound like all the pots and pans in a kitchen falling to a tile floor at once. There was the rumble of thunder and the cracking of ice on a lake. There was a high, thin sound like the screaming of gulls—or maybe that was Mr. Zetes.

And through all the other sounds, underneath them, Kaitlyn thought she could hear music—the kind of music you think you hear when water is crashing through copper pipes.

There was light, too. The kind of light you expect to see just before a mushroom-shaped cloud. Kaitlyn's eyes squeezed shut automatically, and her hand flew up to protect her face, but she saw it through her eyelids.

Colors that her pastels and ink bottles had never prepared her for. Aureolin yellow with a brightness off the scales. Dragon's blood crimson spreading into tongues of lava pink fire. Ultraviolet silvery blue.

They burst like fireworks, sweeping to the edges of her vision, overlapping each other, bright explosion after bright explosion.

And then they stopped. Kaitlyn saw rainbow afterimages, beautiful fiery lattices printed on her eyelids.

Very cautiously she opened her eyes, lifting her hand away from her face.

A cobalt green stain still colored her vision, but she could see again. The great milky crystal was dust on the ground, glassy dust in the shape of a giant stone plant, or a Christmas tree ornament. The largest bits left were pebble size.

Mr. Zetes, who had been touching the crystal at the moment it shattered, was gone. Just gone. Nothing left but the gold-topped cane that had fallen from his hand.

Sasha and Parté King were lying still. Their faces were frozen into a look of empty astonishment—not peaceful, but not anguished, either. In her heart, Kaitlyn was sorry she'd called them the human pupae. They had been human beings.

Everyone else was standing pretty much where they had been before the crash. They were all lifting their heads or lowering their hands, staring.

"It's over," Lewis whispered finally. "We did it. It's over."

Kaitlyn was beginning to realize the same thing. Bri and Renny were gazing around them like sleepwalkers who'd just woken up. Free of the influence of the crystal at last, Kait thought. She looked at Gabriel. He was looking at his hand which had held the shard. The palm was pink, as if he'd been lightly burned.

"Did the shard go, too?" Kaitlyn asked.

He turned his gray eyes on her, as if startled to hear a voice. Then he looked back at his hand again.

"Yes," he said, blinking. "When the crystal did. It felt—I can't explain it. It was like lightning in my hand. I felt the power go *through* it. And the power—it felt like Timon. Like Timon and Mereniang and LeShan—all of them. It was as if they were in there, rushing out." He looked up again, almost furtively. "I guess that sounds crazy."

"No, it doesn't," Rob said, his voice strong. "It sounds right. I believe you."

Gabriel looked at him, just a look. But after that he held his head up, and the startled, furtive expression was gone.

Kaitlyn felt something like carbonated water begin to bubble in her veins. "We did it," she said. She looked at each of her mind-mates, and at Lydia, and suddenly she needed to shout. "You guys, we did it!"

"I said that already," Lewis said with force.

And then it was like a roller coaster gathering speed. Everybody seemed to feel the need to say it, and then to yell it, and then to yell louder to be heard over the other yells. People began to tell one another and then to hug one another or pound one another on the back to drive the point home. Kaitlyn found herself shaking Lydia and kissing Gabriel. Rob, somehow unchained, was wringing Anna's long braids.

Bri and Renny were part of the celebration, punching each other and whooping with gathering intensity. Joyce was crying, clutching with one hand at Kaitlyn's back and whispering something Kait couldn't hear. Lydia was a full member of the winning team, being socked in the arm over and over by Lewis.

But three people weren't. Tamsin knelt by the two dead boys on the floor. Her tilted eyes were wet as she gently closed their eyelids.

And Frost and Jackal Mac were stiff as statues, watching the wild release of energy around them with frightened, hostile eyes. Kaitlyn saw them and raised her arms to Frost.

"Come on," she said. "Don't worry; be happy. Let's all try to deal with each other, okay?"

It wasn't the warmest invitation, maybe, but Kaitlyn thought that under the circumstances it was pretty generous. But Frost's pale blue eyes flashed. Jackal Mac's face turned ugly.

They looked at each other, then with one accord they rushed for the door.

Kaitlyn was too surprised to try to stop them, and by the time she recovered, she wasn't sure she wanted to. The yelling and cheering had died out, and she looked at Rob, who had taken half a step toward the door.

"I think we should just let them go," she said.

He glanced back, then nodded slowly. Gabriel and Lewis settled back reluctantly. Kaitlyn could hear running footsteps up above, then the bang of a door.

Then, silence. In the stillness, Joyce's whispering could be heard.

"I'm so sorry. I'm so sorry for everything."

Kaitlyn turned.

Joyce's aquamarine eyes were red-rimmed. Her face was shiny with tears and perspiration, her normally sleek blond hair ruffled like a baby chick's. Her pink sweat clothes looked damp and bedraggled.

She also looked like a sleepwalker who has just woken up.

"I'm so sorry," she whispered. "The things I've done. The terrible things. I . . . I . . ."

Kaitlyn looked at her helplessly. Then she said, "Tamsin!"

The head with the clustered yellow curls lifted. Tamsin saw Joyce and got up. She looked into Joyce's face, then she took Joyce by the elbow and led her toward the open door.

"The firestones can cast a powerful spell," Kait heard her saying softly. "Their influence can be very strong—and recovery can take a long time. . . ."

Kaitlyn was satisfied. Although Tamsin looked younger than Joyce, there was a sort of ageless wisdom and understanding about her. Joyce was listening as they disappeared.

Kait turned back to find her mind-mates grinning at her.

Good job, Lewis said, and Anna said, *I hope she's okay.*

Bri and Renny were smiling, too. The atmosphere of wild jubilation had quieted, but a kind of dizzy glow remained.

"Let's go upstairs," Rob said, taking Kaitlyn's hand.

"Yes, I'd better change." Kaitlyn glanced down at the bathing suit and grinned wryly. "And I'm sure there are things to take care of—God, the police, I guess. We're going to have to explain all this somehow."

"I wanna get out of here before *that*," Bri said.

Kaitlyn looked behind her, held out her free hand to Gabriel. "Come on, you . . . *hero*. I want to tell you what I think of you."

"So do I," Rob said, golden eyes warm.

Gabriel looked at Kaitlyn's fingers intertwined with Rob's. He smiled, but Kaitlyn couldn't feel his happiness in the web anymore.

"I'm glad you have her back safe again," he said to Rob. He was saying two things with that, Kaitlyn realized.

Suddenly, some of the dizzy glow faded. "Please come up with us," she said to Gabriel, and he nodded, smiling politely, like a stranger.

CHAPTER 16

"So you're not a psychic vampire anymore," Lewis said to Gabriel as they reached the dining room. "I mean, nobody is anymore, right? The Fellowship said if the crystal was destroyed, you'd be cured."

Kaitlyn realized that he was chattering deliberately, filling the silence, trying to help in the only way he could. Gabriel smiled at him, wanly grateful, but Kaitlyn could see the pain behind those gray eyes.

She herself knew that she should be going upstairs, but she couldn't seem to make herself leave. She had never imagined that a person could go from feeling so gloriously happy to so wretchedly miserable in such an appallingly short time.

Wretched, and frightened, and sick with pain. I'm being torn in two, she thought, standing in the sunlit dining room and holding Rob's hand even tighter. I'll never be whole again; I'll never be all right. Oh, God, *please*, please tell me what to do.

She pulled her hand away from Rob, because even her shields couldn't contain the pain. She didn't want him to know.

Anna slipped a jacket over her shoulders and gave Kaitlyn's hand a squeeze. Kaitlyn looked at her gratefully, unable to speak.

Rob was looking a bit lost. "Well—is anybody hurt?" he said, glancing around. "Kaitlyn—?"

"I'm fine. Gabriel's hand, though . . ."

Gabriel, who had just sat down, looked up sharply. "It's all right. Just a little burn." He had been pushing his sweater sleeve off his forearm, scratching under it absently, but now he pulled it down again.

"Let me see. No, I said, *let me see.*" Rob clamped Gabriel's left arm with an unbreakable grip.

"No, leave it alone. It's the other hand!" Gabriel's tone was almost as harsh as it had been in the old days, but Kaitlyn detected a note almost of panic underneath.

"But I feel something here. Stop fighting and hold still!" Rob's voice was equally annoyed. He wrestled the sleeve up by main force—and then stared.

Gabriel's pale forearm was covered with ghastly marks. Angry red cuts, their lips curling open and beginning to bleed again with the rough handling. Burns that were turning brown at the edges and still blistered in the middle. They ran all the way from wrist to elbow.

Kaitlyn felt giddy.

"What happened?" Rob said, with terrible quietness. "Who did this to you?" He lifted clear golden eyes to Gabriel's face, waiting.

"Nobody." Gabriel looked angry, but somehow relieved, too. "It just—happened. It happened when the crystal broke."

There was a silence, a heaviness in the web. Lewis frowned, Anna's lips pulled in at the corners. Bri and Renny had backed off, as if recognizing somehow this wasn't their business. Rob was looking at Gabriel hard.

Kaitlyn was trying to blink dancing spots away. She felt she should know what had happened to Gabriel. She should know, if she could only *think*. . . .

"Well, relax," Rob said finally, evenly. "I can make it stop hurting so much. Make it heal faster."

He put one hand on Gabriel's arm above the elbow and held Gabriel's palm with the other. Kaitlyn could see him feeling with his fingers for transfer points. Gabriel sat, uncharacteristically docile and obedient.

Rob's thumb pressed into Gabriel's palm and he shut his eyes. Through the web, Kaitlyn could feel what he was doing. Sending healing energy through the wounded limb, stimulating Gabriel's own energy to flow, as well. Golden sparks traveling down Gabriel's veins, golden mist enveloping the forearm. Kaitlyn felt warmth, and felt Gabriel relaxing as the pain eased, his muscles unclenching.

With relaxation, barriers go down. Kaitlyn knew that, and

she knew that Rob's healing brought him closer to people. In a minute, she knew that he was doing something else to Gabriel. Probing his mind, looking for something.

Hey! Gabriel tried to jerk his arm out of the steely grip, head lifting, face furious. But it was too late.

They stared at each other a long moment, gray eyes and gold locked as they always had been when the two of them did battle. Locked for endless, time-stretching seconds.

Then Rob's face changed and he settled back on his heels.

Gabriel held his hurt arm to his chest protectively, his own expression defensive and defiant.

"You did those to your own self," Rob said flatly, calmly. Still looking Gabriel in the eyes. "To . . . stay in contact with Kaitlyn." He said the words as if he weren't exactly sure of their meaning. "They were doing something to her and you had to talk to her over a long range. So you thought pain would help you call louder."

Gabriel said nothing, but Kaitlyn felt the truth of it. That was what he'd been concealing when he talked to her in the isolation tank. When he gave her his best memories. She'd felt fatigue and some kind of pain, but he'd shielded most of it from her.

"You used somebody's cigar and a piece of broken glass," Rob said, with growing confidence. "And then later you poked at the sores some more to keep awake."

Yes, Kaitlyn thought, feeling it with Rob in the web. She

could tell he didn't exactly understand what the situation was, but that he was sure about one thing.

"You love her, don't you?" he said to Gabriel.

Gabriel finally seemed able to break their locked stare. He looked away, at the carpet. His face was bleak.

"Yes," he said.

"More than anything," Rob persisted. "You'd crawl on your belly over broken glass for her. Easy."

"Yes, damn you," Gabriel said. "Happy now?"

Rob looked at Kaitlyn.

Kaitlyn's head was swimming, her body racked in so many different directions that she stood still. She couldn't seem to put a coherent thought together. But on top of everything else, holding her precariously in one piece, was the thought that she mustn't hurt Rob. She loved him too much to hurt him. And she knew that Gabriel's eyes on her were saying the same thing.

She now knew that it *was* possible to love two people at once—because you could love them in different ways. The love she felt for Rob now was a burning tenderness, a knowledge that he was the one who'd taught her it was *possible* to love, who had melted the ice of her heart. It was strong and gentle and steady, full of admiration and the intimacy of shared likes and dislikes. It was golden and warm like a summer afternoon.

And if it wasn't the passion and desperate depth of feeling she had for Gabriel, she never wanted Rob to know.

But as Rob looked at her, gazing with those clear eyes full

of light, she realized that her shields were in tatters around her. She had been awake for two days and in agony or terror for nearly as long. She didn't have anything *left* to shield with.

And she could see, she could feel, that he was seeing right inside her. Rob knew.

"Why didn't you tell me?" he asked her after a small eternity.

"I didn't—I didn't feel that way—until—so many things have happened . . ." Kaitlyn faltered. Of all things, she wanted to make Rob all right. Although now she saw that her love for him must have been changing for a long time, gradually, she didn't know how to explain that. "It's probably just—I'll get over it. In a little while . . ."

"Not that, you won't," Rob said. "Neither of you. I mean, I sure hope you don't." He sounded as incoherent as Kaitlyn felt, and he kept swallowing. But he went on doggedly, "Kait, I love you. You know I do. But this isn't something I can compete with." He stepped back. "I'm not blind. You two belong together."

He looked . . . distressed, Kaitlyn realized vaguely. Distressed, but not devastated. Not ruined for life. There was so much more to Rob.

And, as she watched, Anna moved up and put her hand on his back from behind. Kaitlyn looked at her over Rob's shoulder.

Anna smiled tremulously. Her dark eyes were wet but glowing somewhere down inside.

Suddenly a vast, rushing lightness filled Kaitlyn. As if a huge and heavy weight had been taken off her chest. She stared at Anna, and at the way Rob unconsciously was leaning back against Anna's arm. And the effervescent bubbles lifted her skyward.

I just had a precognition, she told Anna silently, a stream of unspoken love and joy. *You will be very happy. Your best friend says to go for it.*

Anna's face was bright, as if someone had set a candle behind it. *You're giving me permission?*

I'm giving you an order!

Lewis laughed out loud. Then he said, "Didn't somebody say something about cleaning up? And how about some food?"

Bri and Renny and Lydia seemed to recognize that as a signal. They followed him as he started for the kitchen. Anna tugged at Rob's arm, gently, to bring him, too.

Rob looked back, once.

I'm glad, he told Gabriel, and Kaitlyn could hear the truth in it. *I mean, it hurts, but I'm glad for you. Take care of her.*

Then he was gone.

Slowly, Kaitlyn turned to Gabriel.

It had occurred to her at the last minute that nobody had really asked him. Maybe, even if he loved her, he'd prefer that the feeling go away. Maybe he didn't want her now that everybody had had a hand in the procedure.

But Gabriel was looking at her now, and she could see his eyes.

She had seen those eyes dark with brooding anger and cold as ice, she'd seen his gaze veiled like a spiderweb and shattering like agate under pressure. But she'd never seen them as they were now. Full of wondering joy and disbelief, and an almost frightened awe.

Gabriel was trying to smile, but the expression kept breaking apart. He was looking at her as if he hadn't seen her for years and years of searching, and had just now walked into a room and come upon her unexpectedly. As if he wanted to look at every part of her, now that he could do it honestly.

Kaitlyn remembered the things he'd given her, the sun-flooded afternoons, and the cool healing ocean waves, and the music he'd written. He'd given her everything that was best in him, everything he was.

She wanted to give him the same back again.

I don't know how you can love me. The words came softly, as if he were thinking them to himself. *You've seen what I am.*

That's why I do love you, Kaitlyn told him. *I hope you'll still love me when you see what I am.*

"I know what you are, Kait. Everything beautiful and brave and gallant and . . ." He stopped as if his throat had closed. "Everything that makes me want to be better for you. That makes me sorry I'm such a stupid mess. . . ."

You looked like a knight with the shard, Kaitlyn said, moving toward him.

"Really?" He laughed shakily.

My knight. And I never said thank you.

She was almost touching him, now. Looking up into his eyes. What she could feel in him was something she'd only felt before when she gave him her life energy. Childlike, marveling joy. Trust and vulnerability. And such love . . .

Then she was in his arms and they weren't separate beings any longer. Their minds were together, sharing thoughts, sharing a happiness beyond thought. Sharing everything.

She never even knew whether he kissed her.

It seemed a very long time later, but the sunbeams falling across the dining room had hardly moved. Kaitlyn had her head on Gabriel's shoulder. She was so full of peace—peace and light and hope for everything. Even the nagging hole in the universe where LeShan had been was filled with light. She hoped that, somehow, he knew what had happened today and was satisfied.

"God make me worthy of you. Fast," Gabriel said. It was something like a command.

Kaitlyn smiled. His arms were tight around her, a feeling she never wanted to lose. But they were no longer outside time, and she could hear banging and shouting laughter from upstairs.

"I guess we'd better see what's going on," she said.

Very slowly, most reluctantly, he let her go, only keeping her hand in his. They walked around the corner to the stairs.

Lydia, though, was just coming down. Bri and Renny were behind her. They'd obviously been going through closets; each had a full cardboard box and at least one bag or suitcase.

"We don't know exactly what we'll need there," Lydia told Kaitlyn. Her green eyes looked out almost shyly from behind her heavy shock of dark hair.

"Go where?" Kaitlyn asked.

"You didn't hear? Oh, I guess not." Lydia headed for the front lab, with Bri and Renny following. Kaitlyn and Gabriel followed *them*.

"Joyce is going with Tamsin back to the Fellowship," Lydia said, dumping her box on a desk. "Ouch. That was heavy."

"Going back with Tamsin?"

"Yup," Bri said. "And we're going with her."

Kaitlyn stared. Renny was nodding, pushing up his glasses with an index finger.

"Tamsin says it'll help Joyce heal from the influence of the crystal," Lydia said. "And Bri and Renny, too. Oh, here they are."

Joyce and Tamsin came in from the kitchen. Joyce's hair was smoothed again, and her lips had stopped trembling. She seemed to be hanging on Tamsin's every word.

"We'd be glad to have you," Tamsin was saying. "And we

can help the children develop and control their powers. Even Lydia . . ."

"I don't have any powers," Lydia said.

Tamsin smiled at her. "You're of the old race. We'll see."

Kaitlyn noticed the sunlight change and realized that Rob was in the kitchen doorway. Lewis and Anna were right behind him, but Anna was closer.

Rob smiled at her, and it was a real smile, with his own gladness and optimism behind it. "Tamsin's been telling us about their place on the new island," he said. "They've got it pretty rough, but they're working on it. It's been hard with Mereniang gone, and now that LeShan is dead . . ." He shook his head, but his eyes were gleaming as if he saw a challenge.

"Rob! Are you telling me—do you want to go, too?"

"Well, I was thinking about it. They're going to need help."

"And leadership," Tamsin said, quietly, without sounding ashamed. "Innovation, new ideas—they don't come easily to us."

Rob nodded. "You help us and we help you. A fair exchange."

And the great task Rob's been looking for, Kaitlyn thought, somewhat giddy with the suddenness of it. Not saving the world, maybe, but fixing a little part of it.

She didn't know what to say. She was remembering Canada, the lush beauty of the rain forest, the open vastness of the sky. The wild blue ocean.

"Of course, the rest of you children can stay here," Joyce was saying. "Not at the Institute—that will be closed for good.

But I think I could arrange for you to have your scholarships after all. Mr. Zetes had the money put aside in a special account; he had to, for the lawyers."

Yes, that was the sensible thing to do. School and then college. Her father would want that. And Gabriel was a city boy. Kaitlyn's fingers tightened on his—and then she felt his thought.

Well, we could just take a vacation, couldn't we? he asked. His gray eyes were sparkling.

Happiness flooded Kaitlyn to her fingertips.

We could—yes, we could, she told Rob and Anna and Lewis. *We could make up the time at school next year. And meanwhile, it would be very educational. . . .*

And we wouldn't break the web, Rob said, and she could feel his joy, too. He and Gabriel were smiling at each other.

Of course, we'll have to break it someday, Lewis said quickly. *I mean, we can't go around this way forever.*

Of course not, Anna agreed solemnly, her owl eyes crinkling at the edges.

But just for now . . . Lewis said.

Just for now, they all agreed, together.

Talk was going on around them. Joyce was moving toward the front door, saying, "What's that?" Lydia was rummaging through her box.

"I forgot to show you. Look what I found!" she said to

Lewis. She was holding two things: an alarm clock shaped like a cow—and his camera.

"Hey, where did you get that? That's precious!" Lewis said, taking the cow.

"I know. I want you to show me what it does." Lydia smiled at him, her new shy smile, and Lewis beamed back. He reached out and squeezed her arm, just once.

"As soon as we get alone," he said wickedly, "I will."

"Kaitlyn! Rob!" Joyce was calling from the front door in a voice wavering between laughter and tears. "There's someone here to see you, and I don't think you should keep her waiting!"

They all went, Kaitlyn and Gabriel and Rob and Anna, with Lewis and Lydia following, and Tamsin bringing up the rear with Bri and Renny. When Kaitlyn got to the porch she stopped in astonishment.

"Oh . . ." was all she could say. Then she said, "Oh, *Marisol.*"

It was Marisol, thin and rather wobbly on her legs, supported on Tony's arm. She was pale, but her tumbled mahogany hair was the same as Kaitlyn remembered, and a smile was trembling on her full lips.

"I came to see the guy who healed me," she said. "And all of you."

"All of them were in it," Tony said proudly. He had a shirt on today, Kaitlyn noticed, and he looked as if someone had just willed him a million dollars.

Kaitlyn hugged Marisol, and then she had to stand back so Rob could do it. And then Lydia was coming forward, and Bri, looking as if they thought Marisol might hate them. But she smiled at them instead, and there were more hugs. Those who couldn't hug Marisol hugged one another.

And Joyce, with her aquamarine eyes on Marisol's face, looked as if healing had already begun.

"We brought you your kitten, too," Tony said to Anna.

"So now everybody's here," Anna said, pressing the kitten to her cheek, then to Rob's.

"Hey, yeah—everybody's here! Wait a minute!" Lewis was running. He was back in a moment. "Everybody, scrunch together by the door. Some of you get down. The rest lean in! Get closer!"

I think we're already about as close as we can get, Gabriel said, and Kaitlyn was surrounded by silent laughter.

"That's it! Hold that smile!" Lewis shouted, and snapped their picture.